BEST CRIME STORIES

OF THE YEAR

NUMBER 1

EDITED BY

LEE CHILD

SERIES EDITOR

OTTO PENZLER

HEAD
of ZEUS

An Aries Book

First published in the UK in 2021 by Head of Zeus Ltd
This paperback edition first published in 2022 by Head of Zeus Ltd,
part of Bloomsbury Publishing Plc

9 7 5 3 1 2 4 6 8

A catalogue record for this book is available from
the British Library.

ISBN (PB): 9781801105750
ISBN (E): 9781801105712

Interior design by Maria Fernandez

Printed and bound in Great Britain by
CPI Group (UK) Ltd, Croydon CR0 4YY

MIX
Paper from
responsible sources
FSC® C171272

Head of Zeus Ltd
First Floor East
5–8 Hardwick Street
London EC1R 4RG

WWW.HEADOFZEUS.COM

BEST CRIME STORIES

STORIES

OF THE YEAR

BEST CRIME STORIES
STORIES

OF THE YEAR

CONTENTS

FOREWORD

Long ago, I came to agree with the brilliant John Dickson Carr, who wisely averred that the natural form of the traditional mystery is not the novel but the short story. It is not uncommon for a detective story to revolve around a single significant clue—which can be discovered, divulged, and its importance explained in a few pages. Everything else is embellishment, and novels have more of this than short stories.

The classic tale, as invented by Edgar Allan Poe, popularized by Arthur Conan Doyle, and perfected by Agatha Christie, is familiar to aficionados and casual readers alike: A crime (usually murder) is committed, law enforcement officers are called in and respond with utter bafflement, and assistance is offered by a gifted amateur, a private eye, or an outlier police detective, who discovers clues, breaks down alibis, and, ultimately, identifies the culprit.

Mystery fiction has changed a great deal over the years, as have all art forms, and as deliciously satisfying as this type of story may be, it is seldom written today. The traditional tale of observation and deduction has largely slipped into the background. The psychology of crime has become the dominant form of mystery fiction in recent years, replacing the whodunit and the howdunit with the whydunit. Those tales of pure deduction may be the most difficult mystery stories to write, as it has become increasingly difficult to find original motivations for murder, or a new murder method, or an original way to hide a vital clue until the detective unearths it.

The working definition of a mystery story for this series is any work of fiction in which a crime, or the threat of a crime, is central to the theme or the plot. The detective story is merely one subgenre in the literary form known as the mystery, just as are romantic suspense, espionage, legal legerdemain, medical thriller, political duplicity, and those told from the point of view of the villain.

I am confident that you will find this to be a superb collection of original fiction about extremes of human behavior caused by despair, hate, greed, fear, envy, insanity, or love—sometimes in combination. Desperate people may be prone to desperate acts—a fertile ground for poor choices. Many of the authors in this cornucopia of crime have described how aberrant solutions to difficult situations may occur, and why perpetrators felt that their violent responses to conflicts seemed appropriate to them.

And what a remarkable job the contributors to this volume have achieved! James Lee Burke has stated that this story is the best he's ever written. How fortunate have we been that an unknown story by the much-loved Sue Grafton was discovered among her papers by her widower and was published for the first time in 2020, four years after her death? David Morrell and Stephen King, two authors whose greatest successes have been on the fringe of mystery fiction, have superb entries that make us wish they wrote more in this category. Paul Kemprecos wrote his very first short story, which is so accomplished that it easily made the cut. Sara Paretsky, who doesn't write nearly enough short stories, proved once again how good they are when she does turn to this challenging form. Doug Allyn is back with another highly professional thriller, as are John Floyd and Jim Allyn. Plus, here's a long story by Joyce Carol Oates, arguably the greatest living writer who has not yet won the Nobel Prize for Literature.

To find the best of these stories is a year-long quest, largely enabled by my invaluable colleague, Michele Slung, who culls mystery magazines, both printed and electronic, for suitable stories, just as she does short-story collections (works by a single author) and anthologies (works by a variety of authors), popular magazines, and, perhaps the richest trove to be mined, literary journals. As the fastest and smartest reader I have ever known, she looks at about three thousand stories a year, largely to determine if they are mysteries, and then to determine if they are worth serious consideration. I then read the harvested crop, passing along the best to the guest editor, who completes the selection process to arrive at the twenty that comprise the book. Ten additional stories are listed on an Honor Roll. Finally, there will be a lagniappe—a bonus story from the past.

Having the right person serve as the guest editor to launch this series is no small thing. Being willing and agreeing to perform this service is an act of extraordinary generosity, certainly not the first such act by Lee Child, the creator of the Jack Reacher series and one of the world's most successful authors. As a national and international bestseller, you may be certain that he is asked to do something virtually every day of his life: write a story, make a speech, sign a book, visit a bookshop or library, provide a quote for a dust jacket, offer advice about how to be a better writer or a more successful one, attend a conference or convention, and even serve as a judge on the Booker Prize committee (which he did last year)—the list goes on.

Child has, at the time of writing this preface, written twenty-five novels in the Reacher series, beginning with *Killing Floor* in 1997 and continuing to *The Sentinel* in 2020, which he cowrote with his brother Andrew. Two novels have been adapted for the screen with Tom Cruise as Reacher: *One Shot*, released as *Jack Reacher* in 2012, and *Never Go Back*, released as *Jack Reacher: Never Go Back*, in 2016. Child had cameo appearances in both. His novels have won numerous honors from the mystery community, and he has been given lifetime achievement awards by the International Thriller Writers, the (British) Crime Writers' Association, and others. In 2019, he was named a Commander of the Order of the British Empire (CBE) for his service to literature.

While I engage in a relentless quest to locate and read every mystery/crime/suspense story published, I live in terror that I will miss a worthy one, so if you are an author, editor, or publisher, or care about one, please feel free to send a book, magazine, or tear sheet to me c/o The Mysterious Bookshop, 58 Warren Street, New York, NY 10007. If the story first appeared electronically, you must submit a hard copy. It is vital to include the author's contact information. No unpublished material will be considered for what should be obvious reasons. No stories will be returned. If you distrust the postal service, enclose a self-addressed, stamped postcard and I'll confirm receipt.

To be eligible for next year's edition of *The Best Mystery Stories of the Year*, a story must have been published in the English language for the first time in the 2021 calendar year. I am being neither arrogant nor whimsical when I state that the absolute firm deadline for me to receive a submission is December 31 due to the very tight production schedule for the book. Sending submissions early is better than sending them later. If the story arrives one day past the deadline, it will not be read. Sorry.

Otto Penzler
February 2021

INTRODUCTION

I was delighted when Otto Penzler asked me to be involved in this new short-story project. I felt the request implied he thought I had something worthwhile to offer on the subject. I'm always delighted to create that impression. But sadly, on this occasion, an impression is all it is. I don't know much about short stories, or their true origins, mechanisms, or appeal. My only consolation is I'm not sure anyone else does either.

What is a short story? Clearly there's a clue in the name. A short story is a story that's short. A *story* is an account of events—in this context almost certainly made up—and the adjective *short* acts to separate the form from other types of accounts that customarily tend to be longer. As a compound noun, *short story* first appeared in print in the year 1877, alongside other compound nouns new that year, including *belly button, coffee table, cold storage, genital herpes, medical examiner, musical chairs, stock option*, and *toilet paper*.

Some of those things were genuinely new in the 1870s—cold storage, certainly, which shook up food supply and started the decline of landed aristocracies by breaking their local monopolies on agricultural production. And coffee table was new as well, I suppose, given the rise of the Victorian middle class, and stock options, and toilet paper, possibly. But others among those things were merely newly *named*—for example belly button, which of course we've all had forever, and probably genital herpes too.

Which category did *short story* fall into—new, or just newly named? The latter applies, as a matter of record. A by-then-established literary form was first called *a short story* in the year 1877. So, newly named. But, without doubt, wrongly named. And far from being new, the form could be the oldest we have ever known.

No one knows when fiction was invented. Or, long before that, the syntactical language that permitted it. Spoken words leave no archeological trace. As soon as their last echoes die away, they are gone forever. All that is left is speculation. Scientific advances in the field of human origins have been spectacular, but scientists don't like to speculate. Just the facts, ma'am.

They will agree, however, on a couple of things. Some explanation is needed, of how a relatively weak and vulnerable and not-very-successful hominid proto-human later came to dominate the whole world and reach outward into the universe. How did that happen?

And scientists will agree that complex, coherent, if-this-then-that language, with a plan B, and a plan C, would have required a big brain. Which they're happy to show us, because that's back in the realm of facts. It's right there in the ground: our brains got big enough less than half a million years ago. There's a vigorous, but very polite, argument whether language colonized a freak mutation, or whether the increase in size was itself driven by the absolute need for language. But either way, that's when it all started.

And it was crucial. A single human was slow and weak. Prey, not a predator. But a coordinated group of a hundred humans was the most powerful animal the earth had ever seen. Tooled up, organized, drilled, rehearsed, if this, then that, plan B, plan C. Language came to the rescue. It made all the difference. We survived. Not that things were easy. Pressures were many and various, and sometimes catastrophic. But we stood a better chance than most. We had lengthy discussions, accurate assessments, correct recall of past events, realistic projections into the future.

In other words, nonfiction saved the day. Language was a lifesaver because it was entirely about truth and reality. It could have no value otherwise. Possibly it stayed that way for hundreds of thousands of years. Then something very strange happened. We started talking about things that hadn't happened to people that didn't exist. We invented fiction.

When exactly? It's impossible to say. The echoes have died away. But we can speculate. Just the guesses, ma'am. We know—because it's right there in the ground, or on rocky walls—that music and representative art date back almost seventy thousand years. Both involved some kind of technical intervention—drums, with stretched skins, hollow bone flutes, with holes carefully drilled for finger stops, pigments found and mixed, twigs chosen and frayed for application—whereas storytelling required no technology. We already had what we needed. We had expressive voices, and sophisticated language. So, it's reasonable to guess storytelling happened much earlier than art or music.

Why did it happen? Not to fill our leisure time. We had none. We were still deep in prehistory, still cognitively premodern, still evolving. Everything we did had a singular purpose: to make it more likely we would be alive tomorrow. Any notion or activity that didn't meet that need quickly died out, literally. How do we square that circle? How did stories make it more likely we would be alive tomorrow?

By encouragement, and empowerment, and subtle instruction, surely. Perhaps the first made-up story was about a boy who came face to face with a snarling saber-toothed tiger. Maybe the boy turned and ran as fast as he could and made it safely back to the cave. Which was encouragement, in the strategic sense of maintaining morale, by delivering the message that not everything has to turn out bad. And also in the tactical sense, in that the specific terrain outside the cave was survivable. Which was the subtle instruction. You had to go out and hunt and gather. A balance had to be struck between reactive caution and proactive boldness, such that the tribe endured.

Then maybe a thousand years later the story evolved to where the boy swings his stone ax and *kills* the saber-toothed tiger. The first thriller, right there. The boldness is turned up a notch. The tribe not only endures, but prospers.

It's worth noting in passing those who neither prospered nor even ultimately endured—our very distant evolutionary cousins, the Neanderthals. On its face, that's a surprise. Compared to us, Neanderthals were faster, stronger, healthier, better toolmakers, better organized socially, and more solicitous of one another. They had bigger brains than us, which surely means they had sophisticated language, possibly even better than ours. Yet they went extinct, almost forty-thousand years ago—granted, after hundreds of generations of extraordinary stress from the Ice Age climate emergency. But we survived it. Why us, and not them?

Those given to fanciful speculation might construct a clue from the actual in-the-ground evidence. Neanderthal settlements tell of occupation by sober, sensible people. They were sporadically nomadic, like all hunter-gatherers, but almost invariably their next settlement was barely out of sight of their last. There is no evidence they ever crossed a body of water without first being able to see land on the other side. The overall impression is one of stolid caution.

Whereas we—Homo sapiens—were nuts in comparison. We were bold to the point—beyond the point—of recklessness.

We ranged thousands of miles into unknown regions. Hundreds of times we launched bark hulls onto giant oceans, and only a tiny percentage can have survived to see the far shore. If any. Our brains were wired differently. The Neanderthals did things we didn't, and we did things they didn't.

Did that include making things up? Nothing about the jump from nonfiction to fiction was biologically preordained or inevitable. It just happened to us. Maybe it just *didn't* happen to our distant cousins. Maybe their sober, sensible, stolid brains couldn't provide the necessary pathway. Maybe wild imagination was required to fire the spark.

What if Neanderthals never left the world of nonfiction? Never entered the land of make-believe? And thereafter, despite their speed and strength and health, and their technical and social skills, what if they didn't make it because of that? Because they didn't have story, to encourage and empower and instruct. Maybe that tiny margin made all the difference.

What do we know about the stories we had and they might not have had? Nothing, of course, but we can speculate. There would have been a strong central strand, be it encouraging, emboldening, instructing, warning, scaring, or whatever else, all wrapped up in context and diversion, and verisimilitude, but not quite. There would have been a rim of unreality, however faint, to expand our experience, which was the evolutionary purpose of story, to take us places we wouldn't normally go, to shine a beam into corners normally left dark. The stories would have been concise, pithy, and focused. They wouldn't have taken long to tell. Survival was a full-time job. Bandwidth was precious.

And now, a hundred thousand years later, you find yourself currently holding in your hands an anthology featuring twenty outstanding contributions from twenty outstanding authors. I know many of them personally. I bet they think this foreword is crazy. I bet they don't agree with a word of it. I bet they all have more plausible explanations. I bet they're going to quote from my first paragraph, right back at me: I don't know much about short stories, or their true origins, mechanisms, or appeal.

But equally, I bet you'll agree their stories fit pretty neatly inside the hundred-thousand-year-old scaffolding described two paragraphs ago. Therefore, you'll also agree the items included here should be called simply *stories*, and those other things their authors produce from time to time should be called *long stories*. Seniority should count for something, after all. Naming rights, at least.

Lee Child

Wyoming

January 2021

Twice an Edgar Allan Poe Award winner, and the record holder in the Ellery Queen Mystery Magazine *Reader's Award competition,* **Doug Allyn** *is one of the best short-story writers of his generation—and probably of all time. He is also a novelist with a number of critically acclaimed books in print.*

The author of eleven novels and more than a hundred and thirty short stories, Doug Allyn has been published internationally in English, German, French, and Japanese. His most recent, Murder in Paradise, *(with James Patterson) was on the* NYT *Best Seller list for several weeks. More than two dozen of his tales have been optioned for development as feature films and television.*

Mr. Allyn studied creative writing and criminal psychology at the University of Michigan while moonlighting as a guitarist in the rock group Devil's Triangle and reviewing books for the Flint Journal. *His background includes Chinese language studies at Indiana University and extended duty with USAF Intelligence in southeast Asia during the Vietnam War.*

Career highlights? Sipping champagne with Mickey Spillane and waltzing with Mary Higgins Clark.

30 AND OUT

Doug Allyn

The sign on the door read Sgt. Charles Marx, Major Crimes. I raised my fist to knock, then realized the guy at the desk wasn't just resting his eyes. He was totally out, slouched in his chair, his grubby Nikes up on his desk, baseball cap tipped down over his eyes, snoring softly. Looked like a class C wrestling coach after a losing season. Edging in quietly, I eased down into the chair facing his desk. When I glanced up, his eyes were locked on mine like lasers.

"Can I help you?"

"I'm Jax LaDart, Sergeant Marx. Your FNG."

He frowned at that, then nodded. "The fuckin' new guy?" he said, massaging his eyelids with his fingertips. "Ah, right. You're the homeboy the chief hired, straight out of the army. I was reading your record. It put me to sleep." He spun the Dell laptop on his desk to show me the screen. "According to the Military Police, you've closed a lot of felony cases overseas, but the details are mostly redacted, blacked out."

"The army'd classify 'Three Blind Mice' if they could. You don't remember me, do you? Jackson LaDart?"

He glanced up at me again, looking me over more carefully this time. Not a comfortable experience. I was in my usual leather jacket and jeans. Not dressed to impress.

"Nah, sorry, I got nothin'. Did I bust you for something?"

"No, but you could have. When I was fourteen, you had me for grand theft auto."

"No kidding?" he said, curious now. "What happened?"

"My cousin and I were working after hours at the Shell station by the freeway, tuning up an old junker Norton motorcycle. Managed to get it running, took it out for a test drive. We made it a few miles, then a tire blew and we cracked it up."

He nodded, didn't comment.

"I banged my face up pretty seriously," I said, jerking a thumb toward an old scar on my forehead. "I'm bleeding like a stuck pig, we had no phone. My cousin runs to the nearest house. Nobody's home, but a pickup in the yard had keys in it, so Jimmy piled me in, drove me into Samaritan Hospital, pedal to the metal. You spotted us on the road, chased us the last few miles with lights and sirens. But at the hospital, you took one look at my face, hustled me inside, and got me some help." I shook my head, remembering.

"Thing is, Jimmy and I were only fourteen, neither of us had a license yet and we'd wrecked a bike and stolen a truck. You could've come down hard on us, but you stood up for us instead. When the pickup's owner came stomping in, yelling he wanted our asses arrested, you took him outside, straightened him out."

"Curly Beauchamp," Charlie nodded slowly, "I remember now. He was half in the bag, all bent out of shape about you two borrowing his piece-of-shit ride. Needed an attitude adjustment, is all. No big thing."

"It was to us."

"I was new to the badge back then," he said with a shrug. "Young and dumb and full of myself. Threw my weight around a lot. Till I learned not to."

"How do you mean?"

"What's that rule about unintended consequences? Something about butterflies?"

"Butterfly Principle," I said. "A butterfly in China flaps its wings, and Hawaii gets a hurricane."

"Except butterflies don't know any better. Cops are supposed to be smarter, but sometimes we're not. That's what the law's for. Draws hard, clear lines, the ones we don't cross."

"You crossed a line for me, back then. If you hadn't, maybe I'd be talking to you from a cage."

"And the world might be a better place."

We both smiled at that. He was probably right. But his grin morphed into a frown as he cocked his head, listening to the loud music wafting up from the street. Rock and roll at concert volume. "Sweet Home Alabama." Lynyrd Skynyrd.

Easing stiffly out of his chair, Charlie moved to the tall window behind his desk and cracked the blinds. I stood at his shoulder, looking down on Valhalla's Main Street, three stories below. Northern Michigan in mid-December. Snow and sleet mixed, stinging like BB pellets in the winter wind.

Down on the street, a funeral cortege was crawling past, a flatbed truck in the lead, carrying a small coffin, escorted by a long queue of pickups and motorcycles, revving their engines, adding to the din of Skynyrd blasting from the flatbed's sound system. Battle flags were flapping wildly in the wind, some trucks flying Old Glory, others flying red rebel flags, the Stars and Bars. The flatbed was flying both, full size banners at the head of the small casket.

"What's all that?" I asked.

"What we were talking about," Charlie said. "How bad things can wind up when you cross a line."

"In a funeral, you mean?"

He nodded without speaking, which was answer enough.

Eyeing the long cortege, I noticed an old man on the flatbed staring up at me. He was maybe sixty, salt-and-pepper beard, wrinkled black suit from Goodwill. I wondered if he was somebody I knew from back in the day. I tilted the blinds for a better look, but the truck was already passing out of our sight.

"Crossing a line can definitely go sideways," I conceded. "But sometimes bending a rule or two is the only way to get a bad guy into a cage. Or in the dirt."

"What was your date of separation, LaDart?"

"A few weeks ago."

"From where?"

"Afghanistan. Why?"

"You're back in the world now, troop, and here we call 'em cells, not cages. And dirt naps—"

"Strictly hyperbole, Sarge," I said. "Just kidding."

"Right," he said, eyeing me doubtfully. Because I wasn't kidding. And we both knew it. I'd come home from a war without rules, where I learned to live by my own. He let it pass.

"Chief Kaz tells me you grew up out in the county."

"I'm a woodsmoke kid," I nodded. "Raised in the deer woods."

"Still know your way around out there?"

"Some, sure, but nobody knows it all. There's eighty thousand acres of state land spread over the five counties, Sarge. Daniel Boone could get lost."

"Which is why our brother officers in the DEA have asked us for a guide. They got a call on their tip line about a motor home parked deep on state land. Their GPS coordinates put it somewhere inside this red circle, but they've got no idea how to get there."

He tapped a computer key, then swiveled his laptop to face me again.

I leaned in, scanning the screen. It took me a moment, but then I recognized a few landmarks. "Their circle's just beyond the north fork of the Black. It's swampy ground, but there's an old logging road just east of it. That road is the only way an RV could make it in. I can get them there."

"Won't be easy. The DEA Strike team will be mostly newbies, recruits fresh out of Quantico. We'll have our hands full with 'em."

"We? You're going?"

"Why wouldn't I?"

"The chief said you're short. Almost out the door."

"Eight days to my anniversary," he said with a broad grin. "Thirty and out. Thirty years from the day I signed on the Valhalla force as a rook."

"It'll be rough going out there, Charlie, and I owe you one. Why not relax, put your feet up for once. Let me handle it."

"You think I'm ready for a rocking chair, LaDart? You're the FNG here, not me."

"I didn't mean it that way."

"Then let's get something straight. A couple weeks back, I got called to the Samaritan Hospital emergency room. Three kids had been dumped off in their driveway, overdosed on meth. They were foaming at the mouth, like *dogs*! *High school* kids! So if the DEA thinks some lab rat's cooking crank on our turf, I'm all over it. If that's okay with you? FNG Sergeant LaDart?"

"Absolutely, boss." I raised my hands in mock surrender. "It's totally fine by me. "

But it wasn't totally fine. The raid was the diametric freaking opposite of fine. Charlie and I met up with the DEA crew at first light at an abandoned motel parking lot just off the interstate. Charlie knew the Agent-in-Charge, Ken Tanaka, but the others were green kids, decked out in full battle rattle, body armor and helmets, M4 automatic weapons, night vision gear clipped to their helmets like snorkels. Looked like fucking starship troopers. They even brought a dope dog along, a black-faced Belgian Malinois bitch half again the size of a German shepherd. She looked more wolf than dog, but she definitely seemed to know her business, cool, calm, and collected. Which was a lot more than I could say for her crew. The young agents were practically jumping out of their skins with excitement, first raid, first action. I was getting a very bad feeling about this.

We divided up into two squads, then scrambled into a pair of camouflaged Humvees to head into the back country. As the guide, I was riding shotgun in the lead vehicle with the DEA boss,

Agent Ken Tanaka at the wheel, a hard-eyed oil drum of a warrior, shaved skull, Fu Manchu. Ken would have looked at home on a steppe pony, riding to war beside Genghis Khan.

Only the Belgian dog was totally calm, alert and aware, but not a bit hinky. Like she'd done this a hundred times before. Which made me wonder about her.

There was no time to quiz her handler about her history, though. The logging road twisted through the hill country like a rattler with a broken back. We stayed with it until we were roughly a half mile from the DEA's red ring, then I called a halt to dismount. Our target should be straight ahead, at the end of the road, but we were in a cedar swamp now. If the meth cooks heard us coming and scattered into the woods, we'd be chasing them all damned day. We needed to locate the lab, encircle it, then tighten the noose.

Good luck with that.

Out of the vehicles, we formed a long firing line, stringing the young DEA agents out for seventy meters on both sides of the road, with Charlie and me holding down the center. It's a Tactics 101 maneuver, should have been easy, but the line has to stay absolutely straight to give everyone a clear field of fire.

No chance. A hundred meters along, we had to stop to realign, then twice more as we made our way through the snowy swamp. The young agents were unconsciously edging ahead, eager to put first eyes on the target. Unfortunately, they were also increasing their chances of getting their heads blown off by their own crew. There's no such thing as friendly fire.

After our second stop to realign, I was seriously wishing I could turn the lot of 'em into dogs. The Malinois maintained her position perfectly, always aligned with the center, her eyes front, sniffing the icy breeze—

"Contact!" one of the agents yelled. "Ten o'clock, straight ahead!"

He was right! A hundred meters down the road, a battered Coachman motorhome had been pulled off the road into the trees. It was well hidden, crudely camouflaged with rattle-can paint, then covered with brush.

Even at this distance, we could smell the rank bite of crystal meth on the wind. For the young agents, it was red meat thrown to a pack of wolves.

Battle tactics required us to extend our line, then surround the motorhome. Instead, the agent on the far end totally blew off his training and headed for the RV at a dead run. A few others raced after him, joining in the chase. Only the rough country and the foot or so of snow on the ground slowed their rush—

And saved their lives.

I dropped to my belly on the road, pulling my weapon, screaming "Down, down, down! Take cover!" into my lapel mike. Tanaka and Charlie Marx dropped instantly, but the younger agents froze in confusion, uncertain as to *why* I was warning them.

For a split second, I wasn't sure why I was yelling either, then it registered. The Belgian! When we'd first smelled the meth, the dog had frozen in place, her tail twitching slowly, alerting us . . .

But then she suddenly dropped to her belly, which sent a far more serious signal. Explosives! IED!

WHAM!

A massive blast smashed the motorhome into flaming splinters, lifting it off its frame, raining fiery debris down around us like a hailstorm from hell! I rose to my knees, dazed, glancing wildly around, trying to make sense of what the hell just happened.

Most of the agents were down, flattened by the blast, but a few were already collecting themselves. Thanks to the Belgian, we were still far enough out that the explosion had roughed us up, but no one seemed to be badly hurt. No one was screaming for a medic or—

A shattered door in the motorhome burst outward as a guy came hurtling through it, sprawling in the snow, shrieking, his face a bloody shambles, his clothing on fire. Scrambling to his feet, he was off to the races, trying to outrun the flames that were burning through his clothes.

"Red light! Red light!" Tanaka shouted. "Hold your fire!"

But the dog handler had lost his leash, and the Belgian instantly gave chase, racing after the runner like a rocket. And after her warning before the blast, I knew what she was, knew what she'd do if she caught him and pulled him down.

She'd tear him apart!

I was up and running, knowing I was already too late. She'd be on him in an instant—

"*Hond!*" I shouted after her. "*Auf! Auf!*"

The Belgian dropped like she'd been shot. Down flat on her belly, but still taut as a drawn bow, teeth bared in a silent snarl, ready to resume her attack on command, her eyes were locked on the runner like rifle sights. I tackled him a few steps later, holding him down as he thrashed around in the snow, which actually helped smother the flames.

Tanaka and Charlie caught up and joined in, grabbing fistfuls of snow, smearing it all over the kid. And he was a kid, a freakin' teenager, bleeding from a half dozen cuts, and clearly in shock. I tried a few questions, but he could barely remember his own name. Had no idea why the RV had been blown to hell. One of Tanaka's newbie DEA agents had EMT training, and took over for us, rendering first aid. The Belgian was still crouched, watching. I picked up her leash, but she didn't even look up, totally focused on the kid. One wrong move and he'd be gone.

Her handler trotted up, a fresh-faced redhead, Kelly on his nametag. He reached for the leash, but I held on to it.

"Where'd this dog come from?"

Kelly glanced a question at Tanaka. "Better tell him," Ken said.

"Overseas," Kelly admitted. "My brother was her handler in the 'Stan. Worked with her for two tours, but he got orders to Iraq and she's maxed out age wise. They were gonna put her down."

"Do you know why?" I asked.

"Her age—"

"—has squat to do with it," I snapped. "She's a war dog, Kelly. I've worked with Belgians, attack dogs, trackers, bomb sniffers. Once they've tasted blood? Chewed up an intruder or tackled a runner? They change, up here," I said, tapping my temple. "After that, they're as dangerous as a brick of C-4. When their handlers rotate back to the states, their dogs stay behind. They retrain with new handlers and go straight back to the war. Over and over, until we get too old or too crazy."

"We?" Kelly echoed.

"It's a running joke over there. Guys who pull multiple tours? Like me? We're called Belgians too. This dog can't be in the field here, Kelly. I'm taking her."

"The hell you are!"

"Jax is right," Charlie said, stepping between us. Look at her, son. One wrong word and she'd tear that kid's throat out before you could—"

A supersonic crack split the air, opening a fist-size wound in Charlie's throat, lifting him off his feet, slamming him to the ground.

"Down, down!" Tanaka roared, as I crawled on top of Charlie, covering him with my body as the rifle report echoed over us, instantly drowned out by the thunder of return fire as the young agents opened up, loosing a hail of lead toward the tree line, whacking down branches, chewing up brush. In the winter wind, they couldn't spot the muzzle blast or gun smoke, had no idea what they were shooting at.

But maybe it had some effect. No more shots came.

Kneeling beside Charlie, I put pressure on the wound, but I could feel the disconnect from his spine, an unnatural flexing, and read his empty stare.

He was dying before my eyes.

"Help me!" I roared at the EMT. "We've gotta get him out of here!"

—⁑—

Our flying column roared into Valhalla Samaritan like the invasion of Iraq. We'd called for an ambulance, but Charlie couldn't wait for it. We loaded him aboard the lead Humvee and tore out of the forest, leaving the young agents to sort through the wreckage and hunt for the shooter.

At the hospital, the emergency team quickly loaded Charlie onto a gurney and rolled him away. Tanaka and I found a bench in a waiting room, but neither of us had much to say, both of us trying to sort out what the hell just happened.

We weren't the only ones asking. A State Police team showed up a few minutes later. Officer-involved shootings are always investigated by another department, but this didn't feel likes standard procedure to me. Two uniformed Staties quickly led Tanaka away to question us separately.

I stayed in the waiting room with two detectives in civvies, a heavyweight sergeant, Haskey, square and gray as a cement block with an attitude to match, and his boss, Lieutenant Sharon Keenan. Haskey's tweed jacket was Sears off the rack. Keenan was in black slacks, black jacket, black turtleneck. Blonde, no makeup, her hair cropped short as a boy's. Haskey had a mouse under his right eye. It looked fresh.

I gave them a quick briefing on what happened, our approach, the blast, the kid running out, then Charlie's shooting.

"So, right after the blast, you, Agent Tanaka, and Sergeant Marx were bunched up?" Haskey asked. "Not too smart. Made a pretty sweet target for the meth cookers."

"I'm not sure it was them. The RV was already blown, the shot came from the other direction and it was definitely a long one. Charlie was already falling when I heard the report. The shooter had to be seven or eight hundred meters out. Helluva long ways for a head shot."

"Actually, the round struck Sgt. Marx in the throat," Keenan said.

"Think center mass, Lieutenant. Normally, you zero in on the heart, but Charlie was wearing a vest. The shooter moved his bull's-eye up to the bridge of his nose and only missed by a few inches. I think he hit what he was shooting at."

"Why cap Charlie?" Haskey asked. "He's at thirty and out, about to retire and everybody knows it. There was even a write-up in the paper about it. If somebody wanted him gone, they only had to wait a few days. But you? You're brand-new on the job when the DEA tip line gets a call about a lab they need your help to find? Did you make that call, LaDart? Or maybe one of your backwoods relatives, trying to make you look good?"

I stared at him. "Me? Where's that coming from?"

"Same place you came from, sport—Afghanistan. Only a trained marksman could make a shot like that. Or maybe a woodsman. Did you make any enemies over there LaDart? Maybe one who followed you here?"

"You think a vet did this?"

"We've been having a lot of problems with Afghan vets," Keenan put in. "Sergeant Haskey mixed it up with one last week."

Which explained the eye, and maybe the attitude.

"We're seeing substance abuse, domestic violence, even suicides—"

"I'm aware," I interrupted. "We call it going Belgian, the same as the burned-out war dogs. A vet would have no reason to kill Charlie."

"Maybe he missed by more than a few inches," Haskey said. "Maybe he missed by a couple of feet."

"Missed me, you mean? How long have you been on the job, Haskey?"

"A lot longer than you, sport."

"Maybe that's your problem," I said, standing up. "This is a lazy interrogation, guys. You're asking me questions without doing fieldwork first, ergo, you don't know if I'm lying or not."

"Are you lying to us, Sergeant LaDart?" Keenan asked.

"Lady, somebody just capped the guy who saved my life, years ago. I want him a lot more than you do."

"This is a State Police investigation, LaDart," Haskey said. "Stay away from it."

"I know the rules, guys. If I accidentally trip over anything useful, you'll be the first to know. But right now, unless I'm under arrest? I need to get some air before somebody gets his other eye blackened."

I half expected an argument, but they let me go. No choice. We all knew they had no cause to hold me.

Out in the corridor, I took the stairs, two at a time, up to the burned cooker's room.

Agent Kelly was on guard out in the hall. "Any news about Charlie?" I asked.

"In surgery, last I heard, Sarge."

"How's the kid doing?"

"Still unconscious. He was a mess before he got burned. Meth head, bad skin, rotten teeth. He'll be a zombie in a year."

"Did he talk at all?"

"Nothing coherent. Between the painkillers they gave him for his burns, and the bat shit he's been snorting, I doubt he knows what year this is."

"Did he say anything about the shooting?"

"No, but I've spoken with the guys who searched the wreckage of the motor home. The only weapons they found were sawed-off shotguns plus a few handguns, strictly street quality. Mismatched calibers, none bigger than a nine."

"No long guns? Anything with a scope?"

"Nah. Tanaka thinks these punks are downstate bangers, Sarge, learned to shoot by watching TV. They don't aim, they pose. Probably couldn't hit a barn from the inside."

"Somebody did," I said. "Last question. Where's your dog, Kelly?"

⚬———⚬

She was down in the parking lot in one of the Humvees, patiently waiting for her next assignment. I gave her some water from the Hummer's canteen, then sat beside her, stroking her great, scarred head as I tried to sort everything out, the raid, the dog, Charlie's shooting, and the Staties' focus on vets.

Hell, maybe they were right. Maybe we all do come home a little crazy. Trying to make sense out of the 'Stan could definitely send you around the bend.

Maybe they should lace our Alpo with arsenic like they'd do to this lady—Damn.

That's exactly what would happen if they found out she was here. Kelly's brother would get jammed up over it, and Kelly too. And the Belgian would definitely be put down. Poisoned, or just shot in the head. And thank you for your service, ma'am.

To hell with this. I'd lost enough friends for one day.

Firing up the Humvee, I headed south out of Valhalla, into the Black River hills, eighty thousand acres of rough country, an area bigger than most nations in the UN. It was a good fifty-minute run, and I needed four-wheel drive to make the last ten miles after the gravel road I was following petered out to a dirt track.

The old farmhouse sat atop a long rise, with a magnificent view of the rolling forest on all sides. From the front porch, Fifi Dumont can watch the morning sun rise, and then see it set again at the end of the day. He can also see anyone approaching a good half hour before they pull into his yard.

He was waiting for me on his porch, a grizzled beer barrel of a woodsman in a checked flannel shirt, cork boots, and hard eyes. He had a long rifle on his lap, an old '95 Marlin, I think. Used to be his dad's.

"Hey, Feef," I said, climbing out of the Humvee. "Long time."

"Jax? What the hell, I thought you was the law."

"I am, bro, but I'm strictly local. Are you and your brothers still growing high grade weed out in the bush?"

"Who's askin'? My high school buddy or Five Oh?"

"Your old bud. You're not in my jurisdiction out here, anyway. Do you still fence in your grows?"

"Some. Chain link keeps the deer off the reefer, but it don't stop the meth heads. They cut their way in to rip us off now and again. Why?"

"I brought a present for you. *Hond! Volg rechts!*" The Belgian sprang out of the Humvee and immediately took up a position beside me. Eyeing Fifi hungrily. His eyes went wide as saucers.

"What the hell is that?" he asked uneasily. "Cross-wolf?"

"No," I said. "She's the answer to your prayers."

I explained exactly what the Belgian Malinois was, and that I'd brought her here because woodsmoke boys treat their dogs like family. He could turn her loose inside his enclosures, and she'd guard his crops with her life, running free in the forest while she did her duty. It wasn't a perfect solution, but it was the best I could do.

I gave him a list of commands in Dutch, the language she was trained in, and we practiced his pronunciation until the dog clearly understood him. And at the end of things, I asked for a favor in return.

"You know Charlie Marx, right, Feef?"

"I heard he got shot," Fifi nodded. "It was on the radio. How is he?"

"Bad. Maybe gone by now. Whoever capped him did it from seven hundred yards out. I've been away awhile, Feef. Who could make a shot like that?"

"I could," he shrugged. "You could. Hell, half the woodsmoke kids we grew up with could do it."

"But why? Charlie was at his thirty and out, almost done being a cop."

"I don't know why it would happen now," Fifi said. "Maybe years ago, but not no more."

"How do you mean?"

"Back in the day, Marx had a rep for roughhouse. If he busted you for beating on your wife, or abusing a kid, you might trip and fall a few times on your way to jail. Or get your head slammed in a door."

"Charlie told me a bust went bad," I said. "I need a name."

He chewed that over a minute, then shrugged. "Broussard," he said. "Or maybe Guthrie."

"Who?" The names meant nothing to me.

"There's a junkyard out on 41, Guthrie's Recycle?"

I shook my head.

"I think the Guthries moved up here around the time you left for the army, ten years ago or so. Bunch of 'em, rednecks from Alabama. Came up to Detroit to work in the auto plants years back, but when the shops closed, they moved up here, to the backwoods. Fit right in. Outside of town, the county's pretty redneck."

"Woodsmoke," I said, shaking my head.

"What's the difference?"

"Not much," I admitted. "Where does Charlie come in?"

"One of the Guthrie girls, Janiva? Gets in a family way with Leon Broussard. Wasn't married, but they're livin' together. But when Janiva gets knocked up, Leon starts knockin' her around. About the third time Charlie gets called out to their place, he beats the livin' hell out of Leon, kicked his drunk ass across his front yard like a dog, I heard."

"Sounds like he had it coming."

"Sure enough. But after Charlie leaves, Leon staggers into the house, grabs a shotgun, and paints the kitchen with his brains."

"Damn," I said.

"Yeah. Naturally, Janiva blames Charlie for it. It's all his fault her drunken boyfriend offs himself, because he got his butt kicked. She's blamin' Charlie while she's still wearin' the shiner Leon give her."

"What happened?"

"There was some kinda investigation, Charlie got suspended a week, that was it. But he definitely calmed down after that, didn't go on the muscle so much."

"What about the 'Bama rednecks? How'd they take it?"

"The Guthries? No problem, far as I know. Leon wasn't family, just Janiva's boyfriend, and a bad one at that. Left 'em a little something to remember him by. A kid, a boy. Never had no luck with him neither."

"Why?"

"He passed away last week. Ten years old. Cancer. Heard his funeral cortege was a mile long. Damn shame."

"Funeral," I echoed, remembering. "Flatbed truck in front, long line of pickups, a lot of rebel flags?"

"That's them Guthries. Do you know 'em?"

"No, I just saw it pass," I said. "From Charlie's office."

I thanked Fifi for the info, warned him again about the lady Belgian, and headed back to town, still chewing over what he'd told me.

Fifi was right. Whatever happened was over and done with way back when. No reason for it to crop up now, years later.

And it wasn't my problem, anyway. It was a State Police case, they'd warned me off, and the lines were clear. I'd been an army cop for most of a decade, I knew all about the lines you shouldn't cross.

But Charlie Marx had crossed a line for me once, and maybe saved my life. If I'd taken a fall for grand theft auto at fourteen, God knows where I'd be now.

Maybe dead. Or doing hard time. Not much difference to a backwoods kid.

I knew I should hand over Fifi's information to the Staties, but I decided to check it out first. At this point, it was only hearsay anyway. An old story told by an old friend. Probably nothing to it.

⚬—⚬

I headed back to the station, but didn't bother to check in. I parked on the street out front instead, waited for a break in traffic, then walked out to the centerline and stood there, looking up. Cars were whipping past on both sides, horns blaring, drivers yelling stuff about my mother.

But it was worth it. Because there was nothing to see.

Looking up from the street, I was standing roughly where I'd seen the flatbed pass with its flags and small coffin. At the time, I thought the old man on the truck was staring up at me, even adjusted the blinds to get a better look at him.

But from down here, with the building in sunlight? I couldn't see squat. The windows were completely opaque in the reflected light. So the old guy hadn't been staring at me at all. From here, all he could see would be the blind windows of Charlie's office.

And when Charlie said that crossing the line can end up in a funeral, he didn't mean just any funeral. He meant this one. The boy's. Which made no sense at all. Because Charlie'd quit muscling suspects years ago. And the sod on this kid's grave probably hadn't taken root yet.

Whatever happened between Charlie and the kid's drunken, wife-beating father went down before the boy was born. Why would it crop up again after all this time?

A horn blared behind me, a garbage truck this time. I crossed the street to the station, but didn't get past the front desk. The duty sergeant had two messages for me, one from Tanaka. Charlie was gone. Never regained consciousness.

It wasn't a surprise. Hell, I'd known from the moment I saw the wound. But it still drilled me like a kick in the belly. Which did surprise me. I've lost friends in combat, once saw a best bud get blown in half. I hadn't seen Charlie Marx in years, we weren't really friends, but he'd had a huge impact on my life. Far more than I'd realized until this day.

The second message was from my boss, Chief Kazmarek. The two Staties had more questions for me. I wadded up that message in my fist, tossed it in the trash.

"Damn shame about Charlie," the desk sergeant said. "Only a week from his thirty and out, you know? Crazy."

"It is," I agreed. "And you didn't see me, okay?"

He frowned at that, but only for a moment. "See who?" he asked.

Route 41 leads northwest out of Valhalla, past the hardboard plant and used car lots, definitely the seedier side of town. Guthrie's Auto Salvage was a sprawling junkyard set back from the main road, acres of rusty cars half-hidden behind a galvanized metal fence. Compared to the 'Stan, the yard looked prosperous. They call it vehicle recycling nowadays. Late model wrecks are worth more for parts than the cars cost new. I guessed this yard held two to three thousand units on a hundred acres. Probably worth a million or more. Wrecks they might be, but junk they ain't.

A few cars were parked in front, with a row of rusty wreckers off to one side. The flatbed truck from the funeral was on the far end, still flying its flags, American and rebel. The only thing missing was the bier. And the small casket.

The office/showroom was built like a fortress, concrete block walls, windows narrow as gun slits, a muddy, rutted driveway that stopped at the front door, the end of the line in more ways than one.

Inside, the lighting was dim, overhead fluorescents winking and buzzing. The room was filled with long rows of shelving units piled high with car parts, some rusty, some new, still gleaming with lube. The air was rank with the stench of burned metal and motor oil. A long counter ran the width of the building at the back of the room. A young guy in greasy coveralls was behind it, Latin from the look of him. Jumpy as a cricket on a griddle.

I headed for the counterman, but veered off when something caught my eye. A rifle rack was bolted to the back wall beside a door that opened out to the yard. The rack held a half dozen long guns, most with scopes. A security chain ran through the weapons' trigger guards, but its padlock was unclasped and the last slot in the rack was empty. A framed display hung beside the rack, and as soon as I saw it, I knew.

It held a long row of medals for expert marksmanship, plus red and yellow combat medals from Vietnam.

The guns in the rack were a serious collection of military sniper rigs. The oldest was a .30-40 Krag that dated from Teddy Roosevelt's charge up San Juan Hill, 1898. Then a '03 Springfield from the War to End All Wars, and a scoped Garand and an M14 from the wars after that. If the logic of the collection held, the missing weapon would be the most modern, a Winchester Model 70 from Vietnam, or maybe an M16. It didn't matter which. Either way, with only my sidearm, I was totally outgunned.

I turned to ask the counterman about the missing weapon, but he'd vanished. I was on my own.

I knew I should call for backup, it was a State Police case now, but I didn't. I wasn't here as Sgt. Jax LaDart, the FNG. I was the kid Charlie Marx stood up for all those years ago.

And however this went down, it wasn't police business anymore. It was personal. I thought about taking one of the rifles in the rack, but the magazines were empty and I didn't see any ammo at hand. I left them.

Instead, I gently eased open the door to the yard, and edged out, to face Harland Guthrie. And if I'd had any remaining doubts, they disappeared.

It was the old man from the funeral flatbed, the one I'd thought was staring at me when he'd looked up at Charlie's office. Same black suit, same wild white hair and beard. Looked like he'd been sleeping in his clothes. His rifle was in much better shape. A Vietnam era Winchester Model 70, a bolt action rifle chambered in 30-06, deadly out to fifteen hundred yards. He was holding it at port arms across his chest, not aimed in my direction, but it didn't have to be. He was leaning against a wrecked Chevy Blazer, maybe sixty meters across the yard from me. If I drew on him, I might get off a round or two, but it would take a miracle for me to score a hit at this distance. Guthrie wouldn't need a miracle. With a scoped Winchester, he could cap me like swatting a fly.

"I know you," he called. "Saw your picture in the paper when you signed on to the force. A war hero, it said."

"We both know better, don't we? The real heroes are buried in Arlington. I just did my job, same as you, back in the day. In Vietnam?"

"Two tours," he nodded. "Sniper with the Airborne. More than sixty confirmed kills. You?"

"Afghanistan, the Sulaiman Mountains. Nowhere near sixty, but way too many, I think now."

"You'd better figure on doing one more, if you're here for me."

"I'm here for Charlie, Mr. Guthrie. I owe him, big. And I've figured out *what* happened, I think. But not the why of it."

"It ain't complicated. Ten years ago, Charlie Marx got called to my daughter Janiva's place, because her live-in, Leon Broussard, was roughing her up. Marx had been there before, but it was different this time, she was pregnant with Leon's child. I guess Charlie figured Leon had a lesson coming, and roughed him up pretty good. I got no problem with that, I'd have beaten the bastard myself if I'd known. Leon was a drunk, mean as a snake when he had his load on. But Charlie crossed the line. Kicked Leon across his own yard, like a damn dog. But he misjudged how drunk and crazy Leon really was, and after he left . . . ?"

"Leon offed himself, like the psycho asshole he was. And you blame Charlie for that?"

"Not then, I didn't. I figured my Janiva was better off without him. And when her boy was born, Todd? I almost forgot where he came from. Todd was Guthrie to the bone. His mother's son. My blood. None of his dad's. Or so I thought, until two years ago . . ." He looked away, swallowing hard. But the gun never wavered. And my heart sank like a stone, as his meaning, and maybe his intent, sank in.

"The cancer," I said.

"The worst kind," he agreed. "In his bones. Couldn't cut it out, chemo hardly slowed it down, drugs couldn't help much with the pain. Todd's only hope was a bone marrow transplant, but he had a rare blood type, AB negative. Like his father. None of us were a match."

"Even with matching blood types, there's no guarantee Leon would have been a match."

"I know, they told me that. But he could have been. That boy needed a miracle, and he deserved one, but he didn't get it because

Charlie Marx wanted to feel like a big man. And he put Todd's last, best hope, his only hope, in an urn on his grandma's mantel."

"Charlie didn't kill your son-in-law, sir."

"He killed my whole damn family! That boy was the last of my blood, last one entitled to bear my name. I'm the last Guthrie now, and I'm going to lay it down a long damn ways from home."

"It doesn't have to be that way—"

"Don't blow smoke at a smoker, son. I don't plan to die in jail. I've killed plenty before, overseas, for my country, same as you. I've thought about that a lot since, same as you, I expect. We killed them on their home ground, in wars that didn't mean spit, in the end. I didn't hate them people, wouldn't take their damned country as a gift, but we dropped 'em anyway, didn't we? They sent us there, and we did what we did. But your Sergeant Marx? He crossed the line, shamed Leon so bad he took his own life, and took away my grandson's last hope. And when I'm suiting up for Todd's funeral, I see this article in the paper, how Charlie's gonna retire on his anniversary, thirty years from the day he signed on."

"Thirty and out," I nodded.

"He's gonna go fishing, maybe sit and rock on his front porch of an afternoon, while the worms are chewin' into my grandson. He done what he done. It was time to pay up for it. Now it's that time again."

"It's not what I want," I said.

"In case you ain't noticed, son, this world don't give a rip what you want—"

And I was off, sprinting straight at him, full tilt, pulling my weapon as I came, trying to close the distance between us, my only hope. Guthrie froze, staring, startled, but only for a moment. Then he shouldered his weapon, snugging it in—to his right shoulder. Right handed. Harder to swing to his right. I dove to my left, landing hard, then rolling back to my right.

He fired! The slug whistled past, so close it cut a notch in my ear, burning a groove where my head had been a split second before. He racked his Winchester—but I was already returning fire, shooting blindly, not aiming, just trying to throw him off stride. But I grew up hunting in the back country. I have gunman's instincts, and serving in the 'Stan made me better. And I was fresh out of a war, much sharper than the old man. On pure reflex, I'd zeroed in on center mass, ripping off a dozen rounds as fast as I could pull the trigger—

And got lucky. Or maybe my desperate run had gotten me just close enough to score two solid hits out of a dozen shots. In center mass.

Dead center.

Guthrie's legs buckled, and he dropped to his knees, staring at me the whole time, as he toppled and fell. Surprised, I think.

So was I, but I didn't waste time on it. I was up and running again in a heartbeat. I knew damned well he was dead, but I kicked him hard in the chest anyway, furious at what he'd done, and what he'd made me do. As he rolled off the rifle, I grabbed it up, racking open the action to make it safe—

But it was already safe. The magazine was empty. He'd fired the only round he had. And missed me. At forty yards. A guy with sixty confirmed kills. Who'd dropped Charlie Marx with a head shot at seven hundred.

Goddamn it! I eased down slowly, kneeling beside his body, trying to read an answer in his glassy, empty eyes.

Had he missed me on purpose? How the hell could I know? All I know is, he put me in a situation, and I did what I had to.

It was his play, he called it, and if I was just a puppet in the old man's swan song, well, so be it.

Fuck him.

He's the one taking the dirt nap.

And in the end, I squared things for Charlie the best I could. He'd gotten his thirty and out, though not the way he'd planned. Or hoped.

Not like this.

Not like this.

They buried old man Guthrie the following Saturday. No flatbed truck or "Sweet Home Alabama" this time. A private ceremony, family only. I was definitely not invited, but I was there anyway, watching, from the far side of the cemetery, still brooding about what happened.

I know damn well it could have me been in that box, dropping down into the deep, dark tunnel to forever. I had a bandage on my ear, covering the notch his bullet put in me, as a reminder.

But that notch wasn't my only cause for thought. That Saturday was an anniversary. They buried Harland Guthrie thirty years to the day that Charlie Marx signed onto the Valhalla force. Thirty and out. He came close, but didn't quite make it.

Nor will I, I think.

My hometown on the north shore isn't the same country I grew up in. It was a quaint little vacation village then. People came to get away for a few weeks in summer, or for hunting season in autumn, or skiing over Christmas break.

The Web has changed all that. Why live in a cramped, dirty city when you can do business from a laptop on your patio? Why not vacation year-round, sell shares from a beachfront cottage or a cozy condo looking out over a glittering lake? Valhalla's population is exploding, and crime's keeping pace with it, and everything is moving so much faster than before.

I have Charlie's job now, boss of Major Crime. But I won't see my thirty and out.

I'll be lucky to make twenty.

Or ten.

---

*The question comes up at every seminar and signing. Where do you get your ideas? We trot out the usual suspects: research, serendipity, even dreams. But this story, "30 And Out"? Came differently.

I was headed home from Flint, one of the most violent cities in America, when up ahead a cop flicked on his flashers, blocking off the intersection to let a funeral motorcade pass.

But this was no ordinary funeral. No hearse, no long, black limousines. The cortege was led by a rusty flatbed truck flying twin rebel battle flags and carrying an undersized casket on a low bier. "Sweet Home Alabama" was thundering out of the truck's massive sound system, loud enough to wake the dead. Behind it, a long train of Harleys and muscle cars stretched out for a mile or more. Outlaw bikers in club colors, rednecks in faded denims and coveralls. Nary a suit in sight. Some of the mourners were armed. NRA to the bone and proud of it.

But the thing that struck me most deeply was the unconcealed rage in their faces, anger at the unfairness of life. A coffin should never be so small. It should be full-sized, large enough to hold a soul grown old, one who's enjoyed a rich, full time on this planet, lived a life that family and friends can celebrate at the end.

Not a lonely little box, just big enough to hold a life ended early. Funerals are never happy, but this one was so clearly unfair that . . . Well.

Where do stories come from? Sometimes they run you right off the road.

Jim Allyn is a graduate of Alpena Community College and the University of Michigan, where he earned a master's degree in journalism. While at Michigan he won a Hopwood Creative Writing Award, Major Novel Division, and also won the Detroit Press Club Foundation Student Grand Award for the best writing in a college newspaper or periodical.

Upon graduation, he pursued a career in health care marketing and communications, working first as a science writer with the University of Michigan and subsequently holding management positions at major hospitals in Michigan, Illinois, and Indiana. In 2009 he retired as Vice President of Marketing and Community Relations at Elkhart General Healthcare System in Elkhart, Indiana.

His first short story, "The Tree Hugger," appeared in Ellery Queen Mystery Magazine in 1993 and was selected by Marvin Lachman as one of the "Best Mystery Short stories of 1993." Seven other stories have been published by EQMM since then, including "Princess Anne," which was selected for inclusion in The Best American Mystery Stories 2014, and "The Master of Negwegon," which was published in The Best American Mystery Stories 2017. Allyn is a US Naval Air Force veteran, having served in a helicopter squadron aboard the aircraft carrier USS Intrepid. He gets valuable insights on law enforcement and things Jarhead from his son Brodie, a Michigan graduate who served in the Marine Corps and is now a federal agent with Homeland Security Investigations in Florida where, among many other responsibilities, he leads a highly active SWAT team.

THINGS THAT FOLLOW

Jim Allyn

F our men were clustered around the form on the stainless-steel autopsy table: two in dark blue uniforms, a homicide detective in a plain dark suit, and the medical examiner in a knee-length white lab coat. The room was cool, sterile, gleaming metal and white plastic. Latex gloves and various instruments of invasion were carefully laid out. A Mr. Coffee was perking happily in the corner.

It was early and quiet, even for the morgue. Sometimes when four or five tables were in use it was almost a locker-room atmosphere, with dark humor the order of the day. But not this morning.

She was a cold, dead, naked teenager, and nobody felt like cracking wise. They didn't know who she was. Her skin was shockingly white. It had the perfection of youth. Her face was that of a child, although she hadn't been a child maybe ever. The tracks on her arms said that. Her face was unremarkable, but not without strength. Her hair was dyed an unnatural deep jet black, black as night, and was streaked with orange and green and yellow like some mysterious tropical bird from a vanishing rain forest. Was she pretty? Hank Sawyer, one of the uniforms, wondered. Often you couldn't tell looking at them dead, the prettiness fading with the pulse. A dark red channel had been carved down her middle. It looked like someone had poured red raspberry preserves from her crotch to her breastbone and now it had dried to a reddish black crust. Hank had seen smaller openings in gutted deer.

"Another lost soul with a nice ass," Carmen Bastio, the homicide detective, said. "Popcorn for perverts and heartbreak for Mom and

Dad." Carmen kept up a good front, but Hank knew these kinds of killings affected him. He had three daughters, the oldest seventeen. Carmen's face was ruddy. He drank too much late in the evening.

"No tats, huh?" Hank said. "That's rare these days."

"She's got a little one on her butt," Carmen said. "A little blue butterfly. Light blue and ragged. Looks homemade."

"Why do you think he opened her up like that?" the other uniform, Joey Sheridan, asked. Joey had the round, smooth, freckled face of a man who would still be called "boyish" at sixty-five. He had recently transferred from public relations to street duty, and the jury was still out. Despite several years on the force, he was still considered green. An unknown quantity. A desk in PR wasn't the street.

"Why does a dentist from Minnesota fly to Zimbabwe to shoot Cecil the Lion?" Daniel Linsky, the ME, asked. "Because it makes him feel good, that's why. There, I just saved the department ten grand in psychological consultation. Be sure to tell them."

"At least Cecil the Lion had a name," Hank said.

"Oh, this girl has a name," Carmen said. "That's the big challenge. Not finding her killer. Finding out her name."

"One thing about a little town like where I'm from," Joey said. "If a young girl ever goes missing, everybody knows her name, everybody knows her family, and everybody goes looking for her. Everybody helps, everybody pitches in." Joey had wavy blond hair, was tall and lanky, and had a kind of yokel look about him. A country boy. " 'Course, this would never happen in my hometown in the first place."

Almost in unison Hank and Carmen and the ME raised their heads from the butchered girl to look at Joey. There was an innocent undercurrent to what he had said, the kind of innocence that if any of them had ever had it had long since been ground away.

It conjured up a magical apple-pie American small town where everyone's a friend and beautiful teenage girls are never disemboweled by vicious freaks. They knew no such town existed, but they weren't sure Joey did.

An awkward silence. Carmen broke it. "Hank, I asked you to stop by because she was found near that area in Campbell where you've been working. You seen her before?"

"If I did, it probably would have been in front of a club," Hank said. He stepped in closer and studied her face. Hank was accustomed to seeing the dead. He'd seen more in Iraq in an afternoon than he'd seen during his entire time on the force. He was beyond shocking, but not beyond anything else.

She looked surprised. Young and surprised for the last time.

It was not a flashback. Not a disorienting, disabling episode. Those were pretty much behind him now. It was a remnant of Iraq, nonetheless. Something in the shape of the girl's sad lips that reminded him of the slain matriarch. A powerful memory that took him back . . .

He was inside the home. The bodies of the Sunni family were lying awkwardly on the floor, twisted and splayed by the bullets that had killed them. Hank was standing alone, black rifle over his shoulder, surveying the silent scene, when a tall, crusty major, a fellow Marine, entered, the oldest-looking soldier he had ever seen.

The major stood next to Hank for what seemed a great while. Together they stared at the bodies. In the middle of the carnage two children were embracing at this, their last moment. Whoever had paid this fratricidal visit, whatever faction or militia or perhaps even the Mahdi Army, they had gunned them down at their evening meal, creating this contorted fatal ring. Blood everywhere, food and shards of bowls and glasses everywhere. Colors and textures splashed across clothing and faces.

The faces were those of individuals, young and old. Their expressions, all different, burned into Hank's memory. His eyes rested and became fixed on the face of the matriarch he had spoken to and warned the day before. She was the wife and mother and grandmother and even in death was the force in the room. The one who was close to them all, had helped them all, had been there for each of them in many different ways. The one who bore their weight.

Suddenly the dead woman's head jerked slightly and a faint sound escaped her lips. Hank took a clumsy half-step forward. The major blocked him with an arm. "Some kind of death rattle," he said. "The weight of the body pushes out gas. There's nothing we can do.

"We've been telling them to clear out for two weeks," the major went on gruffly. "We warned them. We told them to leave. We told them it was dangerous."

"Yes sir," Hank said. If he had learned one thing in the Corps, it was that corporals don't question majors. But he felt compelled to speak anyway: "What if we'd never have liberated this family, Major? Think they'd be any worse off?"

The major glanced sharply at Hank. His face tightened, then instantly relaxed, and he shrugged. "Well, Corporal, there's that, isn't there? There's always that." A long moment went by. "Where you from, soldier?" the major asked softly.

"Michigan," Hank said. "Black River."

The major wore a blank look.

"Northeastern Michigan. About two hundred and fifty miles north of Detroit," Hank said. "Little town right on the coast."

"Ah," the major breathed knowingly. "Ah. The shores of Lake Huron."

"Yes," Hank said.

The wistfulness, the fondness in the major's voice told Hank of the major's intimate knowledge of the region and brought to Hank a painful sense of loss. He might never see the big lake again. Never again see that high blue sky with circling gulls, see the towering white pines, and hear the quiet lapping of waves softly surging up a sandy beach. A gust of dry desert wind came through an open window and brushed his face with the faint scent of death.

The major put his hand gently on Hank's shoulder: "Son," he said, "no matter where your travels take you from here—become an astronaut and fly to the moon—you'll never be any further away from home than you are right now."

"Hank?" Carmen queried. "Anybody home?"

"Sorry," Hank said, then quickly, "There's some around Campbell the same age, same look, but I don't think I've ever seen her. Was she wearing a black leather jacket, high waisted and tight, lots of bangles on it? You know, those shiny trinket-things like on bracelets."

"Charms," Carmen said, looking at Hank appraisingly. "Yeah, she was."

"Well, she's in sort of a club, then, not really a gang, I don't think, just a bunch of young girlfriends dressing alike. It's worth checking out. I'd start at Tubby's about ten. From what I've seen, there's at least five or six of 'em. I'd bet nobody over twenty."

"Okay, good," Carmen said. "Good. I can use that. Thanks for stopping by."

As they left, Carmen motioned for Hank to wait up. "Go ahead," Hank said to Joey and went back to Carmen.

"So that's Joey Sheridan," Carmen said. "I heard about him. If you bring 'em to the morgue again he'll need therapy."

Hank laughed. "You think it's that bad?"

"You know there's a pool on him?"

"Pool for what?"

"For what he'll do if there's real trouble. Melt. Freeze. Puke. Be okay. Lot of guys think he should have stayed in PR, that he's not cut out for the street."

"Yeah? Where's the smart money?"

"You kiddin'? Where do you think? Anyway, I figure if anything happens you'll handle it because you always handle it."

"Like I'll have a choice," Hank said.

"I was sorry to hear about Frankie. How long were you guys together?"

"Six years."

Frankie Cohen passed a physical, then two weeks later had a heart attack. He went from cholesterol being a little high to the cardiologist saying he should think about early retirement to dying at forty-one while reeling in a northern pike. He was a good partner and a good friend to Hank. They took turns watching each other's back. Their relationship had a comfortable rhythm to it.

"Well, I don't think this Joey is going to fill his shoes," Carmen said. "I don't think he understands that we don't always help little old ladies cross the street. Sometimes we have to put her down with an arm bar because she's high on crack and trying to kill her two-year-old grandson. Rose-colored glasses. A sweet man headed for a fall. Better get Butch to transfer him back to PR."

"Got a meeting with him first thing in the morning," Hank said.

⚬━━●

Hank shifted uncomfortably in his chair. He was six foot three and stocky and easily overwhelmed the standard office chair. He had something to say to Assistant Chief Butch Johnson about Joey Sheridan, and he really didn't want to.

If you could draw a soldier—square shoulders, square jaw, determined bearing, sandy hair cut shorter on the sides—that soldier would look like Hank Sawyer. Butch Johnson was a darker, shorter, denser version.

A dark green Marine, Butch was the informal leader of the informal Marine Corps Mafia within the South Bend PD; all the ex-Marines who never really considered themselves "ex." Mostly veterans of Afghanistan and Iraq, they were a close-knit group who hung together and helped each other out. Butch was a busy man. Hank was sure he would consider his concern petty. He hoped he would be wrong.

Among themselves, the Marine Corps Mafia expressed serious doubt about Joey Sheridan. Like Hank, this group of veterans had seen plenty of combat. Yes, it was war, but killing is killing. And if the moment ever came, they weren't sure Joey Sheridan would be up to the task. And none of them wanted to partner with him, including Hank.

"Okay, let's have it," Butch said, recognizing Hank's reluctance to speak.

"I'm not comfortable with the guy."

"What guy?"

"Joey Sheridan."

Butch groaned. "Oh, here we go. Takes a good reason to mess around with assignments, Hank, you know that."

"I don't want to work with him."

"Why?"

"Instinct."

"Oh, well, no problem, there's a reason that will breeze right on through. Joey's okay, Hank. He's been through the same in-depth interviews and foolproof psych evals that we all have." They both laughed. "Look, this is not a small thing. It's going to irritate people for no apparent reason."

"No apparent reason? You heard about the pool?"

"That's a bunch of crap," Butch snapped. "Stupid waste of time."

Hank brought intensity, focus, and seriousness of purpose to any job of work. This Joey thing was a job of work to Hank, because otherwise he wouldn't even have brought it up, and Butch knew he wasn't going to let it go.

"I can't mess with assignments on your personal whim. You kidding me? You want me to give you a choice of air fresheners for your prowler while I'm at it? You like Cinnamon Spice or Wildflowers?"

"It's not a whim," Hank said flatly. "I've learned the hard way not to ignore my gut. I trust my own antenna in some situations, and this is one. I don't want to be a pain in the ass but this guy's trouble. Unreliable. So I'm askin'."

"Let me guess," Butch said. "Because he comes from PR?" He snorted. "You're worried about being with Joey in a shaky situation? Well, welcome to the world, pal. Nobody's reliable until they've proved it, and you know it. Nothing counts except the real deal and you can't simulate that."

Hank didn't know how to push Butch and, anyway, he didn't want to be pushy so he just sat staring into space.

"Give me something," Butch said.

Hank was silent.

"That's what I thought," Butch said.

As he was talking, Butch caught a glimpse of the small, egg-shaped traumatic tattoo on the left side of Hank's chin. It came and went depending on the angle of the light, a whimsical patch of blue or gray or black. Butch remembered it as a larger area of harsh granular red when Hank first came on board. He was still having trouble with it then. Particles of sand, glass, metal, asphalt—anything the shotgun-blast force of the IED had picked up along the way—were embedded there. Aggressive scrubbing under sedation coupled with surgical, enzymatic, and mechanical debridement had got the worst of it out. But microscopic specks of Iraq were still in there, glacially working their way up through the flesh, trying to get out. All scars were like that.

"He's ex–Air Force," Butch offered.

Hank frowned. "Death from Above. Not exactly a recommendation for our kind of work."

"He's won the pistol competition twice."

"Targets don't bleed." Finally Hank said, "Okay, okay, you've got nothing solid to work with. But his reaction to that dead teen in the morgue worries me. It was the way he talked about her. Like she was his sister or something. Carmen said 'rose-colored glasses.' "

"So he failed your and Carmen's half-assed tough-guy test," Butch said. "Big deal. . . . Well, look, best I can do is switch you out in maybe a month or two. Something will open up. Always does. Don't bitch to anybody, just suck it up and keep your mouth shut. Won't do a damn bit of good to have Joey and the others know you think he's shaky. And if you ask me, it's kind of sad that we're talking about somebody maybe bein' a bad cop because he might be too nice.

"I'll move you in a way that won't reflect on you or Joey or me. Might look a little strange, but no one will care. To the degree that it's possible, I'll try to keep you out of hot zones."

"I don't expect you to do that, Butch."

"With your track record, if you trust your gut, maybe I should too."

On a cloudy Monday afternoon Hank Sawyer and Joey Sheridan
were headed for the bad side of South Bend. Hank was quiet. He
knew Joey could feel his reticence, but Joey was content with small
talk and fiddling with time-wasters on his phone.

They were going to talk to Sally Sanchez, the sixty-five-year-
old mother of Mitch Sanchez, a two-time loser who had a habit
of seeking refuge at home, refuge his mom was known to provide
in the past. Mitch had finally hit the big time: He was suspected
of a homicide during an armed robbery. It was a SOP discussion
that Hank knew would be futile. He had talked to Sally before.

They turned into a sinking section of town with mixed light
industry and low-income homes. All the homes in this neighborhood were bowed and bent and fading, the ranches sitting on
slab foundations like they were intended for car habitation rather
than human.

Hank pulled the prowler into the gravel driveway of a typi-
cally nondescript gray ranch. He and Joey stood under a ripped
green-and-white-striped canvas awning that looked like it was
ready to go with the next good blow. Hank pushed the doorbell,
but nothing happened. He knocked.

"Door's open," came a gravelly female voice.

She was sitting at the kitchen table in dull afternoon light
wearing a light blue threadbare cotton robe, a cup of coffee before
her and a Marlboro dangling from the corner of her mouth. Her
hair was dried-out salt-and-pepper. She glanced up at Hank. A
small smile. "You again," she said, a lungful of smoke coming out
in a stream.

"You remember," Hank said. "I'm touched. Here for the same
reason too."

"I haven't seen Mitch. Hasn't called, hasn't been around."

"You said that last time and we picked him up in front of your house."

"He comes and goes," she said. "He's a grown man. Last time you put him in the hospital."

"Wasn't my idea. He came at me." The tats-on-tats gangbanger with God knows what chemicals coursing through his bloodstream had decked Hank with a sucker punch. But Hank got up and Mitch found out why his sucker punch wasn't enough.

"Mitch isn't so easy to put in the hospital."

Hank shrugged. "That's a fact, but I figured better him than me. . . . Listen, Sally, it's different this time. Worse. Armed robbery. Somebody got hurt. Believe me, you don't want a SWAT team rolling in here on a tip. He needs to give himself up or you need to tell me where he is. The only way these things don't end badly is if someone helps us out."

She nodded. "I know. I know that's true. But it can't be me. He trusts me. And anyway, it's Mitch, so it's gonna end badly no matter what." She looked over at Joey. Looked him over, up and down. Studied him.

"Me and Officer Sawyer are having a talk, sonny," she said. "Why don't you go out in the other room with loverboy and watch the game."

Joey looked at Hank. Hank nodded. "I got this," he said. Joey went into the living room.

Sally sipped her coffee. "What is it," she asked, "take your kid to work day?"

Hank laughed. "He's new on the job," he said.

"He's a sweetheart," she said. "Mitch would eat him alive."

"Joey's won our pistol competition twice and he was in the Air Force," Hank said.

Sally smiled hugely. "Right," she said.

"May I?" Hank asked and Sally nodded. He poured himself some coffee and sat down with Sally in her worn robe, her cigarette, her chipped white cup. Traces of the smooth, forgotten contours of youth were still visible in her weathered face. He could imagine her young, pretty, laughing. Full of promise. And she had been once. He used to be brusque with older women, never had time for them. He wasn't like that anymore. Sally Sanchez reminded him of the moms and grandmothers he'd sat with in Iraq, on the floor, trying to gather information, get support, or give them advice, like get the hell out of here before you and your kids get shot or blown up. But they had nowhere to go. They had seen the sprawling squalor of refugee camps that stretched to the horizon. And Sally didn't have anywhere to go either. She was stuck with her chipped white cup and a son gone bad. It seemed to Hank that sons gone bad were a staple of female existence regardless of oceans or religions or race. "You were alone last time I was here," Hank said. "Congratulations."

Sally tossed her head toward the living room. "Right. My loverboy," she said in disdain. "I thought I'd found my soulmate. That's all I been lookin' for, really. Someone to be with me. Love him, you know." She gazed at the white cup. "But he drinks. And when he drinks, he's different. Mean. Ever know anyone like that?"

"Lots." Hank said. "It's half my work and half my family."

"Yes, I thought I'd found my soulmate," she went on. "God, we got along so great." There was a lost passion beneath that aging smoker's skin. A tiny pink bow held her thinning ponytail in place. Hank thought she must have been really something when she was eighteen.

"I get so angry, I mean, really, he told me, 'It's me and you baby, all the way.' And I believed him. Then he turns out to be mean."

"How long have you known him?"

"Three or four months, I guess."

"So is he roughing you up? I can have a talk with him."

She turned furious eyes on him, her voice rising, shrill. "He's not rough with me. I never said that. Roy loves me."

"Oh, oh, sorry. I mean, you said he was mean when he drank. I just assumed . . ."

"No, he isn't mean that way. He watches TV."

"Watches TV."

"Yeah, he comes home from work, pours himself one big drink, plops down on the floor, and lays there watching TV. Every night. Like clockwork. He'll sip that drink till bedtime. He watches whatever. Doesn't matter. Movies. Wrestling. War. Scandals. Sometimes I call to him but he just stays there."

"Does he ever drink more than that?"

"Naw. Oh, on Saturdays he might have two. Doesn't drink on Sunday. Says the Lord doesn't like it. Like the Lord gives a damn about having a drink. Sometimes he goes for hours without saying a word to me. And us fresh in love and all." Her voice trailed off.

"It's natural for things to slow down," Hank said gently. "I'm sure it'll be okay, Sally." He waved his card at her and laid it on the table. "Now listen, if Mitch shows up or contacts you, please call me. He's in deep this time, but we can help him. He's gonna have to do time, but he doesn't have to take the fall for all of it. If you're not careful, that SWAT team will show up, go cowboy, and Mitch will get hurt. It doesn't have to be that way. Together we can keep him from getting hurt."

She smiled at him warmly, lighting another cigarette, and he smiled back, indicating without words that they both knew Mitch would come here, however briefly, and that she would not contact Hank under any circumstances. Pro forma visit over for both parties.

From the kitchen Hank moved into the man cave television gloom. Joey was standing straight, restlessly chewing away at a toothpick, arms folded across his chest, wired and bored.

"Who's this?" Hank asked.

"Tigers and Indians," said loverboy Roy, a big man lying on the floor with his chin on a pillow and a small black cat comfortably curled in the small of his back. "Tigers have talent but only use it when it doesn't matter," he said. "They're like Mitch."

<hr />

Night was here and they were sitting in the worst car in the motor pool, a beat-up, slime green 2010 Honda Civic. It blended nicely with the neighborhood. The only new cars here were just passing through. Plus, they were likely going to sit here all night, so the fact that the Honda might look abandoned didn't hurt. On blocks with no tires or sitting on flat tires, useless cars were as common as unmown lawns. Of the assignments on Butch's sheet, this stakeout was the least likely to yield results and bring the kind of action that Hank was worried about.

They had found a narrow empty lot between two small repair shops. Between the two buildings and from the back of the lot they would be in shadows and had an angled look at the dismal ranch of Sally Sanchez, enough to see the front and side doors.

"You first or me?" Hank asked.

"Go ahead, catch some Zs," Joey said. "I haven't done anything all day and I'm not tired."

"Talked me into it," Hank said, sliding down in the seat. As he dozed off, he knew he wouldn't dream about four-thousand-pound Humvees doing cartwheels through the air, although he'd seen that. He wouldn't dream about buildings turned into hollow-eyed skeletons, although he'd seen plenty of those. He would dream about the Sunni family. His dream was an imagined prequel of something he hadn't actually seen. Those about to be slaughtered were at dinner—chatting, happy, eating, safe—when hooded, shouting, shadowy figures burst into the room. Bullets were sprayed wildly and the noise was deafening. Family members toppled into the positions that he and the major had come upon. And through all the lethal chaos the matriarch with the sad dead face struggles to shield the children until she, too, is among the fallen.

"Wow, you call that sleep? You were like a beagle dreaming about rabbits. Yippin', legs jerkin'."

Joey handed the binoculars to Hank. "See that cat asleep in the window?" With the binos, a thin black shape at the base of the window turned out to be a black cat stretched out between the window and the stained, pearl-colored curtains, which were tightly closed.

"Yeah."

"It's not dead to the world. It's dead period."

"And just how do you know that?"

"We've been here almost three hours. Hasn't budged."

"Interesting, but so what?"

"So we should check it out," Joey said eagerly. "One of us sneak up to the window. See if it's breathing."

"Why would we do that?"

"Because if it's dead, it's probable cause for entry. If we can get in there, Mitch is probably lyin' on the couch drinkin' a beer and watchin' the tube."

"Probable cause? Baloney. How do you figure that?"

"Should be good enough for a good lawyer to get something to fly," Joey said. "We're on a legitimate stakeout, so we have a legitimate reason for watching the place. We see a dead cat in the window. We know it's dead because we've checked it out. It means the person inside can't properly tend to it, so they may be in trouble. One of those 'I've fallen into the tub and I can't get out to feed the cat' kind of deals. So we're going in to help out and oh, by the way, there's Mitch. Or maybe even animal cruelty, abandonment, maybe; dead cat in the window isn't exactly ideal care, isn't exactly business as usual. What I'm sayin' is, a good lawyer can work with something like that."

Hank didn't say what he was thinking, because he thought it might spur Joey on—that there was an extremely slim chance that the right combination of wink-and-a-nod lawyer and judge just might waive the warrant. But he didn't think it could ever survive an appeal. Just too thin.

"Never fly," he said. "Need exigent circumstance for warrantless entry, and the more exigent, the better. Think gunshots. Think screams. Think smoke from the roof. Even if the cat is dead, it's not an emergency. Anything we get will be tainted and tossed.

"Tell you what, let's check our feline friend. I'm gonna put the glasses on 'em for five minutes. Time me." Hank tightened the focus on the cat. He could see it pretty well with the faint rays from a streetlight.

"Time," Joey said.

Hank had seen no movement. "You might be right," he said.

"Okay, so we knock on the door, announce ourselves . . . just want to let them know there's a dead cat in the window and waltz on into the house."

"Jesus, Joey, you don't just waltz into a house. A dead cat in the window doesn't make for a valid search. They'd have no reason to let us wander around the house for that, and a judge would know it. Just let it go, will you, relax. This is a stakeout. We're just looking for Mitch—or at least someone we can claim is Mitch—to be goin' in or out."

"A dead cat in the window isn't business as usual," Joey said firmly. "We can use it."

"We can use it to get our ass chewed off for illegal entry." Hank stretched, still groggy from his restless sleep. He could see Joey was worked up. First time he'd seen that. He decided to try to placate him. No one was in charge here. They were temporary partners, and the fact that Hank was senior didn't matter. "Look, if it's not dead, it's a moot point, right, so I'll go to the window up close and personal and see what's what. If anyone comes out or approaches the place, give me one quick beep on the horn. Don't use the radio."

"Works for me," Joey said, satisfied for the moment to be doing anything but just sitting.

In the brittle moonlight there was a snap to the early morning air as Hank moved along the side of one of the low industrial buildings, then walked briskly in the open right up to the window. The cat's mouth was open slightly, a bit of its pink tongue protruding. Hank rubbed his finger on the window then tapped lightly, something only a cat would hear. Nothing. He watched the rib cage. The rib cage was not moving. The cat sure looked dead. Damn.

Hank returned to the Honda.

"How come you kept lookin' up when you were goin' over there?" Joey asked.

"Did I? Rooftops, I guess. Just a habit. They're great for snipers and for phoning in IEDs."

"That's not much of a problem in South Bend."

"I didn't get the habit in South Bend," Hank said.

"So . . . ?"

"So it looks dead to me, but it's a lame-ass reason to roust the place, and if something does happen it's going to be a mess trying to make it stick. And, okay, maybe it's boring as hell, but we just have to sit here and do our job."

Joey shifted in his seat and looked directly at Hank. Hank had the feeling of looking a strange dog in the eye and having no idea what it might do. Might lick your hand. Might bite it off. It's not growling or showing its teeth, but you're very much aware that you really don't know the animal.

"It's enough to go in," Joey said mildly. "I want to do it. So they throw it out, so what? Maybe we get the guy, maybe we don't, so what?"

"Look, we're partners," Hank said. "We're supposed to agree on a course of action."

"Fine, you can be my partner sitting here in the car doing nothing and I'll be your partner going into that house."

"You know I can't do that. I have to back you and we have to call it in."

"Then do it. Call it in and back me up." Joey got out of the Honda.

Hank was startled. Joey was just going to go ahead and do it. He had to decide: confront him or what. Okay, to keep the peace and follow Butch's advice, he would allow himself to look silly back at the ranch. Half-assed or not, they would at least look like they were cooperating in trying to do their job. He didn't know what confronting Joey might lead to, but it wouldn't be anything good. Hank got out of the car and grabbed Joey by both shoulders, squaring him up in front of him.

"I can't call it in because I don't know what the hell I'd say," Hank said. "If it's necessary, we'll just say we thought the other guy called it in.

"This isn't a lark," he said firmly. "Anything could happen, so we're gonna do it right. First, let's see what we can through all the windows and check the layout. Then we'll figure out the next step. And just for the record, if there's an exigent circumstance around here, it's Butch sticking me with your sorry ass."

"Sure thing," Joey said. "Whatever you say." It was clear that angering Hank did not bother him.

Moving together, they crossed the street, Hank pissed off at how stupidity has a habit of getting its way. As they approached the house, they went left and circled it. The blinds were drawn on the windows. The only variation was the cat at the front window. On the driveway side, a window glowed faintly from a single light. Hank remembered that this was the kitchen. He decided to go in the front, away from the light.

"Okay," he said. "We'll announce ourselves and wait to be let in. If Mitch is there, maybe we'll be lucky and catch him in the open."

"Guns?" Joey asked.

"Not for a dead cat, but be damn ready in case it's Mitch."

Hank beat loudly on the door, and suddenly Joey surprised Hank by putting his shoulder to it. The worn lock gave up easily. "You jerk," Hank breathed. "Now it's forced entry for maybe a dead cat."

The door opened directly into a small living room faintly lit by a plug-in night light. The couch and overstuffed chairs had seen better days. At one end of the room, a backlit archway led to the kitchen. On the other side, a dark shadow of a hallway led to the back of the house. But what captured their attention was someone on the floor apparently asleep in front of the television a few feet away. It was the spot where loverboy Roy had been watching the ballgame. The TV was off.

"Police," Hank said loudly. "Everything okay here?" No response. No movement.

As their eyes adjusted to the half-light, they could see dark ovals on the person's back. Hank drew his Glock and Joey followed suit. "Cover the room," Hank told Joey. He approached the body and knelt. It was loverboy Roy, his white T-shirt decorated with four dark smudges of bullet holes. Hank didn't bother to check for a pulse. He pointed to himself and then the kitchen doorway on the left: He would check that out. He motioned for Joey to check down the hallway.

With his gun up and ready, Hank moved to the open archway.

Bathed in the stark light of a single bulb, Sally Sanchez was sitting at the kitchen table wearing the same light-blue, threadbare cotton robe, a cup of coffee before her and a golden-brown pint of Seagram's VO. A little black Browning .25 auto about the size of a deck of cards was a few inches from her right hand. She turned her head to look at Hank.

"Sally, please don't move," Hank said softly. "Want to tell me what happened?" His gun was at table level, pointing at her body.

"I really loved him, you know."

"So you said. I remember."

Joey appeared in the doorway on the other side of the kitchen. He shook his head, indicating that no one was in the back of the house. He aimed his Glock directly at Sally, who didn't seem to notice. Her focus was entirely on Hank.

"I got so angry," Sally choked. "I mean, I really thought he was my soulmate. I didn't want to hurt him. But he was so mean."

"I'm sure people will understand, Sally."

"Don't you tell them he was beating me. He never did that. Roy loved me."

"I won't tell anybody anything," Hank said. "Sally, you're going to have to come with us."

She didn't move. Hank hesitated. He didn't believe there was any danger. His sense of it was that the violence was over, drained away. He looked into her eyes and saw pain in that aging face—and the pain of other faces—and he saw so much that pointing a gun at her was something he just couldn't do.

"Look, Sally," Hank said gently, slowly and deliberately holstering his Glock. Joey's eyes widened, and in the very moment of that de-escalating gesture Sally smiled ever so slightly and that little smile curled into a snarl of sheer menace. A frightening, twisted face that jolted Hank, as he knew instantly that this was how she looked when she shot loverboy Roy four times. She lunged for her Browning.

Joey's aim was fixed on Sally's heart when she lunged for her gun, but he did not fire. Instead, he took a quick half-step and launched himself across the kitchen. He hurtled through the air for several feet and crashed into the wooden table, collapsing everything, dumping Sally to the floor, and anointing the room with a mixture of Seagram's and coffee. The little black automatic skittered across the yellowed linoleum to the other side of the room.

Joey's face was buried in Sally's warm, soft chest, her robe reeking of cheap perfume and sour sweat, old booze and old smoke. She was motionless. "That damn Roy," she slurred into his neck. Her eyes closed.

Joey got to his feet. His pant leg was torn and he had a small cut on his calf from the sawtooth edge of a broken table leg. He knelt and shifted Sally to a more natural position there on the floor. He eased her limp arms around her back and cuffed her. He turned to face Hank, who was standing stock still, glued to the same spot. His Glock was still holstered.

"She's out, Hank," Joey said. "Probably half drunk and half cold-cocked. We got to call this in, like, right now."

"You call it in," Hank said.

"What do you want me to say?"

"Use your own judgment," Hank said. "Whatever you say will be okay with me. I need a moment. I'm gonna go get the car."

Hank walked through the cool night air lost in thought. He was shaken. He couldn't believe what he'd done. He felt like he should be slapped around and kicked up and down the street. "So stupid," he muttered in disgust. He realized that wherever he had been mentally, it was sufficiently dysfunctional that he wouldn't have reacted fast enough to prevent Sally from getting that gun. But he was a learner. He believed he knew what prompted the dangerous move. A type of thinking had caused him to do something that was potentially deadly. He wouldn't go there again. He would see it coming.

He pulled the Honda well off to the side of the broad gravel driveway, leaving plenty of space for the two prowlers and the ambulance that were quickly on the scene. He watched as officers and paramedics entered the ranch. They brought Sally out on a stretcher and loaded her in. Joey came out with them, said something to them, then walked over to the Honda and stood by the open window. The skinny black cat was in his arms. It was alert and seemed to like him. "Old," Joey said. "Shallow breather. . . . Deaf."

"What did you report?" Hank asked.

"I told them we heard shots," Joey said. "That's why we went in. Couldn't tell how many because they were muffled. We heard shots and went in fast. I didn't mention the cat. Didn't want to screw around with that on a murder case. I said Sally was standing in the kitchen with the gun at her side and I tackled her as soon as we came in. Didn't tell them about you holstering your gun. Didn't want to screw around with that either, and that's not something you want in your record. So that's it . . . everything happened in a couple minutes . . . really fast. . . . If Sally contradicts anything, well, she was drunk, wasn't she? . . . How's that sound?"

Hank nodded approval. "That's damn good. It will save us a lot of explaining and not hurt a thing. Typical stakeout, we hear shots, beat feet to the house, bust the door, and you tackle her as soon as we come in. . . . That was one hell of a body block, by the way. No hesitation. Got to be one of the fastest moves I ever saw. . . . But you should have dropped her, you know. A bullet is a sure thing. A tackle, not so much. . . . You risked both our lives."

Joey laughed softly. "You're talking to me about risk? The guy who holstered his gun in front of an armed murder suspect? She was in my sights. I could have popped her no problem. But I was following your lead. You were trying to finesse her, okay, I get that. You saw something in her that wasn't there or maybe missed something that was. People make mistakes like that every minute of every day. With your record, you get a mulligan. But I'll tell you what, I wouldn't do that again even if the person with the gun is the Virgin Mary."

"Never happened before and won't be back," Hank said. But he wasn't all that sure. Sometimes things that follow catch up.

"Here's how I see it," Joey said. "There was a shooting here tonight and someone got killed. We handled the situation without shooting and without killing. I figure that's the best we can do. We get paid to take chances and the chances we took tonight were the best kind. We tried to save a life. Sally is still breathing, and who knows, maybe she'll invent a cure for cancer in the slammer."

"More likely she'll knife a guard," Hank said.

Joey laughed. "Yeah, you're probably right. Anyway, our first order of business is finding a good home for this old guy. I'd say his support system was pretty much wiped out tonight."

Hank looked up at Joey. Standing there with the cat asleep in his arms, he was perfectly calm, unfazed by the night's events. Hank realized that if he had not followed Joey's lead, they would still be across the street in the Honda deciding where to go to get morning coffee. Just another uneventful stakeout. And then when someone else had to handle the situation with Sally, maybe something terrible goes down and she kills someone else or gets herself killed or both. If they had killed Sally, the mood at this moment would be very different. Trying to get to sleep this night would be very different. Hank believed every cop in the department would have shot Sally Sanchez when she went for that gun. Every cop but one. It slowly came to him, almost as an epiphany, that he was looking at his next partner. It would take some work, but it would work.

"Paper will put up with anything printed on it." So said Joseph Stalin. I don't generally turn to Stalin for inspiration, but I find this particular truism useful. It helps me remember that as a writer you can write anything you want. Anything. Period. I'd been working on "Things That Follow" for a while and had received early feedback from two editors. The feedback was the same and bad: "Too dark. Characters are off-putting."

I'm usually wedded to my characters and my plot. And if you listen to all critics, you won't get out of bed in the morning. But these two I knew I shouldn't disregard. I had no idea how to "tweak" the story. It was solid. So, what the hell, in keeping with the welcoming nature of the blank page, I tried something dramatic. I inverted the characters.

And inverted the plot. Bad cop became good cop. A cop I had envisioned as a sneering asshole became St. Francis of Assisi walking happily down a sunlit forest path with a fawn under one arm and a lamb under the other. A killed cat became a rescued cat. A shot old lady became a saved old lady. A wartime flashback of grotesque butchery was softened to something almost wistful.

This inversion turned out to be engaging and the more I worked on it, the better I liked it. There was still tension, still conflict, still murder, still realism, but the mood music was far different and the ending was altogether different.

It's easy when you're working in this genre to be oblivious to the fact that you're sinking, constantly trying to one-up yourself in dark doings. Like car chases in the movies. Got to have at least one more spectacular crash than the last flick you made. Funny thing, though, identification is paramount in fiction. And I found it far easier to identify with my inverted characters. Thus, I found it easier to empathize with them. I just plain liked them more than my characters who were sinking ever deeper into the darkness. Is there a place for these half-craven characters and stories? Of course. And it's a revered place. Do you always have to write about them? No. That should be a no-brainer but, apparently, it wasn't to me. In the end, then, this challenging inversion turned out to be a useful course correction in my writing and introduced me to characters I liked hanging out with and will be visiting again.

Michael Bracken is the author of several books, including the private eye novel All White Girls, *and more than twelve hundred short stories in several genres. His short crime fiction has appeared in* Alfred Hitchcock Mystery Magazine, Black Cat Mystery Magazine, Black Mask, Ellery Queen Mystery Magazine, Espionage Magazine, Mike Shayne Mystery Magazine, The Best American Mystery Stories 2018, *and in many other anthologies and periodicals. A recipient of the Edward D. Hoch Memorial Golden Derringer Award for lifetime achievement in short mystery fiction, Bracken has won two Derringer Awards and been shortlisted for two others. Additionally, Bracken recently became editor of* Black Cat Mystery Magazine *and has edited several anthologies, including the Anthony Award–nominated* The Eyes of Texas *and the Mickey Finn series. He and his wife, Temple, reside in Central Texas.*

BLEST BE THE TIE THAT BINDS

Michael Bracken

Heather and Robert Connelly held their wedding reception on the expanse of lawn between the Union Revival Baptist Church and the two-story parsonage at the far end of the block. Because Robert could not conduct his own wedding ceremony, his best friend from seminary flew in from Pasadena to do the honors, and the entire congregation turned out to see their spiritual leader betrothed, filling the celebration center beyond official capacity. The lawn was awash with parishioners sporting their Sunday best when the bride and groom finally exited the church following the obligatory post-ceremony photographs, and they applauded when the heavy wooden doors opened, and the newly married couple descended the broad stone steps to join them.

The groom wore a fitted black suit over a white shirt and royal blue tie. Though purchased specifically for the wedding, their finances were such that the suit would soon be seeing duty at the many funerals over which Robert would preside as the pastor of a church with an aging congregation. His new wife was resplendent in a white, floor-length, fitted cap-sleeve gown covered in lace, a dress that would likely never be seen again once it returned from the dry cleaners. Her ash blond hair was swept up into a chignon and held in place with her grandmother's pearl-encrusted comb.

There had been no need to hire a caterer, for the Women's Auxiliary had smothered a long row of folding tables with food prepared in the church's kitchen or brought from their homes. Only the wedding cake, which was nowhere near large enough to serve all the guests, had been professionally prepared, and a variety of home-baked cakes covered the table next to it.

The gift table was equally burdened to overflowing, with several wrapped boxes relegated to the lawn beneath the table, and the gaily wrapped shoebox with the slit in the top proved too small for the number of cards that guests tried to stuff into it.

Heather and Robert were first through the buffet line, and they took their places at the head table, unable to eat as parishioner after parishioner stopped to express best wishes. Once everyone had been served, the best man lifted a glass of sparkling grape juice and toasted the newlyweds, wishing them a long and fruitful life. Later, they cut the wedding cake and posed for the photographer. Then, together and separately, they tried to talk to every one of their guests. When his throat became parched, Robert refilled his glass of sparkling grape juice and was taking a sip when someone behind him spoke softly into his ear.

"You have such a beautiful bride," said the deep male voice. "It would be a shame if anything ever happened to her."

Robert stiffened and turned, too late to see the face of the man who had just spoken. He only saw the back of a dark-haired man in a blue suit walking toward the church parking lot. As Robert started after the man, the church treasurer stopped him. Before Harvey Johnson could speak, Robert asked, "Who was that—the man who was just talking to me?"

"I wasn't paying attention."

By then the dark-haired man in the blue suit had disappeared, Harvey was congratulating him on his marriage, and Heather was on his other side telling him it was time to start their honeymoon. As everyone showered them with birdseed, Heather and Robert ducked into the back of a waiting limousine for the ride to her parents' home, where they changed into comfortable clothing and then drove to a bed and breakfast several hours from home.

They would spend their wedding night in one of six private cabins and, for the first time since accepting the pastorship a year earlier following the unexpected death of his predecessor, Robert would not arise early the next morning to deliver Sunday service. His friend from seminary would perform those honors.

Though Robert had remained celibate since his first day at seminary, he lost his virginity at Bible camp when he was sixteen. So he knew what to expect on his wedding night, but he did not truly appreciate his new wife's beauty until Heather walked out of the bathroom wearing nothing but a sheer white negligee and a shy smile. Though the stranger's comments at the reception weighed heavily on his mind during the drive to their honeymoon cabin, those thoughts, and every other thought, disappeared from

Robert's mind as he took Heather into his arms and they consummated their marriage.

⊶⊷

The following morning, after a breakfast of French toast and fresh fruit delivered to their cabin, they ventured a walk through the woods surrounding the cabins, following a marked trail that meandered downhill, across a creek twice, and then circled back uphill toward the trail's starting point.

Robert realized the previous evening that his new wife had never succumbed to temptations of the flesh and had given herself wholly to him and no one prior. He pondered as they walked whether or not his failure to mention his past indiscretions constituted a sin of omission. His teen years had been filled with activities that went against the teachings of both his church and his parents, and the sealed court records allowed Robert and his best friend Kenny Gilbert to legally deny they were ever involved in the juvenile justice system. He had forsaken his violent past when he entered seminary, and his reward had been his own church, a beautiful bride, and a bright future serving the needs of his parishioners.

His reverie was interrupted by a large dog of indeterminate breed that charged barking and snarling through the woods from a neighboring property.

Frightened, Heather clung to Robert's arm.

Without thinking, he turned and pointed at the dog.

"Go home!" he commanded, in a voice best suited to casting out the Devil.

The dog stopped less than ten feet from them. Robert shook off Heather and strode purposefully toward the animal, still shouting. "Be gone!"

The dog turned and ran away through the woods.

When Robert returned to Heather's side, his new wife wrapped her arms around him and held him tight. Then she stretched up on her tiptoes, kissed him, and whispered, "My protector."

The honeymoon was brief, and they returned home Monday morning. The wedding gifts were in the parsonage awaiting their return, and that afternoon they sat in the living room and opened them. Heather made careful notes about which gift came from which parishioner so that she could write personalized thank you notes to each of them. Having registered at a local department store, they found themselves with eight complete place settings of their chosen china, eight complete sets of flatware, numerous kitchen gadgets, and a variety of things they neither needed nor desired.

When they began opening the cards, making notes about the tens and twenties that fell out, Heather suddenly stopped and looked up at her husband.

"Bobby," she said, an expression of surprise mixed with concern on her face. She fanned out ten crisp one-hundred-dollar bills. "There's a thousand dollars in this one."

"Who's it from?"

"The card isn't signed," she said. "Who would have that kind of money?"

"In our congregation?" he asked. "No one I can think of."

"This is enough to repair my car," Heather said. She had drained her savings account to purchase her wedding dress, and student loan payments had prevented Robert from even opening a savings account.

They set the money and the card aside, intending to learn the identity of their anonymous benefactor so they could express proper thanks. They never did, though, and two weeks later Heather retrieved her car from the repair shop and drove it to the post office to mail thank you cards for all but one of their wedding gifts.

Robert was in the church office one Wednesday, several weeks after his wedding, and he was drafting that Sunday's sermon when his private line rang. The church's telephone system was so old it didn't have Caller ID, and though the church secretary was supposed to screen incoming calls, too many people knew his private telephone number because the pastor's number had not changed since the system was installed. Each time Robert answered his private line he had an equal chance of finding himself speaking to a parishioner or a telephone solicitor. So, he took a deep breath and picked up the phone. "Pastor Bob."

A vaguely familiar voice said, "You're going to see an increase in tithing this Sunday."

"Thank you," Robert said, still unsure to whom he was speaking.

"Be mindful how you spend the money."

"Excuse me?"

But the caller said nothing more, and not until after the conversation ended did Robert realize where he previously heard the caller's voice. After all, he'd only heard it once before as a whisper in his ear.

Union Revival Baptist Church did not pass collection plates during Sunday service, instead relying on parishioners to slip their tithes into a pair of collection boxes mounted to the wall in the vestibule. Just as the caller predicted, the offering boxes were almost a thousand dollars heavier than usual that Sunday, and Robert sat in his office pondering what that might mean. Tithing was up again the following Sunday, and again the Sunday after that.

The church trustees were surprised at the unexpected surge in tithing and began to discuss how they might best spend the windfall. Robert suggested they not make hasty decisions, but during the following weeks, as the surge in tithing continued, the leaking roof was repaired, the parking lot resurfaced, and the parsonage's aging refrigerator replaced, much to Heather's delight. After taking care of the church's few needs, the trustees increased the congregation's donations to the interfaith food bank aiding the poor and homeless.

Union Revival Baptist Church owned an entire city block. The church building occupied one end and the two-story parsonage, built of the same stone as the church, occupied the other. From his office window, Robert could see the parsonage, and he often found himself staring at it. What had once been a cold and lonely place foisted off on him by trustees unable to provide a housing allowance had been turned into a warm and welcoming home. After the previous pastor was killed in a hit-and-run accident, the parsonage had become his residence, replacing the one-bedroom garage apartment provided as part of his compensation package. Pastor John had done nothing to make the place welcoming during his decades-long tenure, and neither had Robert upon taking residence. Heather had overseen the transformation.

That's why Robert enjoyed walking home for lunch each day, even on days when heavy rain might have given him pause if he still lived alone. The walk to the parsonage cleared his mind of church business, and Heather often had lunch prepared, even if only a peanut butter and jelly sandwich accompanied by a cold glass of milk. They sat at the kitchen table sharing idle conversation, the subject matter less important than the company.

When Robert stepped through the door midday one Thursday, already salivating for the leftover meatloaf and mashed potatoes his wife promised him that morning, he was not prepared to find the curtains closed and the parsonage dark as the Middle Ages.

"Heather?" he called. "I'm home."

His wife rushed from the kitchen and into his arms.

Surprised, he asked, "What's wrong?"

"There's been a car parked across the street all morning."

Robert stepped to the living room window and looked out. "I don't see one now."

"The car drove away just before you came home," she said. "I saw it yesterday morning, too, but I didn't think anything about it until I saw it again today. I think someone is watching the house."

"But why?"

She had no idea.

"Why didn't you call me?"

"I was afraid I was imagining things," she said, "and I—I didn't want to bother you."

Robert kissed his wife's forehead. "You're never a bother."

He held her for a bit longer, waiting until he was certain she had calmed down, and then he asked, "How's that meatloaf?"

That afternoon and all day Friday, Robert repeatedly checked the streets surrounding the church property and not once did he see any unexpected vehicles parked near the parsonage. He was not nearly as attentive that weekend. Saturday he was busy with church business, and Sunday he led both the morning and the evening services, for they had yet to find an assistant pastor to fill the position he vacated upon his promotion. Robert had not minded the workload when he was single, for idle minds and idle hands were the Devil's playthings, but as a married man he had many more responsibilities. Those included attending to his spouse's physical and emotional needs.

At lunch Monday, after walking the long way around the block to get home, Robert asked Heather about the mysterious vehicle she had seen the previous week.

"I haven't seen it," she said. "I must have been mistaken."

But he knew she wasn't when he took a phone call in his office that afternoon. Though he had not heard it often, Robert recognized the voice in his ear.

"You've been pastor for almost a year and a half now, haven't you?"

Robert admitted that he had.

"You ever wonder how you got the job?"

He thought about the years spent in college and seminary, the grueling interviews he'd been put through when seeking his first position, and all the hard work he'd done as Union Revival Baptist Church's assistant pastor in the belief that God helps those who help themselves. When the church's beloved pastor was killed in a hit-and-run accident following a visit to one of the homebound parishioners, Robert had been fully prepared to ascend to the vacant position. The trustees and the congregation had agreed. Before he could form a response, though, he learned the answer.

"Pastor John had the courage of his convictions," said the voice. "He wouldn't work with us and we needed someone who would."

"You've been watching my wife."

"She's such a beautiful woman," said the voice. "It would be a shame if anything happened to her."

"You think you can use her to—"

"I know we can, pastor," said the voice. "Heather went shopping this afternoon. Perhaps you should check on her."

Before Robert could reply, the line went dead.

He immediately dialed his wife's cell phone number. He let it ring until Heather's voice mail answered. Then he hung up and tried again with the same result.

The moment he depressed the switch hook, his phone rang. He answered, his voice more irritated than welcoming. "Pastor Bob!"

"Is this Robert Connelly?"

"Who is this?" Robert demanded as he rose from his chair and stared out the window toward the parsonage.

The caller identified himself as a police detective and then said, "Your wife's been involved in an incident."

"An incident?" Robert demanded. "What does that mean?"

"You'd best come to the hospital."

Robert vacated his office without closing the open files on his computer, didn't bother turning out the lights or locking his office door, and was halfway down the front steps before calling over his shoulder to the church secretary who was trying to catch up to him. "Heather's been in an accident."

Only she hadn't.

The black eye, the bloody lip, and the bruises on her arm were the result of a mugging in the parking lot of a big box store where she had gone to purchase laundry detergent and frozen pizza.

By the time Robert found his wife in the emergency room, Heather had already described her assailants to the detectives, and had promised to visit the police station the next day to sign a statement and leaf through a selection of mug shots.

"He took my purse," Heather explained to her husband. "That wasn't enough for him, though. He had to do this, too." The mugger had temporarily stolen her beauty with several well-placed punches that were not life-threatening.

Once they were in Robert's car, she had more to say. "He knew who I was. I told the police I didn't know who he was. I didn't. I don't. But he sure knew who I was, and he said he was sending you a message. What kind of message was he sending you, Bobby?"

"I don't know," he said, shading the truth just a little, uncertain if he was protecting his wife or protecting himself as they completed the trip home in silence.

Robert parked behind the parsonage and followed Heather through the back door into the kitchen.

She screamed.

He pushed past her, ready to do battle with whatever had frightened Heather, but saw only her purse in the middle of the kitchen table.

He turned to her. "I thought you said—"

"I did." She collapsed into his arms. "Why is it here? How did they get in?"

"Your keys were in your purse," he said, a simple explanation for the question easiest to answer.

When Heather calmed down, she upended her purse on the table and examined everything—her keys, her cell phone, her wallet, breath mints, pocket Bible, and an assortment of the detritus that accumulates in a purse not emptied regularly.

"Is anything missing?"

Heather shook her head. "Nothing. Nothing at all."

Then she insisted they change the locks, even though the keys to the parsonage were still on her key ring with all her other keys.

"They could have made duplicates."

Robert called a locksmith, a parishioner who promised to do the job that afternoon without charge once he learned why Robert desired the change.

⊙

Heather was the center of attention at Wednesday evening's church service. She'd done her best to mask her bruises, blackened eye, and split lip, but the locksmith told his wife, she told everyone in the Women's Auxiliary, and from there the entire congregation heard about the mugging. Neither Robert nor his wife mentioned that the muggers had returned Heather's purse, letting everyone believe the reason for changing the locks was fear of some future home invasion.

Robert's sermon that evening was a variation on Matthew 5:39, where believers are admonished to turn the other cheek, even though the anger he felt inside demanded the exchange of an eye for an eye as advocated in Exodus 21:23–25.

He still felt that anger when the anonymous caller phoned the next day. Robert demanded, "What do you want?"

"Your cooperation," said the voice. "You know we can get to your wife anytime we want."

Robert repeated his question. "So, what do you want?"

"We're going to give a lot of money to your church, pastor. We just want to ensure that it gets spent wisely."

"The money comes in dirty and goes out clean?"

"Nothing's cleaner than God's hands."

"What does the church get out of it?"

"The church keeps ten percent," said the voice, "and we don't touch your wife."

Robert said nothing.

"We can push as much as a million dollars a year through Union Revival," said the voice. "Imagine the good you could do with an extra hundred grand each year."

"You know I can't do this alone." He started to explain that every check issued by the church for more than one thousand dollars required two signatures, Robert's and—

"Have a private conversation with your treasurer," the voice said before Robert could finish. "We know where his daughter attends college, and he knows that we know."

"Harvey wouldn't—"

"Who contracted with the roofer and the asphalt company?"

Harvey Johnson had made the recommendations to the board. "And the refrigerator?"

"We didn't make a cent on your refrigerator." The man on the other side of the conversation laughed. "We don't run an appliance store."

<hr />

Retired for almost ten years, Harvey Johnson had served as Union Revival Baptist Church's treasurer for almost thirty, and Robert cornered him after the monthly trustee meeting that evening.

"Why didn't you warn me at the wedding reception?"

"About what?"

"The man I asked you about, the one who spoke to me just before you did."

"I didn't see him," the treasurer insisted.

"He threatened my wife," Robert said. "He may have threatened your daughter."

"Alison's all I have." The church treasurer's only child had been born late in his life to a wife ten years his junior. Cancer had claimed Harvey's wife before his daughter ever entered kindergarten, and he had raised Alison on his own.

"Has he harmed her?"

Harvey didn't answer Robert's question directly. Instead, he asked one of his own. "Is that what happened to your wife?"

Robert nodded.

"I've never seen the man who threatened my daughter," Harvey explained. "He first approached me at Alison's high school graduation. He said I had a beautiful daughter and that it would be a shame if anything happened to her. By the time I turned to see who had spoken, he had disappeared into the crowd."

High school graduation ceremonies had been held two weeks before the pastor's wedding. "One other unusual thing happened that day," Harvey continued. "We held a little reception afterward, with family and friends. My daughter received several nice graduation gifts, including an unsigned card containing ten one-hundred-dollar bills. We never knew who to thank for the money, but we used it as a down payment on a used car for Alison."

Harvey hesitated so Robert prompted him to continue.

"Nothing happened all summer, so I forgot about everything. Then, just after the school year began, I received a call from campus police. My daughter had been mugged, her purse stolen. She wasn't hurt—not like your wife—just a few scrapes from being knocked down."

Harvey looked around to ensure they were still alone. Then he lowered his voice and leaned forward, as if sharing a secret with Robert. "Alison called later that night to say that when she returned to her dorm room, her purse was on her desk, as if she had left it there, even though she knew she hadn't. Then she told me one thing she hadn't told the campus police. She said her mugger told her he was sending a message to me."

"That he can get to your daughter anytime, anyplace."

Harvey nodded. "I've done what he wanted ever since."

"The roofer and the asphalt company?"

"He told me who to hire for those jobs. They weren't the lowest bidders by any stretch of the imagination."

"Have you talked to the police about any of this?"

"No. Have you?"

The two men stared at one another for a moment. Then Robert held Harvey's hands and said, "Let us pray for God's guidance."

"The man who had you mugged wants to launder money through the church," Robert explained. He was sitting with his wife at the kitchen table in the parsonage, and he had to explain what it meant to launder money. "He threatened to hurt you if I didn't do what he said."

"He already hurt me, Bobby." Heather pushed her chair back and stood. "I thought you were my protector."

Robert reached for his wife's hand, but she turned away and left him sitting alone as she climbed the back stairs. He leaned back to stare Heavenward, but he did not pray. Instead, he followed the sound of his wife's footsteps until he heard the creak of their bed as she settled into it.

Then he took his cell phone from his pocket and dialed a number he memorized years earlier and had hoped to never dial.

Thanks to its location near the heart of the city, its attention-getting imposing stone architecture, and its historical significance

as the first church built in the valley, the Union Revival Baptist
Church drew several visitors each Sunday. Some became members, some became regular attendees but never formally joined
the church, and some were just passing through on their spiritual
path. Regardless, all were welcome.

From the pulpit that Sunday, Robert barely recognized Kenny
Gilbert when he slipped in at the last moment and, surprisingly,
found an open seat in the back pew. Robert kept one eye on
Kenny during the service and Kenny kept both eyes on everyone
else. When they'd been released from juvenile detention, their
lives diverged. With a fear of God not nearly as overpowering
as a fear of his father, Robert straightened up, graduated high
school a year late, and squeaked into college, where he majored
in history and minored in English before attending seminary.
Kenny traveled a different path into adulthood, one that found
him solving physically the problems Robert attempted to solve
spiritually.

Until Thursday evening, they had spoken only once since the
day they walked out of juvie together. When Robert graduated
from seminary, Kenny called to offer his congratulations and his
personal cell phone number, a number Robert had memorized but
hesitated to dial until he believed he had no other choice.

Though he barely listened to himself, Robert's message, inspired
by Romans 12:19 and contradicting what was in his heart, was
particularly inspiring that morning, and three people answered the
call, publicly expressing their desire to devote their lives to God
by joining him before the congregation. After speaking quietly
to each of them, Robert introduced them to the congregation and
then handed them off to a trio of deacons who silently joined them
at the front. He closed the service with a prayer and then joined
his wife in the vestibule.

Though Heather had been sleeping with her back to Robert since Thursday night, none but the most astute among the congregation could have ever suspected a rift between the pastor and his wife. In public they were still the bubbly, doe-eyed newlyweds, and they stood beside one another greeting parishioners as they exited the church.

Kenny held back, not approaching the pastor until most everyone else filed out. The two men shook hands, Robert introduced his childhood friend to his new wife without telling her the nature of their relationship, and then let Heather know they would have company at Sunday dinner.

"Pleased to make your acquaintance, Mr. Gilbert," Heather said. "I trust you like pork chops and mashed potatoes."

"Ma'am," Kenny said. "I've not eaten a home-cooked meal in a great many years."

Before she could ask why, Robert directed his guest away from his wife, and the two men made their way to Robert's office. With the door closed, he repeated everything he'd told Kenny on the phone a few days earlier.

"It has to be an inside job," Robert explained. "Someone's using the offering envelopes to slip the money into the offering boxes. Each Sunday since the first call we've found ten crisp one-hundred-dollar bills folded neatly inside one of the envelopes."

A rap on the door interrupted their conversation, and then the church treasurer stepped into the office. He saw the pastor's guest and apologized. "But you wanted to know as soon as I collected the money from the offering boxes. There were two envelopes today."

"Thanks, Harvey."

After the treasurer backed out and closed the door, Robert said. "He's escalating."

"You said he could push a million dollars a year through the church," Kenny said. "Who has that kind of juice?"

"No one I know."

The two men talked a while longer, and then they walked to the parsonage, where Heather had set the dining room table with their wedding china.

After she carried the food to the table and the three of them settled into their seats, Robert said grace.

They ate in silence until Heather asked, "How do you know my husband?"

Kenny glanced at Robert before answering. "We grew up together."

"Really?" Heather asked, surprised. "He's told me so little about his childhood."

"There isn't much to tell," Kenny said. "We spent a lot of time indoors."

Imagining only one possible reason why her husband might have spent his teen years indoors, Heather looked at Robert and said, "You played a lot of video games?"

They had, in fact spent hours doing nothing but playing video games, and a great deal more time reflecting on the capriciousness of justice that led to their incarceration in a juvenile detention center for violent offenders but had not protected Kenny's little sister from the molester they crippled. When they were released they chose different paths to combat evil.

"We did."

Robert interrupted before his wife could further question Kenny. "He's going to be staying with us for a while."

"Here?"

"No," Robert said, "in the garage apartment."

Then he asked his wife about the previous afternoon's Women's Auxiliary meeting, and soon she was telling the two men about the group's plans to expand membership. "We need to recruit more young women, and to do that we need an active social media presence."

Robert agreed, their conversation continued, and Heather never returned to questions about Robert's past or his relationship with Kenny.

When they finished the meal, Kenny thanked Heather and told her how much he enjoyed her cooking. "Robert's a lucky man."

As Heather cleared away the dishes, Robert gave Kenny a key to the empty garage apartment intended for the church's assistant pastor, and he didn't see Kenny again until morning service the following Sunday when he sat in the last pew watching the worshippers. At the end of the service he slipped out to follow a nondescript man who had been attending services at Union Revival Baptist Church since well before Robert and Heather's wedding.

Later, the church treasurer told Robert that anonymous tithing was up to five thousand dollars that morning. "Five envelopes, a thousand dollars in each."

"Did anyone see who put them in the collection box?"

"Most of the parishioners use the offering envelopes, so it's impossible to tell one from another."

"But five envelopes at once?"

⊙━━━⊙

Robert was home Tuesday evening when a police detective visited his wife and showed her a photograph. "Is this the man who attacked you?"

"Yes," she said. She had previously identified her assailant from police mug shots. "I think so. It all happened so fast, but—yes. Have you arrested him?"

The detective shook his head. "He's been killed."

Heather's eyes went wide and she glanced at her husband.

"Do you know anything about it?"

Heather shook her head.

"What about you, pastor?"

"God works in mysterious ways, detective," Robert said.

Satisfied, the detective left the parsonage. As the unmarked police car drove away, Robert gathered his wife in his arms and held her. "He can't ever hurt you again."

That night Heather stopped sleeping with her back to her husband.

There were other deaths in the city that week, including that of the nondescript man Kenny followed from church service Sunday morning, but Robert paid attention to the obituaries when he scanned the newspaper each morning only if he had reason to believe he might be called upon to prepare a eulogy.

He returned to his office Friday afternoon, after lunch with his wife in the parsonage, and he was feeling rather full after finishing off the leftover roast beef, mashed potatoes, and gravy. He was considering the impropriety of taking a brief nap at his desk when his phone rang.

"Pastor Bob."

"We appear to be at an impasse," said a voice that had become all too familiar since his wedding many months earlier.

"How's that?"

"A friend of yours has asked me to place this call. He's under the impression I had something to do with your wife's unfortunate—"

Robert heard the nearly inaudible pop of a silenced automatic, though he did not recognize it as such. Then he heard Kenny's voice.

"It's done."

The line went dead.

Robert did not see Kenny again, and when he visited the garage apartment, it had been wiped clean.

During the following weeks, church trustees were disappointed that tithing had dropped to its previous level.

Police investigating the murder of a man with alleged mob ties never connected the dead man to Harvey Johnson or Robert Connelly, acting on the assumption that it was a hit by a rival mobster. However, after reading news stories about the murder and subsequent stalled investigation, Robert's wife finally put it together.

"I don't know what you and Kenny did," Heather told Robert one night after they slipped into bed, "and I don't want to know."

He pulled his wife into his arms and held her tight as she whispered, "My protector."

Temple and I married the day after Thanksgiving about seven months before I began writing "Blest Be the Tie That Binds," and we spent our honeymoon—brief as it was—in a cabin in Brownwood, Texas. Saturday afternoon, during a brief respite from the rain, we took a leisurely walk through the woods, and a large dog of indeterminate breed came charging at us. I'm no hero, but I stepped in front of my new bride and shouted at the dog until it finally turned and ran back the way it had come. That's when I began pondering how far a man might go to protect his wife.

James Lee Burke has published thirty-eight novels and two collections of short stories. He has won a number of literary awards. His work has been adapted for four films and a fifth is in progress. He and his wife Pearl live on a ranch in Montana.

HARBOR LIGHTS

James Lee Burke

It was in late fall of '42, out on the Gulf of Mexico, just off the Louisiana coast, the water green and cold and sliding across sandbars in the sunset, when we saw the bodies bobbing in a wave, each in life vests and floating belly-down, their arms outstretched, their fingers touching, like a group of swimmers studying something on the floor of the Gulf.

My father was standing behind the wheel in the cabin. He wore a fedora and a raincoat, the redness of the sun reflecting off the water, flickering on his face, as though he were standing in front of a fire.

"Come here and hold the wheel for me, Aaron," he said.

"Are those dead people out there?"

"Yes, they are." There was no change in his expression. At age eighteen he had been at Saint-Mihiel and the Somme, and had been buried alive during an artillery barrage. He still had dreams about the war, but denied their seriousness, even after my mother and I had to shake him awake and put a cold towel on his face lest he injure himself or others.

"They look burned, Daddy," I said.

"Just keep the boat steady. Don't look at these poor fellows."

He went out of the cabin and picked up a long-handled boat hook from the deck, then worked his way up on the bow and probed the figures floating in the waves. He was bent over, his raincoat flapping in the wind, peppered with spray from the waves bursting against the hull, his face sad, as if he knew these men, although I was sure he did not. He put down the hook and gazed at the horizon through a pair of binoculars, then came back into the cabin and picked up the microphone to our radio, his eyes empty. The sun had dipped out of view, leaving behind a sky that seemed filled with soot and curds of black smoke. A solitary piece of reddish-yellow flame wobbled on the horizon, so bright and intense my eyes watered when I looked at it.

"Mayday, Mayday," my father said into the microphone. "Tanker capsized and burning south of Terrebonne Bay. Four visible casualties, all dead."

He laid the microphone on the console and turned off the radio, then looked at the radio blankly.

"You didn't tell them who we are," I said.

He took over the wheel and reversed the engine, backing away from the bodies. "You mustn't tell anyone about this, Aaron."

"Why not? It's what happened."

He cut the gas and squatted down and wrapped me inside his raincoat and held me to his chest, the boat rising on a wave, dropping suddenly into a trough. I could feel the warmth of his breath on my neck and cheek. "There's a great evil at work in the world, son," he said. "All kinds. We mustn't bring it into our lives."

My father was a natural-gas engineer, but like none of his colleagues. He hated the oil-and-gas industry. He scrubbed his hands up to his elbows when he came home from work and never discussed what he did on the job. Nor would he socialize with his fellow employees or even use their names in conversation. He had wanted to be a journalist or a historian, and instead ended up a pipeliner during the Great Depression and hostage to both the job and my mother's hospital bills. Part of that job involved dredging channels through freshwater swamp and marshland, poisoning the root system with saline, and contributing to the erosion of the Edenic wetlands in which he had grown up.

We stayed at the Hotel Frederic in New Iberia, his birthplace, whenever his company sent him to Louisiana. The Frederic was a grand building, four stories high, made entirely of brick and stone and concrete, with a roofed gallery above the entrance and a ballroom and marble pillars and potted ferns and palms in the lobby and a birdcage elevator and wood-bladed ceiling fans and a saloon with batwing doors and a shoeshine stand where a man of color popped a rag in 4/4 time. I loved staying at the Frederic and riding up and down on the elevator and waking to the Angelus. I loved eating breakfast in the dining room with my father, just as I loved everything else we did together in New Iberia.

It was raining when we returned to the hotel. The sky was black, veined with electricity, the fog as soft and white as cotton rolling off Bayou Teche. We ate silently in the dining room. There was no one else in the room except a waiter and two men in suits eating in the corner with their hats on. My father looked casually at the two men, then ordered a bowl of ice cream for me and went into the saloon. When he came back I could smell whiskey and cherries on his breath. "Ready?" he said.

"Yes, sir," I said.

"Was that ice cream okay?"

"It was fine."

"You're a good boy, Aaron. Don't ever forget that. You're the best little boy I've ever known."

We rode up in the elevator, piloted by an elderly black man in a gray uniform and white shirt and a black tie. "Mighty cold out there tonight," he said.

"Yes, it is," my father said.

The black man stopped on the third floor, the skeleton-like structure of the elevator rattling. "Mr. Broussard?"

"Yes?"

The black man's eyes were lowered. "These are dangerous times. That's when bad people tend to come around."

My father waited for him to go on, but he didn't. "Thank you, Clarence," he said.

After we were inside our room, he went to the window and looked down on the street, then pulled the shade and turned on the desk lamp and sat down.

"I owe you an explanation, Aaron."

"About the dead men?"

"A German submarine was out there. I saw its conning tower and periscope go underwater."

"Why didn't you tell the people that on the radio?"

"The government always knows this. But they don't want to share their information."

"Why not?"

"Maybe they're afraid of panic. Maybe they wish to hide their incompetence."

"But they're supposed to tell the truth," I said.

"This is a different kind of situation, Aaron."

"The families of the burned men in the water won't know where they are."

He looked at the design in the rug. The fabric was worn, the colors softened with dust. "They knew what they were doing when they signed on. The world is for the living."

"This doesn't sound like you. Daddy," I said.

"The government is wrong to suppress the truth. If they question me, I'll tell them what we saw. But I'll also have to tell the newspapers. Not to do so would be dishonorable."

"I don't understand."

"The men who start wars never go to them," he said. "They kill people with a fountain pen and call themselves leaders. Never allow yourself to become their servant, Aaron."

That night I dreamed of a giant shark that had a human face. It broke the surface of the Gulf and crunched a toy ship in its jaws, a red cloud blossoming in the waves around its head, pieces of the ship and tiny men washing through the wetlands and into the streets of New Iberia and through the lobby of the Frederic Hotel and up the elevator shaft and into our room, drowning my father and me.

⚓

The next day was Saturday. He took me across the street to Provost's Café & Bar for lunch. That might seem strange in our current culture, but in that era in South Louisiana the pagan world and Christianity had formed a truce and got along well. The ceiling was plated with stamped tin that resembled pewter and was hung with wood-bladed fans. There were domino and bourré and pool tables in back, and a ticker tape under a glass hood below the blackboards where gaming results of all kinds were posted. On Saturday afternoons the floor was littered with football betting cards.

There was no profanity in Provost's, no coarseness, no ill manners. When we went to Provost's we always sat at a checker-cloth table in the corner, and my father always bought me a po'boy fried-oyster sandwich and a side of dirty rice and a bottle of Dr. Nut, the best cold drink ever made. But as soon as I sat down I knew that today was different, that the world had changed, that the sinking of the tanker would not leave our lives. The two men who had been eating in the Frederic's dining room with their hats on came through the front door and walked past us and stood at the end of the bar. One looked like a boxer and had a scar across his nose. The other man was very big, and wore a vest, with a pocket watch and fob. They each ordered beer from the spigot and faced the bar mirror, one foot on the brass rail, while they sipped from their mugs.

I could see my father looking at them and knew he remembered them from the hotel dining room. My father was a handsome man, with soft, dark hair he combed straight back. His eyes were small and narrow, like those of his grandfather, who had been with Stonewall Jackson through the entirety of the Shenandoah campaign, and also at Gettysburg.

"Is there something wrong about those men, Daddy?" I said.

"Pay them no attention."

"Who are they?"

"I think they're police officers."

"How do you know?"

"A gentleman does not wear his hat in a building."

A black man put my sandwich and bottle of Dr. Nut in front of me, then came back with a bottle of Jax for my father.

"They're coming this way, Daddy," I whispered, my eyes on my plate.

"Don't speak to them or look at them. This is our home. Our family has lived on the bayou since 1836."

I didn't have any idea what he was talking about. The two men were now hovering over our table. The man with the scar on his nose was standing immediately behind me, his loins eye level with me. "How y'all doin'?" he said.

My father wiped his mouth with a cloth napkin. "How can we help you?"

"We thought you might have been fishing out on Terrebonne Bay yesterday," the man in the vest said.

"Not us."

"The trout are running," the same man said. His eyes were like brown marbles that were too big for his face, his body too big for his suit and vest and starched white shirt. "I'd like to get me a mess of them."

"My name is James Eustace Broussard," my father said. "This is my son Aaron. We live in Houston. I'm an engineer with an oil and natural gas company there, although I was born and raised in New Iberia."

"You know how to cut to it," said the man with the scarred nose.

"Sorry?" my father said.

"You keep your words neat and tidy," the same man said. "You don't clutter up the air."

"We were having lunch, gentlemen," my father said.

"Put your lunch on hold and take a walk," said the man in the vest. "I'm Agent Hamilton. This here is my partner, Agent Flint. We'll have you back in five minutes."

"I'm afraid I will not be going anywhere with you," my father said. "I'd also like to see your identification."

"I'll show it to you outside," Mr. Hamilton said. He pulled on his collar and rotated his neck.

"I know why you're here," my father said.

"Tell you what," Mr. Hamilton said. He pulled up a chair backward and spread his thighs across it. His teeth were as big as Chiclets. "I'm going to do you a courtesy because of your war record. Yesterday you called in a Mayday on a fire that was put out by the Coast Guard. Right? End of story. You did your good deed and we take it from here?"

"How did you come by my name?" my father said.

"The people at the boat landing," Mr. Hamilton said. "We got us a deal?"

"A deal for my silence?"

Mr. Hamilton leaned forward in his chair. "Lower your voice, please."

"I will not," my father said.

The agent named Flint, the one who looked like a boxer, was still standing behind me, his fly inches from my face. He tugged gently on my earlobe. "You got you a right nice boy here," he said.

My father set his fork on his plate and rose from his chair, his fingers propped stiffly on the tablecloth. "Don't place your hand on my son's person again."

Mr. Flint screwed his finger into his ear, as though he were cleaning it. "Know a lady by the name of Florence Greenwald, Mr. Broussard?"

"I beg your pardon?" my father said.

"She's a looker," Mr. Hamilton said. "Enough to make a man turn his head."

"We're not knocking it," Mr. Flint said. "I've let my swizzle stick wander a few times myself."

"I think you're both evil men," my father said.

"Enjoy your lunch," Mr. Hamilton said. "We'll talk a little later." He winked at me. "See you, little fellow."

They walked out the door. My father sat back down, his eyes out of focus, his hands limp on each side of his plate, as though he had forgotten where he was or what he was doing.

⚬━⚬

I knew who she was. I also knew, without anyone telling me, that I was not supposed to mention her name. There was a great coldness in the relationship of my parents. In my entire life I never saw them kiss, hold hands, or even touch. Sometimes I would wake and hear them arguing in the bedroom, usually late at night after he had come home from the icehouse, bumping against the doorway, scraping against the wall with one shoulder. Once I heard him say, "What am I supposed to do? Go in the kitchen and get a butcher knife?" It wasn't until puberty that I understood what he meant.

Miss Florence worked for the Red Cross and sometimes played bridge with my mother and her friends. For my birthday she gave me a book of stories and illustrations about King Arthur. Then she seemed to disappear from our lives. One evening in the kitchen I asked my father where she had gone. My mother was cleaning the stove, her back to us. She cleaned the house two times a day and washed her hands constantly.

"Miss Florence moved away," my father said.

"Why'd she move?" I said.

Mother scrubbed at a speck of grease next to the gas burner, then realized the burner was hot and grabbed her fingers, her mouth crimped, her eyes watering.

"I'm not sure, Aaron," my father said. "Why don't we go have a Grapette?"

Mother walked out of the room. Then I heard her slam the bathroom door.

But my real knowledge of my father's secret life did not come until weeks later, and to this day I cannot say with honesty that the evidence warranted my conviction. It was one of those moments you have as a child when you suddenly realize there is something terribly wrong with your family, and that the problem will not be corrected, and with a sinking of the heart you realize your life will never be the same.

On a Saturday afternoon, just before our trip to Terrebonne Bay, my father took me with him to the bowling alley. He had no interest in bowling, but the alley had an air-conditioned bar. Part of the Houston *Post* was folded back on the floor of his company car, the shoeprint of someone smaller than a man stenciled on it. The crossword puzzle was exposed. The blank squares had been filled in with pencil. My father had less interest in crossroad puzzles than he did in bowling.

That was when I knew he lived another life. I felt like I was on a swinging bridge above a canyon and the tether ropes had just been severed. I had seen Miss Florence working on a crossword puzzle in the reading room at the rental library in our neighborhood. She was from New Orleans and had been a nurse in France during the First World War. She read books my mother's regular bridge group did not. My father's loneliness hung on him like sackcloth and ashes. His colleagues in the oil-and-gas business had no inkling of his cultural frame of reference, one that included names like Malvern Hill and the Hornet's Nest, which were as real to him as the trench in which he watched a sniper's round mortally wound his best friend on November 11, 1918.

⚬━⚬

The rain was blowing against the window of Provost's Café & Bar.

Men were cheering at the end of the bar. LSU had just scored a touchdown against Ole Miss.

"Aren't you going to finish your po'boy?" I said.

"I think I need another Jax and you need another Dr. Nut," my father said.

I knew he would be drunk by the end of the day, walking off balance in the hotel lobby, an object of pity and shame. I felt as though a giant spider was feeding on my heart.

"Are you crying?" he said.

"No, sir."

"Then why are you looking like that?"

"Why were those men talking about Miss Florence?" He watched the rain running down the window glass. "Is she here, Daddy? Is this where Miss Florence lives?"

"Those men bear me ill will for political reasons, Aaron. I spoke up for a man who used to be a communist because I believed it was the right thing to do. These men are also angry because I don't believe the government has the right to control the news."

"What does that have to do with Miss Florence?"

"Nothing. They harm others because there is nothing else they do well."

The waiter saw my father's empty Jax and came to the table. Then my father surprised me. "We're through here," he said. "Give us a check, please."

"Where are we going, Daddy?"

"To the *Daily Iberian*."

"What for?"

"If a man ever tries to blackmail you, you dial up the newspaper and put the phone in the man's hand and tell him to do his worst. Are you my little podna?"

"Yes, sir," I replied.

I had never been inside a newspaper office. I sat with my father at the editor's desk, which was in a cubicle that gave onto the editorial room and the back shop where the linotype machines and printing presses were. The air was warm and comfortable and had a clean, bright smell like freshly ironed clothes. The reporters wore ties and dress shirts, the copyreaders green visors. The society editor, a large woman in a deep-purple suit and frilly white blouse, had her own cubicle and a big smile for everyone who passed by. I felt as though I were in a special place, a fortress where virtue and truth would always be sacrosanct and would always prevail.

The managing editor was a round man, not fat, just a man who was round, like a series of sketched circles that had been hooked together. He also had thinning sandy-red hair and a soft, kind face. "You saw a submarine sink an oil tanker, Mr. Broussard?" he said, his eyes crinkling.

"I don't know that it was a tanker," my father said. "It burned with the intensity of one. But it could have been a freighter carrying something else."

The editor closed the door to the cubicle and sat back down. He tried to smile. "The sunset can play tricks."

"I saw four bodies. I touched them with a boat hook."

The light went out of the editor's face. "I see."

"Will you run the story?"

The editor shifted in his chair. "These are unusual times."

"You don't think the shrimpers deserve to know there's a Nazi submarine operating a few miles from our shoreline?"

"Your father was an appointee of President Roosevelt," the editor said. "I would think you'd understand, Mr. Broussard."

"My father broke with President Roosevelt when he tried to pack the Supreme Court."

The editor nodded his head but didn't reply.

"Can I buy space for an ad?" my father said.

"An ad?"

"If you won't write the story, I will. I will also pay for the space."

"You're serious?"

"I was just threatened in Provost's by two men who claim to be law enforcement officers."

"The FBI?"

"If the FBI hires thugs."

The editor wiped his mouth and tapped his thigh repeatedly. "They actually threatened you?"

"With blackmail."

"About what?"

"Ask them."

The editor leaned back in his chair, pressing his fingertips to his forehead as though he were trying to flatten the wrinkles in it. "We don't run news stories as ads, Mr. Broussard. But I have the feeling you already know that."

"It crossed my mind."

The editor took a notepad and a fountain pen from his desk drawer. "I wish I had the flu. I wish I had stayed home today. In fact, right now I would welcome an asteroid through our roof. Okay, Mr. Broussard, let's start over."

⚬——⚬

The story ran two days later. It was on a back page and only four paragraphs in length. The story stated no calls to the Coast Guard or the FBI were returned. That evening we ate in the hotel dining room. My father joked with people he knew from his childhood. No one made mention of his statement in the *Daily Iberian*. We walked down East Main inside a tunnel of oaks, past the plantation house known as the Shadows, built in 1832, and past other antebellum homes and Victorian ones, also; one resembled a beached paddle-wheeler and glowed like a candlelit wedding cake in the gloom.

We stopped at the two-story, ivy-grown brick house where my father had grown up. His father had been one of the most admired attorneys in the history of Louisiana, and also the state superintendent of education and the president of the state senate and one of the few men who had the courage to testify against Huey Long during Long's impeachment hearing. One year ago he had died a pauper in this same house, and now the house belonged to others, people from New York City.

The sky was as orange as a pumpkin, striped with purple clouds. Tree frogs were singing on the bayou, and geese honking overhead. My father stared silently at the house, his fedora slanted over his brow. I put my hand in his. "Are you all right, Daddy?"

"*Pa'ti avec le vent*," he replied.

"What's that mean?"

" 'Gone with the wind.' "

"We have a house in Houston."

"Yes, we do," he replied. He stared at his birthplace and at the rolling green lawn that tapered down to the bayou where the mooring chains of Jean Lafitte's slave ship still hung from the trunk of a huge oak tree. "Let's get us some ice cream at Veazey's."

The evening seemed perfect, as though indeed God was in His heaven and all was right with the world. How was I to know I was about to witness one of the cruelest acts I would ever see one man do to another.

Veazey's was on Burke Street, right by the drawbridge that spanned Bayou Teche. I was sitting at the counter with my father, eating an ice cream cone, when a two-door automobile splashed with mud pulled into the parking lot. The bayou was high and yellow and fast-running and chained with rain-rings. The agent named Flint, the one who looked like a boxer, entered the store, mist blowing inside with him. He wiped the damp off his face, grinning. "Recognize somebody out there, Mr. Broussard?"

Miss Florence was in the back seat of the two-door car. She was wearing a blue jacket and a dove-colored felt hat, and sitting stiffly in the seat, as though she wanted to touch as little of her surroundings as possible. She turned her head and looked right at us. My father's face jerked.

"What has she done?" he said to Mr. Flint.

"She's done it to herself," Mr. Flint said.

"Answer my question, please."

"She applied for a job with Navy intelligence. She's a possible fifth columnist."

"Are you insane?" my father said.

"She wasn't in Spain in '36?"

"She was a nurse with the Lincoln Brigade."

"They weren't communists?"

"She's not."

"You're a goddamn liar."

I had never heard anyone speak to my father in that way. Everyone in the ice cream store had gone silent. I wanted my father to get up and hit Mr. Flint in the mouth.

"Daddy?" I said.

But he did nothing. My face felt hot and small and tight.

"I got to run, Mr. Broussard," Mr. Flint said. "Just so you know, we rented space at the women's camp in Angola for your lady friend."

"You can't do that," my father said.

"Tell that to the Japs in those internment camps out West. By the way, we're going to be talking with your wife in Houston. Hope you don't mind."

"Don't you dare go near her, you vile man," my father said.

Mr. Flint stuck a cigarette in his mouth but didn't light it. He looked down at me, then back at my father. "You paid your girlfriend's rent for a week at the motel at the end of town. You take your little boy with you when you're slipping around and judge me?"

I didn't know what some of Mr. Flint's references meant, but I knew he had said something awful to my father. His right hand was trembling on top of the counter as Mr. Flint walked out the door.

"What's going to happen to Miss Florence, Daddy?" I said.

"I don't know," he said, lowering his head to the heel of his hand. "I truly don't."

My father seemed to be turning into someone else. But I was too young to understand that when good people stray into dark water, their lack of experience with human frailty can become like a millstone around their necks. He paid the waitress, then took me by the hand and walked me to the car. The rain had quit and the electric lights on the bridge had gone on, and a tugboat was working its way up the bayou. Through a break in the clouds I could see a trail of stars that was like crushed ice winding into eternity. I wanted to believe I was looking at Heaven and that no force on earth could harm my father and me.

I should have known better, even at my age. Scott Fitzgerald said no one can understand the United States unless he understands the graves of Shiloh. The Broussard family took it a step further. They saw themselves as figures in a tragedy, one that involved the Lost Cause and the horns blowing along the road to Roncevaux, and in so doing condemned themselves to lives of morbidity and unhappiness.

My father hadn't gotten drunk on our trip to New Iberia, but I wished he had. I wished my defining memory of New Iberia would remain the gush of stars beyond the clouds, the red and green lights on the drawbridge, and the water dripping out of the trees on the bayou's surface. I wanted to hold that perfect moment, on the banks of Bayou Teche, as though my father and I had stepped into a dream inside the mind of God.

⊷

In the morning my father sat down with his address book and made several calls from the telephone in our hotel room. First he confirmed that Miss Florence was being held at the women's camp in Angola. Then he tried to get permission to see her. That's when the person on the other end of the line hung up. My father was sitting in a stuffed chair by the window, a slice of yellow sunlight across his face, dividing him in half as though he were two people.

"What is it, Daddy?"

"I don't like to ask people for special treatment. But in our beloved state you get nowhere unless you have friends. So I have to call a friend of mine from my army days."

"What's wrong with that?"

"My friend dug me out of the earth when I was buried alive. I've never been able to repay the debt. He's a grand fellow. I hate to bother him."

"If he's your friend and you need help, he'll want to hear from you, won't he?"

"You're such a fine little chap, Aaron," he said. "One day you'll have a little boy of your own, and you'll know how much that means."

His friend from the Somme got permission for us to visit a place inside Angola called Camp I. We clanged across a cattle guard at the entrance to the prison farm and were met by a man in rumpled khaki clothes and sunglasses and a coned-up straw hat and half-topped boots with his trousers stuffed inside and a nametag on his shirt pocket that said C. Lufkin. His face had the sharpened, wood-like quality of a man who possessed only one expression; his eyes were hidden behind his glasses, his sleeves rolled, his arms sun-browned and dotted with purplish-red spots that looked like burns buried under the skin. He got in the back of our car and shook hands with my father over the top of the seat. He said he was the heavy equipment manager on the farm.

"So where are we going?" my father said.

"I got to check on a n—— in the box at Camp A before we see your friend."

"Sir?" my father said.

"We keep the sweat boxes on Camp A. I had to stick a boy inside three days ago."

My father looked at him in the rearview mirror. "We need to make our visit and be on our way."

Mr. Lufkin leveled a finger at a two-story, off-white building in the distance. "Turn right," he said. "That's it yonder."

Dust was blowing out of the fields, swirling around the building and into the sky, as though it had no other place to go. Mr. Lufkin put a pinch of snuff under his lip. My father slowed the car, then stopped altogether. He looked into the mirror again. "We were not told about any detours."

"Every minute we sit here is another minute that n—— stays in the box. What do you want to do, Mr. Broussard? It doesn't matter to me."

My father shifted the floor stick and drove down a cinnamon-colored dirt road that divided a soybean field. We went through a barbed-wire gate and stopped twenty yards from two coffin-like iron boxes that were set perpendicularly on a concrete slab; each had a hinged door with a gap at the top.

"Didn't mean to upset you," Mr. Lufkin said. "If you knew what that n—— did on the outside, you'd have a less kind view of your fellow man, I guarantee it."

"How about you take care of your obligations and get us out of here?" my father said, his hands tightening on the steering wheel. "I'd be very appreciative."

Mr. Lufkin got out of the car and was joined by two other men in khaki uniforms and straw cowboy hats. Mr. Lufkin unlocked a sliding bar on the door of one box and pulled it open, then stepped back from a horde of flies that rose into the air.

"Watch the bucket!" the man behind him said.

The box was constructed so there was no room to sit down. The man inside was bare-chested and black as obsidian, his skin streaming with sweat, his buttocks pressed against one wall, his knees against another. He tumbled out of the box onto the ground, the bucket that had been placed between his feet tipping with him, his own feces splashing onto his work shoes and his gray-and-white striped pants.

"Goddamn it!" one of the other men said, jumping backward.

My father put his hand over my eyes. "Don't look at this, son. Say a little prayer for the colored man. Then we're going to see

Miss Florence and go home. You hear me? Don't cry. I'm going to write the warden."

A few minutes later Mr. Lufkin got in the back seat of our car. His sunglasses were in his shirt pocket, his hair wet-combed, his face fresh and bright with either expectation or victory. "Head back down the road and keep going till you're almost to the river. I'll show y'all the Red Hat House."

My father began driving down the road, his hands shaking with anger. Mr. Lufkin was leaning forward, looking at my father in the rearview mirror. "The Red Hat House is the home of Gruesome Gertie."

My father looked into the mirror but said nothing.

Mr. Lufkin mouthed the words, *That's where they knock the fire out of their ass.*

"Don't you say another word to me, Mr. Lufkin," my father said. "Not one word."

Mr. Lufkin sat back in the seat, breathing through his nose, his nostrils like slits. "When you're in another man's house, it's not wise to put your feet on the furniture. No-siree-bob, if you get my meaning."

⚬━━⚬

Camp I was a cluster of barracks behind barbed and electrified wire not far from the Mississippi River. Half of the camp was made up of women prisoners who wore both street clothes and green-and-white pinstripe dresses. Mr. Lufkin stayed in the car and a matron escorted us to the dining room. Outside, the sky was the color of orange sherbet, the leaves of the willow trees flattening in the wind along the banks of the river. The women were finishing supper. Miss Florence was sitting by herself at the end of a long table. Most of the women had tangled hair and some had faces that made me think of broken pumpkins. The matron said we could speak with Miss Florence for twenty minutes, then Mr. Lufkin would accompany us back to the front entrance of the farm.

Miss Florence had been in Angola only a short time, but she looked as though her soul had been sucked out of her chest. Her lips were dry and cracked, her face smaller, her eyes recessed. Unlike the other women, her thick brown hair was neatly combed, but it looked like a wig on a manikin. We sat down and my father pushed a package of Lucky Strikes across the table.

"We can't smoke in the dining room," she said. "I can't touch you or take anything from you, either."

"Has anyone physically hurt you?" he asked. She didn't answer.

"Florence?" he said.

She lowered her voice. "This place is Hell. There're convicts buried in the levee."

He put his hand on top of hers. A matron sitting on a stool gave him a look. He took his hand away. "I've called a lawyer. They can't hold you here."

"They can do anything they want. You haven't seen the colored unit."

"I saw the sweat boxes."

She was silent. Then she looked at me. "How is my little fellow doing?"

"Fine," I said.

"You have to forgive me for the way I'm talking, Aaron," she said. "I'm just being a grump today."

A strange sensation seemed to take over me, although I didn't know why. I had always liked Miss Florence. I always associated her with the gift of the book about King Arthur and the Knights of the Round Table. But now I felt I was talking to an intruder who had come carrying gifts out of nowhere and was helping destroy our family. Worse, I felt I was betraying my long-suffering, guilt-ridden, haunted mother.

She had grown up in desperate poverty. Her mother died when she was seven, then her father abandoned her. She was unloved and unwanted and was left to find any shelter strangers might offer. Maybe she had an abortion. Maybe she was molested. She never talked about her childhood, but her memories of it lingered in her eyes like cups of sorrow.

"Is something wrong, Aaron?" Miss Florence asked.

I looked away from her. "I want to go, Daddy," I said.

"We will, son," he said. "Shortly."

"No, now. We're not supposed to be here."

"What do you mean?" he said.

"It's not the way things are supposed to be."

"Don't talk like that, Aaron," he said. "Miss Florence is our friend."

"What about Mother?" I said.

He tried to put his arm across my shoulder, but I got up from the bench and ran through the dining hall to the door. A matron tried to stop me, but I kept running, knocking through a group of colored women, falling to the floor, then getting up and running out the door into the yard, right into the arms of Mr. Lufkin.

"Don't be fighting with me, boy," he said. He dropped me and pressed his palm against his mouth and looked at it. "You just broke my lip, you little shit. I ought to slap your head off."

Then I was running again, all the way to the gate, where a guard grabbed me by the back of my belt and carried me like a suitcase to my father's car.

We drove back to the Frederic in a rainstorm and didn't talk until we reached New Iberia. When I woke to the Angelus the next morning, my father was gone. He had left a note on the desk telling me he would be with a survey team in the swamp all day and that my breakfast was paid for and my cousin would pick me up at noon and take me to her house.

One week later Miss Florence hanged herself in the nude from a showerhead in Camp I.

⚬──┼──⚬

My father and I never spoke again about Miss Florence or the German submarine or Angola or the lawmen who tried to hurt him through Miss Florence. My father died in an auto accident when I was still in my teens. Like him, I lost my best friend in the last days of a war, at a place GIs nicknamed Pork Chop Hill. Unlike my father, at age eighteen I was an inmate in a parish prison ten feet from the death cell, back in the days when the state executioner traveled with Gruesome Gertie on a flatbed truck from parish jail to parish jail. When it arrived, I could hear the condemned man weeping and see flashes of lighting reflect on his face.

I wasn't a criminal; I was simply crazy, just like my mother. I wish I had been even crazier, because I will never forget the sounds of the generators warming up down below on the street and the man being buckled in the chair and a minister reading from a Bible and then the generators growing louder and louder, like airplane engines, and when the electrician pulled the switch the sudden creak of the leather restraints on the condemned man's body stretching so tight you thought the wood and bolts of the chair would explode, even the guards looking at the floor, their arms folded on their chests.

I clamped my hands over my ears and yelled out of a barred window from which I could see the moon and the fog on the

Calcasieu River, so I would not have to listen to any sound other than my own voice. In some ways the river reminded me of Bayou Teche and that perfect moment when my father and I stood in front of Veazey's, believing that as long as we held each other's hand we would never be separated, even by death. However, I try to consign these images to the past and not talk about them anymore. I almost get away with it too. But one night a month I dream about green water sliding over sandbars and a ship burning brightly on the horizon and harbor lights that offer sanctuary from a world that breaks everything in us that is beautiful and good. In the morning I wake to darkness, calling my father's name, James Eustache Broussard, wondering when he will answer.

I think "Harbor Lights" is my best short story. I put everything in my life inside those few pages. I learned early on that there are many forms of pain and many kinds of evil. I know of things that I will not discuss with anyone. I might write about them, but I will not talk about them. I do not believe we all descend from the same tree. I believe gargoyles are real, and are waiting for their time to come round. That's what this story is about. I hope you like it. I'm quite proud of it.

Martin Edwards *is the author of twenty novels, most recently* Mortmain Hall *and* Gallows Court. *In 2020 he was awarded the CWA Diamond Dagger, the highest honor in UK crime writing. He has received the Edgar, Agatha, H. R. F. Keating, and Poirot awards, two Macavity awards, the CWA Margery Allingham Short Story Prize, the CWA Short Story Dagger, and the CWA Dagger in the Library. He has twice been nominated for CWA Gold Daggers and once for the Historical Dagger; he has also been shortlisted for the Theakston's Prize for best crime novel of the year for* The Coffin Trail. *He is consultant to the British Library's Crime Classics series and a former chair of the Crime Writers' Association. Since 2015, he has been President of the Detection Club, and he conceived and edited* Howdunit, *a masterclass in crime writing by members of the Club. His novels include the Harry Devlin series and the Lake District Mysteries; he has published nine nonfiction books and seventy short stories, and also edited more than forty anthologies of crime writing.*

THE LOCKED CABIN

Martin Edwards

"They make a handsome couple," the man murmured as the band struck up "The Lullaby of Broadway."

He was addressing a woman in her late thirties, darkly glamorous in a sequined gown. She sat by herself at the back of the grand ballroom on the *Queen Mary*. Turning her head, she considered the man's long hair, carelessly knotted bow tie, and soft, almost feminine features. Her red lips pursed in distaste.

"I beg your pardon?" she said in an accent unmistakably Italian.

He gave an extravagant bow and said, "Please excuse me, *signorina*. I have a dreadful habit of thinking aloud."

"A dangerous habit, perhaps."

The man's smile suggested he was not easily abashed. "Once again, I must apologize. I was watching Cynthia Wyvern and her charming companion. They dance divinely, don't you agree?"

He spoke with a faint lisp. The woman frowned and said nothing.

"I suppose," he continued, "she is determined to make the most of her freedom while she has the chance. Typical Cynthia. Lovely but headstrong. Mind you, she should have a care. Dancing cheek to cheek with handsome strangers is another dangerous habit. Especially for a young woman in her position."

"I'm afraid you have the advantage of me, sir," the Italian woman said coldly. "I don't know Miss Wyvern and I have no idea what you are talking about."

"Forgive me! I've always had a weakness for gossip." A waiter glided by and the man snapped his fingers. "Another Hanky Panky, please. What may I offer you, *signorina*, as recompense for interrupting your reverie?"

The woman raised her penciled eyebrows.

"I do not drink cocktails."

"Another—what, lime and soda, then? Splendid." The waiter hurried away. "My name's Breen, by the way. Feargal Breen. Dublin-born though now domiciled in Mayfair. Delighted to meet you."

He extended his hand and the woman took it with barely disguised reluctance. His handshake was weak, his palm damp.

"My name," she said, "is Sophia Vialli. And if I may say so without giving offense, I am not here in search of company. I yearn for this crossing to reach its end. At Southampton I shall be reunited with my husband."

"He is working there?"

"We are partners . . . ," she hesitated, ". . .in a photographic business. We travel around the world."

Breen contemplated the splendid curves of her ballgown. "You are his model?"

"I am a photographer," she said coldly, "and I prefer to remain behind the camera. As for Miss Wyvern, I know nothing of her."

"Don't worry," Feargal Breen said. "I'm not one of these dreadful wolves who prowls the decks looking out for beautiful women to take advantage of. Whether or not they are happily married." He tittered and the woman shook her head.

"I'm sorry, Mr. Breen. . . ."

"Feargal, please. Ah, there's no harm in me, I can assure you. I talk too much, that's all. It amuses me to see young Cynthia clinging on so closely to that good-looking fellow. He's certainly enjoying himself. Not an Englishman, I'd say. His swagger strikes me as distinctly American. Mind if I pull up a chair?"

Sophia Vialli gave a shrug of indifference. As he sat down beside her, Breen nodded toward the dance floor. Now the band was playing "I Get a Kick out of You," while Cynthia Wyvern gazed into her companion's eyes as if hypnotized by his smoothly chiseled features.

"Ah well, my lips are sealed." Breen tapped the side of his nose in a knowing manner. "She's a lovely young thing, and it won't be long before her horizons narrow. Algy Neville-Ferguson is so dull he makes ditchwater look like the clear blue ocean. Just as well his pater is worth a mint. And when Algy comes into the baronetcy . . ."

He was interrupted by the arrival of their drinks. "Chin-chin!"

She raised her glass. Scorn had given way to a hint of amusement. "You're a friend of this young English rose, Miss Wyvern?"

"We've bumped into each other several times, but these days she tends to give me a wide berth. I used to contribute an occasional paragraph to the society columns, and since her engagement to Algy, she needs to be on her best behavior. Very tedious, but there it is."

Sophia Vialli sipped her lime and soda. "The young lady does not appear to be wearing an engagement ring."

Breen chortled. "You don't miss much, do you? I can see you're a woman of the world. I spotted that omission myself. Quite deliberate, I'm sure. Cynthia knows what she's letting herself in for with Algy, and if you ask me, she's determined to have a whale of a time before sinking into the quicksand of respectability. A little bird told me that she spent the past fortnight swanning around New York City in her glad rags. Heaven only knows what she got up to. Now the party's almost over."

"I'm sure you do her a disservice."

"Oh, my lips are sealed. At least, I'm not planning to spoil things for her by mentioning anything to the Press. We all deserve to let our hair down once in a while."

Sophia Vialli finished her drink and gave an ostentatious yawn. "Perhaps you are right, Mr. Breen. Anyway, it is past my bedtime. May I wish you goodnight?"

Without waiting for a reply, she stood up and left the ballroom.

—

"I always like a front-toucher!"

The American gave Cynthia Wyvern a cheeky grin. They were playing deck quoits under a high sun.

Blushing prettily, she tried and failed to suppress a giggle. "Ellis, really!"

He spread muscular arms in a pantomime of mock innocence. "Whaddya mean? It's just a technical term. For when the quoit touches the hob."

"Ah."

"Better than a side-toucher or a back-toucher, take my word."

She laughed. "You really are a very bad influence, Ellis. I'll have you know that I'm a very respectable young woman."

"So you keep saying. Butter wouldn't melt, and all that. Hey, this is warm work. Do you fancy taking a turn around the deck? Or four turns, to make a mile? Then we'll really have earned another gin fizz."

"I mustn't drink too much," she said. "It goes to my head."

"You'll be fine," he assured her. "You can trust me. I'm the son of a senator."

❦

"We meet again, *signorina!*"

The first-class lounge was the last word in sophistication, with glass and chrome lamps, Art Deco bronzes, and an end wall that converted into a cinema screen. The upper part of a semicircular, split-level space served as an observation deck, the lower part as an ebony-fronted bar, above which was a large painting that celebrated the Silver Jubilee. This was the hub of social activity on the ship and as the evening drew to a close, the buzz of conversation filled the air. Sophia Vialli stood apart from the throng, drinking orange juice and studying her fellow passengers.

"Good afternoon, Mr. Breen."

"You remembered my name, Signorina Vialli! I'm flattered. And I see you've got your eye on that young couple again."

He gestured to a corner of the bar, where Cynthia Wyvern and her American admirer were having a tête-à-tête. In front of them were two empty cocktail glasses. Cynthia's eyes shone as her companion chattered.

The Italian woman shrugged. "No, no, I only noticed them a moment ago. I recalled our conversation. But—as you say, I mind my own business."

"Not like me, eh?" Breen gave a high-pitched laugh. "He really is a smart-looking chap."

"And the young lady is beautiful," Sophia Vialli said slyly. "Or is she not—well, your *type*?"

With a roguish wink, he drained his cocktail glass. "You do me an injustice. As you can see, I love nothing better than finishing off a White Lady!"

She permitted herself a smile. "I think you like to tease."

"I am a humble fellow, Sophia—may I call you Sophia? I feel that we are becoming friends—but I do claim a talent to amuse. As for dear Cynthia, I agree that she is lovely. No doubt her American swain thinks so too. I'm sure the fellow's well-heeled, but he can't offer a country house or a Rolls Royce with chauffeur. It's just a passing amusement for both of them. A shipboard romance. Delightful. As long as Algy doesn't find out."

Sophia Vialli wagged a finger. "You said you would . . ."

"Keep mum?"

"A peculiar phrase."

He handed his empty glass to a passing waiter. "Indeed. Frankly, it's not much of a story. An innocent shipboard flirtation? There's no real whiff of scandal. It's not as if they . . ."

"And if they did?" Sophia Vialli allowed herself the glimmer of a smile. "This man Algy, he would not turn a blind eye?"

Breen sniggered. "Shocking temper, that fellow. Can't say I'm fond of him. We're both members of the Garrick, and he once said something very rude to me. I'd have asked him to step outside but—well, fisticuffs have never been my way of settling scores."

Cynthia slid her hand across the small table and the handsome American brought it up to his mouth and kissed her fingers. As Breen and Sophia Vialli watched, he withdrew a cabin key from his pocket and put it down in front of her. Then he stood up abruptly and headed for the door.

⚬═══⚬

The first-class swimming pool was suitably opulent, with its mother-of-pearl ceiling and gold quartzite floors. The surface of the water was well below the side. It would never do for spectators to be covered with water if the ship had a sudden roll. Ellis Hart hauled his lean frame out of the pool and stood waiting for Cynthia to join him.

"You won!" she gasped. "I thought you said you weren't much of a swimmer."

His grin showed a lot of white teeth, a tribute to American dentistry.

"I guess it's all relative, honey. I did give you half a length start."

Cynthia giggled. "You rotter, you tricked me!"

"All's fair in love and war."

"You're not about to declare war?"

"Maybe I want to make a declaration of love."

She blushed prettily. "Remember, I told you. I'm entirely respectable. Spoken for."

"You took my cabin key yesterday evening."

"And I left it in your door, without going inside to await your arrival."

"You lost your nerve," he chided.

"I'm not what you Yankees call a pushover."

"I guess not. But you lost the race, and that changes everything."

"How so?"

He grinned again. "Didn't I mention that, either? A winner is entitled to claim his spoils."

<hr />

"We really must stop meeting like this," Breen said. "People will talk."

Sophia Vialli sat in a deck chair, reading a novel from the ship's library while a young couple played tennis nearby. Her glare at the interruption dissolved into amusement. "I'm beginning to suspect you are following me, Mr. Breen."

"The charm of your company is irresistible, *signorina*. I can't deny that I enjoy our little chats."

Breen sat down beside her without so much as a by-your-leave. "It's so refreshing to have a *confidante*. I don't know a soul here other than Cynthia and a dreadful old couple from Holland Park, and there's nothing I like more than a natter." Sophia frowned in bewilderment. "A spot of gossip. Especially as I've made a rather extraordinary discovery about where . . . well, where Cynthia is sleeping."

"You make it sound," she said, "extremely salacious."

"No, no, on the contrary. It's simply rather . . ." Breen's pause was theatrical. "I don't know. Macabre."

Sophia Vialli put her book down next to the Kodak camera at her feet. "I am, as you would say, all ears."

Breen leaned toward her. "Cynthia is occupying one of the finest suites on A Deck."

She shrugged. "You told me she is an heiress. No doubt she can afford it."

"Letty Bohannon died in the very same suite."

The Italian woman's eyes widened. "Letty . . . ?"

"Surely you recall the name?"

"I . . . I'm not sure." She ran a hand through her black hair. "It sounds familiar, but . . ."

"Let me jog your memory." Breen smiled as a loose return sent a tennis ball bouncing toward him. He caught it in one hand and tossed it to the server. "The Locked Cabin Murder Mystery. Now, does that ring a bell?"

She stared at him. "The Locked Cabin . . . yes, I read something in the newspapers, but I'm a little confused. Did I hear correctly? You said *murder*?"

Breen nodded. "Yes, the tragedy occurred during the *Queen Mary*'s third Atlantic crossing. The story created a minor sensation. I was certain that you'd call it to mind."

"It's coming back to me," she said. "Refresh my memory."

"Letty Bohannon was found dead in her cabin by the steward. She was making the crossing to Southampton unaccompanied, just like Cynthia. Give or take a year or two, they were the same age. Like Cynthia, she had everything to live for, but she was shot through the head."

"How dreadful. I'd forgotten her name. But in the case I'm thinking of, the girl killed herself, didn't she? It was a clear case of suicide. Her cabin door was locked."

"So the authorities claimed," Breen said darkly. "Anything else would have been catastrophic. Imagine the lurid publicity. Murder most foul on board the flagship? Unthinkable! No wonder it was hushed up."

"What you say makes no sense. If nobody else was involved, how could there be murder? And didn't she write a suicide note?"

Breen tutted as the serving tennis player double-faulted for the umpteenth time. Game, set, and match.

"Fred Perry has nothing to fear from our fellow passengers," he murmured. "Shall we take a turn around the deck while I tell you about the ghastly business?"

"I'll have you know that I'm highly respectable," Cynthia whispered.

After a game of shuffleboard, she and Ellis were strolling arm in arm in the open air.

"Absolutely," he replied.

"I really can't invite you back to my stateroom. And I'm certainly not going anywhere near yours. What would the stewards think?"

"Aw, honey, you think they aren't used to turning a blind eye?"

"Besides," she said primly. "There's Algy to consider."

"Algy!" He tightened his grip on her arm. "You have the rest of your life to spend with Algy. This is a once in a lifetime opportunity."

His wheedling voice made him sound like a small boy. She shook her head and smiled. "Tell you what. After dinner, we'll take another turn around the deck."

"Under the moonlight," he said enthusiastically. "So romantic."

"Yes," she said, squeezing his fingers. "So romantic."

"What makes you so sure that this woman—Letty—was murdered?" Sophia asked as they ambled along the deck.

"I fancy myself," Breen said airily, "as an amateur psychologist. The way people's minds work fascinates me."

"Can we ever know what another human being is thinking?" She sounded wistful.

"I knew the Bohannon family. They made a fortune out of shipping, although old George Bohannon was terrified that his son would spend it all on fast cars and even faster women the moment he inherited the estate. A wild and impetuous young fellow, Henry, a daredevil and a gambler. He was called to the bar, but couldn't stick the law. Fancied himself as a thespian, but he wasn't much of an actor. I've even heard whispers that he'd chanced his arm as a gentlemanly cat burglar. A second Raffles, no less."

Sophia's eyes widened. "Extraordinary! He was a criminal?"

"Nothing was ever proved. Poor Letty was devoted to the fellow. She was pretty and charming, if rather highly strung. Good sportswoman. At the time of her death she was engaged to be married to a young banker, dull but decent, you know the sort. Pots of money. Everything to live for."

"So," Sophia said, "it comes to this. You can't accept that a well-favored young woman could ever wish to kill herself."

"Precisely!" Breen exclaimed.

Sophia shook her head. "Your loyalty to her memory does you credit, Mr. Breen. But you said yourself that she was highly strung."

"Yes, but . . ."

"Strange things happen on sea journeys." She gestured toward the ocean. "Some of us love the roar of rushing waves. For others, it becomes oppressive, perhaps menacing. Even for those cocooned in luxury on A Deck, a private suite can come to resemble a well-appointed prison. If she was a poor sailor and seasick . . ."

"But she loved sailing! Her death came utterly out of the blue. It made no sense."

"The pistol was her own?"

"Yes," Breen admitted. "It was a birthday present from her brother."

"He has a lot to answer for. Why on earth give her a lethal weapon?"

"Letty was a first-rate shot. She and her pal Winnie would go to Bisley and . . ."

"At all events, who could want to murder her?" Sophia interrupted. "Did she have enemies? Even if she did, surely it's hardly plausible that they were on board the *Queen Mary*?"

"She was rich," Breen retorted. "And about to become even richer. Where there is money, there is envy. People will stop at nothing, not even murder . . ."

"Possibly so," Sophia interrupted. "There are enough examples of sordid crime in my own country. But how could someone get into a locked cabin, commit murder, and then escape without leaving a trace? It makes no sense. It is quite impossible."

"I suppose you're right," he said sheepishly. "Perhaps I've been reading too many detective stories."

"Forgive my bluntness, but I'm quite sure the inquest verdict was correct. She must have killed herself. We can only presume that the balance of her mind was temporarily disturbed."

"You think so?" Breen sounded weary, old beyond his years.

"Of course," Sophia said, "what other explanation can there be?"

"I'm . . . I'm afraid for Cynthia."

"Superstitious nonsense!"

"But don't you see? She occupies the selfsame stateroom. It seems like an omen!"

Sophia halted in her tracks. "Shhh . . . they are coming toward us."

She tugged his sleeve. The couple they had watched on the dance floor were approaching from the other end of the deck. They were smiling fondly at each other, as if neither of them had a care in the world.

⚬━⚬

"You shouldn't be here," Cynthia said. "Clearly you're not a true gentleman."

Ellis Hart laughed. They were sitting beside each other on the settee of the sitting room in her suite. On the small table in front of them stood a champagne bottle in an ice bucket and two glasses, filled to the brim.

"Say, tell me this. All that baloney about being worried that the steward would think you were a hussy. When did you ask him for the bubbly?"

Cynthia giggled. Over dinner, attentive waiters had already plied them with drink, although she hadn't attempted to keep pace with her companion. She handed Ellis a glass and clinked hers against it.

"We need a toast," she said. "*Carpe diem!*"

"*Carpe diem!*" he echoed.

"Like it?" she asked, indicating their surroundings.

The Cunard Line had spared no expense in ensuring that passengers with the deepest pockets enjoyed the last word in luxury. The close carpeting was supplemented by woven rugs, while illumination came from lights concealed in troughs of molded glass. The furniture was quilted maple, the paneling light mahogany. The door to the bedroom was wide open, affording a provocative glimpse of pillows and bedspread of ivory satin, their pink and green ribbon appliqué a perfect match for the sitting room curtains.

He savored his champagne. "Love it. How the other half live, eh?"

"You're no pauper, Ellis." She brushed her fingers along his leg. "Not if you can afford to travel on the *Queen Mary*."

"I can't complain."

"You certainly can't, young man," she said coquettishly. "Invited to the stateroom of a pretty fellow passenger. Plied with champagne. I only hope you have a good head for drink. Perhaps you shouldn't have any more."

"Life is short," he said, draining his glass in a single gulp. Deferential as a chambermaid, she refilled it.

"Would you excuse me for a few moments?" she asked. "I just need to freshen up."

He laughed. "Honey, you're the freshest thing on this whole damn ship."

She stood up and considered him. "I hope this doesn't seem forward, but I may slip into my pajamas. I like to get to bed early, you know."

"Hey, you won't need to wear pajamas tonight, baby."

She wagged a finger in admonition. "Patience, Ellis. You know what we say in London? Everything comes to he who waits."

"I don't care to wait too long," he mumbled. "I'm a . . . man of action."

She lifted her glass again. "Then let's drink to *action*."

He watched with bleary admiration as Cynthia shimmied into the bedroom and, with a sly glance over her shoulder, shut the door. Hearing a key turn in the lock, he took another drink of champagne.

"How much . . . longer?" Ellis Hart demanded, putting down his glass. His jacket and tie were on the settee. His shirt was unbuttoned, his hair rumpled.

"I've been making myself beautiful for you." From behind the bedroom door, Cynthia's voice was muffled but seductive. "I'm coming out now."

The key turned again and the door swung open, revealing Cynthia in blue Chinese silk pajamas. The black trim of her jacket was embellished with scrolling embroidery; each of the cuffs had an exotic floral motif. Only two of the four closures were fastened, allowing a generous display of pale pink flesh.

"Worth the wait, I hope?" she asked.

For a few seconds Ellis was motionless, as if paralyzed by the sight of her. Then he gave a short whistle.

"Sure . . . sure is."

He stumbled toward her, and she turned her face up to his. As their lips met, the door of the stateroom was flung open.

"So this is what you get up to when my back is turned!"

Sophia Vialli was standing in the doorway, camera in hand. Taking a step into the room, and kicking the door shut behind her, she took a photograph. As the flashbulb popped, Cynthia screamed.

Ellis pushed her through the open door and on to the ivory bedspread. He slumped down beside her. Cynthia wailed in dismay. Sophia followed them into the bedroom.

Another flashbulb popped.

"Harlot!"

"What . . . what is happening?" Cynthia sobbed. "Ellis, talk to me!"

He pushed a hand through his hair. "Honey, you shouldn't have led me on the way you did. It's not right . . . you being all but married, and all."

"You wanted me! You said . . ."

"Never mind what he said," Sophia snapped. "The camera never lies. And I have the evidence of my own eyes. You have been committing adultery with my husband."

"*Husband*?" Cynthia turned to the American. "Ellis, is this true?"

He dropped down on the bed beside her. "Yeah, it's . . ."

"Slut!" Sophia hissed. "Wait till the newspapers hear about this. The supposedly respectable Cynthia Wyvern betraying her fiancé by seducing a naive young American."

"Please!" Cynthia cried. "I'll do anything! Is it money you're after?"

Ellis gave a foggy smile. "Now you're . . . talking, honey."

"My silence will not come cheaply, you understand," Sophia said.

"How . . . how much?"

"You are a rich woman." Sophia named a figure. "Where is your checkbook?"

"It's too much! That amount will ruin me."

"What is marriage to your beloved Algernon worth? What price your future happiness?" Sophia bared her teeth in a fierce grin. "Regard it as an investment."

Cynthia opened the drawer of the dressing room table and lifted out a checkbook and pen. She turned to face Ellis. "You tricked me, didn't you? It was all a ploy, so that the pair of you could blackmail me."

He grinned stupidly. "I guess . . ."

Sophia tried to yank him to his feet. "What's the matter with you, Joel? Don't tell me you're drunk! I thought you had a harder head."

"It wasn't . . ." he began.

The door of the wardrobe swung open. Standing there, dressed in a cabin steward's white uniform, was Feargal Breen. In his hand was a small black gun.

"The man's right." The Irish accent had vanished and he sounded as if he'd just stepped off the playing fields of Eton. "It wasn't ordinary champagne. I slipped in, if you'll forgive a vulgar phrase, a Mickey Finn."

Cynthia reached under a pillow and took out a snub-nosed revolver. "Don't move an inch, either of you."

Sophia blinked. "What is the meaning of this?"

"You've left it too late for a show of dignity," Breen said. "I gave you your chance as we strolled along the deck. If you'd showed a degree of contrition, things might have been different."

On the bed, Ellis groaned. His eyes were shut and he was holding his head.

"What are you talking about?" Sophia demanded.

"I told you. This concerns the murder of Letty Bohannon. My sister." He smiled as the woman absorbed his words. "That's right, I'm Henry, the scapegrace son with a taste for acting. Rather a ham, I'm afraid, but not to worry. I do hope you appreciated my mincing Irish gossipmonger."

"You tricked me!"

"Sauce for the gander. Your lover set out to seduce Letty so that the pair of you could exploit her. You travel the high seas in search of prey. Rich victims with a great deal to lose. On that occasion, however, you went too far. You threatened Letty with ruin and in a fit of panic, she shot herself. Yes, this stateroom was locked, but you killed her, just as surely as if you'd pulled the trigger yourself."

"She was neurotic."

"She was distraught," Henry said. "That was clear from the note she left. Thank the Lord, the coroner didn't make its contents public. Poor Letty had suffered enough humiliation. She didn't know your real names, naturally. The enquiry agent I hired discovered the truth. You believed you were beyond the reach of the law. There was no independent evidence that either of you had committed a crime. The police weren't interested in pursuing you. But we were. I loved my sister."

"And I am Winnie," the girl said. "Her dearest friend."

"So what do you want?" Sophia was defiant. "We have no money to pay you back. The Bohannon girl's check was useless, her death made sure of that."

"We have plenty of money," Henry said. "These staterooms don't come cheap."

"What, then?"

"We want justice."

⊶

For a few seconds, Sophia was silent. Her brow furrowed. Henry had spent long enough at racecourses to know she was calculating odds. The woman was another gambler. In a tight corner, she'd risk everything if she thought she could get away with it. She couldn't hope for help from the American. He'd lost consciousness while sprawled across the bed.

"What do you mean?"

"We want you to write a confession," Henry said. "Admit to what the two of you did to Letty. You must tell the world everything. And don't try blaming it all on Joel Dyson here, alias Ellis Hart. You're the brains behind the partnership, aren't you, Sophia? Or should I call you Maria Mancini?"

"Words written under duress," she said with a dismissive gesture. "They are worthless in a court of law."

Her voice was curiously flat, as if her mind was elsewhere.

"Watch her!" Winnie shouted.

At that moment, Maria Mancini sprang forward. Her sharp fingers became talons clawing at Henry's eyes. As he fell back, she leapt upon him, trying to wrench the revolver from his hand.

"Let him go, or I'll shoot," Winnie hissed.

"You won't dare," Maria spat. "You'll hit him, not me."

She was strong and sinewy and Henry fought to keep hold of his gun. Winnie jumped forward.

In the confines of the bedroom, the noise of the shot seemed deafening.

Maria screamed in horror. In the struggle, her lover had been shot in the chest. Blood oozed over his shirt. Henry seized hold of her wrist, only for the gun to fire again.

The second bullet hit the side of Maria's head at point blank range.

꘎

Winnie sobbed as Henry checked the blackmailers' pulses and found no sign of life. He laid a hand on her shoulder.

"You must keep calm. There's work to be done."

Still wearing the steward's uniform he'd bought in London, he strode out into the corridor and headed for the laundry room. It was in darkness, as he'd expected. Hinting that he planned a surreptitious liaison with a fellow passenger, he'd given the steward a lavish tip to make himself scarce.

The wicker basket he'd spotted the previous day stood in an alcove. He lifted the lid to make sure it was still empty before dragging it back to Winnie's suite. She was drying her tears.

"Give me a sheet to keep the blood off the basket," he said.

"What . . . what will you do?"

He pulled a pair of gloves from his pocket. "I'm taking these bodies back where they belong."

"You can't throw them overboard!"

"I could, but I won't. Tidy up and make a bundle of the blood-stained bedclothes. Chuck it over the side of the ship while I shift the corpses. Thankfully their cabin is only down one flight of stairs and pretty much underneath us. But I'll need two journeys. This wretched basket isn't big enough for both of them."

⁌—✦—⁍

"Are you sure people won't suspect?" Winnie was breathless. The past hour had been a frenzy.

"There's a sporting chance," Henry said. "If we hold our nerve."

"But the angle of the second shot . . ."

"Is consistent with a self-inflicted wound," he said. "Just about. When their steward finally opens the cabin, he'll discover a macabre tableau. What happened will be obvious. A violent quarrel got out of hand; these Latin women are tempestuous types."

"People have seen me in his company," she said.

"Hence the quarrel."

"They've also seen you talking to her. If the authorities ask the right questions . . ."

"We have answers." Henry clasped her hand. "After you left the lounge with him, I noticed her following. There was a confrontation in the passageway. Raised voices. You made your excuses and left them to it. Meanwhile I did my best to cheer you up and refused to let you out of my sight. A perfect alibi."

"Only if they take our word for it."

"Who can contradict us? Thank your lucky stars for good old British reserve. The only two people on board who thought of us as Miss Wyvern and Mr. Breen rather than Henry and his pal Winnie will never utter another word."

A thought struck her. "What if someone heard the shots?"

"There's no better-built ship than the *Queen Mary* on the seven seas, remember. The stateroom walls are solid and I'm your next-door neighbor. Everyone else on A Deck is still waltzing the night away. The band is loud and if anyone did hear shots, they might easily suppose they came from our friends' cabin. It's almost exactly below us, don't forget."

"Whatever the ship's officers may think, the police . . ."

"Are likely to take the easy way out," he interrupted. "Legal jurisdiction on the high seas is as clear as sea mist. Or so I recall from my tedious year in chambers."

"You're sure everyone will believe . . . ?"

"That just like Letty's death, it's a tragedy rather than a mystery?" He gave a dark smile. "People believe what they want to believe. Just as Mancini and Dyson were only too happy to believe in Cynthia Wyvern and the mischief-making Irishman."

She remained quiet for a few moments. "Am I stupid to believe that you intended them to die all along?"

"You could never be stupid, my dear." He paused. "Blackmail was their sport. They reveled in it."

"You planned all this, didn't you?" she murmured. "You love playing for high stakes, whether you're burgling or . . . that's why you took an impression of his cabin key before I put it back in his door, isn't it?"

"Don't worry. Ten minutes ago I threw my copy of the key into the waves."

"You never meant to use it simply to snoop around for evidence of their crimes."

"Call it poetic justice," he said softly. "The authorities will realize it's impossible that anyone else was involved. A plain case of murder and suicide. Maria shot her faithless lover and then turned the gun on herself. Their bodies were found inside a locked cabin. And to prove it, the key is lying on the floor for all to see."

---

*In 2019, I was invited to give a series of lectures to American crime fans on the Queen Mary 2. As we crossed from New York to Southampton, I wandered around the ship, reading the wall panels which recounted events in the history of the original Queen Mary in the 1930s. One fascinating snippet suggested the raw material for a short story, but a further spark was needed to give it life. A few months later, I undertook a second Atlantic crossing. At the time, I was toying with the possibility of writing some form of locked-room mystery. Rather than contrive a puzzle for purists, I wanted to take a familiar trope and play a game with it. But what sort of game? As I took another look at the story on the wall panel, the two elements, historic anecdote and locked room, coalesced in my mind. The result was "The Locked Cabin." And as a tip of the hat to Anthony Boucher, an American novelist and critic who loved locked-room puzzles, I gave one of my characters a name that recalls a detective who features in three of Boucher's impossible crime stories.

John M. Floyd's work has appeared in more than three hundred different publications, including Alfred Hitchcock's Mystery Magazine, Ellery Queen Mystery Magazine, The Strand Magazine, The Saturday Evening Post, *and three editions of* The Best American Mystery Stories. *A former Air Force captain and IBM systems engineer, John is also an Edgar nominee, a four-time Derringer Award winner, the 2018 recipient of the Edward D. Hoch Memorial Golden Derringer Award for lifetime achievement in mystery fiction, and the author of nine books.*

BILOXI BOUND

John Floyd

"You're right," Mitchell White said. "We should move."

He swiveled on the stool behind the cash register and looked through the rectangular serving window into the kitchen. His brother Danny, two years older than Mitch and twenty pounds heavier, was sweating like a racehorse as he slapped a burger and a handful of sliced onions onto the grill.

Without looking up, Danny said, "I thought you were set on staying."

Mitch shrugged. "I was. But I've been thinking."

"And?"

"And I figured someday you'd come up with at least one good idea. Maybe this is it."

"Yeah, I'm just a cook. Thank God we've got you to sit out front and think and put on a pretty face for the customers."

"And talk to 'em. Don't forget that. I engage them in meaningful conversation."

Danny nodded. "That's probably the reason they're leaving and not coming back." He glanced past his brother at the tables. Mitch turned to look also. Only two were occupied, one by a single man in a gray business suit and the other by an older couple, all of them almost finished with their meals. Seven thirty at night, the place ought to be bustling with diners.

"Maybe it's your cooking that's running them off," Mitch said. Their eyes met through the window and both chuckled. Might as well, Mitch thought. It was either that or cry. The White House had been losing business for months.

"You know the problem, don't you?" Danny looked at him and pointed a spatula. "It's that new restaurant down the street."

"It's not just that," Mitch said. "Everything around here's going downhill, everything except crime. Those places that got robbed the other day, and the murders, right here on this block? Nothing like that used to happen here. A cop friend of mine—Nick Posey, remember him? He told me last week a mobster from Chicago's in the area now, came here to stay."

"Came here how? Retired?"

"Retired, fired, on the run, I don't know. Posey just said he's here."

Danny frowned at the sizzling burger. "You mean, like, an assassin? An enforcer?"

"Beats me. He could've kept their books, for all I know. An accountant, like Duvall in *The Godfather*."

"Duvall was a consigliere. An advisor. Not an accountant."

"Who cares?" Mitch said. "They're still crooks."

"I hear you. The neighborhood's going bad." Danny stood up straight, rolled his shoulders tiredly, and leaned over to adjust the heat on the grill. "Is that what you been building down in the basement? A bulletproof room where we can go hide when the bad guys take over?"

Robbie Stanton, the kid they'd hired to help out in the kitchen, stuck his head around the corner with a mop in his hand and said, "What bad guys?"

Danny shot him a get-back-to-work look and Robbie vanished as fast as he'd appeared.

"We don't need a hideout," Mitch said to Danny. "We just need to *leave*. And what I've been working on in the basement is none of your business."

"The hell it's not. It's my house. If I recall, you're living there rent free."

"Biggest mistake I ever made," Mitch mumbled. "After working with you all day, it's not easy being around you at night too."

"You love it and you know you do," Danny said, both of them grinning now. He fell silent a moment and when he spoke again his voice was serious. "This new resident you heard about, this mafia dude. You don't think he's that guy we been seeing, do you?"

Mitch knew whom he meant. For almost a week now, a thin man in his forties with dark eyes and dark clothes and a black baseball cap had been stopping in between seven thirty and eight. He never ate anything, never stayed more than a few minutes, never spoke at all except to order a cup of coffee, which he drank in silence in one of the corner booths. He was definitely spooky, but Mitch hadn't given him much thought—probably since the man's recent appearance in their lives had coincided with that of Mary Del Rio. A new regular, Mary had a way of occupying Mitch's attention. She was also the reason for all those hours he'd been spending with his woodworking tools in the basement. But that was another matter. Now Mitch found himself wondering if

Danny was right: could their mysterious customer be the Chicago guy Officer Posey had told him about?

But why would anyone connected with organized crime be interested in Mitch and Danny White? They weren't wealthy—they never even had much cash on hand except around Thursday or Friday, before the Saturday morning run to the bank to deposit the week's proceeds. Mitch supposed he and his brother could be considered potential sources for "protection" money. He'd heard of that happening elsewhere. Again, though, the White House wasn't doing a booming business—surely someone who stopped in every night could see that extortion payments from this place wouldn't be reliable. No, probably the biggest threat was getting caught in the crossfire if someone tried to whack the guy.

"If whoever Posey was talking about *is* retired," Mitch said, "our Mystery Man coffee-drinker looks a little young for that."

Danny snorted. "I don't think age matters in that line of work. It's not like they get a gold watch and a pension."

"I still doubt it's the same guy. Anyway, it seems like he's a no-show tonight—it's almost eight."

"Maybe he's home watching *Goodfellas*," Danny said. He flipped the burger, squirted something on it, and stirred the onions around. They smelled good. Danny's cooking always smelled good. As Mitch watched, Danny took a long look around the kitchen as if seeing it for the first time and said, "So if we move . . . where you figure we should go?"

Mitch shrugged again. "You're the one suggested it. You don't have a place in mind?"

"Somewhere down south. Someplace warm."

"How about a specific answer?"

"Hawaii," Danny said.

"Why?"

"You said you wanted a Pacific answer."

"A *specific* answer. Smartass."

"I'm thinking the Gulf Coast. They like food down there even better'n we do. But not Florida, with all the crowds and the overpricing—I been reading up on it." As he talked, Danny drained a small basket of French fries and piled them into a white take-out box.

"Where, then?" Mitch asked.

"Biloxi."

"That's what, Mississippi?"

"Yeah. There's thirty miles of white sand beach from there to Bay St. Louis. Casinos and fancy hotels, plus down-homey fishermen and country folks. Sort of a combination of ritzy and laid-back. Some crazy people there, for sure, but nothing like South Florida or California."

"What if they already got a White House?" Mitch asked. "Lots of places do."

"Then we'll call it something else."

"Big waves down there? I like big waves."

"Nope. There's a string of barrier islands. Not much surf." Apparently satisfied, Danny scooped the burger and the onions onto a bun, piled on some lettuce, loaded the result into the box with the fries, and called, "Robbie? Bag this up and take it down the street to Joe Watson. Tell him he owes us for last night's too."

The teenager, probably glad for something to do, propped his mop against the kitchen wall and hurried over.

"Barrier?" Mitch said. "Against what?"

"The ocean. The open sea."

"That didn't help much against Katrina, did it? Or Camille." Danny frowned. "Camille?"

The bell dinged above the front door and Mitch rose from his stool, picked up a menu, and said, "I think you need to do some more reading."

Only then, on his way around the end of the counter, did he see who had just come in. She was taking a seat in a booth near the door. Mitch smiled at her and she smiled back.

Mary Del Rio was probably, he figured, their only regular customer. She had short copper-colored hair, green eyes, and was about his age, late forties. For almost a month she'd been coming in several nights a week around this time, limping heavily and carrying a rolled-up newspaper under one arm. She usually ordered coffee and a sandwich and worked the daily crossword puzzle while she ate. The first few times she'd been quiet, but lately she'd opened up a bit, telling Mitch that she'd recently discovered that the White House—she loved the name—was right on her way as she walked home from her part-time job at the library. After hearing this, Mitch had solemnly agreed that shelving books all day sounded like hungry work and he was rewarded with a delightful laugh. They'd talked more and more each visit—she'd even mentioned her limp, the result of a recent but permanent injury, she said—and he'd begun looking forward to seeing her.

Especially tonight.

"Hey, Mary," he said, handing her the menu. "Snowing out there yet?"

"No, just cold." She shrugged out of her coat. "Guess I should be used to it by now."

"You never get used to it," Mitch said. "What'll it be?"

"BLT this time. Wheat bread, extra mayo."

"Comin' up." He paused. "Also . . . I have something for you."

"What is it?" She smiled.

He hurried back to the cash register, gave Danny her order, and waited until his brother turned back to the fridge for the bacon and lettuce. Mitch quickly pulled a narrow four-foot-long box from under the counter and returned to Mary's table. There he paused to glance furtively around the room, but the older couple was deep in conversation and the lone diner was studying his cell phone intently. Mary sat looking up at Mitch, clearly puzzled.

Unceremoniously, he slid the box across her table. "For you."

She studied it a moment, then opened it. Inside was a hand-made walking stick with a crook at the top and a rubber tip on the bottom. The word MARY had been carefully etched into the polished and gleaming wood on the top of the handle. She stared at it for a long moment, her fingers touching the letters of her name. When she raised her head to look at him, she had a huge grin on her face.

"You told me," he said, "that you don't use a walking stick because you haven't found one you liked. Well, you might not like this one either, but . . . who knows? It's a little heavy, but it's balanced and solid."

"It's perfect," she whispered. She reached up and took his hand. "I don't know what to say."

Mitch lightly squeezed her fingers. "Say you'll give it a try." From the corner of his eye, he saw the gray-suited man rise from his table. "Be right back," Mitch said. He picked up the empty box and headed for his post at the cash register.

When the diner had paid and left, Mitch glanced at Danny, who—always watching—grinned and rolled his eyes. Then Mitch poured a cup of coffee from the pot on the countertop and took it to Mary Del Rio's table. She was still examining the cane, turning it over and over in her hands.

"What a kind and wonderful thing for you to do," she said quietly.

He smiled and put down her cup and saucer. "My pleasure. I like to make things, and I wanted to give it to you now because . . . well, we might not be here long, my brother and me."

She blinked. "You're closing?"

"Moving." He sat down across from her and told her what he knew so far, about their plans, and when he described them aloud he realized they sounded a little half-baked. "Nothing's definite yet," he added.

"Biloxi's a good place," she said. "I have a sister in Mobile."

"How far away is that?"

"Different state, but just fifty or sixty miles. And it's bah-LUCK-see, not bah-LOCK-see. Say it wrong and they'll run you out of town."

He laughed. "Good to know. I just found out what a barrier island is."

"They weren't much of a barrier to the last few hurricanes."

"My thoughts exactly." He paused. "But I think I'd rather get blown away by a storm than by a hopped-up teenager with a gun. Or a gangster."

"Gangster?"

He shook his head. "Never mind. I've been listening to too many rumors. What I do know, though, is that it isn't as safe around here as it used to be." He leaned forward, holding her gaze. "I'd hate for you to stop coming here, whether Danny and I own the place anymore or not, but walking home from work after dark . . . well, that might not be a great idea."

She stayed quiet a moment, then said, "You're a good man, Mitch White—"

"That's what I keep telling my brother."

"—but I go where I want, and when I want. Okay?"

He smiled again. "Okay." He hesitated, then almost said something more, but didn't. He liked that she was brave, and stubborn. She reminded him of Emily. He felt the beginnings of tears in his own eyes. He could hardly believe she'd been gone three years now.

The scrape of chairs snapped Mitch out of his thoughts. The elderly couple had finished and were rising to leave. "Your sandwich'll be ready in a minute," he said to Mary, as he stood up to go back to the counter—and she surprised him by standing also.

"I'm headed to the ladies' room first. Besides, I want to try out the cane."

Two minutes later, after Mitch had tucked the old folks' cash payment into the drawer of the register and watched them shuffle out into the night, he heard his brother set a plate down with a clatter in the service window behind him and say, "One BLT for the pretty lady."

As Mitch picked up the plate, he and Danny exchanged a look, and Mitch couldn't help smiling. She *was* pretty. Later, he wouldn't be able to remember why he hadn't heard the dinging of the bell above the front door, though it was probably because the old couple had only just exited.

Mitch turned back to the counter—and straight into the barrel of a gun.

The bill of the baseball cap was pushed back a bit, and he saw Mystery Man's face clearly for the first time. If eyes could look cold and soulless, this man's did. Mitch felt a chill run down his spine. Behind him, on the kitchen side of the window, he could hear his brother humming a tune. Danny hadn't yet seen what was happening.

The man waved the pistol—a heavy revolver—at the window and said, "Get him out here. And put that down."

Mitch set the sandwich plate down on the countertop, turned, caught Danny's eye, and waved him out front. He was careful not to look at the hallway that led to the restrooms.

If the gunman didn't know Mary Del Rio was here, Mitch wanted to keep it that way.

Danny could now see the man on the other side of the counter, could see the gun and the look on Mitch's face, and didn't ask questions. A moment later the two brothers were standing side by side, staring at the dark stranger.

"I know tomorrow is deposit day," the man said. "I also know how much business you've done this week. Hand it over."

Mitch's mind was whirling. As his trembling hands took out the stacks of bills, he found himself wishing fervently that he'd paid more attention to this guy. But how could he have suspected, much less prevented, something like this?

"Now," the gunman said, pocketing the loot, "as for you two—"

He never finished the sentence. Mitch heard a WHOP like a palm slapping a tabletop and saw the man's cap fly off and his eyes roll backward. He teetered there for a second, his face slack and shoulders slumped, and then fell forward across the counter and lay still.

Only then could Mitch see what had happened. Standing behind the man was Mary Del Rio, her walking stick high over her left shoulder and her upper body twisted in a follow-through like a batter after a home-run swing. Slowly she lowered the cane, switched ends so she was holding the crook, and looked at the brothers. "You guys okay?" she asked.

Mitch's brain couldn't seem to form words. Danny, whose mouth was hanging open, finally said, "Lady, you 'bout knocked his head off."

"I was trying to," she said, looking down at the gunman. Sprawled facedown across the counter with his head and arms hanging off one side and his legs off the other, he looked like a drunk cowboy flung over a horse's back to be carried home to the bunkhouse.

"I better call the cops," Danny said. As he hurried to the phone, Mary hobbled around the counter to stand beside Mitch and leaned forward to examine the man's face.

"How long you think it'll take 'em to get here?" she asked.

Mitch swallowed. "The police? Maybe ten minutes. There's a station two blocks away." Then, as the thought occurred to him, he said, "What if he wakes up before then?"

She was studying the guy as if in deep thought. Finally, she straightened up again. "You know that thing on an alarm clock that you push so you can sleep a little longer?"

"The snooze button?" Mitch said.

"Yeah." Calmly, she gripped the cane with both hands as before, stepped forward, and bashed the guy in the head again. "That should do it."

Both she and Mitch stood there a minute, staring at him.

"Is he still alive?" Mitch asked, when he found his voice.

"Probably." Mary Del Rio, leaning once more on the cane, raised her head and looked him in the eye. "Listen to me, Mitch." When he'd focused on her, she said, "You listening?"

He nodded.

"I wasn't here tonight," she said. "While this jerk was robbing you and Danny, some guy off the street you never saw before came in and hit him in the back of the head with a baseball bat. Understand?" She paused. "If you tell the truth, I could lose my job."

Mitch blinked several times, not quite following, but suddenly a more urgent thought occurred to him. "You could lose more than that. If this stranger is who I think he might be . . . Yeah. You weren't here. That's a good idea."

"Make sure Danny understands too. Make up a description of your rescuer, get together on it, and stick to it. Okay?"

"Okay."

She sighed then and gently touched his cheek with her palm. Her hand was warm and steady. "Go south," she said. "Get out of here. And don't forget me."

"I won't," he said.

He watched dazedly as she used the cane to walk to the door, pausing only long enough to retrieve her coat and purse and newspaper from her booth. Then she was gone.

⚯

Officer Nicholas Posey arrived in twelve minutes to find the robber still unconscious and still in possession of the contents of the café's cash drawer. Mitch and Danny, faithful watchers of all the *CSI* shows—even the reruns—had been understandably reluctant to touch the guy, but they had no trouble convincing Posey to dig the stolen money from the guy's pants pockets and return it to them. It wasn't as if there was no further evidence against him. The White brothers presented a believable, if entirely false, account and Posey could find no reason to question it. As unlikely as it might seem, an anonymous Good Samaritan had swooped in at exactly the right time, or, from the head-battered robber's perspective, the wrong time.

After the perpetrator had been carted off to the hospital, from where he would eventually be carted off to jail, Officer Posey allowed himself to be persuaded to sample a slice of Danny White's apple pie and—in return—to answer a few questions. The first was the most obvious:

"Was he the guy you told me about?" Mitch asked.

"What guy?" Posey replied, chewing.

"You said someone with mafia connections had relocated here in the past month or two. Was that him?"

"No. Why do you think it was?"

"I don't know—he was a stranger, acted sneaky, and looked dangerous, I guess."

"He *was* dangerous," Posey said. "And you guys were lucky. I'm thinking he's the one who killed those people the other night."

"But . . ."

"He was just a thug. Retired mob figures don't usually hold up small mom-and-pop—"

"Brother-and-brother," Danny corrected.

"—brother-and-brother eateries. No offense."

"None taken," Mitch said. "But why are you so certain?"

"That your thief wasn't the gangster?"

"Yeah."

"Because your thief was a man."

"So?"

"The Chicago underworld is apparently an equal opportunity employer."

"What do you mean?"

"The mob guy I told you about," Posey said, "was a woman."

"What?"

He nodded. "Walked with a limp."

It was suddenly very quiet in the café. Posey took another bite of pie and chewed awhile before realizing Mitch and Danny were staring at him.

"A limp," Mitch said.

"Yeah. She was shot not long ago, in the left knee. Or so I'm told." He finished off the pie, wiped his mouth with a napkin, and pushed his chair back from the table. Standing, he hitched his gun belt a little higher—it slid right back down—and studied the two brothers, who remained seated. "You boys okay?"

It was almost exactly the same thing Mary Del Rio had said to them half an hour earlier, after stepping up behind the robber and knocking him cold. Thinking of that, Mitch cleared his throat and nodded. "We're fine."

He and Danny stood, shook hands with Posey, and thanked him. After the cop left, the brothers silently cleared the tables. The CLOSED sign they'd put on the front door when Posey arrived stayed in place. They didn't want any more customers tonight. When they were done, they stood together for a moment behind the counter, each lost in his own thoughts.

"She was a good actor," Danny said. "Good liar too."

Mitch was still shaken. "She didn't lie about her leg. She told me it was a recent injury."

"She didn't tell you it was a gunshot wound. You still think all she did was balance their books?"

"No."

"Me either. Accountants die of boredom—they don't get shot."

"Neither do librarians, I guess."

A long silence passed. The only sound was the murmur of evening traffic in the street.

At last Danny said, "You're not thinking about looking for her, are you?"

"Looking for her?" Mitch took a long breath and let it out. "No. How could I look for her, now?"

Danny didn't reply.

After another silence, Mitch rubbed his eyes and checked his watch. "You ready to go?"

"Let me hit the bathroom."

A moment after Danny disappeared down the hallway, the front door opened and Robbie Stanton walked in.

"Robbie?" Mitch said, glancing at his watch. "You left before eight. Where you been?"

"Across the street, sittin' on the curb between two cars. Watching."

"Watching?"

The teenager stuck both hands in his pockets and started shuffling his feet. He looked about nine years old. "And waiting," he said.

Mitch walked around the counter and leaned back against it. "Tell me everything."

Robbie shrugged. "Not much to tell. I was out front, walking back here after delivering Mr. Watson's order, when a lady came out—that good-looking lady who's been here most every night. Except tonight she was using a walking cane."

"And?"

"And she recognized me. She told me I might not want to go in right then. She said the police were on their way. Then she left."

"So you did what she said?"

"Oh hell yeah. The police and me, well . . ."

Mitch held up a stop-right-there hand. "I don't want to know. What'd you do then?"

"I went over and sat in the dark and watched. Sure enough, a cop car came about ten minutes later, and then more cops, and then a guy got hauled out the door. He looked dead."

"He wasn't," Mitch said. "What then?"

"I kept waiting. Finally, the first cop came out again, got in his car, and drove off. I waited a few minutes more, and here I am." Robbie paused, looking worried. "What happened?"

"We almost got robbed. I'll fill you in tomorrow. This lady—did she say anything else?"

He shook his head, then brightened. "But she gave me a note. Wrote it while we were standing there and told me to give it to you."

Mitch took the folded slip of paper from him and said, "Go on home, Robbie. And be careful *you* don't get robbed."

"Okay, Mr. White. Thanks."

Mitch watched him leave, then looked down at the note. Slowly, his heart thudding, he unfolded it and was reading the message when he heard the restroom door swing open.

"Talk about timing," Danny called from the hallway. "You and me were standing here earlier tonight, talking about the rising crime rate—and then all this happens. Nothing like getting a gun pulled on you to speed up a decision to sell out and leave, is there?"

Mitch, staring at the note, didn't reply.

Danny ducked into the kitchen and came back out with his leather jacket. "I vote we look for a new owner tomorrow—Ned Dunaway's still interested, I think—and start checking out places for sale, or a lot to build on, in the Biloxi/Gulfport area. What do you think?"

When Mitch still didn't answer, Danny looked at him and paused, one arm inside his jacket and one out. "What's the matter with you?" he asked.

"Nothing," Mitch said, looking up. "Why?"

" 'Cause you look like the cat who caught the canary, that's why." He finished putting his coat on. "Who were you talking to a minute ago?"

"Robbie. He stopped in to bring me something."

"Watson's payment for his burger orders, I hope."

"No—I forgot to even ask for that."

"We'll get it tomorrow. I'm just glad Robbie wasn't here for all the excitement."

Mitch paused, focusing. "I don't think he was meant to be here," he said. "I think our robber wanted as few people on site as possible, and he'd already been here enough to find out about Robbie's nightly delivery. I figure that's why he didn't know Mary was here tonight. He was probably watching the back door so he'd know when Robbie left, and she came in through the front about the same time Robbie went out the back. Then he waited until he saw the other customers leave."

"Makes sense. I guess we were lucky all the way around." Danny turned up his coat collar and said, "What's that you're holding?"

"A note Robbie brought me." Mitch gave it to Danny, who fished a pair of reading glasses from his shirt pocket and held the paper up to the light.

It read, in a neat feminine hand:

I really do have a sister in Mobile.
I'll find you.

Danny looked up at his brother in amazement. "Well, well," he said. "What do you think about that?"

Trying not to smile, Mitch took the note back, refolded it, and put it in his pocket. All of a sudden, he felt like a kid again, a kid on the first day of summer vacation. "I think you're gonna have to learn how to make gumbo," he said.

He fetched his own coat, joined Danny at the door, and both their faces went solemn for a moment. They took a long look around, at the tables and booths, the windows, the counter, the floor they'd swept a thousand times, the lights they'd worked so hard to mount just right.

Without turning, Mitch said, "You said people are crazy down there, huh?"

Danny nodded. "We'll fit right in."

He walked out then, and a second later Mitch turned out the lights and followed.

One of my favorite subjects as a suspense writer has been the ordinary guy with an ordinary job who suddenly finds himself in a desperate situation. In the case of "Biloxi Bound," my protagonist is one of two brothers who operate a small diner in an unnamed northeastern city. When their neighborhood becomes a hotbed of violent crime, they decide they should move to the slower-paced (and warmer) Mississippi Gulf Coast. That's an area familiar to me, since I once lived on the beach there and have spent most of my life not too far away.

To this scenario I added a retired mobster, a friendly cop, a mysterious regular customer at the café, and several plot reversals. When I finished writing the story—crime does of course arrive at the diner before the brothers can relocate—I sent it to The Strand Magazine, *which has always been receptive to tales with multiple plot twists and surprises.*

I'm glad I did.

In 1995, **Jacqueline Freimor** won first prize in the unpublished writers category of the Mystery Writers of America's 50th Anniversary Short Story Competition. Since then, her short stories have been published in Ellery Queen Mystery Magazine, Alfred Hitchcock's Mystery Magazine, Rock and a Hard Place Magazine, Red Herring Mystery Magazine, and Murderous Intent, among others, as well as in the e-zine Blue Murder and at akashicbooks.com. Two of the stories received Honorable Mention in The Best American Mystery Stories, the first in 1997 and the second in 2000. Jacqueline's most recent story is forthcoming in MWA's 2021 anthology, When a Stranger Comes to Town, edited by Michael Koryta. She lives in Westchester County, New York, and is a musician and music teacher.

THAT WHICH IS TRUE

Jacqueline Freimor

At nine o'clock that morning a court officer ushered us twelve jurors and two alternates into a windowless jury room at 111 Centre Street. Silently, we shuffled around a large, scarred conference table, and each of us claimed a seat. My fellow inmates looked disturbed, probably because we'd had to check our cell phones at security. I wasn't upset by that, but then again, I belonged to the one-wall-phone-in-the-kitchen-with-a-twenty-five-foot-long-cord generation. The twenty-somethings in the room looked like they wanted to set their hair on fire.

What bothered me was that I'd been selected in the first place. I was so sure they would strike me. I was betting nonrefundable tickets to Maui on it.

"Mrs.—" the defense attorney had said, his eyes flicking from his clipboard back up at me—"Tannenbaum."

"Ms.," I said.

He paused. "Ms." He managed to sneer with his eyes; neat trick. He checked the clipboard again, then looked up, frowning. "That's *Norma Jean* Tannenbaum?"

"Jeannie." Mentally, I dared him to tell me Norma Jeane was Marilyn Monroe's real name, but he wisely moved on.

And on. The questioning continued at a glacial pace while I squirmed in my seat. Finally he got to the good part.

"Would you state your occupation, Jeannie?"

There it was—my get-out-of-jury-duty-free card. "I'm a private investigator." I hid a smile. I could smell the ocean. I could taste the mai tais.

He raised a bushy eyebrow. "Really."

"I'm under oath, aren't I?" I knew why he was surprised, though. I was a woman of a certain age, which meant I held no appeal for most men, which meant I was invisible. I wasn't offended. Invisibility was my superpower. And the lawyer didn't appeal to me, either, a middle-aged man with dull gray hair and a paunch that even his expensive bespoke suit couldn't hide.

Not that I was looking. I had Harry. And Harry and I were going to Hawaii next week—if I could get out of jury duty.

The attorney scribbled something—hopefully *Strike! Snarky PI!*—on his clipboard. He pursed his lips. "So, um . . . Jeannie, would your experience as an investigator adversely affect your ability to keep an open mind about my client?"

I was tempted. Sorely tempted. I even opened my mouth, the *Yes* ready to slither out from between my lips like the lying snake it was. "No," I said, and the lilting strains of "Aloha 'Oe" faded into the ether.

Now the court officer, a stocky white woman with the shoulders of a linebacker, took attendance, and I took the opportunity to size up the other jurors. We were a diverse group, age- and ethnicity-wise, and about evenly split between women and men. Most were dressed in degrees of casual, but the slender, metrosexual black guy sitting next to me was dressed like Henry Fonda in *Twelve Angry Men*: white button-down shirt, belted gray pleated slacks, and a skinny tie—with an actual tie clip. He caught my gaze, raised an impeccably shaped eyebrow, and gave a tight smile. I smiled tightly back. He and I were the only ones taking the measure of the group. The rest seemed to have decided that the only rational response to this situation was to pretend we were on the subway and studiously ignore one another.

The court officer snapped her folder shut, and we all looked her way. "All present and accounted for," she said, "and on time. Good." She consulted a giant black watch on her thick wrist. "I'll be back in about an hour to take you to the courtroom. Restroom's over there." She left, closing the door behind her.

Someone sighed, and everyone got busy, rummaging in their bags and backpacks and spilling out all manner of food, drink, and reading matter on the table. Among the bottles of water, soda cans, and granola bars, I spied the latest blockbuster novel, a Bible with a worn black leather cover, and a Sudoku book, as well as a bunch of trashy and highbrow magazines. One scruffy young white guy was fiddling with pieces of a plastic toy in his lap—how old was he, ten?—and an elderly woman had pulled out a deck of cards and was setting up a hand of solitaire. It was charming. I thought everyone played solitaire online.

Mr. Metrosexual leaned toward me. "Is your name really Norma Jean?"

"Yes. But the 'Jean' is spelled without a final 'e.'"

He placed a slim hand, fingers splayed, over his heart. "Just a coincidence? Or were you named after MM?"

I sighed inwardly. "I was named after her. My mother is an actress, and she knew her."

His eyes widened and he slapped at my shoulder. "Get out!"

"Ow. No, it's true."

"Sorry, but this is so exciting! MM is my idol. I'm an actor too."

Clearly, everyone could hear us, but just as clearly, they were pretending not to. The woman sitting on the man's other side—our foreperson, because she had been seated on the jury first—glanced at me briefly and turned away. She looked familiar, but I couldn't place her. What did the lawyers call her—Judy? Jody? She seemed about my age and was blonde, skinny, and tan in a way that owed more to money than to genetics.

The man offered me his hand, nails trimmed into shiny, buffed ovals. "I'm Antoine. Antoine Dubois."

We shook. "Nice to meet you."

Antoine leaned his elbow on the table and rested his chin on the back of his hand, like he was settling in for the long haul. "So. How did your mother know La Monroe? What's her name? Your mother, that is."

"Stella Mann—born Estelle Tannenbaum. She was an uncredited extra in *Some Like It Hot*."

Again, I caught Judy-Jody glancing at me and quickly looking away. What was up with that?

Antoine inhaled deeply. "Oh, honey, that's fabulous! I would give anything to have met Marilyn. Did you have an absolutely glamorous childhood? Where did you grow up? Hollywood? Oh, tell me it was Hollywood!"

Hardly. I debated describing being shuttled from one foster home to another for most of my early life but couldn't bring myself to vandalize the beautiful portrait Antoine was painting. "Well, it was Queens, actually. And my childhood was . . . okay."

Judy-Jody looked at me again.

Enough was enough. "Hello?" I said. "Do I know you?"

Her eyes widened, and she blinked rapidly. "I don't think so."

"Are you sure? I could swear I've seen you before."

"I *said*, I don't *think* so." Her lip curled and her nostrils flared.

That sneer—could it be? Oh my God—it was. In an instant, forty years melted away, and I was in junior high school again, facing Jodi Auerbach, Queen Bee of IS 47, chief architect of the prison of pain in which I served my adolescence. Pretty, popular, nasty Jodi Auerbach, who'd befriended me the first day of seventh grade just so she could drop me a month later.

My stomach clenched. My hands started shaking. I put them in my lap under the table and squeezed them into fists. For three solid years, Jodi and her minions had made my life a misery. They ignored me when I was standing right next to them. They left nasty notes and, once, a used sanitary pad, in my locker. One would say sweetly, "Going on a trip?" as I walked up to the blackboard, and another would obediently stick out a foot and send me flying. The teachers either didn't see or didn't want to see. Jodi's parents were rich, and her dad was on the school board, while I was a foster kid, at the mercy of strangers. The last day of ninth grade was literally the happiest day of my life.

Now Jodi gazed at me, and I saw her blank out the recognition in exactly the same way she willed me into nonexistence all those years ago. I struggled to control my breath and keep my voice steady. "My mistake," I said, enunciating like a drunk pretending to be sober. I shrugged as though I hadn't a care in the world and turned back to Antoine.

"*Any*way," he said, "tell me everything. I want all the deets."

I knew that I opened my mouth and words fell out, but I had no idea what I was saying—I was too busy beating myself up. For years, I'd thought about how I'd react if I ever saw Jodi Auerbach or her posse again, my fantasies ranging from shaming them in public to impaling them on a pike. But here was my chance, and what did I do? Not a thing. Stupid, stupid, stupid.

The scruffy young guy at the end of the table plonked his toy down. "Oh, for the love of Mike!" he shouted. "Would you shut up already?" He lurched to his feet, almost overturning his chair.

Every head swiveled to stare at him. "What?" I said.

He picked up the toy and pointed it at me and Antoine. "Yap, yap, yap, blah, blah, blah—Gawd! I should just shoot the two of you right now."

It wasn't a toy. It was a gun. Plug-ugly and made out of plastic, but a gun nonetheless.

I froze, my hands and feet turned to ice. Oh my God, oh my God! How had he gotten a gun past security? I thought he was playing with a toy, but was he actually putting plastic pieces together to assemble a weapon? Jesus.

The guy backed away from the table and, pivoting on his heel, swept the thing in an arc around the room. Someone gasped, and we all shrank back in our seats. "Keep quiet and stay still," he said, "and I won't have to kill you." No one moved. "And you, motormouth"—he waggled the gun at me—"crack the door open and stick your head out. Tell that lardass to lock us in, or I'm gonna start shooting."

I sat, paralyzed.

"Now!" he screamed, and leveled the gun.

I bolted up from my chair and held out my hands, as though my palms could repel bullets. I backed to the door, slivered it open, and poked my head out. The court officer was sitting behind a desk ten feet away, filling out forms.

"Excuse me?" I squeaked. My teeth were chattering.

She looked up. "Yes?"

"One of the jurors has a gun and is threatening to shoot us unless you lock us in the jury room."

She stared at me. I knew how she felt. I couldn't believe this was happening, either.

"Seriously," I said. "You need to lock us in." I withdrew my head and closed the door.

"Good," the guy said. "Sit down." I returned to my seat and folded my trembling hands on the table.

Still no one moved. It was like we were playing Statues—Nightmare Edition. Someone started breathing audibly and someone else sobbed. What would happen if the court officer burst in? Would this nutjob start shooting? I didn't want to find out. *Please, lady*, I thought, *please. Just do what he says*.

The door shifted slightly in its frame like someone was leaning on it. A shadow flicked in the narrow space between the bottom of the door and the floor.

"Hey!" the guy yelled. "I know you're listening. Lock the goddamn door, or one of these people dies."

A beat. The court officer called back, "Is everyone okay? First tell me they're okay."

Crazy pants looked at me. "Tell her."

"We're fine," I said loudly. "Please lock the door."

I heard the thunk of a key turning a bolt. "It's locked," the court officer said. "Now what? What do you want?"

"What I *want* is for you to go away. Go back to your desk." Nothing happened. "Do it! Do it now!"

I could feel her hesitation. The shadow at the bottom of the door disappeared, and although I knew she must have gone to summon help, it struck me like a fist to the gut that we were truly on our own. Tears threatened to spill. I blinked them back.

"So," the guy said. "Here we are." His green eyes glittered with malicious glee, or maybe he was just high. He bore an uncanny resemblance to the pre-swastika'd Charles Manson—small face with a high forehead, long shaggy hair parted in the middle, small goatee.

"Look," said a Latino man sitting at the far end of the table. "You want money? We'll give you money. Just don't hurt us." He looked around, and several heads nodded.

Charlie danced over to him and shoved the gun under the guy's chin. Charlie was shorter and skinnier than I'd thought; he must've loved the power the gun gave him over men who were bigger than he was. Color drained from the man's face and he stared up at Charlie, a muscle near his eye jumping.

"What's your name, man?" Charlie said.

"Oscar." It was a whisper.

Charlie lifted Oscar's chin with the barrel of the gun. "Well, Oscar, if I wanted money, I'd've taken it already, right? *Right?*"

"Right," Oscar said faintly. He closed his eyes and his Adam's apple twitched as he swallowed.

"Damn right," Charlie said, slapping Oscar's cheek lightly with the gun and bounding back to his seat at the other end of the table.

He was definitely high—which meant he was erratic, which meant he was even more dangerous than I'd thought. And here I'd been worried about junior high school bullying forty years in the past.

"So, friends, now that we've gotten that out of the way, let me tell you what happens next. I got a letter here"—Charlie fished in his back pocket and pulled out a folded rectangle—"that I need someone to push under the door for me. Volunteers?" He held the note up and looked around the room. "No? Then the winner is . . . Norma Jean! Come here, Norma Jean. Not too fast, though."

Oh, God. I took a deep breath, stood on wobbly legs, and slowly walked toward him, my eyes locked on the gun. A rivulet of icy sweat trickled down my spine as I reached for the paper. Once I had it firmly gripped between thumb and forefinger, I just as slowly made my way to the door and squatted, sliding the note under it. Thank God for those Pilates classes. If I was going to die, I'd do it with a fine-looking pair of glutes.

Still trembling, I slunk back to my seat. Under the table, Antoine pressed his knee against mine, and I pressed back. Mentally, I shook myself—hard. I was not going to die. No one was. I had survived equally dangerous situations before, and I was going to figure a way out of this one too. But how?

Charlie sat back in his chair and threw one leg over the arm, foot jiggling, the hand holding the gun resting in his lap. "Good job, Norma Jean! I knew you could do it." He smiled. "So now we're gonna wait for the police. We're gonna have plenty of time together, so let's get to know each other! We all met Oscar here, and Norma Jean and her new buddy Antoine, but what about the rest of you? Around the table—you! What's your name?"

He pointed the gun at the curvy young red-haired woman seated immediately to his left. She sank in her chair, the freckles on her face standing out in stark relief against the paleness of her skin. "Um, my name's Darlene," she said in a small voice.

"Darlene," Charlie said. "Dar-lene. And what are your hobbies, Dar-lene?"

She stared. "My hobbies?"

"Yeah, your hobbies. Although I think everyone can see what you do for fun, right, all those nights alone, sitting in front of the TV?" He mimed shoving food in his mouth. "Do you 'eat your feelings,' Dar-lene? Huh? Do you?" He guffawed.

A fiery blush rose steadily from Darlene's chest to her hairline. She ducked her head, but I could see she was biting her lip. A tear slid down her cheek.

Charlie faux yawned. "Ho hum. Too easy." He shifted the gun to the woman sitting to Darlene's left—Jodi. "Next!"

Jodi started and blanched under her tan, but there was defiance in the way she stuck out her chin. "Jodi Greenberg."

"And what do you do for a living, Jodi Greenberg?"

"I'm a realtor."

I almost laughed. Of course she was.

Charlie pursed his lips and squinched his eyebrows in a parody of deep thought. He stroked his goatee. "Hmmm, that's really . . . boring. Right, everyone?" His stare was a searchlight scanning the room. "Right?"

The group murmured something that could have been assent. What a sick bastard. He was enjoying this.

Charlie turned his attention back to Jodi. "Everyone agrees that's pretty boring, hon. Say something interesting."

I had to hand it to her; she looked him straight in the eye. "Like what?"

The gun swiveled between me and Jodi and back again. "How about, like, how you know Norma Jean here? She says she knows you." He rested his chin on the back of his hand and batted his lashes in a nasty imitation of Antoine. "I need all the *deets*."

I felt Antoine tense up. Jodi gave me the side-eye, then turned her gaze back to Charlie. Backbone of steel. "I don't know her."

I looked at Charlie, sitting three people away from me—Antoine, then Jodi, then Darlene. I was getting an idea. It was a huge risk, but this guy was so unpredictable, I wasn't sure the cops could get to us before he shot someone anyway. But could I do it? My heart jackhammered in my chest, my throat so dry I could barely swallow. I had no choice.

Teeth clenched, I responded before Charlie could. "Sure you do," I said. "Jodi Auerbach, right? From IS 47?"

She whipped her head around to stare at me. She wasn't ignoring me now. She snarled. "I don't know you. How many times do I have to say it?"

Charlie leaned forward in his chair, grinning. "Ooh! Grab your popcorn, folks! We got us a catfight!"

I shook my head. "Wow, Jodi. That really hurts. We were friends! Don't you remember the pranks we pulled on the girls we didn't like?" I held her gaze, willing her to understand me.

Jodi narrowed her eyes and watched me warily.

"Pranks!" Charlie said. "What kinds of pranks?"

I shrugged, hoping it looked casual. "They were pretty fun. We wrote notes to these losers telling them nobody liked them and they should kill themselves."

Charlie inclined his head. "Not bad. What else did you do?"

I spoke only to Jodi. "We put, uh, used feminine products in their lockers."

Charlie laughed. "Ew. That's a good one."

"We also used to send them on trips." I raised my eyebrow at Jodi and awareness flooded her face. She nodded slightly and turned back to look at Charlie.

"Trips?" Charlie said. "What does that mean?"

This was it. My body electric with fear, I stood up, flinging my chair back. "Figure it out, asshole. Or are you too stupid to understand one-syllable words?"

He froze. Rage darkening his face, he jumped out of his seat and charged at me, arm extended, gun lifted at shoulder height.

"Now!" I yelled.

Jodi stuck out her foot.

<hr>

As it turned out, the gun wasn't even loaded. According to the newspaper, Charlie—ironically enough, his real name—had mastered 3D printing and assembling most of the weapon's components before learning that even plastic guns require metal bullets and, crucially, a metal firing pin to help discharge them. He knew he'd never be able to sneak those parts past the courthouse's metal detectors, but he decided to go ahead anyway, counting on the presence of the gun itself to intimidate the cops into giving him what he wanted.

It was a good thing, too, that there were no bullets. After Jodi tripped him, Charlie flew a couple of feet, hit the floor, and landed on the gun. If it had been loaded, he might have shot himself in the belly, or it might have exploded, injuring him and the five jurors who sat on his back to restrain him. Antoine was first to pile on; I heard a crack, and Charlie screamed. "Oops," Antoine said. "My bad."

The newspapers also reported that in the note I had shoved under the door, Charlie said he was going to hold us hostage until New York State released his incarcerated brother from Sing Sing. It was a ridiculous plan, destined to fail, but it seemed to me Charlie's special skill was cruelty, not intelligence.

As was Jodi's. I had mixed feelings about her. Despite the horrible things she did to me in junior high school, I thought what she did in the jury room that day was pretty brave. And when it was all over and we jurors were sitting on the long benches in the courthouse hallway, waiting to be interviewed by the cops, I told her so.

"You too," she said, tapping her foot and glancing at her watch.

I cocked my head. "What's amazing, though, is that you understood I wanted you to trip that guy. I mean, considering you've never seen me before."

Jodi stopped fidgeting and looked me straight in the eye, then shrugged. "I really don't know what you're talking about."

I stared at her. "Seriously? After everything that happened today?" I shook my head in disgust. "Although, if you wouldn't admit it even at gunpoint, you never will. Jesus." I started to rise.

She glared at me. Then she tapped my hand. "Wait."

I sat back down and folded my arms across my chest. "Yes?"

She blinked rapidly and sighed. "Those popular girls?" Jodi said. "I think they were wrong to do what they did. I think they were probably just really, really immature. In fact, if they were here now, I think they'd probably apologize."

"Oh, you do, do you?" I examined her face, searching for a hint that she was messing with me, but she seemed sincere—embarrassed, even.

"If they were here." She shrugged. "Hypothetically."

Any further nonapology she might have made was interrupted by the appearance of a uniformed cop, who said he was ready to take her statement. Without another word, she stood up and followed him down the corridor.

I shook my head. What a piece of work. But as I watched Jodi disappear down the hall, a funny thing happened. I felt some of my anger go with her. I felt lighter. I felt good.

And when I hit Waikiki Beach with a mai tai in each hand, I'd feel even better.

---

*A few years ago, I discovered that open-source blueprints for printing 3D guns could be downloaded from the Internet. After my initial shock about the implications for our society, I started toying with the implications for, of course, a short story. If untraceable, unregistered firearms could be smuggled through metal detectors, then many of our relatively "safe" public spaces are vulnerable—including our courts.

Setting a story in a courtroom was intriguing to me because during one of my stints of jury duty service in New York City, I discovered how irrational and, frankly, terrifying my fellow jurors could be, even without firearms. How likely was the jury-selection process of voir dire—"to speak that which is true"—to ferret out different kinds of threat? Like most crime writers, I'm interested in capital-J Justice. But I wanted to explore other kinds of justice too.*

Alison Gaylin has written eleven books, including the Edgar Award–winning If I Die Tonight, *and the Shamus Award–winning* And She Was. *A* USA Today *and international bestselling author, her work has been published in numerous countries, including Japan, Germany, the UK, and France. Her twelfth book,* The Collective, *was published in the spring of 2021 by William Morrow.*

THE GIFT

Alison Gaylin

DAY ONE

When the first call comes in, Lyla McCord is at the London premiere of her new film, *Desire of Annabeth*. She is posing on the red carpet, done up in freshly highlighted beach waves and heavy false lashes that make her eyes sting, about five inches of high-def makeup, and a skintight Elie Saab dress that would have been a lot more comfortable had she opted to remove a few ribs before putting it on. She resents this. All of it. It was bad enough caking on the foundation and squeezing into getups like this one when she was just another girl on a teen TV show. But she's a serious actress now, an Oscar winner. Will there ever be a point in her life when she doesn't feel as though she's being examined under a microscope?

Lyla is smiling, though, because that's what's expected of her. She sticks a spray-bronzed leg through the slit of her torturous dress and strikes a pose for the bank of British photographers and reporters and smiles until her lips start to spasm.

She does notice the vibration of her phone in the borrowed $500,000 diamond-encrusted Chanel clutch—but only as a nuisance that momentarily throws her off her game. She wishes she'd given her phone to someone else—her UK publicist, Claude; her assistant, Gigi; one of the bodyguard detail. Anyone.

Who could be calling? Actually, she never asks herself that question because she doesn't care. Her daughter, Fidelity, never calls; she texts or FaceTimes, and Fidelity is the only one who matters to Lyla. So when the Chanel clutch begins vibrating yet again, Lyla is irritated, nothing more.

A Cockney-accented reporter shouts, "Where's Nolan?" and Lyla recovers. She aims her emerald eyes at him and gives him that smoldering gaze she's practiced in the mirror hundreds of times since she was a teenager, the *Lyla Look*, as it's been dubbed in the press. "He's home with our baby," she says.

For a moment, she envisions the three of them, back when Fidelity truly *was* a baby. Lyla, Nolan, and Fidelity, all in their pajamas. A lazy Sunday morning watching Elmo on TV, as close to real as she's ever felt. "I miss them." She says it unprompted. The reporter eats it up. "I miss my family."

Her phone vibrates again. Lyla feels like throwing the clutch to the ground and stomping on it till it shatters.

⚬━━⚬

After she thanks the British press and before she goes into the theater, Lyla slips the phone out of the purse and turns it off. And so she doesn't see the dozen consecutive calls, one minute apart, all from the same number: Fidelity's nanny.

As she makes her way to her seat, Lyla receives a standing ovation from the audience. This is far from a normal occurrence, but advance buzz has been that good for *Desire of Annabeth*, the story of a young woman on death row for killing both her parents. *Thanks to the truly gifted Lyla McCord*, the *Variety* critic had written, *what could have been a downer of a film turns out to be a revelation.*

Lyla is basking in the glow of the ovation, the word *revelation*, the very beauty of it, lighting up her mind, when a man in a dark suit approaches, tapping her politely on the arm. Behind him stand Claude and Gigi, wearing identical grave expressions. She holds a finger up at this trio, takes a bow for the cheering audience, and lets the lights go down before following them up the aisle and into the theater's lobby.

"Ms. McCord." The man's voice is as dark and somber as his suit. "I'm Inspector Harrison. Scotland Yard."

"Is there a problem?"

"I'm afraid so."

Lyla takes a deep breath—the last one she'll be able to take for a long time. "What does this problem concern?" she says.

"Your daughter, Fidelity," he says. "It appears she's gone missing."

The inspector keeps speaking, about the New York State Police and being contacted by the FBI and providing an escort to the airport. But soon his words turn to fog, and all Lyla can hear is the thump of her own heart. She drops her bag. Her legs give out from under her. Claude and Gigi catch her before she hits the floor.

DAY TWO

By the time Lyla arrives at her country home in the tiny Catskills town of Shady, she hasn't slept or eaten in more than twenty-four hours. Everything feels blurry and surreal—the brightness and cool of the early spring day, the crunch of her sneakered feet on the gravel driveway as she hurries to the door, Gigi trailing after her. As she runs, she notices two parked police cars and a few dark sedans she doesn't recognize.

"God," she whispers, wanting to pray herself awake. *Please let this be a dream. Please let this just be a terrible dream . . .*

She disables the alarm and pulls open the front door, her breath echoing throughout the empty great room, the house heavy and dull from the lack of her, the lack of Fidelity, her Fidelity. Her baby. *What would I be without her? What sort of horrible thing would I be?*

She hears her own voice, calling out her daughter's name. And then another deeper one booming from the kitchen.

"Ly! Is that you?"

She follows the voice. *He's here. Nolan's here.* Nolan Carnes, her husband. *Her soul mate*, she's called him in the press, which has, in turn, fused their names. *Lylan. Nola. McCarnes.* Ironic, really, since Lyla and Nolan, the human beings, aren't fused at all. In fact, they're rarely in the same zip code.

The magazines ship you and Daddy, Fidelity told her once last year. Fidelity, fluent in preteen speak, even at the age of seven. When Lyla had asked her what that meant, Fidelity had said, *It makes them happy to think of the two of you together.*

Do you feel that way too? Lyla had said. *Do you ship me and Daddy?*

Fidelity had just giggled. *You sound funny when you say that, Mommy.*

Lyla calls out Nolan's name. It feels strange on her lips. For the past six weeks, he's been in the wilds of the Arizona desert, some bleak spot with patchy cell phone service, shooting an as-yet-untitled Netflix movie that takes place after the apocalypse. She hasn't spoken to Nolan or even texted with him in more than two weeks.

Thinking about him during the plane trip back to New York, Lyla had wondered if Nolan even knew about Fidelity's disappearance. She imagined it might have been difficult even for the police to track him down.

Lyla had pictured her husband with a prop gun in his hands, sweat stains sprayed onto his tight, ripped T-shirt, acting out a pretend crisis as a real one unfolded back at home. She'd texted him herself. Left voice mail messages. But all went unanswered.

"*Nolan,*" she calls out again, her voice cracking as she moves into the kitchen, where her husband sits at the long table they'd had custom made from the door of an eighteenth-century barn, the bright pool of the skylight pouring down on him. Nolan is bearded and rangy from the pretend crisis of his movie, and for the briefest of moments, she doesn't recognize him. But then he looks up at her, his eyes red rimmed and shattered, and he's Nolan again. The father of her child.

Also at the table are Fidelity's nanny, Courtney; two uniformed police officers; Nolan's bodyguards, Aziz and Jerry; and a staid-looking group of suits Lyla has never seen before—three young men and one young woman, all staring at her as though she's a bomb about to detonate. By now Gigi is in the room, too, and Lyla feels surrounded. She wants to scream.

Nolan moves toward Lyla and takes her in his arms. She smells the sweat on him, the panic, and everything shifts focus—from a nightmare to something awfully, unquestionably real. *Fidelity is gone. Fidelity is gone. Fidelity is gone.* Lyla's stomach clenches up, her vision blurs, and her head turns swimmy. She feels as though she may faint again but wills herself not to.

"What happened?" she says.

Nolan's breath is warm at her neck. "We'll find her. She's our baby. We have to."

Lyla pulls away from him and looks at Courtney—pale, wan, by-the-book Courtney, whose only job was to keep Fidelity safe. Out of the knot of emotions tearing at Lyla's insides, anger emerges. Her hands ball into fists; her teeth clench. She can actually feel the veins pressing against her skin. It's a relief, really, the anger, compared to everything else. It is, at least, something she's experienced before. She says it again, directly to Courtney. "*What happened?*"

"I went to pick her up at school, and she was just . . . she was gone. No one saw her leave. Not her teachers, not anybody. They think it happened during recess."

"Wait, what?"

"I went to pick—"

"She was gone when you got there? The teachers . . ." She whirls around to Nolan. "Isn't that why we moved here in the first place? To keep her safe? Oh my God. Oh my God! Oh dear God I want to . . . *Where the fuck is she?*"

"Shhh."

"*Don't you dare fucking shush me, Nolan.*"

Lyla can feel dozens of eyes on her. She wants to put her fist through a wall. To break everything in the room and burn it down, burn the whole house down and disappear. Again. "Where is Fidelity?" she says.

The young woman approaches her. "Ms. McCord, I'm Shelby Martin, and I'm with the state police. These gentlemen are with the FBI, and I assure you, we are doing everything in our power to find your daughter."

Lyla blinks at her. She looks about twelve.

"It's still very early. The officers here have canvassed the area around your daughter's school. Every member of the faculty and staff has been questioned. It's a private school in a very quiet loca—"

"I know where my daughter goes to school."

Nolan gapes at her, but Shelby Martin remains unfazed. "What I'm saying is, there were no reports of any strange people or cars in the area." She says it very calmly. "It's possible that your daughter simply walked away from the school of her own accord. We're spreading out into the woods behind the school. The woods are quite deep, so this may take some time."

"She wouldn't do that," Lyla says. "She wouldn't walk away. She wouldn't do that to us."

"That's what I told Detective Martin," Courtney says. "It's not like Fidelity to do something like that."

Lyla glares at Courtney. Grits her teeth.

Nolan says, "She could have gone exploring and got lost."

"Fidelity doesn't explore," Lyla says. "She stays where it's safe. She's been taught that. I've—we've taught her that. Haven't we, Nolan?"

Shelby Martin says something about Fidelity not having a cell phone they can track, and Lyla's reply sounds more indignant than she intends it to. "She's *eight*."

Nolan says, "We wanted her to have as normal a life as possible. It's why we live here and not Hollywood. It's one thing we've agreed on, ever since she was born."

This is all press release stuff, none of it true. Fidelity had asked for a cell phone at six, and Nolan, FaceTiming from Madagascar, hadn't thought it such a bad idea. When Lyla had said no—thinking more of trackers and hackers than preserving her daughter's childhood—Nolan had called her paranoid, sparking a huge fight over Nolan's lack of sensitivity and understanding when it came to the very real emotional issues that Lyla had battled, issues that affect many women, many human beings. *What's next?* Lyla had yelled at the screen. *Are you going to call me hysterical?*

Honestly, there are few things that can make a person feel emptier than arguing with one's abnormally laid-back husband on FaceTime. And yet he's here. And Fidelity is not . . .

Lyla says, "Is there anything we can do to help?"

Shelby Martin has large doe eyes and full apple cheeks. Even with her hair slicked back into a tight bun and the high-collared gray silk blouse she wears with her black suit, she still looks more like a babysitter than a detective—a teenager, dolled up for a school play. Lyla is probably five years older than she is, at the most. But Lyla feels as though the gap could be measured in decades. Centuries. "Keep communicating with us, ma'am," Shelby Martin says. "Tell us everything you know about Fidelity. Everything you remember."

DAY THREE

It's strange how equalizing fear can be. Lyla and Nolan are stars by any definition, with an Oscar and four Golden Globes between them and a combined net worth of $250 million. But alone in their dark kitchen at 3:00 A.M., their cell phones and the landline as silent as the night, they are a couple with a missing child, like any couple anywhere with any missing child. They have nothing.

Lyla gazes up at the skylight, the stars shining down on her like mocking eyes. *Please bring her back. Please don't make me live without her.*

"Ly," Nolan says. "Do you think Fidelity was unhappy?"

Lyla closes her eyes. "Why would you say that?"

"Detective Martin said she may not have been kidnapped. She may have run away."

"Yeah, well, Detective Martin is a child."

"That FBI guy said it too."

"Who trusts the FBI? I think we should hire a private investigator."

"But she could have," he says. "Fidelity could have run away. We don't know what's been going through her mind."

"Fidelity loves us. We've given her a great life. She wouldn't run away. Why would anybody with so much to be grateful for just . . . disappear . . ." Lyla stops herself. She knows what Nolan is going to say.

"You did, Lyla. You disappeared."

Lyla exhales. He's right, of course. Nine years ago, she walked off the set of a hit teen TV show, ending not only her career but a budding relationship with her sweet and handsome costar. She disappeared, leaving behind reports of addictive behavior and severe mental health disorders, speculation that she'd joined a cult in the California desert, an ashram in Tibet, that she was homeless on the streets of Toronto, that she was dead. There were threats of a lawsuit from the show's producers, endless speculative items on TMZ and in the tabloids, hundreds of unanswered texts from her manager and her agent and, of course, from the sweet, handsome costar. She never responded to any of it. Instead, she stayed disappeared until all the fuss faded and people stopped caring or even thinking about her, and she realized that it was even worse than being under the microscope, the feeling of being invisible. Only then did Lyla text the costar, whose name, of course, was Nolan Carnes.

I had a baby. It's yours.

Nolan begged her to come back. And when she did, with their baby, he proposed.

Lyla married Nolan in a private ceremony on the grounds of a French château owned by a music mogul, their six-month-old daughter, Fidelity, the only guest. They took a few photos, which they sold exclusively to *People* magazine for $1.2 million, donating it all to a charity for orphaned children.

Before the ceremony, after, and in all the years since, Nolan has never asked where Lyla went for that year or how she managed to stay hidden before and after she'd had the baby. She's given one short interview about it, to *People*, the same day as the wedding—and even that contained no specifics. *It was the year I found myself*, she told the reporter. *It was the year I became a mother.*

"Are you saying that running away from a good life is genetic, Nolan?"

"No, Ly." The reply is so quiet, she can barely hear it. "I'm just saying that it's possible."

Day Four

It's Nolan's idea to see the psychic, but Lyla is on board. Nolan is Southern California born and bred, the son of a holistic doctor and a yoga teacher, and so he's always been the woo-woo one in their relationship. But while Lyla has rolled her eyes more than once over her husband's regular visits to astrologers and crystal healers and Reiki masters, she's willing to try anything to find Fidelity. At this point, she believes in psychics more than in the growing team of state police detectives, feds, and hired private investigators who have now joined Shelby Martin and company in not finding their daughter.

Lyla wakes up from an Ambien-induced half sleep just before sunrise, her phone alarm chirping furiously in the midst of a wispy dream about a crystal ball floating in space.

Without speaking, barely making a sound, she and Nolan throw on their incognito clothes—baseball caps, sunglasses, dark, baggy sweats—and leave the house while their staff is still sleeping. They slip into their most nondescript SUV in the chill of early dawn and drive four and a half miles to the storefront in Woodstock where the psychic resides—a one-story cement eyesore that looks like someone plucked it out of some Florida strip mall and dropped it into arty, picturesque Woodstock, halfway up a forgotten side street, between a vacant lot and a cemetery.

"Nice." Lyla is standing outside the building, staring at the plastic bead curtains, the yellow letters on the faded purple sign:

PSYCHIC READINGS, TEA LEAVES,
PAST LIFE REGRESSION.

There's something off about the sign, something not entirely trustworthy, like a bottle of pills that's slightly past its expiration date. Just before they ring the bell, Lyla turns to Nolan.

"How did you hear about this psychic?"

"Aziz."

"Your bodyguard."

He nods.

"Since when did Aziz get into that stuff?"

"Keep an open mind, Lyla."

"I'm trying."

"Listen, I spoke to the psychic over the phone. Before I even said my name, he knew I was looking for my daughter."

"He?"

"Yeah?"

"I was picturing a woman. Aren't psychics usually women?"

"Only in movies, Lyla."

A man opens the door before anyone knocks, maybe as a display of his gift. He's short and frail, with stringy gray hair, a beak-like nose, and bashed-in-looking cheeks. "I'm Carl," he says.

Lyla frowns. *A psychic named Carl.*

Nolan says, "Thank you for meeting us. I know it's early—"

"It's never too early for the truth." Carl speaks in a cigarette rasp. If he dressed better, he could pass for an aging rock star. But in tattered drawstring pants, bare feet, and an inside-out T-shirt with a faded Nike logo, he looks more like an escaped patient of some sort—most likely mental, though he could have walked out of any hospital ward. "I dreamed of you last night." He says this to Lyla.

"You did?"

"You're in a lot of pain."

Lyla levels her eyes at him, thinking, *Of course I am. My kid is missing. Is this supposed to be impressive?*

He holds her gaze. His eyes are watery and bright and strangely riveting. The longer Lyla looks into them, the more uncomfortable she feels—as though he's trying to page through her brain. "Being Fidelity's mother," he says. "Protecting her. It's why you're alive."

Lyla swallows hard. She's had this exact thought more than once within the past four days, though she's never dared say it aloud. Before her lost year, Lyla used to believe she was born to be an actress, that it was the only truly good thing about her, her talent. But then Fidelity came into her life, and the veil lifted, and she could finally see what she was put on this earth to do.

All the acclaim she's gotten since then—the plum roles, the magazine covers, the Oscar, even . . . Without Fidelity, it's meaningless. Without Fidelity, she has no business being alive.

Carl says, "Why do you feel so guilty, Lyla?"

"Excuse me?"

He smiles, but it doesn't quite reach his eyes. "Don't mean to pry," he says. "Occupational hazard."

"I don't feel guilty."

"You don't?"

"No. Why would I?"

Carl shrugs. "Sometimes my senses fail me."

He turns and lets them inside, Lyla staring hard at his back. *Who are you?* She can feel Nolan watching her, but she pretends not to notice.

"Excuse the look of the place," Carl says. "I only returned to town a few days ago after being gone for more than a year. I haven't had the chance to clean. My clients don't even know I'm back . . . that is, if I still have any clients."

The psychic's work space is small and gloomy and smells of cigarettes and stale incense. It's mostly empty, save for a few folding chairs and a metal table that looks as though it were stolen from an interrogation room, a lineup of multicolored crystals at its center.

Lyla says, "Where does a psychic go for more than a year?"

"Here and there. I move a lot. Places don't matter to me."

"What does matter to you? Friends? Family?"

His gaze burns on Lyla's face. "I don't have friends or family," he says.

Carl takes one of the folding chairs, Nolan and Lyla two others. Lyla finds herself drawn to the dust motes floating on the light that oozes through the purple-and-gold beaded curtain. She feels as though she's in a movie, lit by a kind cinematographer. "So what brought you back to Woodstock?"

"Same thing that's brought me anywhere. I felt a call."

Sunlight strokes the side of Lyla's face, and she can almost hear the soundtrack swelling. She knows what Carl means. She's felt that call. It took her out of her life nine years ago, and then it brought her back. Maybe it really is genetic. Maybe Fidelity felt it, too, and that was why she left school, and all they need to bring her back is another call. The right call.

Carl says, "Did you bring something of hers?"

Nolan opens his messenger bag and pulls out one of Fidelity's T-shirts—pale pink, with a glittery Hello Kitty riding a bicycle on the front. Lyla bought it for her in Japan last year. It's one of Fidelity's favorites, and seeing it now, the shirt without Fidelity in it, takes Lyla out of the movie.

It's been four days. Four days without a ransom note or a reliable sighting or a single lead that's panned out. Four days without Fidelity. How many times has Lyla gone into her room, praying to find her there scribbling in her diary or playing games on her laptop? How many times has she stood in Fidelity's closet, inhaling the fading scent of her daughter's clothes and feeling only the lack of her, a black hole at the center of her chest, swallowing everything else?

Fidelity's pink laptop. Her fuzzy diary. The police have taken both of them, and Lyla may not ever get them back. Her daughter. Her only child . . . *Why do you feel so guilty, Lyla?*

She hears herself say, "Please let her be alive."

Carl clutches the shirt in his gnarled hands. His eyes are shut. He starts to hum softly, his head swaying back and forth. Lyla plucks a pink crystal from the table and cups it in her hands. It's very heavy, with sharp, dagger-like edges, and lovely to look at.

They're supposed to soothe fears, the pink ones. Rose quartz, she recalls Nolan saying, is a calming stone. She listens to Carl hum and cups the rose quartz, its surface grainy with dust.

Finally, Carl says, "She's alive."

Nolan puts a hand over Lyla's, and her breath catches, the tiniest spark of hope . . .

"Where is she?" Nolan says. "How can we find her?"

Carl opens his eyes. They make Lyla think of spotlights. "She's screaming," he says. "She's screaming for her mama."

Nolan says, "Is she in pain?"

"It's fuzzy," Carl says. "All I can hear are the screams. And I see something. A train."

"A train?"

"With eyes. A train with eyes."

Lyla's mouth goes dry.

"Does that mean anything to you?" Carl says. "A train with eyes?" He's staring straight at her.

She clutches the crystal. Its edges bite into her palms. "No," she says.

"Are you sure? It's getting clearer. A blue train. With—"

"I don't know what you're talking about."

"Who's Leslie?"

"What?"

"Leslie? No, wait. Lisa."

"I don't know."

"Lisa. Lisa. Leeeesaaa . . ." Carl's voice pitches up an octave. He sounds like a girl. "Leeeeeessaaaa . . ." A tear slips down his cheek.

Nolan grips Lyla's hand. She can't breathe.

"The blue train has big black eyes."

Lyla says, "I want to leave."

"She needs her mother. She's screaming for her."

"Stop!"

"She's so young. So small and helpless. She doesn't like being taken away from her mother."

"*Stop now!*"

Nolan says, "Are you all right, Lyla?"

Lyla tastes copper in her mouth, the warm, sick slickness of it. "I'm fine." She's bitten her lip so hard it's bleeding. She puts the crystal down, her palms scratched, bleeding too.

Carl opens his eyes.

Lyla feels her husband's hand on her shoulder.

"You're—"

"I'm fine, Nolan. We need to go now."

She wipes her palms on her sweats and stands up. Nolan says a few words to Carl. He replies. Lyla hears none of it. She makes a point of not listening to Carl. She'll never listen to him again.

Lisa, what are you doing?

Lyla heads for the door and waits there for Nolan, Carl's blue gaze burning through her back.

⚬────⚬

"I don't like him." Lyla says it to the windshield, the peachy-pink sunrise.

"I don't know. I thought he was . . . I don't know . . ."

"What, Nolan? You thought he was what?"

"Real."

"Well, he's not. He's a rip-off artist. A con man. I'll give him one thing, though. He's a terrific actor. That performance in there . . . That was, like . . . goals." She forces out a laugh. It sounds natural.

"You don't know anyone named Lisa? Maybe one of the other moms from the school. Or a nanny, or—"

"I don't know any Lisas."

Nolan lets out a long, wounded sigh. "I don't either," he says. "And a train with eyes. What the hell is that supposed to mean?"

Lyla stares out the window and shakes her head. Acting may not be her purpose in life, but it is a gift, she knows. For years, acting has provided her with a generous livelihood. But more important, it enables her to keep secrets. In her mind, the memory resurfaces. The train's round, staring eyes, the heat tearing through her . . . *Why, Lisa, why?* Her muscles tense with it. The heat. The rage. In her throat, behind her eyeballs, tears start to well. But thanks to her gift, Lyla's expression remains serene. What is acting, she wonders, other than lying? And what is lying other than a way to survive? "I have no idea what it means," she says.

⊶——⊷

Everyone's awake by the time Nolan and Lyla arrive home—the gardeners and the housekeepers and the security detail, the feds and state detectives, checking on nonexistent leads. Even in Fidelity's absence, the house feels noisy and alive—a contrast to the dead quiet of the psychic's lair.

Their personal chef, Sydney, is preparing breakfast smoothies in the kitchen, and Lyla chokes one down for the sole purpose of being able to stand upright. She's hardly eaten or slept since Fidelity disappeared. Courtney is sitting at the kitchen table, the same spot she was in four days ago, staring at her hands like a kid in detention. Lyla wants to ask her: *Why are you still here? In my kitchen, in my house, in my life?* Her gaze shoots from the spindly, dull-eyed girl to the rack over the stove. The heavy copper pots they'd imported from Germany. How easy it would be to grab the skillet by the handcrafted handle, to raise it high over Courtney's useless head and bring it down . . .

Lyla takes several calming breaths, the cuts on her palms stinging. She makes small talk with Sydney and waits for Nolan to finish his smoothie and head off for the home gym. And only then, once this feeling has subsided, her skin no longer prickling with it, is she able to look at Courtney again. "You're fired," she says. "Pack your things and get out."

Courtney says something, but Lyla doesn't care enough to listen. She leaves the kitchen and sets out from the house in search of Aziz.

She circles the house a few times before finally finding Aziz on the running track, completing what must have been the latest of many laps. Aziz is very disciplined. While other members of their bodyguard detail spend their breaks playing video games or in the home cinema watching movies, he's always lifting, running, cross-training. Building his strength. He's always seemed so practical minded to Lyla, which is why it strikes her as odd that he recommended a psychic to Nolan.

Lyla waves to Aziz as he crosses the finish line, and he slows his pace to a trot. Before heading over to her, he swipes a towel off the bench and mops his forehead, though once he's closer, she sees that he's barely broken a sweat. "Ma'am?"

"What can you tell me about Carl?"

He stares at her for several seconds. Then he says it again, in the same flat tone, like a rewound tape. "Ma'am?"

"The psychic? In Woodstock. Nolan said you recommended him, and I'm just wondering what you know about him."

For several seconds, Aziz says nothing. His expression doesn't change. The sun gleams off his bald head, and Lyla imagines wheels spinning beneath his skull. *Does not compute. Does not compute . . .* "Oh, wait," he says. "You mean Mr. Budowitz."

"I don't know his last name."

"He said he could help find Fidelity. He wanted to speak to Mr. Carnes, but I didn't recommend him."

"You didn't?"

"No, ma'am," he says. "I don't mean to offend, but I don't believe in psychics."

"Then why did Nolan say you told him about Mr. Budowitz?"

"All I did was relay a message," he says. "Mr. Budowitz approached me."

Lyla's eyes widen, but only for the tiniest instant.

"Did you go to see him?" Aziz asks. "Was he helpful?"

Lyla gives him a slight smile and shakes her head slowly. "You should trust in your belief system," she says. "He wasn't helpful at all."

***

Lisa. Lisa. Leeeesaaa . . .

Lyla grips the steering wheel, the psychic's voice looping through her mind, the shrill, familiar punch of it. She's alone in the parked SUV, staring at that cheap sign. She's told no one that she's left the house, so she needs to do this fast. In less than an hour, Nolan will be done with his workout, and she doesn't want him looking for her.

She opens the car door, then stands next to it, steadying herself. *Mr. Budowitz approached me.* That's what Aziz had told her. Carl Budowitz, itinerant psychic, had spotted a big, bald, terrifying-looking man standing in the checkout line at the health food store the previous afternoon and clocked him as *Lylan*'s bodyguard. He strode up to Aziz without hesitation or fear. *I know who you work for*, he had told him, pressing a purple business card into his hands. *I need to speak to them. I've been getting visions. They relate to their daughter.* "He walked as though he had purpose," Aziz had said to Lyla. It was why he hadn't figured him for just another crisis opportunist and told Nolan about him instead. It was that driven, determined step.

He was determined all right, Lyla had told him. *He was determined to rip us off.*

Good thing you saw through him, ma'am.

"Good thing." Lyla slams the door to the SUV and hurries across the empty street. By the time she gets to the door, it's open, Carl Budowitz standing in it, as though he's been expecting her. Apparently, he has no need for a doorbell.

She pushes him inside. Shuts the door behind her. She had planned on staying calm, as though she has nothing to hide, but she can no longer control herself. The gift has failed her. Lyla's fingers grasp Carl's thin T-shirt. She grabs him by the shoulder, her nails digging into his skin. "Where is Fidelity?"

Carl gapes at her, like someone watching a movie.

She shoves him to the ground. The fall is almost graceful. When he hits the cement floor, a grim smile plays at his lips.

"What do you want?" Lyla rasps. "Money? How much?"

"What?"

"You want a book deal? Your own TV series? I know people. I can make it happen."

"I don't want any of those things."

"Bullshit."

"Spirits speak to me. They tell me truths. I have to—"

"Where is Fidelity? Where are you keeping her?"

He says nothing.

"*Tell me!*" Lyla's throat is raw. Her muscles are clenched and coiled, her hands balled into fists. She closes her eyes and takes a long, shuddering breath. *Calm, calm, calm . . .* When she opens them, Carl hasn't moved.

"Look," she says. "I don't know who you are or what your deal is." She crouches on the floor. She speaks quietly. "The one thing I do know is that you're trying to scare me."

Lyla kneels next to Carl. Moves in close enough for him to feel her breath on his skin. Through the beaded curtain, the sunlight warms the back of her neck. She uses it to get into character. *I'm in control. I have the power.* She makes herself stare into those laser-blue eyes, and she gives him the look, the Lyla Look. "I don't scare, Carl."

He stares back at her. "I can't help the fact that I can see what you are."

"Where is she?"

"I told that bodyguard the truth. I had a vision."

"Where is Fidelity?"

"I keep having visions. They're getting clearer, every day. But they're not telling me where Fidelity is. They're telling me who she is. Who you are."

"Who the fuck are you? What do you want?"

"It's a gift I didn't ask for," he says. "You have to believe me. I don't want to know the truth. I never want to know the truth. But the truth finds me. And it won't leave me alone until I . . . reveal it."

Lyla lifts herself from the floor, her gaze darting around the dusty space. She sees a door in the back corner of the room and hurls herself at it, throwing it open. "Fidelity?" she shouts. "Are you in there?"

The room is small and dark. She finds a light switch and flicks it on, but all she sees are a few cardboard boxes, a sleeping bag on the floor next to a faded rug with a Mexican print, a paperback Carlos Castaneda book lying on top of it. The only other things in the room are the huge crystals, placed around the sleeping bag like sentries. The largest one is close to a foot tall, jagged as an iceberg, and pink. Rose quartz.

There's nothing in this room that would belong to Fidelity or to any little girl. She whirls around, looking for more doors, a staircase leading up or down. She throws herself against the walls, pressing against them, shouting Fidelity's name. But this isn't a movie, and she isn't a heroine. She presses her forehead against the wall, wanting to cry, to collapse. The words scrape at her throat. *"Where is my daughter?"*

She feels warmth at her back. Carl is standing now, and when he speaks, it is in a voice that's quiet and calm enough to be a guide for meditation. "She's not your daughter," he says. "You know that, Lisa."

He had to have been a con artist. A blackmailer. A bad guy with a plan. How else would he have known the name that Lyla had used during her lost year spent homeless on the streets of Toronto? How else would he have been able to imitate a voice she hasn't heard in nine years?

Lisa! Leeesaaaaa, what are you doing?

Carl sounded exactly like her, a girl whose name Lyla had once known. A girl with short, spiky hair and rough hands and a bad temper. A homeless, hysterical girl with a beautiful baby who was suffering because of her . . . *You seem stressed*, Lyla had said back then. *Please don't take it out on the baby. I can help you take care of her. Let's travel together.*

You look so familiar. Do I know you?

I have one of those faces. My name is Lisa.

"Were you there too, Carl? Did you follow the three of us? Were you hiding in the public bathroom? Has it taken you all these years to track me down?"

Lyla is in her car now. Speaking to no one. Asking questions no one can answer, not anymore. She's on her way home, but she's taking the long way, following the body of water that runs through these western Hudson Valley towns. The Esopus River the locals call it, though it's always struck Lyla as strange, calling it a river when it's so slim and weak in parts—a creek, really. Calling the Esopus a river is like calling Carl a psychic, or that girl a mother. They're frauds. All of them.

She never deserved that baby. What mother dresses a daughter like that? A T-shirt at least three sizes too big, Thomas the Tank Engine on the front. Everyone knows that Thomas the Tank Engine is for boys.

The blue train has big black eyes . . .

"You can't scare me anymore, Carl."

There is one section of the Esopus Lyla knows about. It's deep and heavily shaded, and Lyla often comes here to meditate when she's preparing for certain roles. It's on no one's private property, and there's a narrow road that leads down to it, presumably for swimmers, though the shade makes it an unpopular swimming hole, even in the peak of summer, far away as that feels.

Lyla heads down the narrow road in her SUV. The water glistens in the morning sunlight—yes, it's still morning. Seven forty-five, according to the clock on the dashboard. Lyla finds that hard to believe.

She parks the car and hauls the sleeping bag out of the trunk. When it falls to the ground, she rolls it until it reaches the water. It's slow work, not so much because of Carl's body as the heavy crystals she's used to weigh it down. But Lyla is smart and Pilates strong, and, as Carl might have said if he were still alive, she's been here before. She gives the bag a final push and watches it sink into the water.

Strange how the world works. How people and memories can disappear, only to resurface at the oddest moments. Lyla thinks of the crystal she'd zipped into the sleeping bag. The pink calming one she'd placed by Carl's head. Carl, who had no friends or family. *No one to miss him or mourn him or ask after him* . . . Hopefully that heavy crystal will bring him some peace. *Rose quartz*, she thinks. And then, *Rose*. That was her name. Rose. Fidelity's mother. Nine years, and she's just remembering that now.

It's eight thirty by the time Lyla pulls up her long driveway, a string of excuses running through her mind. *I went for a drive to clear my head / took a walk in the mountains / went looking for Fidelity / needed to be alone* . . . Any of these will work. Lyla has a gift, after all. And that gift makes people believe in her. Besides, there's no one in her life these days who questions her actions.

Leaving her car, Lyla is so deeply in character that she doesn't notice the extra police cars in her driveway, though when she opens the front door, she's aware of their voices. "She's here," one of the officers says. And before she can come up with a plan, or even open her mouth to speak, Nolan is rushing at her, tears on his face.

Lyla's stomach drops. He pulls her to him. She hears the crackle of police radios and feels his strong arms around her, squeezing her so tightly she can barely breathe.

"What ha—"

"They found her." Nolan says it again and again and again. "They found Fidelity." And then, finally, "She's alive."

DAY FIVE

"Are we going home now, Mommy?" Fidelity says. Her voice sounds like music, and her cheeks are pink again. She's no longer dehydrated, and she's already gained back a couple of pounds. Four days spent lost in the woods . . . Incredible how resilient children are.

"Yes, honey," Lyla says. She gently hugs Fidelity. She's followed by Nolan, the *People* magazine photographer capturing the moment, the nurses applauding.

"Fidelity," the *People* reporter says, "are you glad to see your mommy and daddy again?"

And Fidelity's face goes serious. "Yes," she says. "I'm sorry. I'm so, so sorry I made them worry."

It's the latest of many times Fidelity has apologized since they were first reunited, and it troubles Lyla a little bit. When you apologize that much, there's something you aren't saying.

Once the hospital staff have left and Nolan has gone to the waiting room for a follow-up interview with the reporters, Lyla brings it up with Fidelity as she helps her get dressed. "Honey," she says. "I just want to know. Why did you wander off in the first place?"

Fidelity looks at her with big, grave eyes. "You promise you won't get angry?"

"Promise."

She takes a breath, then speaks very quietly. "I went looking for the ghost."

Lyla stares at her.

"Bethany said there was a ghost in the woods. She said he was old and skinny with big blue eyes. I didn't believe her, but then I saw him. I mean . . . I think I saw him, but it could have just been in my head. I saw him standing in the woods, and I thought I heard him say something . . . something bad. Then he ran away, and I went after him, and . . . I guess I got lost."

"What did the ghost say?"

Fidelity closes her eyes. "He said you aren't my real mom."

I don't want to know the truth. I never want to know the truth. But the truth finds me. And it won't leave me alone . . .

"Is it true, Mommy?" She opens her eyes, and Lyla sees something in them. A spark of fear that brings back memories.

"Of course it isn't true," she says. "And you know what else? There's no mommy in the world who loves her daughter as much as I love you."

Fidelity throws her arms around Lyla's neck. Lyla holds the little girl close, remembering her fingers around Rose's neck, the rasp of her fading breath . . . and then Rose's neck becomes Carl's neck, his hands clawing at the air. *It's a dream*, she tells herself, getting into character. *It's only a dream.*

"I love you, Mommy," Fidelity says, and it *is* a dream. Just a bad dream, sunk deep in the darkest water, soon to be forgotten.

Hush, which includes "The Gift," was edited by the wonderful Jonathan Santlofer, who gave the authors involved one directive: all the stories should involve a lie or the act of lying. I thought it was a great assignment. In the fiction I like to write, lying is either a means of survival or the thing that does you in, but usually it's both. What fascinates me most are characters who lie to themselves and do it so effectively that the truth, when it reveals itself, is like a bomb going off, destroying the false world they've worked so hard to create. "The Gift" involves a Hollywood actress whose path intersects with that of a storefront psychic when her young daughter goes missing. But really, it's about lying. I hope you enjoy it.

Sue Grafton was the author of the famous "alphabet" series, beginning with "A" Is for Alibi in 1982 and ending with "Y" Is for Yesterday in 2017, when she died. Her introduction of her series private detective, Kinsey Millhone, was one of the most significant events in the history of American detective literature as it was instrumental in opening the door for women to write in the hard-boiled genre. A beloved author, both personally and for her books, she was a fixture on the New York Times Best Seller list for two decades, as well as one of the bestselling detective novelists internationally.

IF YOU WANT
SOMETHING
DONE RIGHT . . .

Sue Grafton

Lucy Burgess waited her turn at the Rite Aid pharmacy counter. The pollen count had soared and she'd gone to the drugstore to pick up Burt's allergy medication, his bronchodilator inhaler, and a new brand of antihistamine he'd seen on TV. What a baby. Apart from his being an alcoholic and chronically unfaithful, he was becoming tedious. He was constantly misplacing his personal belongings—cell phone, car keys, glasses, wallet—making it her responsibility to locate the lost items. Really, there was no excuse for his being so disorganized. He was a high-profile divorce attorney who battled for his clients as though his life depended on it. He said that in the fight-or-flight stakes, he was all fight, which was what made him such a dangerous opponent. He claimed his stress levels were what kept him on top of his game.

His high blood pressure did actually worry the doctors, and the asthma he'd suffered all his life was hard on him, but the rest of his ailments were ridiculous. Burt was highly suggestible, but she hadn't realized how paranoid he was until the trip to India came up. This would be their twenty-fifth wedding anniversary, and for years he'd promised her a trip to India. They'd reserved a large stateroom on an elegant cruise line that would take them from the Bay of Bengal around Cape Comorin to the Arabian Sea. Burt had set aside the time—two full weeks in August—which he hadn't done in years. She thought everything was fine, but then he'd started kicking up a fuss. First he worried about exposure to infectious diseases. Then he fretted about the filth, the vermin, tainted food, and the risk of contaminated water.

Then, just last week, he'd canceled his reservation altogether, leaving her to go by herself. What kind of anniversary celebration was that? Not that she cared. Why pay good money just to hear him complain? He was probably carving out time for his latest lady-love, but how could she call him on it when she had no concrete proof?

The most irksome consequence of his cancelation was that now, in addition to her preparations, she had to make sure he'd be comfortable on his own, which included two weeks' worth of meals, refills on all his medications, and a list of emergency numbers as long as her arm. Orderly as usual, she'd bought a slim pocket-size notebook in which she kept a running tally of all the errands she had to run. The notebook was perfect for slipping in and out of her handbag, allowing her to utilize time that would otherwise go to waste. Standing in line at the gourmet market, she worked on her to-do list, checking off the stops she'd already made.

Bank. Check.

Drugstore. Check.

The journal was divided into two sections. The first was devoted to things to be accomplished before she left town. In the second section, she kept a running list of ways to kill Burt. She'd come up with the idea as a form of idle amusement. Imagining his demise helped her tolerate his many loathsome qualities, among them his need to always be right and his tendency toward verbal abuse. He would never lay a hand on her, but he put her down every chance he got.

Under **Possibilities,** she'd written:

Gun? Where to acquire?

Poison? Possible, but how to administer?

Car wreck? Also possible, but difficult given ignorance of auto mechanics. Who to consult?

She didn't write down **garrote,** because she didn't have the strength.

She and Burt had no children. She was ten years younger than he. Early on he'd lobbied for a child, but thank God she'd had the sense to say no. Turned out Burt demanded her total focus. Moody, petulant, and self-centered, he was a man who'd do anything to maintain control. She suspected infidelity was his means of tranquilizing himself, because every time he launched a new affair, his temperament improved. Suddenly, he would become kinder and more attentive, much as he'd been in recent months.

The first indication of a new dalliance was his staying late at the office, where a series of soon-to-be-divorcées paraded past his desk. These women were vulnerable. He had the power to make or break them financially, which made them oh-so-eager to suck up, so to speak. His current extramarital fling had lasted longer than usual. Burt was easily bored, so most of the women he bedded disappeared within weeks, but this liaison had gone on for months. Lucy had begun scrutinizing his phone bills, looking for a pattern of frequently called numbers. She didn't want to learn the woman's identity, because she knew from experience that once a name and face were attached, the affront would be harder to ignore.

In the interest of keeping tabs on the situation, she searched his desk drawers at home. She checked his calendar for initials and cryptic references. She steamed open the bank statements, studied his expenditures, and then made copies of his canceled checks and all his credit card bills. She kept a record of the hotel rooms, the many expensive meals out, and the flowers he lavished on his paramour. If nothing else, he'd taught her the value of documenting items for later use as ammunition. The week before, she saw that he'd made a cash withdrawal of five thousand dollars, probably to buy jewelry, his modus operandi. Lucy was relieved. Usually, the jewelry came close to the end, like a form of severance pay.

She'd assumed she was home free until she ran into Laird Geiger, their estate attorney, as she emerged from the dry cleaners that day—yet another item she could check off her list.

He'd greeted her warmly and bussed her on the cheek. They chatted amiably and were on the verge of parting when Laird said, "Oh, I nearly forgot. I ran into Burt last week and he said he needed to come in for a chat. Have him give Rachel a call and we can set something up. I gather he wants to bring his will up-to-date. Is everything okay?"

"Oh, we're fine. You know him. We're leaving on a cruise, and he wants to make sure he has all his ducks in a row. I'll deliver the message. Better yet, I'll call Rachel myself and get it on the books."

"Do that," he'd said. "I'll be out of town this next week, but Rachel can slot you in as soon as I get back."

Before he was even out of sight, Lucy could feel the chill descend. They'd had no discussion at all about their wills. Clearly, Burt was up to no good. All she needed was for him to cut her out of his estate, removing her as his executor and prime beneficiary. For the first time, she understood he must be serious about the woman, whoever she was. If talk of divorce was not far away, he'd make sure she got creamed.

That night in bed, Burt watched *CSI* while rubbing salve on an imaginary rash. Smelling the ointment, she began to think in more concrete terms about killing him. She propped her journal against her knees, tapping her lip with her pen as she analyzed the choices.

Hit-and-run? Hard to pull off without witnesses.

Bludgeoning? Ugh. All that bone and splattered brains? No, thanks.

During a commercial, she caught Burt peering over at her. "You've had your nose stuck in that thing for weeks," he said. "What's so fascinating?"

She closed the journal, a finger on the page to save her place. "Just some ideas I had about the silent auction for the charity luncheon next year. I wasn't happy with the format."

"They suckered you into doing *that* again?"

"I insisted. Brenda was in charge this year and completely botched the event. She was all over the place, dropping the ball right and left. Pathetic. We could have made a lot more money if she'd done as I said."

He gave her the indulgent smile he used when he was systematically betraying her. "I have to hand it to you, kid. You may be a cold fish, but you're efficient as hell."

"Thank you, Burt. That means a lot to me."

Burt had the good grace to laugh while she went back to her list. **Stabbing** would be nice.

On Tuesday, she drove into Beverly Hills to Saks Fifth Avenue. At the makeup counter, she watched as a saleswoman named Marcy smoothed a drop of liquid foundation on the back of her hand. She and Marcy discussed the virtues of "Ivory Beige" versus "Medium Beige." Lucy made her selection and when she reached for her wallet, she realized her handbag was gone. For a moment, she stood perplexed. Had she set it down somewhere? Left it in the shoe department when she was buying her Ferragamos? Most certainly not. She remembered distinctly that she'd placed the bag on the glass counter near the perfume display. Someone had come along and lifted it. A wave of intense irritation swept over her as she thought how much work it would take to replace her driver's license and close all her credit card accounts. Fortunately, she'd put her car keys in her jacket pocket so at least she could get home.

Marcy called store security and in the confusion that followed, Marcy admitted with embarrassment that they'd had a rash of purse snatchers working in the store. Lucy scarcely listened because the contents of the journal had just popped into her head. She could feel dampness forming at the nape of her neck. How explicit were her notes? The only items she could remember with absolute clarity were her name, address, and phone number neatly printed on page one. Anyone finding it could read the lengthy scribbled debate about the virtues of **electrocution** versus **miter saws** and other woodworking tools. Dear god. Marcy was chattering away, apologizing for not warning her, but Lucy was intent on the possible ramifications of the theft.

The answer came soon enough. The next day, the phone rang and a man with problem adenoids introduced himself as Mr. Puckett. He told her he'd found her purse in some shrubs and he thought she might want it back. She assumed he'd swiped the bag himself, removed all the cash, and would be angling for a reward for returning the very bag he'd stolen. He didn't sound very bright, but neither did he sound sinister. She suggested they meet at the public library, where there was no danger of running into anyone in her social circle.

She waited in the reference department, as agreed. At the first sight of him, she nearly laughed aloud. He was such a bandy-legged little jockey, he should have been wearing silks. He couldn't have weighed more than 122 pounds. He was in his fifties, his sparse hair combed straight back, widow's peak kept in check by a malodorous gel. He seemed perfectly at ease as he passed the bag across the table. She murmured a word of thanks, wondering if a twenty-dollar bill would suffice, when he pulled the journal from his pocket. "The name's Puckett," he remarked.

"So you said on the phone," she replied with all the chill she could muster.

He smiled, leaning toward her. "Mrs. Burgess, I'd cut the atti-tude if I was you. What you got here ain't nice. Doubtless, you'll intuit the subject matter to which I refer." He opened the journal and read a few telling lines in a theatrical tone. Two patrons at nearby tables turned to stare.

"Please keep your voice down."

He dropped into a whisper. "Excuse me. I must've forgot myself in my haste to communicate."

She held out a hand. "I'll have that now."

"Not so fast. You got a real problem here, judging by what you've wrote."

She tried to stare him down. "There's a very simple explanation. I'm writing a play."

"You ain't writing a play."

"Well, I'm thinking about one."

"You're an amateur at this, right?"

"I don't know what you're referring to."

"You're gonna blow it *big*-time. Just my opinion as one who would know."

Voice low, she said, "Not to contradict you, Mr. Puckett, but I've done years of community service, and my planning skills are highly regarded. Once I've made up my mind to do something, I never fail."

"Mrs. B, it's dirty work whacking someone. Much trickier than puttin' on a charity lunch. Murder's a serious crime, in case you hadn't heard."

"You're a purse snatcher. You're a fine one to talk."

"Correction. You left said reticule on the counter at Saks. Thinking it was lost, I sought to return the alleged bag to its rightful owner. In casting about for some means of identifying same, I inadvertently disinterred some data that would suggest you're formulating a plan that might be expeditionary to your hubby's untimely end."

One of the two nearby library patrons gathered his belongings and moved to a table some distance away.

Lucy said, "You made copies, I'm sure."

"Strictly for my own protection. Any individual who'd ponder such acts might decide to eliminate a person like myself, who now has advanced and intimate knowledge of same. I hope you don't mind my asking, but what'd hubby do to generate such rage?"

"Why is that any of your business?"

"Because I'm in possession of certain tangible information that I'd be distressed to see fall into the wrong hands, namely his. Such an unfortunate turn of events might result in a failure to activate."

"I'm sure we can come to an understanding. I'm willing to pay you . . . within reason . . . if you'll return the journal and any copies you made."

"You misunderstand. My taking your money in return for this here would constitute the *corpus delicti* of the crime of blackmail. You're hoping for a corpus of another kind, or so I surmise."

"I wish you'd just say what you mean."

"I have a suggestion."

"I can hardly wait."

Her sarcasm seemed to go right over his head.

He said, "Keeping my remarks entirely famatory, every matrimonial association is defeasible, am I right? So why not take that route? I'm talking divorce here, in case you're not getting my drift."

"Thank you for the clarification. Divorce has a cost attached that I'd prefer not to pay. California is a community property state. Most of our assets are tied up in real estate. Burt's ruthless. If we divorce, I'll be crushed underfoot."

"So what I hear you saying is that you and him are engaged in a parcenary relationship of which you'd like to see his participation shifted to the terminus."

"Precisely. He's a drunk and he's had numerous affairs. He's also on the verge of changing his will. He had a chat with our estate attorney, who happened to mention it earlier this week. I pretended I knew what was going on, but that was the first I'd heard of it. If Burt cuts me out of his will . . ."

"Lady, I'm way ahead of you. You're hoping the turd will expire before such changes are made."

"Close enough."

"I think you might find me a valuable ancillary to your ruminations. Once we come to an agreement, you show me a picture of the man you want severated, and I'll handle it from there."

"Severated?"

"You know, like his head from his neck." He drew a line across his throat.

"Decapitated? That's vile. I couldn't live with myself."

"I don't mean to sound misapprobative, but you're favoring a claw hammer. I seen it on your list."

"It was the only thing I could think of at the time."

"If you wouldn't take unkindly to some direction, I have at my disposal a certain pharmaceutical substance which if mixed with a certain foodstuff or perhaps inculcated into a common household product changes from inert to extremely ert. It's like a certain particle of speech that in itself may not look like much, but in conjecture with its opposite can have a deleterious effect."

"Meaning what?"

"Ingest one iota and the recipient susperates his last. The only known unction is extreme."

"If he's stricken, why wouldn't he use his cell phone to dial 911?"

"Easy. Turn off the ringer and toss it in the trash. Next question."

"Will he suffer?"

"Not that much. On the other hand, you wouldn't want to be there. This form of expiration is often accompanied by encopresis."

"Enco . . ."

". . . presis. Victim shits himself."

"I see."

"A further advantage to this toxic substance? There's no known anecdote. And the best part is this—no one will ever know. It looks entirely natural, like a sudden heart attack or a massive stroke."

"You mentioned putting this substance in food. Won't he taste it?"

"Negatory, but if it worries you, I can add a dollop to one of his personal hygiene products, like maybe his shaving gel."

"Or maybe the container of wet wipes," she said, helpfully. "He's always swabbing down the counters because he's phobic about germs."

"Now you're thinking like a champ. So what do you say? Are we in this together or are we not?"

She considered his proposal, quickly assessing the pros and cons. As crude as he was, she could see the virtue of delegating this particular job. She was a capable woman, but she wasn't at all certain she'd be good at murder. She might get rattled and betray herself. On the other hand, if Puckett was experienced and had access to an undetectable poison, she could avoid doing anything distasteful.

Cautiously, she said, "The police are thorough. How can you be sure the poison will defy detection?"

"Because I've seen to such situations in the past. The forensic experts can expiscate all they like. They'll never cop to this."

"And you'd do this in exchange for what?"

"Why don't we say equipotent compensation."

"Which is how much?"

"Ordinarily, we're talking five grand . . . a bargain, even if I say so myself."

"I'm sure it is, but if my husband dies—"

"Correction. *When* hubby dies . . ."

"Suppose I come under suspicion? The police will examine my bank accounts. I can't afford to show a large cash withdrawal. How would I explain?"

A flash of annoyance crossed his face. "I'm not asking for dough. Did I say a word about that? Jesus, lady. That would be unpropitious, to say the least."

She put a finger to her lips, shushing him again.

He lowered his voice. "You're an educated woman, am I right?"

"I graduated from Smith. I assume you've heard of it."

"Of course. With a common name like that? So what it ain't Harvard? It's nothin' to be ashamed of. Now me, I'm a self-educated sort."

"I never would have guessed."

"It surprises a lot of people, but it's the truth. I've been studying you. Just while we been sitting here, I'm picking up clues. You may be hoity-toity, but you're not a bad egg. You got a good life that you're just trying to protect. If hubby don't treat you right, you gotta take the situation in hand. I got no quarrel with that."

"I appreciate your support."

"So I'm thinking there's more than one woman in your position. We could make a deal on the if-come. I do for you and in exchange, you give me a referral should another housewife of your acquaintance express an interest in the process of spousal peroration."

"Like a loss leader."

"Right. I'm out the bucks on this one, but the deal will be effective at bringing in the trade."

"How do I know I can trust you?"

"How do I know I can trust *you*? Truth is I do. You know what I sense about you? You're a nice lady. I mean, aside from your desire to take a lead pipe to hubby's skull, I'd say you're a peach."

She studied him briefly. "I leave on Tuesday for two weeks in India. Our anniversary trip. If you can take care of this while I'm away, I'll have the perfect alibi."

"Good move."

"So how do we proceed?"

"Simple. You have an alarm system at your place?"

"Yes, but we hardly ever use it."

"Fine. You give me a house key and the code. I already got the address off your driver's license, so I know where you live. I'll keep an eye on the place, and at some point when hubby's out, I'll let myself in and insinuate a generous serving of the you-know-what where it'll do the most good. And don't pin me down. The less you know the better. When the time comes, you want to be able to fake your genuine surprise."

"And my genuine horror and grief."

"That too."

"Perfect. I'll give the housekeeper the time off, as well, so you won't have to worry about her." She removed the house key from her key ring and dropped it in his palm. "One more thing. How will I know when the job is done?"

"Easy. I'll leave the key underneath the doormat in front. The key ain't there, you know the job ain't been done. It's there, then all your troubles evaporate."

<hr />

For Lucy Burgess, the cruise was magical. Knowing the pesky business with Burt was finally under control, she felt lighter and freer than she had in years. She slept late, alone in the luxury of her stateroom. She made friends, sunned herself, danced, played bridge, and sat in the bar drinking pricey champagne. On the various shore excursions, she scarcely noticed the loathsome lepers and crippled children begging her for coins. She was dreaming of what awaited her when she got home: the properties, the house. She could get a dog, now that she didn't have Burt's allergies to worry about.

She did entertain the faintest whisper of uneasiness where Puckett was concerned. There was no guarantee that he would do what he said. She believed in backup plans, keeping a little something in reserve. Delegating work was all well and good, but if the other person failed to perform, you had to be prepared to step in. She pondered this for days with no clear sense of how to protect herself. Then in Goa, on the final day ashore—her silver anniversary of marriage to Burt, by happy coincidence—she went on the tour of a local factory, and the answer presented itself.

On her return that Saturday, when Burt wasn't at the airport to meet her plane, she was thrilled. Wonderful! Divine! He was doubtless *d-e-a-d*. Giddy, she took a taxi to the house. Once her luggage was on the porch and the driver had pulled away, she lifted one corner of the mat. There lay her house key, glinting in the sun. *Hallelujah*, she thought. *It's over.* The deed was done.

She unlocked the door, breathing in the familiar scent of the rooms. The house felt gloriously empty. Colors seemed brighter and every surface shone. The very air seemed sweet. She made a cautious circuit, knowing the body was somewhere on the premises. She hoped he wasn't sprawled on the bedroom floor, where she'd have to work around him when she unpacked her bags. She was also hoping he hadn't been dead so long that putrefaction had set in, though they probably had cleaning services to eradicate the ooze. She found herself tiptoeing, as though playing a game of hide-and-seek, peeking around corners to make sure the coast was clear. Guest room, hall, foyer bathroom. Really, how aggravating. She was running out of rooms.

"Hey, babe. Why didn't you tell me you were getting home today?"

She whirled, shrieking.

There stood Burt, alive and well, and apparently in perfect health. In addition to looking fit, he seemed rested, probably from screwing his brains out the whole time she was gone. Her heart was pounding and she thought she'd weep from disappointment, but she had to carry on as though everything were fine.

She recovered sufficiently to fake her way through the rest of the day. Sunday came and went. She waited, but there was no sign whatever that Burt was on the brink of death. He must have spent every minute at his girlfriend's place. Clearly, he hadn't ingested or applied poison of any kind. She wondered where it was. Puckett had mentioned food, personal hygiene items, and common house-hold products, but he hadn't said which. How could she avoid poisoning herself by mistake? He could have put the fatal dose in anything. She realized with dismay she had no way of reaching him. Originally, he'd called her—and had neglected to give her a contact number in return. Whatever he'd done, wherever he'd put the poison, she was now as vulnerable as Burt.

When two more days passed and they continued to coexist, her anxiety began to mount. Burt showered and shaved, slapped cologne on his face, and went merrily off to work. When he came home, he'd fix himself a drink while she prepared dinner as she usually did. While his appetite was hearty, she couldn't eat a thing. The only products she used were those she removed from her own suitcases, sitting in the bedroom still packed and kept under lock and key. She bathed with newly opened bars of soap and ate all her breakfasts and lunches out. She avoided room fresheners, laundry soap, and scouring cleanser, even though the sinks were turning gray. No shampoo, conditioner, or styling spray for her. She made certain no toothpaste, dental floss, or mouthwash crossed her lips.

Meanwhile, Burt was in the best of spirits. Lucy was mystified. What if he'd already been exposed to the poison and somehow managed to avoid harm? Maybe he was naturally immune to whatever it was. Occasionally, she thought he might be toying with her. He'd start to eat a handful of nuts, and then change his mind. Or he'd fix himself a sandwich and end up throwing it in the trash. The suspense was getting on her nerves.

By the weekend she decided it was time to move on to Plan B.

Saturday night, the two retired early. Lucy read the paper, catching up on the news while Burt lay beside her, watching one of his boring TV shows. She noticed him wincing as he cleared his throat. "Scratchy. I think I'm coming down with a cold."

"Poor you," she said.

"Yeah, poor me. There's all kinds of shit going around these days. Client came in yesterday and coughed all over me. Office was a cesspool of germs. I sprayed everything as soon as she left."

Lucy snapped the paper, folding it back so she could check the weather page. "Highs in the nineties tomorrow. How unpleasant is that?"

"What's the pollen count?"

"Way up," she said.

He looked over at her. "They're talking weeds?"

"Weeds and grass. Molds are moderate, but trees are off the charts."

"Shit." He got out of bed and padded barefoot into the bathroom where she heard him opening the medicine cabinet. Lucy rolled her eyes.

Sunday morning, Lucy went into the big walk-in closet and got out her walking shoes. She couldn't bear it. She had to leave the house or she'd go stark raving mad. She was beginning to regret the agreement she'd made with Puckett, which was harebrained at best. The man was a moron. She took off her robe and was pulling on her sweats when Burt stuck his head in. "So, how about Sunday brunch? I thought you could rustle up some bacon, eggs, and toast."

"I was just going for a walk."

"Come on. Indulge me. It'll be just like the old days. I'll walk with you afterward. How's that for a deal?"

She shoved her feet down into her running shoes and laced them, then followed him down the stairs. His proposal was the first nice thing he'd come up with in recent memory. Eggs must be safe. Surely, Puckett hadn't used osmosis to get poison through the shells. She didn't give him credit for the imagination it would take to inject a dose into the hermetically sealed package of bacon they'd had for a month. She made a pot of coffee. She poured Burt a glass of orange juice while he sanitized his hands and downed his echinacea. For once, his fussiness seemed more eccentric than annoying. She had quirks that probably annoyed him no end. She cooked his bacon, eggs, and toast. She opened a jar of his favorite strawberry jam and spooned it into a dish.

She put his plate in front of him, and then sat across the table watching as he read the Sunday paper and wolfed down his meal without saying a word. He was still in his robe and pajamas. He didn't shave on Sundays so he was disheveled—unusual for him.

He looked up, noticing for the first time she wasn't joining him. "You're not having anything?"

"I'm not hungry."

"Something wrong with you? You've hardly touched a bite since you've been home."

"I haven't been feeling well. My digestion's off. I'll fix something for myself later on."

He wiped his mouth and crumpled the paper napkin as he pushed his plate aside. "You picked up a bug. I hear some parasites can live in your guts for life. I warned you about that. You better have the doc run some tests."

Lucy took his dirty dishes and put them in the sink. She ran water, but she couldn't bring herself to add detergent, which might be the agent Puckett had selected to deliver the you-know-what. On second thought, she added detergent. No danger there. Puckett must have known Burt had never washed a dish in his life. Behind her, she heard him snicker. She assumed he was reading the funnies, but when she turned she saw him looking at her with barely suppressed mirth. She turned off the water. "What's so funny?"

"Nothing," he said solemnly, and then cracked up again. "No, wait. This is rich. This is killing me. Maybe it's time to end your misery."

"Misery?"

It took him a minute to compose himself. Finally, he took out a handkerchief and mopped his eyes. "Whew. I didn't mean to lose it there. I just couldn't help myself. This past Friday, I ran into a pal of yours, who said to tell you hello."

"Oh? And who was that?"

"A fellow named Puckett. He says the two of you had a meeting before you left town." Burt was making an effort to keep a straight face.

Lucy frowned. "The name doesn't ring a bell." She leaned her backside against the counter and crossed her arms, keeping her distance from him. "How do you know him?"

"He was referred by one of the other attorneys in the firm. I said I needed a little job done and his name came up."

"What sort of job?"

Burt left her hanging for a moment while a smile played across his lips. "Let's put our cards on the table for a change, okay? Just this once."

"Fine. Go ahead. I'm fascinated." In truth, she felt a touch of uneasiness settle in her gut.

"I knew you were up to something so I paid this guy Puckett five thousand bucks to steal your purse and hand it over to me. You might have noticed the cash withdrawal when you were snooping in my desk."

"I don't know what you're talking about."

"I was curious why you were so engrossed in that journal of yours. Every time I turned around, you were scribbling away."

"That's how I'm able to stay organized. You know how I am."

"Come on, Luce. I read it from beginning to end. You were planning to have me iced. Puckett spilled the beans about the deal you made."

"Burt, I'd never heard of this Puckett fellow until you mentioned him just now."

"Get off it. The cat is officially out of the bag. He left the key under the doormat like he said he would. When you got home from the cruise, you thought I was dead. I watched you creep around the house with me ten steps behind. You should have seen the look on your face when you turned around and spotted me. You screamed like you'd seen a ghost."

Lucy smiled politely. The joke was always on her. She wanted to protest, but she couldn't see the point.

"You want to know how I survived?" He began to laugh again, so tickled with himself he started to snort. "The guy's an actor. He does improv. There isn't any poison. That was all bullshit." On he went, chortling to himself while she stared, her smile fading. "Sorry, but I got such a kick out of watching you this past week. You were so worried about poison you wouldn't sit down on the toilet seat. You had to squat to pee."

Lucy faltered. "An actor?"

"Get a clue. With all that phony lingo, you didn't pick up on it? Nobody talks that way. I told him to play it straight, but he insisted. Guess he fooled you anyway, huh."

"Oh, Burt. It's not funny."

"You know what your problem is? You have no sense of humor. God, you're gullible. It really cracks me up. Hook, line, and sinker, you swallowed every bit of it."

She turned back to the sink and washed his plate. Her hands shook badly and as she moved the plate to the draining rack, it slipped out of her hand and shattered on the floor.

"Goddamn it!" She leaned her hands on the counter. "Jesus, Burt. You should have told me before."

"Well, you don't have to get *mad*. It was a prank, okay?"

She returned to the breakfast table and sat down. "There's something I have to confess."

"Great. I'm all ears."

Lucy put a trembling hand against her lips, then placed it palm down on the table. "You know how particular I am, how I hate to delegate . . ."

"Jesus, you're telling me? You're a pain in the ass."

"I wasn't sure I could trust Puckett so I came up with a backup plan . . ."

"What's wrong with electrocution? Drop a radio in the bathtub. I liked that."

She leaned forward, clasping his hands in hers. "Don't make jokes. We're in serious trouble here. I thought you were having an affair."

"Nah. The bimbo? I dropped her."

Lucy studied his face with a worried gaze. "But you told Laird you wanted to rewrite your will."

"Yours, too. It's been ten years since we signed those things. You think our financial situation hasn't changed?"

"Why didn't you tell me? You should have said something at the time."

"Gee, sorry. I didn't realize it was such a big deal."

Lucy sank to her knees beside him. "Listen. You have to trust me. We need to get you to a hospital . . ."

"What for?"

"You need medical attention."

"No, I don't. Are you kidding?"

She shook her head, her voice barely audible. "When I was in Goa the last day on shore, we took a tour of a castor bean processing plant. There's a poison called ricin that's made from the leftover waste. I bought some on the street."

"Ricin? Perfect. I never heard of it."

"I'd never heard of it either so I did a bit of research as soon as I got home. Do you remember that Bulgarian journalist who died in London after he was jabbed in the leg by an umbrella tip?"

"Sure. He turned out to be a spy, offed by the other side."

"Ricin was what killed him. A puncture wound is just one way of delivering a fatal dose. You can also dissolve it in liquid or add it to food. If the ricin's inhaled, it takes longer, maybe twelve hours or so before the symptoms appear. After that, it's quick."

He rolled his hand to hurry her along, as though she were telling a joke and he was impatient for the punch line.

"I'm sorry. Honestly. I planned on leaving the house early, but then you insisted on breakfast and I realized I'd made a mistake. If we can get to the ER, you still have a chance."

He reared back in disbelief. "I can't go anywhere. I'm in my robe."

"You're not hearing me. I'm trying to help you."

Burt studied her, picking up the word she'd used a couple of sentences before. "What do you mean, if it's inhaled? What's that got to do with it?"

"Don't you remember? Last night you asked if the pollen count was high. I said yes and you went straight to the medicine cabinet and took your inhaler out. You sniffed five or six times. I could hear you from the bedroom, even with the TV on."

He tried to laugh, and then stopped. "Seriously. You put poison in my inhaler?"

Lucy wouldn't meet his gaze. "How was I supposed to know you and Puckett were in cahoots? He said he'd take care of it. I was only being thorough in case he didn't follow through."

"I don't believe you."

"Shit. You're an idiot. I knew you wouldn't take my word for it so I got on the Internet and printed out the information from the CDC." She got up and crossed to the planning center, where she took a folded paper from her Day-Timer. She flattened it on the table and pushed it over to him.

"You're lying. I feel fine. There's nothing wrong with me."

"Let's hope. This doesn't really specify how much poison you have to use so maybe you're okay."

Burt's face began to flush as his eyes traced the lines of print. It was clear her message had sunk home as he was now short of breath. "For god's sake, quit yammering and dial 911."

"I can get you to the ER quicker if we take my car. You can read that on the way."

She went to the hall closet and pulled out a coat that she handed him as she passed him. She grabbed her handbag and her car keys and opened the door to the garage.

"I hope you know what you're talking about. I go traipsing in there when nothing's wrong, I'll look like an idiot."

"Oh, believe me. There's something wrong with you."

She activated the garage door and slipped into her Mercedes on the driver's side. Burt paused to close the kitchen door behind him. He'd pulled the coat on over his pajamas and he was buttoning it in haste. She started the car, revving the engine in frustration. "Jesus, would you get in!"

He let himself into the car on the passenger side, the information from the CDC in hand. Perspiration had appeared on his face like a fine mist. He lifted one shoulder, using his coat sleeve to dab at the sheen. His fingers made damp spots on the paper. He glanced down at it. "Symptom number two—excessive sweating." His look full of pleading. "But why would you do this to me?"

Lucy eased through the traffic light at the intersection, and then hit the freeway on-ramp and floored it. "You set this in motion. It wasn't me. Laird told me you were going to change your will. This was all I could think to do. It's only two more exits."

"What if I don't make it? You'll end up in jail. They'll run a toxicology report. Don't you know they test for shit like this?"

Lucy changed lanes abruptly, causing Burt to brace himself against the dashboard. He yelped as the vehicle next to them swerved just in time. "Christ! Slow down. You're going to kill us. Not that you'd care."

"Would you stop blaming me? I told you I didn't meant to do it."

"Suppose you never told me. Suppose I just died. How'd you expect to get away with it?"

Lucy's tone was reluctant. "Ricin's unusual. I knew it wouldn't show up on a routine screening panel. Anyway, why would it even occur to them? With your history of hypertension, I figured it would look like a heart attack."

"Jesus, Luce. What else do I have to look forward to?" His gaze dropped back to the page. "After the heavy sweating and the respiratory distress, the victim develops a blue cast to the skin." He tilted the rearview mirror so he could see himself. "I'm not blue. Do I look blue to you?"

She glanced at him quickly. "Not that much, really. You're not in pain?"

"No."

"Good. That's a good sign. I think we're okay. When we get there, I'll tell them . . . well, I don't know what I'll tell them, but I'll make sure you get the antidote."

"What a pal." He placed a hand against his shoulder and massaged his arm. His breathing was heavy and had a raspy sound. "I don't know how to say this but something's going on. Feels like I got an elephant sitting on my chest."

"Burt, I'm so sorry. I know it was horrible, but you really gave me no choice." She looked at him. Sweat trickled down his face, soaking his shirt collar. Two wide half-moons of dampness had appeared underneath his arms.

He began to pat his pockets. "Where's my cell phone? I'll call and tell 'em that we're on our way."

"Your cell phone? Puckett said I should put it on vibrate and throw it in the trash."

He was gasping. He swallowed hard, his gaze turning inward as he struggled with the urge to heave. He used his handkerchief to mop his face. He leaned heavily against the car door, his breathing labored. "Pull over here, I'm going to be sick."

"Hang on. Just hang on. We're almost there."

"Open the window . . ."

She fumbled for the window control on her side and lowered the window, as grateful as he was for the chilly stream of fresh air.

"Luce . . ." He held out his left hand.

She reached across the front seat, grabbed his hand, and then quickly released it. "You're all clammy," she said with distaste. Burt was fading before her very eyes.

By the time she pulled into the receiving area at the ER, he was breathing his last. She parked under the ER overhang, prepared, in a moment, to honk her horn, summoning help.

Burt was slumped against the car door. Lucy watched the light drain out of his face.

"Burt?"

Burt was beyond hearing. He gasped once in agony, and then ceased to breathe.

She glanced up as the doors swung open, and a doctor and two orderlies emerged at a dead run. She leaned closer. "Hey, Burt? Talk about gullible—try *this* on for size. You can't buy ricin in Goa or anywhere else. You did it to yourself, you freakin' hypochondriac."

By the time the orderlies snatched open the car door, she was sobbing inconsolably.

When the Mystery Writers of America wanted to celebrate its 75th anniversary with a commemorative anthology, Deadly Anniversaries, *editors Marcia Muller and Bill Pronzini were able to unearth an unexpected treasure, a previously unpublished story by Sue Grafton. Why it was never published before remains a mystery that would need Kinsey Millhone herself to solve.*

Paul Kemprecos says he owes his writing career to pirate Samuel Bellamy, whose treasure ship Whydah broke apart off a storm-beaten Cape Cod shore in 1717. Paul was writing newspaper articles about attempts to salvage the wreck and thought at first that the story might make a good nonfiction book. Instead, he used the shipwreck saga as the inspiration for a novel entitled Cool Blue Tomb. Drawing on his experience as the son of immigrants, Paul created a philosophical fisherman, diver, and part-time private detective named Aristotle "Soc" Socarides. The Private Eye Writers of America chose the book for a Shamus award. Paul wrote five more Socarides books before being asked by Grandmaster of Adventure Clive Cussler to collaborate on the new NUMA Files series. He coauthored eight bestselling novels, and then wrote two adventure books on his own. The Minoan Cipher was nominated for a Thriller award by the International Thriller Writers. After a fifteen-year hiatus, he revived the Socarides series with the release of Grey Lady, a novel of madness and murder on the island of Nantucket, and Shark Bait, nominated for a Shamus award by the PWA. His first stand-alone novel, a mystery-thriller that pairs famed artist Edward Hopper with a festering World War II secret, will be released in 2021 by Suspense Publishing. He and his wife Christi live on Cape Cod.

THE SIXTH DECOY

Paul Kemprecos

Elmer Crowell had a sharp eye and a sharper blade. He could take a block of wood and cut away everything that didn't look like a bird, creating a masterpiece that looked as if it could quack, waddle, or take flight. Some people say he was the best bird carver in the world.

Ol' Elmer was an authentic American genius, no doubt about it. He was also a humble man from what I've heard. He would have dropped his whittling knife if someone told him the carvings he turned out in his ramshackle shed would bring millions of dollars at auction. And his gentle soul would have been burdened if he knew the desire to possess the things of beauty that sprang from his mind and his hands could lead to bloodshed.

Crowell had been dead more than a half century before the golden, late fall day when I crossed paths with his ghost.

I had spent the morning scrubbing down the deck and cleaning out the galley of my charter fishing boat *Thalassa*. The rods and reels were stowed in the back of my pickup truck. I'd scheduled a forklift to raise the boat out of the water and lower it onto a wooden cradle to be tucked under a plastic blanket for a long winter's nap.

The fishing season had been as good as it gets. Nantucket Sound teemed with schools of hungry striped bass, and every one of them had a death wish. The skies were sunny, the seas gentle, and the tips generous.

Hooking fish wasn't something I thought I'd be doing for a living, but as the ancient poet Homer once said, our destiny lies on the knees of the gods.

The Immortal in charge of my fate must have had restless leg syndrome, because I fell off his knee, cutting short my college education in philosophy for a lesson in life, and death, paid for by the US Government in Vietnam.

After mustering out of the Marines, I became a cop and worked my way up to detective in the Boston Police Department. I was engaged to be married to a beautiful and intelligent woman whose only blemish was her judgment in men.

I might have weathered a corruption scandal at the BPD if I kept true to the code of silence, but I lost my will when my fiancée died in a car accident.

After the funeral I got in my car and headed south from Boston with a bottle of vodka, driving until the road ended at a deserted Cape Cod beach. After a few slugs from the bottle, I fell asleep in the lee of a dune. I woke up to the cries of hovering gulls and the rustle of breaking waves. I staggered off the beach and was sobering up in a coffee shop when I met an old fisherman named Sam. He was looking for a crewman. I said I might be interested in the job.

Either Sam had been desperate, or he'd seen the desperation in my face, because he simply nodded and said, "Finestkind, Cap."

Fishing was tough, but cheaper than stretching out on a head-shrinker's couch. More effective too. Rolling out of bed at three in the morning to catch the tide, commuting twenty miles into the Atlantic Ocean, and working a twelve-hour day forces your mind to ignore the little demons of regret tap-dancing in a corner of your brain.

The wind, and sun reflecting off the glassy sea, had burned most of the sadness from my face and darkened my skin, hiding the lines of bitterness lurking at the corners of my mouth, even though they were still there. Sam accused me of going native when I went for the pirate look, with a gold earring, and a droopy mustache that decorated my upper lip.

More often than not my mouth was set in a grin as Sam gossiped about townspeople, fish, and the cooking prowess of his wife Mildred. When Sam retired I took over his boat, but couldn't cut it on my own. I cleaned up my act, mostly, and bought a charter fishing boat with a loan from my family.

Every day was an adventure. I had to make sure my clients didn't fall overboard or hook themselves instead of a fish—a state of alertness that had called for a higher degree of sobriety than I was used to. I'd been busy from sunup to sundown, subsisting on Mountain Dew and peanut butter and jelly sandwiches.

In the off-season I'll earn a few bucks with an occasional commercial diving job. There's not much demand to go underwater during the winter. I've held on to the private detective license I got after leaving the Boston PD, but there's even less call for a PI.

With my boat coming out of the water, and no jobs in the works, money would soon be tight. I set a course across the marina parking lot for a waterfront bistro named Trader Ed's. I was thinking that a frosty beer might help me come up with an idea how to keep the boat loan payments to my family flowing during the lean months. I was about halfway to my barstool when a silver Mercedes convertible pulled up beside me and braked to a stop. A woman wearing a dark gray pinstripe suit got out from behind the steering wheel.

"Excuse me," she said. "I'm looking for a boat captain named Aristotle Socarides. The harbor master pointed you out."

"That's me," I said. "How can I help you?"

"I'd like to retain your services."

"Sorry," I said, shaking my head. "I'm done fishing for the year. My boat will be out of the water in the next day or so."

"That's not a problem." She removed her sunglasses to reveal coral-colored eyes under arching brows. "My name is Bridget Callahan. I'm an attorney. I know that you're a retired police officer and that in addition to running a charter boat, you sometimes take on cases as a private detective."

"Word gets around."

"Thanks to modern communications technology."

She held up a cell phone. On the small screen was the face I see in the mirror during the morning shave. The earring and mustache of my pirate days were gone. I was now a serious businessman. The photo of me at the wheel of the *Thalassa* was from the business section of the *Cape Cod Times*. The headline was: "Former Cop, Charter Captain Moonlights as Private Eye."

"I mentioned the private eye thing to the reporter as an aside," I said. "I don't have a lot of clients."

"All the better. You'll have time to take a case for a client of mine."

"Depends, Ms. Callahan. I don't do divorce investigations. They're too dangerous."

"Nothing like that. My client would like to recover some valuable property."

She tucked the phone in her pocketbook and handed me a business card. The words embossed on the card in gold told me that Bridget Callahan was a partner in a Boston law firm that had more ethnic names than the United Nations.

"Big legal powerhouse, as I recall," I said. "Making partner couldn't have been easy."

"It wasn't. It took talent, hard work, and a willingness to deal with difficult clients."

"Congratulations. Does this case involve one of those difficult clients?"

She nodded.

"Why come to me? My last big case had to do with oyster poachers. Your firm must have staff investigators."

"We do. One of them gave us your name. He said you'd be perfect for this job. That you take unusual cases."

She mentioned a retired detective I knew from the BPD.

"He's a good cop," I said. "What makes this so unusual he can't handle it?"

"The client is a bit eccentric."

"In what way?"

"He's a collector," she said, as if that explained everything.

"Does this eccentric collector have a name?"

"His name is Merriwhether Ruskin the Third. He wants to meet you."

"Send him over. I'll be here for at least another hour."

She brushed a curl of silver and auburn hair back from her face as she collected her thoughts. "Mr. Ruskin doesn't get out much. He has, um, peculiar health issues. It's hard to describe. He'd like to talk to you in person."

I glanced up at the clear blue autumn sky. The raw north winds and slag gray clouds of winter seemed far away, but it would be spring before I earned another paycheck. Meanwhile, the boat loan statements would arrive with the regularity of waves breaking on the shore. A job for a rich client would get me through a few months, maybe longer.

Trader Ed's would have to wait. "I'm ready when you are," I said.

"Wonderful," she said. "Let's go for a ride."

<hr />

Bridget's client lived twenty minutes from the marina on the shores of Nantucket Sound, in a gated community of sprawling silver-shingled houses hidden behind tall hedges that protected their owners' privacy as effectively as castle ramparts. The only things missing were moats and drawbridges. A long gravel driveway led to a two-story mansion surrounded by manicured lawns of impossible green. A white-trimmed porch bordered with hydrangeas ran along the full length of the house.

On the drive over, Bridget talked about growing up in the gritty working-class enclave of South Boston, making her

Harvard law degree even more impressive. I talked about my roots in the former factory city of Lowell and my stint in the Marines. We were chatting like old friends by the time we got to the house. She snapped the switch into business mode as soon as she parked behind a black Cadillac sedan in the circular driveway.

"This is it," she said.

This was a mega mansion that looked to be at least ten thousand square feet in size. I had to crane my neck to take in the whole length of the front porch and the three-story height.

"Nice little shack. What does Mr. Ruskin do to pay the lighting and heating bills in this place?"

"He doesn't have to do anything. He comes from an old New England family that made its fortune years ago in labor procurement, energy, and pharmaceuticals."

Bridget answered the question with a straight face, but the airy lilt in her voice sent me a different message. "I get it. The skeletons in the closet of many a respectable Yankee family. Slavery, whale butchery, and the opium trade, in other words."

"Yes. In other words. Mr. Ruskin currently dabbles in nation-building."

I had to think about that. "Gun running?"

"Guns, missiles, and bombs. And people to use them." She cocked her head. "I think I like you, Mr. Socarides."

"Soc. My friends call me Soc."

"Very well, Soc. I answer to Bridge. Shall we?"

The slightly stooped man who answered the front doorbell looked like the greeter in a funeral parlor. Gray hair, grayer face, and matching four-button suit, all the color of fog. Speaking softly in an undertaker's voice, he said, "Follow me to the visitation room."

He led the way down a long hallway, opened a door, and ushered us into a rectangular space around twenty feet square. Three walls were plain. The fourth was covered by a hanging tapestry that showed a medieval hunting scene of sharp-toothed dogs taking down a unicorn. The fact that the victim was an animal that never existed did little to ease its pain at being ripped apart.

The gray man pressed a wall button. The tapestry slid silently aside to reveal a glass window. He pointed to a leather sofa facing the window, then left us alone.

The lights on the other side of the window went on seconds after we had taken our seats. We were looking into a big room. Directly in front of us was a metal and plastic desk and chair.

The room was a zoo of the dead. Animal heads of every kind festooned the walls. Their eyes were glassy and their expressions far from happy. Antelope, mountain goats, bear, some big cats.

Bridget was silent.

"You've seen this before?" I said.

"Yes," she said. "I think it's kind of creepy."

"Ever wondered what hunters do with the rest of the animal?"

"That's even creepier."

"What is this place?" I asked.

Before she could answer, a door swung open between a pair of tusked boar heads at the far end of the room. A ghostlike apparition entered the room, made its way in our direction, and stopped next to the desk. It wore a hooded white suit, like the kind worn to protect against hazardous materials. A white gauze mask covered the lower part of the face. The feet were encased in fabric pull-ons.

"You're right; Ruskin is eccentric," I murmured.

"That's not him," Bridget said. "That's his valet." She put her finger to her lips, then glanced at a red plastic globe on the wall above the window. "That's a camera and a microphone that is very, very sensitive."

The door opened again. Another man entered, leisurely walked the length of the room, and stood next to the figure in white.

"Ruskin?" I whispered.

Bridget nodded.

I'd pictured Ruskin as a raw-boned flinty-eyed Yankee with a mouth full of horse teeth, mop of unruly hair, and a profile that looked as if it had been carved from a granite quarry. Bad call. Ruskin was as bald as a bullet, had a neck that belonged on a cartoon bully, and looked as if he chewed steroids as candy. He was wearing a snug T-shirt and shorts that showed off a buff physique. His hands looked as if they could hurt someone.

He said, "Thank you for coming, Mr. Socarides. Please pardon the unusual meeting arrangements. This is a protected environment. I suffer from a number of acute allergies, all potentially life-threatening. It's a rare, progressive affliction particular to the Ruskin family. This gentleman is an employee of mine. The suit he has on is to protect me from outside allergens that would cause a severe reaction."

Despite his mauler looks, Ruskin spoke with a cultured accent that carried echoes of an English boarding school.

"No different than talking over the phone," I said, although it was a lot different. "Ms. Callahan said you need a private detective to recover some valuable property."

"Correct. Tell me, are you familiar with the work of Elmer Crowell?"

"The bird-carver?"

"That's right, although he was much more than that. Anthony Elmer Crowell is considered the Father of American Bird Carving. He was the master of a unique form of American art who has been called the Cezanne of waterfowl carvers. Another question. Have you heard of Viktor Orloff?"

I would have to have been stuck in a cave not to know about Orloff. His face had been in all the papers and on TV. "Sure. Orloff was the financial guy who conned his clients out of millions of dollars. Were you one of them?"

Ruskin's lips twitched in an almost-smile.

"I knew better than to invest money with that slimy old grifter. We had a business arrangement. He had agreed to sell me a preening merganser."

"Come again?"

"It was a carving, part of a set of six half-scale models that Crowell had carved for special friends. I own the other five. I paid Orloff for the decoy, but before I could pick it up he was arrested and put in jail. The judge denied bail because Orloff was a flight risk. His house was sealed with all its contents."

"Including the bird?"

He nodded. "As you probably know, Orloff was convicted and went to prison. He had my money but I didn't have the decoy."

"No chance of getting your money back through legal channels?"

"Unlikely. Even if I could dig it out of whatever black hole Orloff had hidden it in."

"I see the problem. There must have been a long line of people trying to get their investments back."

"I wasn't an investor. I could prove that I owned the bird. I didn't *want* my money. I wanted the decoy to complete the set. An intact set of Crowell decoys would be worth millions, but the bird was desirable to me as a collector."

"Any chance you could get the house unsealed?"

"Yes, under ordinary circumstances, but the house burned down before my lawyers could file a claim. Cause of the fire is still unknown. Then Orloff died in prison of a heart attack, which surprised many people who didn't think he had a heart."

"The decoy?"

"It supposedly went up in flames."

"You sound like you have doubts."

Ruskin whispered to the man in the white suit, who went to a wall cabinet and slid open a glass door. He reached inside and came out with a large plastic cube. He carried it back to Ruskin, who set the container on the desk, flipped the lid back, took something out, and held it above his head like an offering to the gods.

The carved bird in his hands was around half the size of a real one. Its copper-colored head was turned back in a graceful curve with the long, sharp beak pointed at the tail. The gray and white feathers painted on the wooden wings looked so real they could have riffled in the breeze.

"The preening merganser has everything Crowell was famous for," Ruskin said, lowering his arms. "Attention to detail, accuracy, and beauty."

"You're confusing me, Mr. Ruskin. You said the merganser is missing, presumably burned."

"It *is*."

He turned the bird over and brought it to the window, close enough for me to see the black oval sticker on the bottom. Printed on the sticker in silver letters were the words: "Copy of A. E. Crowell Preening Merganser. Product of China."

"A Chinese rip-off?" I said.

"Yes. A well-done fake, but still a fake."

"What does it have to do with the missing bird?"

"*Every*thing, Mr. Socarides. Only someone with access to the Crowell carving could have made a reproduction that is so accurate in every respect to the original."

"Not sure I understand."

"Ms. Callahan?" Ruskin said.

Bridget explained.

"The reproduction was advertised for sale in a collectors' publication. It was purchased for a hundred and fifty dollars. My firm's investigators traced the bird to a manufacturer in Hunan province, China, which specializes in making wooden reproductions of all kinds. The original piece is scanned digitally and the data fed into computer-guided laser carving machines. Skilled craftsmen do the final detailing."

"That would mean the Chinese had access to the original?"

"Indirectly," she said. "A company in upstate New York does the scanning and transmits the data to China."

Ruskin rejoined the discussion. "And I believe the American and Chinese companies used the real decoy to manufacture the fake."

"Do you know who contracted for the work?"

"No. Someone dropped the carving off, waited while it was scanned, and picked it up. Payment was in cash."

"Could they have copied it from a photo?"

"Yes. But not as accurately as this," Ruskin answered. "Crowell knew bird anatomy from years as a professional hunter, and his birds were accurate in every detail. Moreover, he imbued his models with life. This is good for a fake, but without the hand of the master it is just a prettied-up piece of wood."

"Have you been able to run a trace on the magazine ad?"

He put the carving back into the case, closed the cover, and handed the container to his valet, who carried it from the room. Ruskin lowered his athletic body into the swivel chair, leaned his elbows on the desktop, and tented his fingers.

"The ad was placed by something called Elmer's Workshop. No email address. Orders went through PayPal. The ad listed a post office box in the town of Harwich, Massachusetts, where, coincidentally, Crowell lived and worked."

"Any idea who rents the PO box?"

"No. It's since been closed."

"Any chance the reproduction was made *before* the fire?"

"The records at the New York and Chinese operations show that the reproduction was made after the fire, indicating that the original survived the blaze."

"What would you like me to do, Mr. Ruskin?"

"I believe finding the source of the fake will lead you to my property. You may have some contacts locally. Having city detectives poking around would attract unwanted attention. You understand the need to be discreet, of course."

The job seemed like an uncomplicated one, except for the Orloff angle. The charming old bandit had left suicides, divorces, and bankruptcies in the wake of his stealing spree. And his greedy fingers were still reaching from the grave. Ruskin was unsavory, but he wouldn't be the first client of dubious character that I'd worked for. Any doubts I might have entertained went up in smoke when Bridget handed me a check made out in an amount triple what I would have charged.

I rubbed the check lightly between my thumb and forefinger. "I'll see what I can do."

"Good," Ruskin said. "Let me know as soon as you hear something."

He rose from his chair and, without another word, headed for the door.

Hiring interview was over.

Seconds after Ruskin left the room, the old gray man showed up and pushed the wall button. As the unicorn tapestry slid across the window, he handed me a cardboard box.

"Mr. Ruskin thought this might assist you in your work," he said. "He wants it returned when you are through. It is not to be taken from its protective container."

He led us back the way we came. We stepped onto the porch and the door clicked shut behind us.

"Was that for real?" I asked, taking a breath of fresh air. "That stuff with the allergies?"

"Mr. Ruskin could be a hypochondriac, I suppose, but he's gone through a lot of unnecessary trouble and expense modifying this house if he's simply imagining his allergies. All his food is prepared in accordance with his allergy issues. The butler is a bit of a gossip. He told me Ruskin is allergic to everything you can think of."

"Does he ever leave the house?"

"Not very often, the butler says; only for urgent matters, and when he does he wears a hazmat suit. He usually goes out only at night."

I set the cardboard box down on the porch and peeled off the sealing tape. Then I lifted out the transparent plastic container that held the reproduction decoy Ruskin had shown me. The lid was secured with a padlock.

I jiggled the lock. "Ruskin is very protective of his property."

"Mr. Ruskin is deathly afraid of contaminated things or people coming into the main house. When it comes back this box will go through a clean room where it will be wiped down and sterilized. Anyone coming into the living quarters from the outside has to wear a throwaway suit."

"Like the valet?"

"Yes. His name is Dudley. That's all I know."

I put the bird container into the cardboard box and Bridget gave me a ride back to the marina.

There wasn't much small talk. I was thinking about Ruskin's strange request. She was probably mind-counting her retainer. She dropped me off in the parking lot. When I got out of the car, she handed me a brown, eight-by-ten envelope.

"This report was prepared by our staff investigators. I'll call you at some point to see how things are going. Mr. Ruskin's phone number is inside. He has asked that you contact him directly as the investigation moves along. I'll be in touch."

She put the car into gear and left me standing at about the same spot she stopped my trek to Trader Ed's. This time I made it all the way to a barstool. My personal alcohol meter was on empty, but I decided to stay sober. Sipping on a club soda with cranberry juice and lime, I went through the papers inside the envelope Bridget had given me.

I skimmed a history of the Crowell decoys and read that his workshop was still standing. It had been moved from the original site to the property of the Harwich Historical Society at Brooks Academy, which was a short drive from where I was sitting.

Seemed like a logical place to start. I tucked the papers back into the envelope, slid off the barstool, and headed for my pickup truck with the cardboard box tucked under my arm.

◦—+—◦

If you looked at a map of Cape Cod you'd see that the town of Harwich is near where the elbow would be on the peninsula, which curls out into the Atlantic like a bent arm. Harwich is an old seafaring town with Nantucket Sound at its doorstep, so it's no surprise that it once had a school of navigation.

The school was housed in a graceful, nineteenth-century Greek-revival building named Brooks Academy that had been turned into a museum run by the Harwich Historical Society. I parked behind the academy and walked across the parking lot to a low shingled building.

Hanging over a sliding barn door was a black quarter board with the words "A. E. Crowell, Bird Carvings" in white letters. On a shelf above the door to the shop was a carving of a Canada goose. The workshop was closed, but a pleasant, middle-aged woman working in the museum opened it up for me. She accidentally set off an alarm and had to shut it off. I stepped through the entrance to the workshop and into a room with wall displays that told about Crowell and his work.

I tossed a couple of bills into the donation box and said I carved birds for a hobby. I jokingly asked if the Canada goose was a Crowell. She laughed. "It wouldn't be out there if it were."

The museum had a few Crowell decoys in its collection, she said, but nothing like the carvings that were bringing a million dollars.

The shop contained a workbench, wood working tools, a pot-bellied stove, and what looked like an antique sander and band saw. A half-dozen miniature bird models with minimalist details sat on a shelf.

A carving on a workbench caught my eye. It looked identical to the fake bird sitting in the box on the front seat of my truck. I asked where it came from.

"A bird carver named Mike Murphy donated the reproduction. We had it in the museum where it would be more secure, but since it's only a reproduction someone suggested we put it out here. As you may have noticed, we have a burglar alarm in the barn, but there's nothing in the workshop that's really valuable. Even the tools are borrowed."

I thanked her, put another couple of bills in the donation box, and walked back to my truck. I leafed through the folder Bridget had given me and reread the investigation report where they interviewed someone named Mike Murphy.

A guy with the same name had been the caretaker of the Orloff mansion. He told the investigators he had seen the merganser in Orloff's study. The bird was there when the marshals sealed the place. He assumed it had been burned in the fire. He couldn't say for sure because he got to the fire after the house had burned down. Someone at the fire department had called him.

The investigators left it at that. I might have done the same thing, except for Murphy's donation to the historical society. It suggested that he had more than a casual interest in the preening merganser, fake or not. And I wanted to know why.

Murphy lived in a one-story ranch house in a working-class neighborhood that was probably never fashionable, nor ever would be. I parked in the driveway behind a beige Toyota Camry and knocked on the front door. The stocky man who answered the door stared at me with inquisitive blue eyes.

"Can I help you?" he said.

"My name is Socarides." I pointed to the *Thalassa* logo on my blue polo shirt. "I run a charter boat out of Hyannis. I'm also an ex-Boston cop and I pick up a few bucks on the side as a private investigator for insurance companies. I wonder if I could ask you a few questions about Viktor Orloff."

He gave a weary shake of his head. "Orloff is the gift that keeps on giving. Wish I never heard of the guy."

"From what I know of Orloff, you have a lot of company."

Murphy grinned. He had a wide jaw cradling a mouth filled with white, even teeth.

"Come on in," he said with a sigh.

Before I accepted his invitation I went to the truck and got the cardboard box. He gave the carton a curious glance, then ushered me into a living room paneled in knotty pine. He shooed away a gray long-haired cat from a wood-framed chair and told me to take a seat.

He sat on a sofa, picked the cat up, and stroked its head.

"This is Gus," he said. "Gotta keep him inside because coyotes come through the yard once in a while, but he doesn't seem to mind being a house cat."

Gus looked as if he didn't mind anything. I glanced around the living room. There was art on every wall, most of it prints of waterfowl. Wooden decoys were scattered on shelves and tables around the room.

"Quite the collection," I said.

"Thanks," Murphy said. Then he crossed his arms and gazed at me. "How can I help you?"

"My client is a rich guy named Ruskin. He bought a Crowell decoy called the preening merganser from Orloff, and paid a lot of money for it, but the law took your former boss off to the clink before he could make good. Then Orloff died in prison and his house burned down, along with the decoy."

Murphy nodded. "I already talked to the cops. What does your client want to know that isn't in the record?"

"He thinks maybe the merganser didn't burn up."

Murphy scoffed. "That's because he didn't see the fire."

"You did?" I remembered from the file that Murphy told the interviewer he lost his job when Orloff was arrested and hadn't been back to the house since it was sealed.

"I didn't see the actual fire," he said, catching himself. "I saw the TV stuff and came by the house later. It went up quick, like it had been set."

"The investigation didn't say anything about arson."

"A guy like Orloff would know people who could do a smart job. Everything had been reduced to cinders. *Everything.* I don't know where Ruskin would get the idea that the bird wasn't burned up."

"From this." I opened the carton, extracted the plastic case, and set it on the coffee table. "Made in China. Ruskin saw an ad in a magazine and ordered this Crowell reproduction."

"Chinese are pretty clever at copying stuff," he said.

"Ruskin says a copy this good could only have been made from the original. Which means the authentic Crowell didn't burn up."

"Orloff could have had the fake made before the real bird got burned."

"That's not what the record shows. The repro was made *after* the house fire."

He shrugged. "Can I take a look?"

I handed him the encased bird model. He ran his fingers over the plastic surface of the box.

"Where did you get this?"

"Probably the same place you got the one you gave to the museum."

"You stopped by the museum?"

I pointed to a photo of the Crowell workshop that hung over the fireplace mantle.

"They moved the decoy to the woodworking barn," I said.

His hand stopped stroking the box. "No kidding. Why did they do that?" He sounded almost startled.

"Thought it would add to the workshop's authenticity. The lady at the museum said you were a bird carver."

"I carved most of the birds in the house, but I'm no Elmer Crowell. I've taken a few courses and have the tools."

"That makes you an expert compared to me. How does the mail order repro stack up against the original?"

"Technically, it's very good, but it doesn't have the soul you'd see in a Crowell. I figured I'd never own a real one, so I bought the reproduction. I must have seen the same ad as Ruskin. I ordered one just to see what they'd done."

He put the box down on the coffee table, which is when I noticed the blurry blue tattoo on his forearm. I could still make out the eagle, globe, and anchor of the Marine insignia. That explained the military buzz cut of his white hair.

"Semper fi," I said, and pushed my sleeve up to show him a smaller version of the EGA on the top of my arm near the shoulder.

"I'll be damned," he said. "Where'd you serve?"

"Up by the border mostly. You?"

"I spent a lot of time around Pleiku. Got a Purple Heart. What about you?"

I shook my head. "Only wounds I got were psychological. Worst one was when a village got shelled after I told everyone they were safe. Now I think real hard before I make a promise."

A knowing smile came to his lips. "Sometimes you don't see the forest for the trees."

Murphy seemed more relaxed. He told me that after the Marines he had married and gone into the postal service like a lot of vets, retired early after his wife got a bad disease that eventually killed her, and started a small company keeping an eye on summer houses when their owners weren't around. That's how he met Orloff, and went to work for him as a full-time caretaker until the time his boss got arrested.

"Did he cheat you?" I asked.

"He owed me a month's salary. They say he only went after big accounts. But he stiffed little guys like me. He even cheated a fund for handicapped kids that didn't know he was handling its money. He was like somebody's uncle, people trusted him right to the end."

"Speaking of the end, this looks like a dead one," I said. I gave him my business card. "Let me know if you remember anything else."

"I'll keep my eyes and ears open. Come by to see me anytime. I don't go out much and stay up late. Maybe I'll hear something from the bird carver crowd. You never know."

"That's right," I said, getting up from the couch to shake hands. "You never do."

The investigative report said the fake decoys had been mailed from Harwich. I stopped by the post office, went up to the desk, and asked the postal clerk what the cheapest rate would be for sending out a box like the one in my hands.

"Depends on weight, of course. Parcel post is the cheapest, but it's also the slowest," she said.

"I was talking to a friend named Mike Murphy. He's got a PO box here and sends out a lot of packages, but I don't remember what rate he used."

"We've got a few Murphys. I don't recall anyone doing a lot of shipping."

"I'll talk to him and get back to you."

I remembered that there was more than one post office in town. I got back in my truck and drove a few miles to the pint-sized West Harwich post office. I went through the same routine with the postmistress, and this time I struck gold.

"Mike uses straight parcel post to send boxes that look just like that," she said. "Haven't seen him for a while, though. Not since he closed his box."

"I'll tell Mike you miss seeing him," I said.

⚊⚊

Twenty minutes later I drove down the potholed dirt driveway that leads to the converted boathouse I call home. Chez Socarides was part of an old estate when I bought it and rebuilt it into a year-round residence. The place is still just short of ramshackle, but it's got a million-dollar water view of a big bay and distant barrier beach.

My cat Kojak ambushed me as soon as I stepped inside. I poured him some dry food, grabbed the phone, went out on the deck, and tucked the box with the fake bird under a chair. Then I dialed the number for Ruskin. He answered right away.

I told him about my talk with Mike Murphy, his connection with Orloff, and the visit to the post office.

"Do you suspect Murphy knows more about my decoy than what he's saying?"

"Yes, I do, which is why I want to go back to talk to him again."

"When you do, tell him he'd better say where it is, or else."

"Or else what, Mr. Ruskin?"

"I'll leave that to your imagination."

I didn't like what I was imagining. Ruskin was suggesting that I threaten Murphy.

"I don't work that way, Mr. Ruskin."

"Well, I do," he said. "And I have found my methods extremely persuasive."

"I can tear up your check or send it back to you, Mr. Ruskin. Your call."

There was a pause on the other end of the line, then Ruskin laughed.

"No need to do either. You don't think I'm serious. I've decided to offer a reward."

I should have been suspicious at Ruskin's fast turnaround. But I was put off by his conciliatory change of tone.

"It's worth a try. How much of a reward?"

"Oh, I don't know. How about ten thousand dollars?"

"That will definitely get his interest. I'll go see Murphy tomorrow and make the offer."

"Yes," Ruskin said, after a pause. "That should work."

He hung up. I went back into the house and came out onto the deck with a can of Cape Cod Red beer. I popped the top and took a slurp, thinking about my conversation with Ruskin. He said his rash suggestion to lean on Murphy was a joke, but I wasn't so sure. I sipped my beer, letting my mind zone out as the late afternoon sun painted the bay and beach in autumn pastels.

After the beer can went dry, I went back into the house. I pulled together a Greek salad for dinner, then worked a few hours on some paperwork for the charter operation. The figures looked so good that I decided to call my family in the morning to tell them about my accounting.

My eyes were tired from looking at numbers. I had another beer, then I stretched out on the couch and fell asleep. The chirp of my phone woke me up. I groped for the phone, stuck it in my ear, and came out with a groggy "hello." I heard a wet gargle on the other end and a second later the phone went dead. The caller ID said Mike Murphy had called. I hit the redial button and got a busy signal.

The phone's time display said it was after midnight.

I splashed cold water on my face and headed for the door.

⌖

Murphy's house was in darkness. I parked in the driveway behind the Toyota Camry, went up to the front door, and knocked. No answer. I knocked again, louder this time. No one came to the door. I rang the doorbell. No one answered the ring, but something brushed up against my leg.

I looked down at Murphy's cat, Gus. Funny. Murphy said Gus stayed indoors because of the danger from coyotes.

I tried the knob. The door was unlocked. As I opened the door Gus scuttled past me into the darkness. I stepped inside and called Murphy's name. No answer. I tried again. This time I heard a low moan. I felt for the wall switch and flicked on the lights.

Murphy was stretched out on the couch, one arm dangling limply toward the floor. The lower part of his face looked as if it had been smeared with ketchup.

I snatched a phone from the floor next to the couch and called 911. I said I was Mike's neighbor and that he needed medical help. Then I knelt next to Murphy. I put my face close to his, and said, "You're going to be okay, Mike. Rescue squad is on its way."

He opened his mouth and I got a knot in the pit of my stomach when I saw that his beautiful Irish smile had been ruined. Something or someone had hit him in the jaw with a force powerful enough to knock out his front teeth. There were bruises on his left cheek. I guessed he'd been worked over with a blackjack.

Anger welled in my chest.

"Who did this to you, Mike?"

He tried to talk. The best he could manage was a wet gurgle similar to the one I had heard over the phone. I asked him again. This time he said what sounded like *goats*. I tried again. The same answer. His dazed eyes looked past my shoulder. I turned and saw he had fixed his gaze on the fireplace photo of the Crowell barn. Then, mercifully, he passed out.

I had done all I could for Mike. I didn't want to explain to the police who I was and why I was there. I went outside, got in the pickup, drove half a block and parked where I could see the house. Minutes later, I saw the flashing lights of an ambulance coming down the street.

It was clear to me who'd worked Mike over. Ruskin made no secret that he would crack heads if necessary to get his hands on the decoy. Thanks to my big fat Greek mouth, he knew Murphy held the key to its whereabouts. I had handed Mike on a platter to a dangerous man.

Maybe I should tell the cops what I knew. Lousy idea. Ruskin had the money to hire a team of lawyers who would say that there was no evidence. And Ruskin had the perfect alibi. He never left the house because of his acute allergies, poor guy.

I watched the rescue squad bring Mike out on a stretcher and put him in the ambulance. I followed the ambulance to the hospital emergency entrance. I waited outside a few minutes, but there was nothing I could do while Mike was in the ER, so I drove home.

When I drove up to my house I saw I had company. A black Cadillac was parked in front. I pulled up next to the car and got out of the truck. The caddy's door opened and a tall man emerged from the car. His silver hair was combed back from a broad forehead. He had a sharp-jawed face with a chin like a shelf. He stood there with his arms folded.

"Ruskin sent me," he said. He had an accent that was neither English nor Irish. I figured him for Australian.

The black running suit didn't hide his broad-shouldered physique any better than the white coverall did when I first saw him in the trophy room. "You're his valet. Dudley."

If he was surprised I knew his name he didn't show it. His expression looked as if it had been carved in ice.

"Yeah, that's me. How'd you know my name?"

"Ruskin's butler."

"He talks too much."

"I almost didn't recognize you without your hazmat outfit."

"What? Oh yeah. The spook suit. I put it on after I've been out of the house. Ruskin worries about bringing in bad stuff."

"I'd ask you in for a cup of tea, Dudley, but the place is a mess. What brings you by this time of night?"

"Mr. Ruskin wanted me to tell you you're off the case. He doesn't need you anymore."

"Funny, he didn't say anything about firing me when I talked to him a few hours ago. He suggested I offer a reward to a source who might be able to lead him to the decoy."

"Save your energy. You're done."

"Does that mean he's found the decoy?"

"He knows where it is. You're out of the picture."

"He paid me a lot of money to snoop around."

He sneered. "Don't bother cashing the check. He's going to put a stop payment on it."

"Mr. Ruskin is stiffing me?"

"You didn't find the bird. That was the deal. He had to take matters into his own hands. I'm here to pick up the fake bird."

"It's a fake. What's the hurry?"

"Mr. Ruskin doesn't like other people to have his property."

"People like Mike Murphy?"

"Whaddya talking about?"

"I told Ruskin that Murphy might know where the decoy was. A few hours later someone put him in the hospital."

Dudley smiled. "So?"

"So maybe the police might like to know the connection between your boss and Murphy getting beat up."

"That would be stupid on your part."

"Tell Ruskin I'll drop the duck off tomorrow. Maybe we can talk about my paycheck then. Thanks for coming by, Dud."

Calling him Dud was my first mistake. Turning away from a violent thug was my second. He moved in, and I saw him unfold his arms from across his chest a second before something hard slammed into the side of my head. My legs turned to rubber and I went over like a fallen oak.

I didn't even have the chance to yell, "Timber!"

———

A groan woke me up, which wasn't surprising because it was coming from my throat.

I pushed myself onto my elbows, then onto my knees, got my legs under me, and staggered into the boathouse. The right side of my head was on fire. I had trouble focusing, but I saw that the inside of the house looked as if a bulldozer had gone through it. Only not as neat.

I called Kojak's name and sighed with relief when he sauntered out of the bedroom. I splashed cold water on my face for the second time that night, put ice in a dish towel, and held it tenderly against my head where it helped numb the pain.

I went out on the deck. The box was where I left it, behind the chair. The bird container was still inside.

Dudley said his boss knew where to find the Crowell decoy. I stood on the deck and recalled my conversation with Murphy, and the startled look on his face when I told him his gift to the museum had been moved to the barn.

I remembered, too, the way he had stared at the Crowell barn photo when I found him with his teeth smashed in. It was a deliberate gesture that must have caused him some pain but he did it anyhow.

Sometimes you don't see the forest for the trees.

You can get so involved in the details, you can't see the whole picture.

Whether he intended to or not, Mike's wry comment told me he had found a safe place for the original Crowell. Right in the open, where no one would suspect it to be.

It was a short drive from my house to Brooks Academy. The black Cadillac was parked on a side road in the shadow of some trees.

I dug a filleting knife out of its case, snuck over to the car, and stuck the blade into all four tires. The car slowly slumped onto its rims. About then, I heard the sound of an alarm from the workshop. Dudley was making his move. I got back in my truck and drove to the police station around a half mile away. I went in the front door and hurried up to the dispatcher's desk.

"I just went by Brooks Academy and heard an alarm going off," I said. "There's a car parked nearby. Looked kinda suspicious."

The dispatcher thanked me, and while she got on the phone I slipped out of the police station. I sat in my truck and saw a cruiser drive away from the station toward the museum. A minute later another patrol car raced past, going in the same direction.

I waited ten minutes, then drove by the museum. Four cruisers with roof lights flashing were parked near the museum. Some police officers were talking to a tall man. He had his back to me so I couldn't see his face, but his hair looked even more silvery in the harsh beam of headlights.

On the way home I stopped by the bank ATM and deposited the check from Ruskin. The transaction went through, thanks to the warning from Dudley.

I was still thinking about Dudley when I stepped into the boat-house. He'd probably say he got drunk and broke into the workshop by mistake. Ruskin would spring him from jail before the arresting officers got off their shifts.

A guy like Dudley doesn't make his way through life without leaving tracks. I called the best tracker I knew. If John Flagg was surprised to hear from me at three o'clock in the morning, he didn't show it. He simply said, "Hello, Soc. Been a while. What's up?"

Flagg seems to function without sleep. Which may have something to do with his job as a troubleshooter for an ultra-secret government unit. We'd met in Vietnam and bonded over our New England heritage. He was a Wampanoag Indian from Martha's Vineyard whose ancestors had been around for thousands of years. My parents came to Massachusetts from the ancient land of Greece.

"Ever heard of a guy named Merriwhether Ruskin the Third?"

"Sure. He runs one of the biggest mercenary ops in the world. Bigger than the armies of lots of countries. Why do you ask?"

"He hired me for a job."

"Never figured you for a soldier of fortune, Soc."

"Me neither. That's why I'm no longer on his payroll. Ruskin has another guy working for him. First name is Dudley. Maybe Australian. I know that isn't much."

"Give me a minute. I'll look in the bad guy database." He hung up. I could imagine him tapping into the vast intelligence network he had at his fingertips. He called back after three minutes. "He's an Aussie named Dudley Wormsley, aka 'The Worm.' Interpol has a pile of warrants out for him."

"I thought as much. Wonder if there is any way to let the FBI know that 'The Worm' is sitting in the Harwich, Massachusetts, police station, under arrest for breaking and entering."

"I'll take care of it. When we going fishing?"

"Charter boat's coming out of the water, but there's my dinghy. As you know, I don't bait my hooks."

"Suits me," Flagg said.

I hung up and thought about Mike. He said he'd been attacked by *goats*. Dudley had referred to the hazmat suit as a *spook* suit. Spooks equal ghosts. Which meant plural. Which meant he wasn't alone. Which meant the second ghost was Ruskin.

With Dudley out of the way, Ruskin was an open target, if I could get to him, although that was unlikely given the airtight fortress he lived in. When I got home I retrieved the box from the deck and brought it inside. I took out the plastic case protecting the merganser, put it on the kitchen table, and stared at it, taking in the graceful lines of the bird's body and neck.

"Talk to me," I said.

Early the next morning I got up, poured some coffee into a travel mug, and called Ruskin's number. The butler answered the phone and said his boss was busy. I said that was all right. I merely wanted to drop off Mr. Ruskin's decoy. He said to leave it at the gatehouse.

After hanging up, I got a small leather case out of a duffle bag I keep in my bedroom closet. Inside the case was a full range of lock picks. After a few tries, I popped the padlock and lifted the box lid back on its hinges. I remembered how Ruskin had reached into the box for the carving and lifted it above his head.

Then I took the decoy out of the box, put it in the sink and got a jar of peanut butter out of the refrigerator. I spooned some butter out of the jar onto the bird carving and smeared it all over the wooden feathers with my hands. Then I nestled the glistening fake bird back into its fake nest. I padlocked the box again and carried it out to the truck.

As I drove away from the gatehouse after dropping the box off for Mr. Ruskin, I thought what I'd done was rather sneaky and not very nice. Maybe Ruskin was allergic to peanuts. Maybe not. But I didn't like being played for a patsy, especially when innocent people are hurt. It happened at a village in Vietnam, and with Murphy. It wasn't going to happen again.

I stopped by the hospital on the way home. Mike was out of the ICU and sleeping. The nurse in charge said he was doing fine.

Bridget called me that night to say that she had been trying to reach Ruskin, but his butler said he wasn't available. She said she would keep me posted. I didn't know what Ruskin was allergic to when I returned his decoy. Maybe I just got lucky.

Mike got out of the hospital a few days later. I drove him home and checked in on him while he healed and popped painkillers. When I asked why he had called me instead of 911, he said it was because Marines stick together.

Once he was able to talk at length we discussed what to do about the Crowell decoy.

He confessed that he'd taken it from the Orloff mansion for payment of back wages. When he found out the bird was worth maybe a million dollars, he knew he couldn't sell it. He read about Chinese reproductions somewhere and went into the fake decoy business for himself. He had the original scanned in New York and made in China. He sold out the first batch except for the one he kept. But he started to get nervous about attracting attention to himself and wanted the Crowell bird out of the house. He hid it in plain sight at the historical society museum, never figuring they'd put it in the Crowell barn.

"Legally speaking, the bird may belong to Ruskin," I said. "He told me that he paid Orloff for the merganser, but I have only his word for that. It's quite possible no money exchanged hands, which means that the sale never went through. In that case, Orloff was still the owner. Did he have any heirs?"

"None that I know of. He left lots of folks holding the bag. Including me. But if I admit I took it from the house, I could get into trouble."

Mike was right. He'd removed the bird without permission. His sticky fingers saved the carving, but it was still grand larceny. If the debtors heard about the bird, they'd want it put up for auction so they could get a cut, no matter how small.

I thought about it for a minute. "You mentioned a fund for handicapped children that Orloff cheated," I said.

"Big time. They'll never recover."

"They might," I said. "Suppose we contact their lawyers and say we have the bird. Tell them that Orloff felt remorse over cheating the fund, and he wanted to donate proceeds from the sale of the Crowell at auction."

"Great, but how does that explain me having the bird?"

"You're a bird carver. Orloff let you take the bird so you could prepare a prospectus at auction. When he went to jail and the house was sealed, you didn't know what to do. Orloff called and told you he wanted to move ahead with the sale, then he died."

"That old bastard never said that. Never would."

"Maybe, but that's the way you understood it. It makes him look good, and helps a bunch of kids who need it. Splitting it among the debtors would only make the lawyers rich. Look at it this way: the Marines have landed and the situation is well in hand. Semper fi."

Mike shook my hand with a lobster grip.

"Semper fi."

Mike's new implants look like the real thing. They should. I used Ruskin's check to help pay for them. It was the least I could do, but left me with nothing for the boat loan. I was drowning my sorrows in a beer at Trader Ed's one night when another boat captain offered me a job crewing on a charter boat in the Florida Keys. I said I'd take it. The timing was good. Bridget called the other day to let me know the Ruskin job was permanently off.

Sometimes I wonder what Crowell would have made of the whole affair. He'd be puzzled at all the fuss over one of his birds, but I think he'd be pleased how things turned out with the preening merganser.

The knees of the gods, as Homer said.

Or my partner Sam used to say after a good day of fishing: "Finestkind, Cap."

*The idea of writing a mystery centered around master bird carver Elmer Crowell had rattled around in my skull for years. I frequently drove by his former workshop and I had read that wealthy collectors paid millions for some of his rarer pieces. People have killed for far less and it seemed to me that a missing Crowell bird carving or carvings might be a good basis for an Aristotle Socarides book. When Suspense Publications asked me to contribute to an anthology entitled Nothing Good Happens After Midnight, I decided to use the Crowell concept. It was my first short story and I had to ask a longtime writer friend named Brendan DuBois how long it should be. Crowell is not well-known outside of collector circles. I'm hoping the story will make more people aware of this remarkable self-taught America genius.

Stephen King has been one of the world's bestselling authors for four decades, most of his work being in the horror, supernatural, fantasy, crime, and suspense categories. Among the many films and television series made from his books are Carrie, The Shining, Misery, The Shawshank Redemption, It, *and* The Stand.

THE FIFTH STEP

Stephen King

Harold Jamieson, once chief engineer of New York City's sanitation department, enjoyed retirement. He knew from his small circle of friends that some didn't, so he considered himself lucky. He had an acre of garden in Queens that he shared with several like-minded horticulturists, he had discovered Netflix, and he was making inroads in the books he'd always meant to read. He still missed his wife—a victim of breast cancer five years previous—but aside from that persistent ache, his life was quite full. Before rising every morning, he reminded himself to enjoy the day. At sixty-eight, he liked to think he had a fair amount of road left, but there was no denying it had begun to narrow.

The best part of those days—assuming it wasn't raining, snowing, or too cold—was the nine-block walk to Central Park after breakfast. Although he carried a cell phone and used an electronic tablet (had grown dependent on it, in fact), he still preferred the print version of the *Times*. In the park, he would settle on his favorite bench and spend an hour with it, reading the sections back to front, telling himself he was progressing from the sublime to the ridiculous.

One morning in mid-May, the weather coolish but perfectly adequate for bench sitting and newspaper reading, he was annoyed to look up from his paper and see a man sitting down on the other end of his bench, although there were plenty of empty ones in the vicinity. This invader of Jamieson's morning space looked to be in his mid to late forties, neither handsome nor ugly, in fact perfectly nondescript. The same was true of his attire: New Balance walking shoes, jeans, a Yankees cap, and a Yankees hoodie with the hood tossed back. Jamieson gave him an impatient side-glance and prepared to move to another bench.

"Wait," the man said. "I sat down here because I need a favor. It's not a big one, but I'll pay." He reached into the kangaroo pouch of his hoodie and brought out a twenty-dollar bill.

"I don't do favors for strange men," Jamieson said, and got up.

"But that's exactly the point—the two of us being strangers. Hear me out. If you say no, that's fine. But please hear me out. You could . . ." He cleared his throat, and Jamieson realized the guy was nervous. Maybe more, maybe scared. "You could be saving my life."

Jamieson considered, then sat down, but as far from the other man as he could while still keeping both butt cheeks on the bench. "I'll give you a minute, but if you sound crazy, I'm leaving. And put your money away. I don't need it, and I don't want it."

The man looked at the bill as if surprised to find it still in his hand, then put it back in the pocket of his sweatshirt. He put his hands on his thighs and looked down at them instead of at Jamieson. "I'm an alcoholic. Four months sober. Four months and twelve days, to be exact."

"Congratulations," Jamieson said. He guessed he meant it, but he was even more ready to get up. The guy seemed sane, but

Jamieson was old enough to know that sometimes the woo-woo didn't come out right away.

"I've tried three times before and once got almost a year. I think this might be my last chance to grab the brass ring. I'm in AA. That's—"

"I know what it is. What's your name, Mr. Four Months Sober?"

"You can call me Jack, that's good enough. We don't use last names in the program."

Jamieson knew that too. Lots of people on the Netflix shows had alcohol problems. "So what can I do for you, Jack?"

"The first three times I tried, I didn't get a sponsor in the program—somebody who listens to you, answers your questions, sometimes tells you what to do. This time I did. Met a guy at the Bowery Sundown meeting and really liked the stuff he said. And, you know, how he carried himself. Twelve years sober, feet on the ground, works in sales, like me."

He had turned to look at Jamieson, but now he returned his gaze to his hands.

"I used to be a hell of a salesman—for five years I headed the sales department of . . . well, it doesn't matter, but it was a big deal, you'd know the company. Now I'm down to peddling greeting cards and energy drinks to bodegas in the five boroughs. Last rung on the ladder, man."

"Get to the point," Jamieson said, but not harshly; he had become a little interested in spite of himself. It was not every day that a stranger sat down on your bench and started spilling his shit. Especially not in New York. "I was just going to check on the Mets. They're off to a good start."

Jack rubbed a palm across his mouth. "I liked this guy I met at the Sundown, so I got up my courage after a meeting and asked him to be my sponsor. In March, this was. He looked me

over and said he'd take me on, but only on two conditions: that
I do everything he said and call him if I felt like drinking. 'Then
I'll be calling you every fucking night,' I said, and he said, 'So
call me every fucking night, and if I don't answer talk to the
machine.' Then he asked me if I worked the Steps. Do you know
what those are?"

"Vaguely."

"I said I hadn't gotten around to them. He said that if I wanted
him to be my sponsor, I'd have to start. He said the first three were
both the hardest and the easiest. They boil down to 'I can't stop on
my own, but with God's help I can, so I'm going to let him help.'"

Jamieson grunted.

"I said I didn't believe in God. This guy—Randy's his
name—said he didn't give a shit. He told me to get down on my
knees every morning and ask this God I didn't believe in to help
me stay sober another day. And if I did, he said for me to get down
on my knees before I turned in and thank God for my sober day.
Randy asked if I was willing to do that, and I said I was. Because
I'd lose him otherwise. You see?"

"Sure. You were desperate."

"Exactly! 'The gift of desperation,' that's what AAs call it.
Randy said if I didn't do those prayers and said I was doing them,
he'd know. Because he spent thirty years lying his ass off about
everything."

"So you did it? Even though you don't believe in God?"

"I did it and it's been working. As for my belief that there's no
God . . . the longer I stay sober, the more that wavers."

"If you're going to ask me to pray with you, forget it."

Jack smiled down at his hands. "Nope. I still feel self-conscious
about the on-my-knees thing even when I'm by myself. Last
month—April—Randy told me to do the Fourth Step. That's

when you make a moral inventory—supposedly 'searching and fearless'—of your character."

"Did you?"

"Yes. Randy said I was supposed to put down the bad stuff, then turn the page and list the good stuff. It took me ten minutes for the bad stuff. Over an hour for the good stuff. When I told Randy, he said that was normal. 'You drank for almost thirty years,' he said. 'That puts a lot of bruises on a man's self-image. But if you stay sober, they'll heal.' Then he told me to burn the lists. He said it would make me feel better."

"Did it?"

"Strangely enough, it did. Anyway, that brings us to this month's request from Randy."

"More of a demand, I'm guessing," Jamieson said, smiling a little. He folded his newspaper and laid it aside.

Jack also smiled. "I think you're catching the sponsor-sponsee dynamic. Randy told me it was time to do my Fifth Step."

"Which is?"

" 'Admit to God, to ourselves, and to another human being the exact nature of our wrongs,' " Jack said, making quote marks with his fingers. "I told him okay, I'd make a list and read it to him. God could listen in. Two birds with one stone deal."

"I'm thinking he said no."

"He said no. He told me to approach a complete stranger. His first suggestion was a priest or a minister, but I haven't set foot in a church since I was twelve, and I have no urge to go back. Whatever I'm coming to believe—and I don't know yet what that is—I don't need to sit in a church pew to help it along."

Jamieson, no churchgoer himself, nodded his understanding.

"Randy said, 'So walk up to somebody in Washington Square or Central Park and ask him to hear you list your wrongs. Offer a few bucks to sweeten the deal if that's what it takes. Keep asking until someone agrees to listen.' He said the hard part would be the asking part, and he was right."

"Am I . . ." *Your first victim* was the phrase that came to mind, but Jamieson decided it wasn't exactly fair. "Am I the first person you've approached?"

"The second." Jack grinned. "I tried an off-duty cab driver yesterday and he told me to get lost."

Jamieson thought of an old New York joke: Out-of-towner approaches a guy on Lexington Avenue and says, "Can you tell me how to get to City Hall or should I just go fuck myself?" He decided he wasn't going to tell the guy in the Yankees gear to go fuck himself. He would listen, and the next time he met his friend Alex (another retiree) for lunch, he'd have something interesting to talk about.

"Okay, go for it."

Jack reached into the pouch of his hoodie, took out a piece of paper, and unfolded it. "When I was in fourth grade—"

"If this is going to be your life story, maybe you better give me that twenty after all."

Jack reached into his hoodie with the hand not holding his list of wrongdoings, but Jamieson waved him off. "Joking."

"Sure?"

Jamieson didn't know whether he was or not. "Yes. But let's not take too long. I've got an appointment at eight thirty." This wasn't true, and Jamieson reflected that it was good he didn't have the alcohol problem, because according to the TV meetings he'd attended, honesty was a big deal if you did.

"Keep it speedy, got it. Here goes. In fourth grade I got into a fight with another kid. Gave him a bloody lip and nose. When we got to the principal's office, I said it was because he'd called my mother a dirty name. He denied it, of course, but we both got sent home with a note for our parents. Or just my mom in my case, because my dad left us when I was two."

"And the dirty name thing?"

"A lie. I was having a bad day and thought I'd feel better if I got into a fight with this kid I didn't like. I don't know why I didn't like him—I guess there was a reason, but I don't remember what it was. Only that it set a pattern of lying.

"I started drinking in junior high. My mother had a bottle of vodka she kept in the freezer. I'd swig from it, then add water. She finally caught me, and the vodka disappeared from the freezer. I knew where she put it—on a high shelf over the stove—but I left it alone after that. By then it was probably mostly water, anyway. I saved my allowance and chore money and got some old wino to buy me nips. He'd get four and keep one. I enabled his drinking. That's what my sponsor would say."

Jack shook his head.

"I don't know what happened to that guy. Ralph, his name was, only I thought of him as Wretched Ralph. Kids can be cruel. For all I know, he's dead and I helped kill him."

"Don't get carried away," Jamieson said. "I'm sure you have stuff to feel guilty about without having to invent a bunch of might-have-beens."

Jack looked up and grinned. When he did, Jamieson saw that the man had tears in his eyes. Not falling, but brimming. "Now you sound like Randy."

"Is that a good thing?"

"I think so. I think I'm lucky I found you."

Jamieson discovered he actually felt lucky to have been found. "What else have you got on that list? Because time's passing."

"I went to Brown and graduated cum laude, but mostly I lied and cheated my way through. I was good at it. And—here's a big one—the student adviser I had my senior year was a coke addict. I won't go into how I found that out, like you said, time's passing, but I did, and I made a deal with him. Good recommendations in exchange for a key of coke."

"As in kilo?" Jamieson asked. His eyebrows went up most of the way to his hairline.

"That's right. He paid for it and I brought it in through the Canadian border, tucked into the spare tire of my old Ford. Trying to look like any other college kid who'd spent his semester break having fun and getting laid in Toronto, but my heart was beating like crazy and I bet my blood pressure was red-lining. The car in front of me at the checkpoint got tossed completely, but I got waved right through after showing my driver's license. Of course things were much looser back then." He paused, then said, "I overcharged him for the key too. Pocketed the difference."

"But you didn't use any of the cocaine yourself?"

"No, that was never my scene. I did a line or two once in a while, but what I really wanted—still want—is grain alcohol. When I got a job, I lied to my bosses, but eventually that gave out. It wasn't like college, and there was nobody to mule coke for. Not that I found, anyway."

"What did you do, exactly?"

"Massaged my sell-sheets. Made up appointments that didn't exist to explain days when I was too hungover to come in. Jiggered expense sheets. That first job was a good one. The sky was the limit. And I blew it.

"After they let me go, I decided what I really needed was a change of location. In AA that's called a geographic cure. Never works, but I didn't know that. Seems simple enough now; if you put an asshole on a plane in Boston, an asshole gets off in LA. Or Denver. Or Des Moines. I fucked up a second job, not as good as the first one, but good. That was in San Diego. And what I decided then was that I needed to get married and settle down. *That* would solve the problem. So I got married to a nice girl who deserved better than me. It lasted two years, me lying right down the line about my drinking. Inventing nonexistent business appointments to explain why I was home late, faking flu symptoms to explain why I was going in late or not at all. I could have bought stock in one of those breath-mint companies—Altoids, Breath Savers—but was she fooled?"

"I'm guessing not," Jamieson said. "Listen, are we approaching the end here?"

"Yes. Five more minutes. Please."

"Okay."

"There were arguments that kept getting worse. Stuff got thrown occasionally, and not just by her. There came a night when I came home around midnight, stinking drunk, and she started in on me. You know, all the usual jabber, and all of it was true. I felt like she was throwing poison darts at me and never missing."

Jack was looking at his hands again. His mouth was turned down at the corners so severely that for a moment he looked to Jamieson like Emmett Kelly, that famous sad-faced clown.

"You know what came into my mind while she was yelling at me? Glenn Ferguson, that boy I beat up in the fourth grade. How good it felt, like squeezing the pus out of a boil. I thought it would be good to beat *her* up, and for sure no one would send me home with a note for my mother, because my mom died the year after I graduated from Brown."

"Whoa," Jamieson said. His good feeling about this uninvited confession took a hike. Unease replaced it. He wasn't sure he wanted to hear what came next.

"I left," Jack said. "But I was scared enough to know I had to do something about my drinking That was the first time I tried AA, out there in San Diego. I was sober when I came back to New York, but that didn't last. Tried again and *that* didn't last, either. Neither did the third. But now I've got Randy, and this time I might make it. Partly thanks to you." He held out his hand.

"Well, you're welcome," Jamieson said, and took it.

"There is one more thing," Jack said. His grip was very strong. He was looking into Jamieson's eyes and smiling. "I did leave, but I cut that bitch's throat before I did. I didn't stop drinking, but it made me feel better. The way beating up Glenn Ferguson made me feel better. And that wino I told you about? Kicking him around made me feel better too. Don't know if I killed him, but I sure did bust him up."

Jamieson tried to pull back, but the grip was too strong. The other hand was once more inside the pocket of the Yankees hoodie.

"I really want to stop drinking, and I can't do a complete Fifth Step without admitting that I seem to really enjoy . . ."

What felt like a streak of hot white light slid between Jamieson's ribs, and when Jack pulled the dripping ice pick away, once more tucking it into the pocket of the hoodie, Jamieson realized he couldn't breathe.

". . . killing people. It's a character defect, I know, and probably the chief of my wrongs."

He got to his feet.

"Thank you, sir. I don't know what your name is, but you've helped me so much."

He started away toward Central Park West, then turned back to Jamieson, who was grasping blindly for his *Times* . . . as if, perhaps, a quick scan of the Arts and Leisure section would make everything okay.

"You'll be in my prayers tonight," Jack said.

---

* "The Fifth Step" is a hard story to talk about without spoiling it, so let me just say this: I've been a Friend of Bill, as we call ourselves at AA meetings, for over thirty years. It's a wonderful, lifesaving program, but as my longtime readers know, I can find the dark side of almost anything. (Even that may be saying too much.) I've been doing this job for forty-five years, and as the old farmer up the road from me says, "I ain't tired of it yet."

Janice Law is an Edgar-nominated (for The Big Payoff) and a Lambda award–winning (for Prisoner of the Riviera) novelist. She has written two series of mysteries, as well as contemporary fiction and short stories that regularly appear in Alfred Hitchcock Mystery Magazine, Ellery Queen Mystery Magazine, Sherlock, and Black Cat. Her work has also been featured in a variety of anthologies, including Paraspheres (fantasy), Enter the Apocalypse, and Echoes of the Natural World (Sci-Fi), Best American Mystery Stories, Vengeance (MWA), and several Level Best editions. Her most recent novels are Mornings in London (mysteriouspress.com) and Homeward Dove (Wildside Press).

Besides fiction, she has published two history books, journalism pieces, and scholarly articles, the latter reflecting a twenty-year-plus career in college teaching.

THE CLIENT

Janice Law

Edith Wing lived in a three-story Victorian, a complicated business with porches and a turret and a lot of millwork that you couldn't duplicate today for love or money. The street was once home to the upper management of the silk and linen mills. Now the relics of the comfortable and house-proud were subdivided into shabby apartments or under expensive and doubtless time-consuming repairs.

Not so Ms. Wing's. She lived alone in the house, which was sound but well-worn and cluttered with an accumulation of mismatched furniture, family photos, and souvenirs. The wallpapers were yellowed but holding on, much like the owner. Though easily the oldest of my clients, Edith Wing was sharp and spry. I wouldn't like to have bet on her age, which could have been sixty as easily as seventy-five or older.

She was eccentric in a number of ways, but I suspected loneliness was what brought her to Wilde Investigations and my employment. Understand that we don't get a lot of complicated crime in our town. We're more apt to have drunks motoring on a Saturday night, teens breaking windows, or family disputes that end in black eyes and broken noses. Generally, my clients want the goods on a straying spouse or a larcenous employee; they want to find a runaway child or a dropout sibling. Nothing really too different from the little jobs that Edith had given me over the last few years, such as the location of her strayed terrier—the dog pound one town over—and the fate of her black and white spotted cat—dead by the roadside.

There was also an occasion when she suffered petty harassment from some neighborhood kids—a visit to their parents and their school principal settled that, and overall, I believe Edith was satisfied. So was I. If the jobs she put my way were in the foothills of my profession, she paid promptly and sometimes put in a bit extra "as a little thank you for your time." As far as I was concerned, she was a sweet old lady.

Lately, though, she'd branched out, tasking me with some Internet searches, supposedly looking up old friends and "interesting people." It was such basic stuff that I hated to take her money, but when I pointed out that Google, Facebook, and the Internet Yellow and White Pages could do the job for free, she shook her head. "Oh, I can't get used to all that computer business," she said and added, "My eyes, you know."

She did not even email me the names; either she dropped a note at the office or asked me to stop by on my way home. Mostly

I stopped by. Edith might have trouble with her eyes, but she whipped up mean scones and muffins, and her brownies weren't bad, either. But one afternoon I was so busy with a bona fide stakeout that I asked Robin to enjoy afternoon tea chez Wing for me. Robin is the bookkeeper at the big auto body shop, but she does my books and handles my billing on the side, and she gives me lots of good business advice that I mostly ignore.

That was how I learned something that cast Edith's requests in a different light. Robin looked in the next morning on her way to the auto body shop. As she put a list of names on my desk, she said, "Bit odd. You know she has a MacBook Pro sitting in the living room."

"Really? Hers? She always says she can't see the screen and can't bother to learn the programs."

"It's probably the only thing in the house that is hers," Robin said, turning to go.

"What do you mean?"

"That's the Latour house. Old local money. My grandmother used to cook for them, and I was in the house once or twice as a child when the old lady was alive. Nothing's changed. I recognized the pictures, the furniture, even the family photos."

"But Edith has lived there a while, right? Long as I've been here."

Robin thought a minute. "Ten years at least, probably more. She must have bought it furnished. But who lives with someone else's photos? Paintings, maybe, but personal photos?"

"Clearly Edith Wing," I said, though this seemed beyond eccentricity, and when I next did some Internet searches for her, I indulged a little old cop curiosity. My client had asked for address, email, and phone number, but just for the heck of it, I plugged one Bruce Horman's name into a criminal conviction site I use.

I was thinking, *I don't have time for this*, when my screen blossomed: Our man Bruce had convictions for grand larceny, armed robbery, assault, and firearms violations. Some old school friend. As I went down Edith's list, each name not only turned up a big-time rap sheet but, if I was reading between the lines correctly, connections to a notorious mobster, a real monster who'd dominated the Boston rackets for decades and currently resided in a maximum security prison. By the time I was finished, I had some serious questions—and not just about Edith Wing's alma mater, either.

Whether and how to ask them was my problem, one I had not settled by the time I arrived at her house.

"Oh, Ray, how nice to see you," she said.

The low afternoon light emphasized the lines in her face, but she stood very straight and, as always, she was well groomed, her white hair nicely cut, her nails immaculate. Previously, I had focused on her age and on the job at hand. Now I realized that she was still handsome and suspected that she had once been a real looker. Was that important in some way?

"Do you have time for a little snack?"

"If you have some of those muffins, I have the time." I followed her into the kitchen, old-fashioned—obsolete, to be honest, but with glass-fronted cabinets and tall windows that made a charming impression, like a stage set for some period piece. It struck me how formal my interactions with Edith were. We said the same things and went through the same motions. For the first time I wondered what was underneath and asked myself what was the real point of my employment.

"I brought you the addresses and numbers you asked for." I laid the envelope on the table.

She put on a pair of reading glasses to examine the list. I should mention here that Edith does charming welcomes and mild irritation very well. She showed genuine relief when I returned her old dog and real sorrow about the loss of her cat. Otherwise, she has perfected an all-purpose poker face. You have to know her for quite a while to read her emotions, and that day, to my surprise, I realized that she was not only deeply concerned but frightened.

What to do about that was the big question. Clients sometimes want no more than they've asked for. Still, because I liked Edith, I ventured to ask if something was wrong.

"No, no," she said. "I was noticing a pattern, is all."

"Mostly Boston area," I said.

"But one in Woonsocket and"—she tried for indifference and did not quite manage it—"one in Brockton Heights."

She glanced at me as she spoke. Woonsocket was closer to our fair town than Boston, and Brockton Heights was our next-door neighbor. "Did you really know them at school?" I knew I sounded skeptical.

"In a manner of speaking." Her expression, eloquent a moment before, shut down. "Another muffin? These are a new recipe with orange rind. I have good hopes for them."

The moment had passed. I knew that even if I asked about those extensive rap sheets, I would get no answer. The business would—and should—have nagged at me, but I got a contract from a local big-box store with an unacceptable level of shrinkage, and for several weeks I was just swamped. Robin was delighted with what she took to calling "our cash flow," and the eccentricities of Edith Wing and the criminal careers of her schoolmates faded into the background.

A month later, Edith called late one rainy afternoon. Though she invited me to try an "interesting new cake," I knew her well enough to sense a disguised appeal for help. I was right. The cake, like all Edith's confections, was superb, but as soon as she put a slice on my plate, she said that she wanted to find out if Archie "The Ox" Shaunessy, the Brockton Heights resident on our list, was really living in town and what he was doing in the area.

I said that the lemon topping was outstanding and that she should tell me what this was all about.

She thought for a minute, and I waited to see if she was going to reveal that Shaunessy was an old gangster, that she feared her school friend had gone bad, that she'd had a girlish crush on him decades before—whatever.

"He's no friend of mine," she said, "and he's been around here. Here in town. I can feel it."

I couldn't think why Edith Wing, ultracorrect single lady, pillar of the preservation society, and devoted communicant of St. Mary's, was worried about some superannuated gangster. "Lot of Brockton Heights people shop the Big Y. And the Walmart," I said. Our center has declined from its glory days but the big retailers like the cheap land on the outskirts.

"But what's he doing here in the first place?" she asked sharply. "He's a Boston man, a big-city guy."

"People retire. They look for cheaper living."

"They go to Florida," she said in a scornful tone. "They aspire to die in the sun." Her expression suggested that snowbirds let down right living and the entire northeast.

"He may remember the old days," I said carefully. "There used to be a dog track in Brockton Heights."

She did not take this hint about old-time gambling. "It wouldn't be hard for you to find out what he does, though, would it?"

"Time and money, Edith. I can ask around, but real surveillance means time and money." I hated to charge her for what I was sure was nonsense, and I feigned busyness, although my big-box job had been successfully concluded. Certain folk in their shipping department had serious legal troubles, and tough new policies were in place.

She produced her checkbook. "I want to know if he is working, if he has an interest in some business—legitimate or otherwise. In short, is he is living an ordinary life?"

"He's sixty-four, Edith. He may well have a heart condition and emphysema."

"Archie? You must be kidding." Indignation got the better of discretion for an instant. "Fitness obsessed. You be careful with him."

She wrote a check for a high three figures and passed it across the table. "And some cake," she added, once again my charmingly eccentric client. "I'll wrap a piece for you to take home."

Thus obligated, I worked the phones for a bit and met an old colleague for a late breakfast at the roadside joint on the fringe of Brockton Heights. Result? The Ox was not gainfully employed. He had a room with kitchen privileges just off the state highway, and so far as he went anywhere, he visited the two big casinos.

"A creature of habit," I told Edith. "Just an old guy passing the time."

"Did you get a look at him?"

I'm not good at lying to clients; I confessed I had not.

"Take a photo," she said. "I know he's been in town. I know it."

Why this was important, she did not tell me, but her checks were good and, as I didn't see another big job coming up any time soon, I spent a couple of uncomfortable days in my Jeep Cherokee keeping an eye on The Ox. Edith was right: He was an impressive specimen, six feet of heavy bone and muscle with a shaved head and the slightly pigeon-toed gait of a man who could move fast when he needed to.

He was alert too. Checking the area whenever he left his apartment, I swear he sensed me around because on the third day he departed from his usual route to the Mohegan Sun, his preferred casino, in what looked to me like an attempt to lose a tail. I let him think he'd succeeded. I had his routine down. I had photos, too, and as per instructions, I printed them out and took them to Edith.

She was interested in his trips to the casinos, the location of his apartment, and especially the fact that he liked to take a couple of beers and drink in the state park off Route 6. "And he shops here?" she asked.

"Yes. The market and the smoke shop."

She raised her eyebrows. The smoke shop is on Main Street, two blocks from Edith's house. "I knew it."

"He went straight back to the highway," I said, but when she pressed me, I had to admit that he had taken the longer route, which passed her street.

"Well," she said. "Thank you, Ray. Now about Mark Keane in Pawtucket. I think you should get me the same information."

I balked at this. I felt that I was exploiting a lonely old woman's fears.

"Please," she said. "You're the only one I can trust with this. I wouldn't know how to go about finding a reliable detective in Pawtucket."

I was not deceived by this show of helplessness, but if she was determined, I might as well get the profit. I said that I would start the next week when I had wrapped up some loose ends on other investigations. Edith said that would be fine; there was no immediate hurry.

Very good. It was actually two weeks later before I got up to Pawtucket, where Keane proved to be a regular at a shabby Irish pub near the ballpark. He was as thin as his former associate was muscular, with a hatchet face and a long, horsey jaw. Though he had a slight limp, he favored long walks, moving through town with a surprisingly rapid gait. He walked in the early morning and quite late at night. "An unquiet spirit," I told Edith, who nodded her head with what seemed to be satisfaction.

She took the information and thanked me. "You've been such a comfort."

"I'm sure you have nothing to worry about."

"Not anymore," she said.

Just over a week later, I picked up the morning paper. Here in the east, we don't get much coverage, but I like to keep an eye on the rascals in the legislature and to read the latest about the big college teams. The murder in Brockton Heights made the front page, just one column with the runover inside. I knew the face. Archie "The Ox" Shaunessy had been killed with a single shot while communing with nature at the state park. No details were forthcoming, but every sign was that this was a professional job, one of those belated hits that are a drawback of the mob life.

"A guy with plenty of old enemies," said my contact on the Brockton Heights force.

"I'd heard he was some scary guy," I said, but I really wished I had never asked any questions about Shaunessy, because now he said, "And your client? What exactly was his interest?"

"She. Her interest. A nervous old lady who reads too many crime novels," I said, and with a flash of inspiration, added, "I think she's going to try her hand at one herself."

"She sure picked a winner with Shaunessy. I tell you Ray, this is a case of addition by subtraction, if you know what I mean."

I did, but I'll admit I was not entirely easy, although Edith remained gracious, eccentric—and secretive. I turned to the Web, but there Edith Wing had stepped lightly. She was not on

Facebook, she didn't tweet, and as far as I knew she'd refused email and Tumblr and all the rest of the electronic time wasters.

No one else mentioned her either, except for our local mill preservation society, which listed her as a board member, and the website of the local diocese, which thanked her for the chairmanship of the annual rummage sale at St. Mary's. What she had done before she landed in our town was a closed book, and I soon realized she was not about to enlighten me, not when her worries seemed to have lifted. Except for the delivery of an excellent batch of fancy cookies around the holidays, I didn't hear from Edith for half a year.

As for her "old school friends," they were forgotten until the day Richard "Dicky Boy" Ahern had his demise splashed across the front page of every paper on the news rack. Ahern had been residing at the fed's expense for twenty years, but he'd maintained a long reach. Some said it extended from the federal pen at Otisville all the way to the backstreets of Boston where he'd been a mob kingpin since his early twenties.

The old monster died in his bed at eighty-three, which was more than you could say for his associates. The story provided a list of colorful names, stretching back to the "old days," including a few I recognized. Others, foot soldier casualties of more recent mob warfare, meant nothing to me until I came across Shaunessy and Mark Keane, the sallow-faced old crook who'd walked obsessively in Pawtucket. Shaunessy was old news, but Keane's death hadn't made our local papers. A little research in the Pawtucket *Times* and *The Providence Journal* revealed he'd also been a victim of what was termed a "mob style" hit, dispatched with a single shot as he walked home one night from his favorite watering hole.

That afternoon, I paid a visit to Edith Wing, carrying a copy of *The Boston Globe*. The *Globe* had done its native son proud, recounting his life from cradle on its mean streets to power and influence, before betrayal, incarceration, and death. Better than most novels, I had to say.

"Ray, how nice to see you."

Was it my imagination or did Edith look a decade younger? Certainly there was a spring in her step and a cheerful note in her voice that had not been there during the months—years, actually—that she'd been my client.

"Come in. It's been too long." She seemed completely at ease, adding, "Oh, you read the *Globe* too. I try for it at the gas station, but delivery's not reliable since the newsstand closed. A big loss."

She insisted on tea, apologizing that the cake was yesterday's. "I didn't expect you."

"No? I thought with the story this morning you might. I just learned about Mark Keane. You'd been concerned—for some reason."

She let that hang in the air.

"Ahern's life," I said after a moment. "An epic of massacres and assassinations."

"His reputation for ruthlessness was surely well known in law enforcement circles." Edith poured the tea, her hand steady.

"He might have been gunned down, too, had he not been in prison," I suggested.

"Very true. Odd how things work out. I suppose one could say his companion saved his life by turning him in. Of course, he'd betrayed her first—according to the story. The classic case of a younger, prettier woman."

"She disappeared, his longtime mistress, I mean. Vanished. Maybe into witness protection with a new identity?"

"She'd have needed to, wouldn't she?" Edith turned the paper that I'd set on the table and looked at the illustrations. "From what I read, Ahern would have murdered her in a heartbeat."

Her hand rested beside the big photo of "Dicky Boy" Ahern somewhere warm and fancy with Patricia Burns, his longtime companion. Ms. Burns looked svelte in a two-piece swimsuit with a wraparound skirt. She had a lot of fair hair above a wide forehead and even features. Not a beauty, exactly, but her firm chin and perfect posture suggested a strong and able character such as I'd come to know.

"He was residing at the fed's expense in Otisville, New York," I said.

"But according to the papers, he still had serious mob connections. I'd hate to think the *Globe* isn't strictly accurate."

"His connections, as you call them, have been decimated over the years."

She tapped the paper. "A costly division of the spoils, I'd imagine."

"Yet supposedly Ahern was calling the shots, even from his cell."

"Plenty violence to go around with one thing—and another." Her face hardened. "He would have died rather than concede defeat. And sacrificed his faithful lieutenants for his revenge. He had lines to corrupt officials, even within law enforcement, even within witness protection. You can take my word for that."

"Shaunessy and Keane?"

She hesitated before she said, "The last throw of the dice, so to speak."

"You could have moved on instead, Edith."

"I was tired of moving on." She paused and looked reflective. "In certain lives, the only dignity lies in loyalty and courage. If loyalty is lost—or rejected—courage is all that's left." She was silent for a moment, before she once again became the woman who made superior cakes and helped with church fundraisers. "Besides, I like Edith Wing, don't you? She is perhaps what I was meant to be."

I couldn't quite see that but I said, "Perhaps what you could have been—with other choices."

"Poor girls in South Boston didn't have many choices and few of those were good. But this is a fine place to be old. I'm here for the duration."

I could see that she meant every word.

"Don't feel too bad about your part—which you need to remember, Ray," she continued. "Questions are more likely to be asked about a private investigator, former cop, and crack shot than an elderly volunteer, aren't they? Besides, you're a public benefactor. Although you surely couldn't anticipate it, defeat most likely killed Richard Ahern."

I raised my eyebrows.

"He couldn't stand to lose. Not to anyone, especially not to a woman. I think losing one more time just finally stopped his heart."

"So this is the end?"

"I do believe so. The rest are sheep without a leader. But," she added, putting another slice of cake on my plate, "old habits can die hard. I'll keep an eye open, and I'll be sure to let you know if anyone suspicious turns up."

I always find the genesis of a story mysterious, but in the case of "The Client," I can point to two houses, both in an old mill town near where we live. The great water-powered textile and thread mills of eastern Connecticut created prosperity well into the twentieth century. Their loss brought hard times to the area and to Ray Wilde, the first professional detective I have written about since I ended the Anna Peters series.

Ray was actually devised for an anthology edited by Paul D. Marks, Coast to Coast, Private Eyes from Sea to Shining Sea. *Geographic* variety was imperative, and a little story-and-a-half house behind our bank's parking lot provided not only a venue for my half-formed plot but suggested a weary ex-cop sitting through a boring surveillance.

The resulting story was about mostly decent people caught in small crimes, and I figured one and done for Ray. Still, I liked his style and his turn of phrase, and another house, a large, imposing home gently going downhill, gave him a client.

Edith Wing, a courteous eccentric, pillar of the library board and the local church, is an unlikely person to lead Ray into deep water. He likes her and I like her too. Although the mystery genre may be kinder to older females than it used to be, women of a certain age are still usually victims or accessories if they appear at all. Edith Wing gave me an opportunity to create an intelligent, morally ambiguous character, an elderly woman who, as she puts it to Ray, knows that sometimes there are few good choices.

Dennis McFadden, *a retired project manager, lives and writes in a cedar-shingled cottage called Summerhill in the woods of upstate New York. His collection* Jimtown Road, *winner of the 2016 Press 53 Award for Short Fiction, was published in October of that year; his first collection,* Hart's Grove, *was published by Colgate University Press in 2010. His fiction has appeared in dozens of publications including* The Missouri Review, New England Review, The Sewanee Review, Crazyhorse, The Antioch Review, The Saturday Evening Post, Ellery Queen Mystery Magazine, Alfred Hitchcock Mystery Magazine, *and* The Best American Mystery Stories. *A Pushcart Prize nominee, he was awarded a Fellowship at the MacDowell Colony in 2018.*

THE TRUTH ABOUT LUCY

Dennis McFadden

This happened in Hartsgrove a long time ago. A middle-aged spinster by the name of Lucy Wilson was raped and murdered one night in the railyard signal tower at the edge of town where she worked all alone. A man named Oscar Huffman, stout as a bear but nowhere near as smart, was arrested and sent to the chair, although a good number of people believed his uncle, George, smaller, smarter, and greasier, was the real killer. That number included George's wife, Elsie. She ended up braining George with an iron skillet and running away a few years later with a barnstorming pilot who barnstormed right on out of the area and into history.

None of it would wash off George's and Elsie's son, Henry. It clung to him like a bad smell. Memories are long and suspicions run deep, and nearly sixty years later there were few of us old-timers in town who could look at Henry Huffman without a shiver, without feeling a creepy-crawly sense of bloody murder, of sudden, violent death in the middle of a lonely, black night. Poor Lucy. Poor Henry.

That wasn't even all of it. Henry's papa, George, ended up burning himself to death (or so it was ruled) a few years later in a house fire of suspicious origin. Around the same time, the only girl Henry Huffman had ever fallen for dropped him like a rotten spud the minute she found out his cousin, big, dumb Oscar, had been executed for the murder. The girl's name was Gracie Wolfgang. It turned out that Oscar's (or George's) victim, Lucy Wilson, was her dear auntie—small world! Gracie had come from out of town, the same as her Aunt Lucy had, and that was the reason she hadn't known it right from the get-go, like everybody else in town did. We almost felt sorry for Henry. Almost.

One thing we've learned, us old-timers, is that on your way to oblivion—or to heaven, as the hopeful souls among us like to think—you first have to pass through invisibility. You reach a certain age—not measured in years so much as in gray hair and age spots, turkey skin and wrinkles, loose flesh and a slower step—when the youngsters of the world no longer see you. When they look straight through you, like the ghost you're bound to soon become. Not so for Henry Huffman. Huffman was lucky, or unlucky, enough to skip the invisible stage on his way to oblivion. Word had been handed down from generation to generation, and he could never shake loose from the shadow of his family's reputation. Him, the young people of Hartsgrove could see. Him, they tried not to stare at.

When Henry Huffman wasn't taking long walks up and down
the hills of Hartsgrove in the early morning hours, or wasn't in
his basement tying flies, or out along the creeks and streams in
the deep woods using the flies he tied—he seemed to like to be
alone, mostly—he sometimes joined us for Bingo or canasta or
some other nonsense at the Harvest Senior Center, or a bus trip
down to a Pirates game, usually with his buddy, Earl Radaker.
Earl's wife, Gwenda, had passed away a few months before, and,
after Gracie'd taken off like a spooked colt, Henry'd never got
around to marrying. He wasn't a bad-looking guy; he'd stayed in
decent shape over the years. He had a head that protruded a bit
in back, and he kept his hair—still mostly red, sprinkled with
a little gray by now—close-cropped, a buzz cut, like he always
had. He had a habit of putting his hand on the back of his neck,
as if to rest his head—or, when he was walking around town,
like he was pulling himself forward to take another step, getting
himself through another mile, another day. Seldom did more pass
between us than a hello-how-are-you or two, the odd harmless
jibe, the usual complaints about bowels and bladders and joints
and hearts. We almost felt sorry for him, some of us did. We tried
to like him. But when you tried to make the connection, when
you tried to look into his eyes that were brittle and brown, there
was always something there that ran away. And if it wasn't Lucy
Wilson all battered and butchered up in that dark signal tower,
what else could it be?

Most of us have lived in Hartsgrove all our lives, and most of us
wouldn't have it any other way. It's a pretty, leafy little town on
seven rolling hills, and the pinks and blues of sunrise, the fog

lifting out of the trees on a far hillside, make a body as content as can be to live in this place at this time. Three creeks converge at the bottom of town where the ball fields sprawl out in the after-noon sun, and Main Street looks pretty much the same as it did a hundred years ago, although the horses, wagons, and buggies have been replaced by cars, trucks, and pickups. The stately red brick courthouse and its tall white dome with the four clocks on the four sides can be seen from just about anywhere in town. So can the hospital perched up on the highest hill, and the green steeple of the Catholic church like tarnished brass sitting high on a southside hill. It's not a place where crime feels at home. The streets are safe enough to stroll down in the light of the streetlamps and moon, or in the early morning hours. Every decade or two though, every generation or so, along comes a crime that makes you sit up and take notice, a crime like the killing of Lucy Wilson, to remind us that we're not, after all, immune. That they're still out there, even in small, pretty towns.

The murder of Lucy Wilson was one. What happened to Smokey Bowersox close to a half century later was another.

Smokey Bowersox was a piece of work, a big, ugly piece of work, drunken, cussing, brawling, barely smart enough, but plenty intimidating enough, to avoid jail for any long stretches. He was known to host the occasional flea infestation, and lice were pretty much in permanent residence. You didn't want to cross paths with him anywhere, in Jum's or any of the other bars and junkyards where he spent most of his time, but especially not out in the woods, hunting. Strange things have been known to happen in those hills. Bowersox was around when Lucy Wilson was killed, and it was him in fact that first gave the nickname *Killer George* to Henry Huffman's father, even before his nephew, Oscar, had been executed. Just to be mean. Just to cause trouble. But it caught on.

For years Bowersox got away with his bullying, until the day the woman he lived with figured enough was enough. That was Edna Harriger. She looked for all the world like Grimelda the Witch, and when she wasn't praying or chattering incoherently—often one and the same—she was cooking and baking. She was purt near as famous for her cooking as she was for her weird, witchy ways. One day when Smokey brought her home a little girl's pet cat to bake up in her leberkäse—she used all kinds of meats in her leberkäse—she decided to conk him over the head and bake him up in it instead. His just deserts, so to speak.

Quite a few folks in town got a taste of Bowersox before the main ingredient was found out. He actually didn't taste too bad. What finally tipped it off was when the fat banker, Alexander Fiscus, mentioned how smoky Edna's leberkäse tasted.

Edna's reward for her prize leberkäse recipe was a life of leisure in the loony bin up in Warren. She spent the rest of her days strolling the hallways and grounds, muttering for the most part, and praying, eyes often as not rolled halfway back up in her skull. They wouldn't let her near the kitchen, which, word had it, broke her heart. When she died a little while back, Edna's older brother called Sheriff Rote. The sheriff in turn called Chief Toole.

"Hey, Chief," Rote said. "I just got a call from Beesie Harriger."

"You mean D. W.?" His name was Garfield Abraham Harriger, but everybody knew him as D. W. Everybody except for the ones who called him Beesie.

"Beesie—lives out there in the woods above Jimtown Road. Edna Harriger's brother."

"Yeah. That's old D. W. What'd he want?"

"You knew his sister, Edna, passed away up there in Warren?"

"I did. Yep. A mercy."

"Seems he was going through some of her things and he found a box with Smokey Bowersox's name on it."

"The hell you say."

"Yeah. Says there's something in it we ought to see."

"*We*? Or you? He called you up, didn't he?"

"Yeah, but Smokey Bowersox and Edna—figure it probably has something to do with her cooking him up in that pie, and that was on your patch."

"That wasn't no pie, it was more like a meatloaf. That was quite a while back."

"I figured you'd want to have a look."

Chief Toole thought it over. He was one of us, an old-timer. He was tired, about ready to hang 'em up, but this one took him back and made him perk his ears up. He could still taste the smoky flavor of Edna's prize leberkäse on a corner of his tongue. It was never going to go away. "The hell you say."

Garfield Abraham D. W. Beesie Harriger was a hermit. He lived alone in a little shack with a rusty tin roof and warped green shingles the color of moss deep in the woods north of town. He must have been near eighty but still ran a string of traps and hunted and planted a few tomatoes. He had the odd visitor now and then, an old hunter or fisherman, and he made the occasional trek into town. It wasn't so much he disliked people, just that he never had much use for them. He kept dogs, he'd always kept dogs, two or three or four at a time—them, he had use for. He always kept them a little bit hungry. He figured it kept them more on edge, which was good in case of a bear or other trespasser with bad intentions, but there was more to his fancy plan than that: He didn't like the idea of keeling over dead some day and laying there rotting, stinking up the place to high heaven, so he figured his dogs would do what there was no undertaker there to do, dispose of his body for him by eating him and shitting him back into the dirt. To him, it was just another version of dust to dust.

When Hiram Mackey, one of his rare visitors, asked him what would happen if he was just incapacitated but still alive, that gave old Beesie some pause. But it didn't make him change his plan any.

Chief Toole and Sheriff Rote took along a couple of men. They weren't too leery about old Beesie himself, but the dogs were another story. Beesie greeted them at the door of his shack. He only had a little hair left, but it was on its own, wisps and strands sticking out this way and that, and his bony, spotted forehead glowered over the caves of his eyes. "Don't pay 'em no mind," he said as the men approached through the trees and over the fallen logs. The dogs were barking and snarling, but keeping an eye on Beesie, too, and keeping their distance.

"What do you got for us, Beesie?" Chief Toole said. Toole, his Clark Gable mustache all gone to gray and scraggle now, his jowls all droopy and spotted, was the closest to Harriger's age, and he knew him some, so he took the lead. Sheriff Rote, young, polished, and cocky, looked like he didn't belong in any woods. Young folks nowadays, all of them hardly ever look like they belong in any woods.

"In here," Beesie said. On the floor of the shack—it was hard to tell whether it was a dirt floor or a board floor caked with dirt—by the rough wood table sat a cardboard box that was falling apart. There were three or four other boxes like it, but this was the only one had *Smokey's* scrawled on it. "In there."

"Check it out," the chief said to Rote, nodding toward the box.

"I ain't sticking my hand in there," Rote said. "You check it out."

"Deemer," called Toole to one of his officers. "See what's in that there box."

Officer Deemer, a little fellow who was used to being picked on, stepped up, sighed, shook his head, and knelt down in front of the box. He hesitated. "What am I looking for?" he said.

"A big glass doohickey," Beesie said.

Deemer groped his hand in holding his breath as though he was performing an autopsy, and pulled out something blue. He held it up. It was glass. It was big and heavy, a deep, dark blue color, murky with age. "Appears to be an old inkwell," he said.

"What the hell's an inkwell doing in Smokey's stuff?" said Toole. "I didn't think that dumb bastard could read, let alone write."

All Rote could do was shrug. He only barely remembered the adventures of Edna and Smokey, what he'd read in the papers well over a decade before.

Beesie's glowering brow took a dark turn. "None of you fellas remember when that woman was killed up there in the railroad signal tower? Back around '35, '36, around in there?"

"Can't say as I do," Rote said, "but I wasn't even a gleam in my daddy's eye back then."

Toole, however, the old man, was nodding, rousting old memories.

"Lucy Wilson, I think her name was," Beesie said. "They nabbed a fella name of Oscar Huffman, sent him to the chair for it." Toole remembered. He'd barely been born when it happened, but he remembered the talk through much of his young life, hell, through all of his life—they still talked now and then about Hartsgrove's Crime of the Century. Toole was impressed by Beesie's memory. The old man's mind was still sharp as the claws in his traps.

"Yeah," Tool said, "It was Lucy Wilson." Then he looked at the blue inkwell on the table where Deemer had dropped it like a petrified turd. "What the hell's that got to do with this?"

"Shit," Beesie said, "why you boys is even dumber'n you look, the whole pack of you. Ain't you supposed to be coppers? Ain't you supposed to be able to put two and two together and solve a crime when a body hands you a goddam clue?" Toole and Rote and Deemer just looked at one another and frowned and looked back at Beesie. The deputies and officers in the doorway outside the cabin looked away and whistled.

"The murder weapon up there at the signal tower," Beesie said. "They figured it was a blue glass inkwell that was missing from off of her desk. They never did find the damn thing."

Beesie glowered at the men, one after the other, then he glowered at the inkwell. "Not until now, they didn't," he said.

The Harvest Senior Center was, fittingly enough, in an old sagging building with a swayback roof that used to be a grocery store back before it went bust. It was down at the bottom of town near the ball fields, past Proud Judy's Bar and Dan Tucker's Candies and Ice Cream. The Senior Center was packed to the gills at the potluck lunch that Wednesday. It was probably twice as many people as what normally showed up, an even bigger turnout than the Fourth of July square dance. Even though that shindig was over two months before, the crepe paper was still up, red, white, and blue. Buzz about Smokey Bowersox and Lucy Wilson and the Huffman family, the old murder up at the signal tower way back when, had lit a fire. We had to bring out extra chairs and tables from the back room.

"Don't eat the meatloaf!" That was Charlie Waters. Waters was a loudmouth and his little joke took some of us a while to get—the thinking caps don't fit quite as snug as they used to—before we connected the dots from the meatloaf to Edna Harriger's leberkäse. Charlie Waters wasn't by any stretch the first man to make a smoky meatloaf joke, but he might have taken more satisfaction in it than most, since Smokey Bowersox had beat him up, damn near killed him, not too long before he up and got himself baked. Hattie Hetrick, though, didn't get it. It was her meatloaf. She took some offense and asked her husband, Harvey, what was the matter with it. Harvey just shook his head and patted her hand.

"I ain't the least bit surprised," Annie Westphall said. "I remember a story about him groping and grabbing this waitress out at Vowinkle—oh, what was her name?"

"Vowinkle used to have some damn good fish fries," said Chet Emerick.

"I don't believe she was the only one, either," Elva Plotner said. "Women were afraid to say anything back in those days." Her husband, Jacey, a grizzled old ball player, was there too, much to everyone's surprise, but he didn't say anything. He never said much. Matter of fact, he hardly ever came out at all, but we figured the lure of the gossip was too strong.

"Heck, a lot of 'em still are," said Harvey Hetrick.

"You should have seen the bruises on poor Edna," said Myrna Sayers. She lived near the old witch's haunted house. "Every day she seemed to be sporting some new ones. I couldn't hardly blame her a bit for what she done."

Ron Bullers said, "You know he tried to get on with the Shawmut, but they wouldn't hire him. They didn't want nothing to do with him. He had a reputation even way back then."

"I remember when he beat up the brakeman up there, I forget his name." That was Earl Radaker. "Wonder if it might've had something to do with that, with him not getting on."

"I ain't the least bit surprised," Joe Milliron said.

"Who brought this succotash?" said Chet Emerick.

There was more talking than eating going on. A lot of the dishes still had the tin foil on the top. The chatter put you in mind of the low rumble you used to get up in the Moonlight Roller Rink, and you couldn't hardly hear the music from the record player up front. Sinatra mostly, a little Bing Crosby. Most of it was about what they'd found out, what Chief Toole had told the paper. Turned out the fingerprints on the inkwell matched the other fingerprints they found in the box, on the boots and the belt and the billfold and the belt buckle. Turned out the tiny trace of blood you couldn't even hardly see deep in the chipped corner of the inkwell was the same type as Lucy Wilson's. It was all gift-wrapped with a pretty white bow.

Smokey Bowersox was the son of a bitch that killed Lucy Wilson.

It wasn't Oscar Huffman. It sure wasn't George either. Sure as hell was Oscar that got fried for it, though. That was sinking in. That, and that it was Henry Huffman who bore the brunt of it down through all the years ever since.

"Oh, Lordy, Lordy," said Annie Westphall, "that poor man."

"Which one? Oscar or George?"

"Or Henry?"

"Well she sure as hell ain't talking about Smokey."

"Why, yes, the Huffmans. All three of them, I suppose."

There was an awful lot of headshaking going on. We knew Earl Radaker was as close to Henry Huffman as anybody, probably the only buddy he had. Ron Bullers said, "Hey, Earl—you know if Huffman heard about it yet?"

Radaker had his mouth full. "Yep," he said, "I stopped on up to see him. He wasn't too impressed. Said what difference does it make. Said it's all water over the dam bridge."

"You should've asked him to come on down."

"I did. He said he'd sooner go fishing."

It was quiet for a minute while everybody felt bad for poor Henry.

"I wonder if there's anything he can do about it," Milliron said. "His cousin getting fried for something he didn't even do."

"He ought to be able to sue 'em," Jacey Plotner said. That caused a few double takes, not on account of what he said, but on account of he said anything. Jacey hardly ever said two words.

"And everybody blaming his dad. And him wearing it like a crown of thorns."

"Wasn't him that got electrocuted, though. His cousin—I don't even think they consider that immediate family."

Earl Radaker said, "Hey, Elva—what was the name of that girl?"

"You mean Gracie?" Elva Plotner said. "Gracie Wolfgang?"

"Yeah, that was her. She still alive, I wonder? Wonder if she heard about it?"

"We still exchange Christmas cards," Elva said. "I'll make sure she knows."

"He was crazy about her," Radaker said. "Only woman he was ever crazy about."

It was quiet then as it settled in, just silverware clinking on china, the groaning and creaking of tables and chairs, and underneath it all, from up front, Sinatra singing "I'll Never Smile Again" from fifty years ago.

⌀

Just after Radaker's wife, Gwenda, died here a few months back, Henry Huffman went up to see him. It was early. Radaker was always an early riser anyhow, in the building business, and so was Huffman. Every now and then, in the early morning light, we'd look out our window over the first cup of coffee and see Huffman walking by. He liked to get out early to enjoy the fresh air before everybody else used it all up.

Huffman told him he was sorry he didn't make it up to the funeral. Radaker put the posies he'd brought in an old jelly jar with some water, poured them a cup of coffee, and they sat down at the kitchen table and looked out the window at the big maple in the yard where he'd made a tree house once for his stepdaughter. The sun was just peeping up, and the morning shadows stretched across the dewy lawn. Huffman told him he was real sorry about Gwenda.

"You know what they say," Radaker said. "Only the good die young."

Gwenda was a good ten years younger than him. Fit as a fiddle too, or so everybody thought right up till the minute she dropped a carton of eggs on the floor in the middle of the Golden Dawn Supermarket, then dropped dead right on top of them. Aneurysm, they said. "I guess," said Huffman. "Or only the lucky."

They'd been friends over forty years. Exactly how they'd managed that nobody knew for sure, since Huffman really didn't have another friend, but it might have had something to do with their parents, or lack of them. They had that in common. Radaker's had taken off on him when he was little and left his Uncle Shorty to raise him, and Huffman's parents—well, we all knew about them, about Elsie bashing George with a frying pan after his nephew had been fried for killing Lucy Wilson. Then running off with that barnstorming pilot. Back in the day, Radaker and Huffman used to hang out, have lunch together, a beer after work, shoot the breeze, damn near every day, but after Radaker got married

(Huffman never did, after Gracie flew the coop), they didn't get together near as often, even less the older they got. But when they did, it was like they never left off. Radaker said, "Like your cousin Oscar? Was he one of the lucky ones?"

"Maybe," Huffman said. "Apparently he wasn't one of the good ones."

Radaker shrugged. "Me, I'd rather be lucky than good."

"Well, looks like you ain't either. You're still alive and kicking."

"Alive, I guess. Ain't too sure about the kicking."

Huffman took a sip of his coffee, made a sour face. "I remember squabbling over comic books with him when I was little. Joe Palooka was his favorite. I still got 'em—that's all they sent us after they executed him—just his comic books."

"Maybe be worth some money someday," Radaker said.

Huffman still lived in the house up on Hastings Street not far from the old railyard where he'd shared a room with his cousin Oscar right up till the day they took him away for the murder. The same house where he stayed with his addled father, minded him, changed his dirty pants, after his mother had run off. The same house a fire burned down with his father inside it, a fire they figured he must have started himself by accident. They had no proof of anything else. Huffman had it rebuilt with the insurance money, and moved back in as quick as he could. Why, we couldn't figure. Why he'd want to live back there, after all that had happened, none of us was ever too sure about. He was still looking out the window at the tree house tree and shaking his head. "I could never fathom how a man whose greatest passion in life was Joe Palooka and Fritzi Ritz could take and bludgeon a woman to death. He was always so careful not to wrinkle the pages."

Turned out he was right, of course, his cousin Oscar never did bludgeon anybody to death, as we found out a few months later with the blue inkwell and all. When we found out it was Smokey Bowersox who'd killed her all along. But at the time all Radaker said was, "Let's go up to the graveyard. I want to show you where I buried her at. It's a real nice spot."

The cemetery is on top of a hill on the north side of town, and from where they'd laid Gwenda to rest you could look out across and see the steeple of St. Mary's poking up out of the trees on the one hill, and the hospital perched on the top of another. Radaker pulled over to the side of the dirt drive, under the branches of a big old shade tree, and they walked across toward Gwenda's plot. The dew on the long grass soaked Radaker's boots and Huffman's sneakers. Birds were fussing and chirping and flitting about from one tree to the other, none too happy about the intruders. It was early, and they were surprised to see someone across the way, Myrna Sayers, visiting her parents' grave. They gave her a wave, but she never looked up, her head bowed down.

"I sometimes wonder where my parents ever ended up buried," Radaker said.

Huffman didn't have anything to say to that.

Radaker said, "You ever wonder where your mum's buried at?"

Huffman shook his head. "Naw," he said, "I don't. I buried her a long time ago."

"You done what?"

Huffman looked at his friend like he was just a little bit surprised. "In my head, Earl. In my head, she's dead and buried."

Radaker nodded in relief. "Probably ain't the only place," he said.

When they got to Gwenda's plot, they took deep breaths and stared down at the stone. Myrna Sayers had disappeared from sight, but the flittering, chirping birds were just as suspicious as ever. Huffman shook his head and sighed again and said, "That's just not right."

"You know what they say," Radaker said. "Here today, there tomorrow."

Two names were carved into the fancy stone, three years: *Gwenda Radaker / 1941–1995* and *Earl Radaker / 1930 –*. Huffman pointed at the stone. "Lookee there—you're missing a date. You ought to go and get your money back."

"I was going to have 'em go ahead and put it on," Radaker said. "I was thinking *2036*."

"Yep," Huffman said. "Only the good die young." Radaker had a chuckle.

They looked up and all around the graveyard and Huffman put his hand up to the back of his neck. A blue bird with yellow wings fluttered down to a nearby limb that was bright in the morning sunlight and chirped straight at them. The fussing of the other birds had settled down to a regular melody. "Sure is pretty up here, anyways," Radaker said.

On a rise a little ways off, three big, black crows thudded down to strut among the stones like soldiers, cawing at the top of their lungs, like bullies and braggarts. "Listen to them," said Huffman, nodding, "look at 'em—nothing pretty about that."

"Sure there is," Radaker said, "if you don't take it personal."

"That's your wife laying there. You can't help but take it personal."

Radaker let that sink in, looking back down at the stone. He wasn't convinced. "Some leafs fall off the tree in September," he said, "some of 'em hold on all winter long."

"So what? They're dead on the limb already. They're dead the minute they're born."

Radaker looked over. Huffman's face was clenched up like a fist, angry, sure, but he couldn't be sure he didn't see a tear in there too. He went over to him. Huffman looked away from Gwenda's marker, away from Radaker, who put his arm on his friend's back, his hand on the back of his neck so he wouldn't have to. In forty years they'd hardly ever touched. Huffman took a deep breath and held it, and they looked down across the town to where the church steeple was poking up through the trees like the blade of a knife.

Turned out Gracie Wolfgang had her own tale of woe, damn near as bad as what Henry Huffman had lived through. Some folks had to shake their heads, tisk, tisk, tisk, and whisper about star-crossed lovers and the like, about being born under some kind of a hex sign. They wondered why does God forsake some of his children while he so richly blesses others, and not always the most deserving ones at that. Some just chalked it up to dumb luck. Some figured they must have had it coming, Henry and Gracie. They must have somehow got what they deserved.

Elva Plotner dropped Gracie a note and then drove on down to Cranberry to see her. A pretty long haul for a woman pushing eighty, but she didn't want to just call her up on the phone, not with news like that. She'd been Gracie's only friend in town—they were both nurses up at the hospital at the time—the one Gracie confided in during her short spell in Hartsgrove. The one she told about her crush on Henry Huffman, the one she revealed her horror to after she found out his cousin had murdered her aunt. The only one she said goodbye to. Elva and her had kept in touch a little, but the Christmas cards had tailed off over the years.

They met at a little lunch counter in an old storefront on Cranberry's broad Main Street. Gracie was a good bit younger than she was, and Elva was bothered by how old she looked—the years hadn't been very kind to her. She was still tall, but her shoulders weren't back near as far as they used to be, her back was a little bit stooped, and her beautiful black hair was turning a dusty color of gray. When they hugged—Elva had to reach up, she was so much shorter—Elva thought she felt almost fragile. That surprised her, worried her. Wasn't until later we found out Gracie was suffering from a bad heart.

"My goodness," Elva said through a great big smile. "Look at you!"

"Yes," said Gracie. She was smiling too, but kept her teeth hid. "Look at me."

They sat in a wood booth that was probably as old as Elva. Over the years kids had carved their initials in it and hearts and such. There was a high tin ceiling and the light coming in through the windows in front threw shadows across the scuffed white tiles on the floor. Elva was hungry and ordered a grilled cheese and tomato sandwich and a cup of coffee. Gracie just got hot tea. They talked and talked, or at least Elva did, at first. She wanted to blurt right out with the news about Henry Huffman and Smokey Bowersox and how Henry's cousin had been put to death for a crime he didn't commit, but she decided to wait a little, hold it back till they caught up on everything else. Such big news.

Elva knew Gracie'd never married after she left Hartsgrove, but she had a son not long afterwards. Elva couldn't be sure what kind of eggshells she might be tromping on. There'd been pictures of the little boy in the earlier Christmas cards, a note or two about him, but that all stopped a while back, about the same time Gracie quit reaching out to Elva much at all. But what it came down to was this: Elva figured Henry Huffman had to be the only man she ever really fell for. She remembered the glow on Gracie's face, a once-in-a-lifetime glow, talking about him way back then. And when she gave birth just a year or two after she left town, it was proof enough, in Elva's mind, of a broken heart and an unhappy rebound.

Elva told her about Jacey (just as quiet and stubborn as ever) and about her son, Jimmy (doing fine in upstate New York). "He comes down to see us almost every month," Elva said. "You ought to see his granddaughter, Emma—she's just the cutest little thing."

Gracie didn't say anything. She tried to smile sweetly, but it came out kind of sour.

"How's your boy?" Elva said. "I haven't heard much about him in a while. What was his name? Luke?"

"Yes, Luke." Gracie's face was pale and drawn, like old parchment paper. "He's dead."

"Oh, how awful! How? What happened?"

"He got killed," Gracie said.

He'd been found in his girlfriend's apartment, his head bashed in—right about here, Elva started getting a sense of déjà vu, once removed. Luke's girlfriend, a waitress, was arrested and tried for the crime, but she was turned loose when her alibi seemed to hold up.

"I'm so sorry," Elva said. "I can't even imagine—first your Aunt Lucy, then your son."

Gracie sighed, gave her head a little shake, and took a sip of her tea. "Some people just have all the luck," she said.

Some folks might have been at a loss for words, but not Elva. Elva never was. "Well, I have some news," she said, "It's about Oscar Huffman. And about Henry, too, for that matter."

Henry's cousin Oscar had not killed Gracie's aunt, Lucy Wilson. It had been another man, a man named Smokey Bowersox. She doubted Gracie even remembered who he was.

She told her about Edna and Beesie Harriger and the blue inkwell, all about Smokey Bowersox. About the rest of it, too, things Gracie already knew about, if she remembered, about poor George, *Killer George*, about his wife running off and leaving him with the addled brain she'd inflicted, all on account of Oscar and Lucy Wilson, and about Henry having to live his whole life with the stain of it all over him. All of it so unfair, so undeserved. Poor Henry.

While she was listening, Gracie's face started to change. The color came back. She seemed to come alive again. When Elva was coming to the end of her story, the questions started tumbling out of Gracie. *How did Henry take the news? What did Henry have to say?* Elva told her she couldn't say for sure. Earl Radaker—did she remember him?—he's the one who told Henry, and all he said was Henry didn't seem too excited about it. She didn't tell Gracie that it seemed to her—it seemed to all of us—that Henry didn't seem to much care. It was almost like he'd given up.

Gracie had another question, but she didn't ask it at first. Instead she asked how Henry was after all these years. *He must be, what, close to seventy by now? Is he still working in that women's clothing store, oh what was the name of it? Is he still living in the same house? Did he rebuild it after the fire?* Elva told her no, he left Siebert's a long time ago, worked for the county, or the state, maybe it was DMV, for a lot of years before he retired. Yes, he still lived in the same house, up on Hastings Street. He had it rebuilt.

Then Gracie held her breath like somebody tiptoeing up to the edge of a high cliff. *Did he ever get married?* she said. *Does he ever talk about me?*

⁕

Before she passed away, Lulu Hidinger used to say Elva Plotner, her neighbor up in the Queen Anne Apartments, was never at home because she was always out somewhere building up her obituary. Besides being a Senior Warden in her church, Elva was also the Senior Citizens Advocate to the Hartsgrove Borough Council, real active in her bowling league, and a member of the VFW Ladies' Auxiliary. Just the opposite of her husband, Jacey, maybe figuring she ought to make up for what he lacked in sociability. She was also President of the Senior Citizens Association of Hartsgrove and it was mostly that bunch of us who got together and decided we ought to do something for Henry Huffman. After everything he'd been through, the injustice him and his family had suffered, we figured the town owed him something.

Huffman Family Day was what we came up with. None of us felt any real personal responsibility for what had happened to Oscar Huffman—that was all our parents' generation's doing—but we figured we ought to at least try and clean up some of their mess. None of us figured they did it on purpose, but we figured they weren't real diligent either. Blaming an innocent man, the first dumb palooka they came across—the Huffmans being German probably didn't help, being between the wars and all—and letting the real killer keep on swaggering and bullying and terrorizing folks around town for another fifty years ought not to have happened. Something ought to be done. We got to work. Elva and Annie Westphall talked to the Mayor and went before the Borough Council and got them on board. Ron Bullers got Buster Clover aside up at the Rod and Gun Club and talked him into running a piece in the paper—Clover ran the *Hartsgrove Herald*. Everybody pitched in, even if it was only tearing down the old red, white, and blue crepe paper in the Harvest Senior Center, and putting up new decorations, maroon and black, maroon being one of the school colors. We picked a date a month off, in early October. Buster Clover got a picture of Oscar Huffman from the front page of the paper in 1936, taken the day they arrested him, and we got it blown up to poster size. We worked with the Mayor on his Proclamation of Huffman Family Day, and helped the Borough Council draft a Resolution with a bunch of whereases and therefores and resolved-that's declaring Oscar Huffman was an innocent man unjustly put to death. Joe Milliron talked to his old hunting buddy, Harry Jameson, Esq., who'd been Borough Attorney for a number of years, about going down to the Court House and filing a brief, or whatever they call those things, whatever it was they needed to go about getting a posthumous pardon for Oscar Huffman.

We were all set. Now the tricky part would be to get Henry Huffman to show up. And Gracie too.

Earl Radaker wasn't so sure Huffman would go for it. He'd been a loner so long, an outcast, he couldn't picture him being the center of attention, let alone guest of honor, at least not willingly. It seemed like something Huffman would shy away from.

As for Gracie, well, Elva was working on her. She called her up a couple of times to tell her what we were planning. Gracie was real interested. She was nibbling, Elva said, but whether or not she'd be able to reel her in was another story.

In the end it didn't work out as good as we hoped.

Gracie wouldn't come. She just couldn't face Henry after what she'd done to him, she told Elva, especially not after so much time had passed, after forty years. She'd like to see Henry again, she was curious as all get-out, but what if he just took one look at her and turned around and walked away? Would he even recognize her, she'd got so old? Did he even remember her? A lot of water had gone under the bridge. There was more than one of us who'd fallen in and out of love a few times in the last forty years, some of us who'd fallen out of love and never back in it again. Wasn't life like that? What were the odds they'd still be crazy about each other, that they could pick right up where they left off? Some of the more hopeful souls among us liked to think it might happen that way, but for the most part we knew real life was not like any fairy tale. Happy-ever-afters are damn scarce.

In the end we didn't even get a chance to see.

Neither one of them showed. Radaker went up to his place the day before Huffman Family Day to try to talk him into it one last time, at least to get an answer out of him one way or another. When he didn't answer the door, Radaker walked right on in, headed down to the cellar where Huffman was busy tying his flies. Huffman looked up from his table and vise, looked up at his friend with a not real friendly look, magnified by the glass he was wearing over his eye to tie the tiny threads. Radaker knew he didn't especially like him coming down to his cellar—he figured he was real fussy about his fly-tying setup, the way he had everything all neat and laid out right where he wanted it—but he needed to get an answer. We were putting a lot of pressure on him to get one.

Huffman said, "I'm not going."

"Why not?" said Radaker.

"Let's go upstairs," Huffman said. Radaker was fine with that. It was dark in the cellar and the air tasted like it had already been breathed in and out over and over. The cement floor was always cold, and the curtains on the windows up high on the walls, just under the low ceiling, heavy, dark curtains, were always drawn tight. The only light was the bright splash on the table from the gooseneck lamp over the vise.

Upstairs in the kitchen, Huffman said, "I'll tell you what—you tell 'em if they can get Oscar there, I'll come too. He's the one they owe."

"That ain't real likely."

"Then it ain't real likely I'll go either. It's *not* real likely."

"They'd sure like to see you. *We'd* sure like to see you."

"You want a cup of coffee?" Huffman said, but Radaker didn't smell any coffee brewing. "Listen, I know they mean well—you all mean well—but I just can't quite see it. They're just trying to ease their guilty consciences over what happened to Oscar."

"You ask me, I think you ought to forgive and just let live."

"Easier said than done." Huffman put his hand on the back of his head. "All their lives most of those folks can't look at me without looking like they're biting into a lemon. And now they want to kiss and make up like nothing ever happened. I don't think so."

"Did you know Elva's been in touch with Gracie Wolfgang? Your old flame?"

That caught his attention. "No. Is that right?"

"Yep. Told her all about it. About Smokey Bowersox and about poor old Oscar going to the chair for something he never done. She told her about the shindig we been planning, too, trying to talk her into coming up for it."

"And is she? Coming up for it?"

Radaker swallowed hard, wishing he could backtrack, realizing he'd dug the hole deeper. "I ain't exactly sure."

Huffman leveled his gaze. "You're not prevaricating here, are you, Earl?"

"I sure hope not. I just got my blood pressure checked."

"She's not coming up, is she?"

"I don't think Elva quite got her talked her into it. Yet."

"Well there you go," Huffman said.

⚬━⚬

Huffman Family Day at the Harvest Senior Center was somber if not downright glum. It was supposed to be somber anyways,

commemorating a grave miscarriage of justice, but it was supposed
to be a feel-good kind of thing, too, recognizing the injustice
for what it was, putting it on the record, trying to do something
toward setting it right. The feel-good part was missing. We've had
more people than what showed up that evening show up for the
potluck lunches, and the Mayor, who doesn't exactly socialize with
the likes of us anyway, looked around the room like he smelled
a gas leak, read his Proclamation, and got the hell out of Dodge.
Elva Plotner read the Borough Council's Resolution herself, and
Harry Jameson got up and said he'd filed a writ or some such of
a thing down at the Court House to try and get that posthumous
pardon for Oscar Huffman rolling. Big, dumb Oscar Huffman
himself stared out over the room in his bib overalls, a lost look on
his face, wondering what the hell was going on, just like he did
on the day he was arrested, the day the picture was taken. Earl
Radaker stood up and showed everybody the fancy new Orvis
rod and reel we pitched in and bought for Henry, said he'd take
it up and give it to him tomorrow morning, while Buster Clover
snapped a bunch of pictures for the paper. A lot of us couldn't help
but wonder what it might have been like if Huffman and Gracie
had showed up, if there mightn't have been a little less gloom,
maybe even a little magic. Then somebody turned on the record
player and put on a Bette Midler record, and everybody sat down
and had some coffee and pie.

⚬━━━⚬

Clover's story ran the next Thursday, and we figured that was probably pretty much the end of it. Most of us figured we'd be dead
before Oscar Huffman's pardon ever came through, if it ever did
at all, and we wondered if it made any damn difference anyways.

He'd still be just as dead. The town settled back down to its normal sleepy ways, and chatter about the Huffmans—Oscar, George, Henry—and Gracie Wolfgang began to die out, and the mother in the picture, Elsie Huffman, who'd run away all those years before, who was all but forgot about in the first place, drifted even further away with all the rest of it. That came to an abrupt end a couple of months later—it was a little bit before Christmas—when a hot spot flared up. The hot spot flared up when Elva Plotner spotted Gracie Wolfgang in the Golden Dawn Supermarket. She was there shopping for her groceries with Henry Huffman.

Huffman had reached out to her, and they'd got back together on their own.

Elva and Gracie hugged. Elva scolded her for not letting her know. Gracie said she was sorry, she just hadn't had the time, it was a whirlwind, and at her age—they'd just got hitched and she was still moving her things up from Cranberry. Elva thought she looked as happy as she could be—but at the same time she looked paler and frailer than ever. She was walking with a cane. Earl Radaker didn't know about them getting together either. They'd kept it to themselves. Radaker found out about it when he stopped up one afternoon with a box of chocolate chip cookies he'd bought—it was buy one, get one free—that he thought Huffman might be able to put to good use. Gracie answered the damn door.

For a while then, through most of the winter anyhow, a lot of the chatter at the Harvest Senior Center—all around town, for that matter—was about Huffman and Gracie sightings. There was a little bit of magic after all, especially there around Christmas time. A couple of us invited them to stop down and join us at the senior center, and they said they would, but they never did get around to it. For a while Gracie went out a few times in the early morning with Huffman on his walks, but the walks were a lot shorter and slower—Gracie with her cane—and then the big snows came, and by spring the walks had stopped altogether. By spring he was pushing her around in a wheelchair, Huffman was, when they ever got around at all.

Then came another fire. The morning of the Fourth of July, Independence Day, in the middle of the night, Huffman's house up on Hastings went up in flames again, same as it had forty years before. That time it had killed George. This time it killed his son, Henry. Smoke inhalation, the coroner said. Gracie's body was found snuggled up next to Henry's, but she was already dead—heart failure—before the fire ever got started. How it got started they couldn't say for sure, but of course we all knew.

Huffman left a will. He'd gone down to a firm in Pittsburgh to have it made out. In it were real plain and simple instructions to dig up the floor in his cellar and it even said exactly where to dig, right underneath his fly-tying table. Then, in the next paragraph, it said he wanted his mother buried in the plot that he'd bought a long time ago, the plot right next to his. That big-city lawyer down in Pittsburgh had no way of knowing of course that the two paragraphs were related. He might have wondered why the damn fool would want to go and have his cellar floor dug up after he was dead—maybe he figured there was buried treasure there or something—but he had no way of knowing that the buried treasure was his mother's bones, the bones he wanted buried next to his.

How'd she get there in the first place? When? The coroner said it was probably around the time she disappeared. Didn't take no

genius to figure out ol' Ace Barnini—that was the barnstorming
pilot's name—didn't have nothing to do with it. Only two people
who could have: George Huffman—all of sudden his old nickname, *Killer George*, took on a whole new light—or his boy, Henry.
Or maybe the both of them.

A lot of people got to feeling put out. They got to feeling they'd
been snookered. Maybe it wasn't no Huffman that killed Lucy
Wilson, but it sure as hell was one that killed Elsie. Coroner said
she'd died of a blow to the skull. The kind of blow an iron skillet
would make.

Huffman Damn Family Day.

---

* *The nineteen stories that make up my two published collections,* Jimtown Road *and* Hart's Grove, *are set in the fictional western Pennsylvania town of Hartsgrove (based on my hometown, Brookville) and
are interrelated. Each collection is a novel-in-stories. While* Hart's
Grove *revealed the circumstances surrounding the mysterious disappearance and murder of a popular high school cheerleader,* Jimtown
Road *unveiled the fate of two little girls who vanished into the woods,
never to be seen again.*

Why stop there? A third collection didn't seem like such a bad idea.

This collection (working title: The Signal Tower: A Mystery in
Stories) *consists of ten additional interrelated tales (also set in Hartsgrove, and also linked, in many instances, to the stories in the first two
collections) that unravel Hartsgrove's "crime of the century," the rape
and murder of a middle-aged lady in an isolated railroad yard, and all
that was left in its wake. "The Truth About Lucy" is the tenth and final
installment of that new collection and, being equally a final chapter
and a stand-alone story, it presented unique advantages and challenges
different from the normal process of crafting short fiction.*

On the one hand, most of the heavy lifting that goes into character-ization, the creating of living, breathing people, was already done—all the Huffmans (Henry, George, Elsie, and Oscar), Elva Plotner, Earl Radaker, Gracie Wolfgang, Smokey Bowersox, Edna Harriger, nearly all the characters with a speaking role in "The Truth About Lucy" (and even a few of the cameos) were already alive and kicking, inhabiting the previous nine stories. About all that was left was to invent a Greek chorus of old fogies to keep an eye on the fresh goings-on.

On the other hand, the storyline was a bit trickier. After all, these folks weren't just sitting on their hands in the earlier stories, twiddling their thumbs and whistling "Dixie." They were up to their ears, acting and reacting, scheming and plotting, loving and living. In those earlier stories, Lucy was murdered and Oscar was arrested and walked his last mile; Elsie brained George with an iron skillet and split for parts unknown; the star-crossed love affair of Henry and Gracie went down in flames; Smokey got himself baked in a meatloaf by Edna, and passed all around. All manner of assorted vicissitudes took place. This all had to be accounted for in the grand finale. Not only accounted for, but woven into a neat little tapestry and hung on the wall.

Moreover, the mystery that was hatched in story number one, the mystery that shouted and whispered and tiptoed and barged and stalked and lurked here and there, behind this corner and that, down through all the subsequent tales, had to be resolved in "The Truth About Lucy." It was a lot of fun. I'm thinking about a fourth.

David Marcum *is the author of nearly eighty published Sherlockian pastiches, appearing in various anthologies, magazines, and his own books, which include* The Papers of Sherlock Holmes, Sherlock Holmes and A Quantity of Debt, Sherlock Holmes—Tangled Skeins, *and* The Papers of Solar Pons. *He has also edited over sixty books, many of which are traditional Sherlockian anthologies, such as the ongoing series* The MX Book of New Sherlock Holmes Stories *(featured in* Publishers Weekly*), which he created in 2015. The royalties for this collection, now up to twenty-four volumes and over six hundred new stories (with more in preparation) go to the Stepping Stones School for special needs students at Undershaw, one of Sir Arthur Conan Doyle's former homes. Marcum has contributed numerous essays to various publications and is a member of a number of Sherlockian groups and scions. He is a licensed Civil Engineer and lives in Tennessee with his wife and son.*

THE ADVENTURE OF THE HOME OFFICE BABY

David Marcum

The occasion of my marriage had in no way served to effectively diminish contact with my friend, Mr. Sherlock Holmes. A few months before the happy event, I had been fortunate enough to locate a medical practice in the Paddington district, only a few blocks east of the great station itself. Though quite modest, it was well established by a doctor quite respected in the neighborhood, and he was generous enough to allow me to work alongside him during the gradual transition, in order that his patients might come to know and trust me, before he took himself off to a well-deserved retirement on the southeast coast.

The practice itself, on the Edgware Road end of Praed Street, also served as the newlywed home for Mary and myself, and she set about making a wonderful residence for us upstairs while I labored on the ground floor.

Through careful organization, I was able to both build the practice and also find time to assist Holmes in a number of investigations, including that of the Sixth Finger, which so terrified a pair of spinster sisters, and the incredible discovery in the Iron Age fort near Llandysul, which must remain unknown except to scholars, until such time as its implications can be determined. (Heaven help us if word should ever surface, but I do have permission from Holmes to make a record of it, to be stored away in the tin dispatch box that I keep at Cox and Company for just such cases that should not be forgotten, no matter the risk.)

That box contains the records of a number of other unique circumstances, including this particular narrative, which will be placed there when I have finished preparing it. I was reminded of it by a recent article that appeared in the popular press detailing the unexpected death of the principal figure involved, and while the specifics can never be published, I'm moved to record this, a true account of the additional and unknown facts.

It was in late November of 1889 when I found myself passing through Baker Street. My feet knew the way quite well, and I nodded to a number of acquaintances, shopkeepers and mothers, landladies and cabbies, who made up that little community of which I had been a part for so long. I had known them well before marrying and moving elsewhere earlier that year, and old friendships were not quickly forgotten simply because I now resided in a different part of the city.

It had been a dark overcast morning when I reached the door of 221, but the fog was lifting and the morning light quickly waxing. I used my old key to enter, as it had been made clear to me, both by Holmes and Mrs. Hudson, that the simple fact of no longer lodging there did not mean that my right to enter was in any way diminished, and I was grateful for it.

Calling out as I entered, I was gratified to hear Mrs. Hudson make her way from the back of the house, wiping her hands. I could smell something baking, and her pleasure at seeing me was matched by mine at seeing her, as well as knowing that something pleasant would soon be pulled from her oven. My timing, indeed, was serendipitous.

Informed that Holmes had just come in, I climbed the steps, irritated that I could no longer avoid counting them. A year or so earlier, Holmes had pointed out, as an example of the observational mind, that I had previously climbed those steps thousands of times without making note of their number. He, of course, knew exactly how many there were. I saw his point, but unfortunately, I now logged each step nearly every time that I ascended to the sitting room. Often I found myself doing the same upon other stairways as well—which had surprisingly been of use during the unfortunate affair of the greedy minister and the four bags, in which it will be remembered that Holmes broke the man's alibi because it wouldn't have been possible for him to make the number of trips up and down the stairs with his burdens in the time that he testified—a small fact, but it was the thread that unraveled his entire story.

"Come in, Watson!" cried Holmes, whom I found standing by the mantel. He was holding a cup, and he turned it up and finished its contents with several swallows. "You are just in time. Tea?"

"Just in time for tea? It's a bit early, isn't it?"

"When you've been out all night as I have, picking up the last pieces of the Brune Street killing from under Athelney Jones's nose, there is no right or wrong time. And by 'in time,' I meant that you are in time for my expected visitor."

Holmes stepped to the table, where a tray held a pot and several clean cups, and poured for me while I shed my coat, hanging it upon one of the pegs behind the door alongside his Inverness and fore-and-aft cap. I accepted the cup and crossed the room toward my old chair by the fireplace, clearing my throat to ask the particulars of his involvement in the case that was on the front pages of every newspaper, but in vain, for even then the doorbell rang. In just a moment, I heard voices, and then steady footsteps climbing to the sitting room from more than one person—too jumbled to accurately count to seventeen when each one landed. Setting down my cup, I stood and turned toward the door, only to see a young lady enter, followed by our old friend, Inspector Lestrade, who complimented Holmes on identifying the murderer earlier that morning—a story whose details had still eluded me. *Did this new visitor have relevant information?* I wondered. I was soon to learn that she was there regarding an entirely different affair.

Mrs. Hudson followed the two visitors almost immediately with the product of her baking, a fine mound of scones, along with another fresh pot of tea. As everyone was settled and served, I had a chance to observe our visitor. She was in her midtwenties, tall with dark brown hair. She had a wide forehead with striking blue eyes, and a small but rather distinctive mole about an inch to the left of her mouth. Later I would see that, when she spoke, it seemed to vanish within a dimple. She appeared to be a bit nervous, but that was typical of many visitors to that sitting room. Still, she seemed as if she did not want to be there. I could see that her simple outfit was of fine quality, although not expensive, and several years out of style. It was still serviceable, however, and would be of use for many a year to come if she chose to retain it, even as fashion changed.

"Mrs. Aiken," said Holmes, gesturing for her to take the basket chair, usually claimed by Lestrade. He didn't seem to mind, finding a place on the nearby settee. I sat down, curious as to what we would hear.

"The inspector's note indicated that you had presented an interesting problem," Holmes continued, "and fortunately I have recently returned from another investigation." Then he glanced my way. "But the poor doctor is in the dark, as he arrived unexpectedly just a moment before you did. Please, Mrs. Aiken—relate your story." And then he dropped into his chair, crossed his legs, and closed his eyes while steepling his fingers before his face.

The young lady looked surprised, a pair of attractive vertical lines forming on her forehead between her eyes. She looked to Lestrade for guidance. He nodded and said, "Perhaps I should speak first." Holmes, eyes still closed, waved a hand in acknowledgment, and the inspector began, although looking at me as he spoke.

"Doctor, what do you recall of the Home Office Baby?"

I frowned, having some vague recollection of it. Without opening his eyes, and as if sensing my puzzlement, Holmes murmured, "Check the index, Watson."

I rose and moved behind my chair to the shelves that held Holmes's scrapbooks. Since long before I'd met him, he had maintained these repositories of information related to past cases, as well as facts concerning people or events that might be useful in the future. His collection was a long row of books, each fat with pasted-in clippings or loose items such as theater programs, train tickets, handwritten notes, telegrams, sketches, and the occasional obscurely purposed object like a bird feather or a small envelope filled with a pinch of sand, cryptically labeled "*Pagham—November '78*."

Holmes's filing system might charitably be called "eccentric," but I gambled upon the simplest of choices and pulled out the *H* volume, finding—without too much time wasted—his notes upon the incident. I carried the book with me back to my fireside chair, sat down, and summarized the facts aloud.

"In 1884," I stated, "a Reverend Mirehouse of Colsterworth, in Lincolnshire, wound up in a dispute that went all the way to Gladstone's Home Secretary, Sir William Harcourt. It seems that a local graveyard had been proposed for closure without making a new cemetery available for the parish, and there were difficulties in finding designated and consecrated grounds in which to bury the bodies."

Seeing what came next, I glanced up at Mrs. Aiken, but she seemed to be made of sturdy stuff, and unlikely to be shocked—especially if her business somehow related to this affair. "In early November," I continued, "Reverend Mirehouse, in protest, sent through the mail the body of a stillborn infant, packed in a starch box without telling the family what he had done. He marked it 'Perishable.' It set off quite a tempest. There was an inquest, and the coroner, Mr. Braxton Hicks, thought it to be incredibly indecent, and that the minister ought to be reprobated, but Judge Phillimore was of the opinion that no known canon law was violated, and that Reverend Mirehouse could not be punished. Still, he was severely censured, in spite of his full apology, and he was forced to pay the expenses for his journey, as well as that of his witnesses, up to London for the inquiry." There was nothing further, and I started to close the book, but Holmes opened his eyes and motioned for me to hand it to him. He glanced over what I had read and then set it beside his chair before looking expectantly back toward the inspector.

"As you can imagine," Lestrade explained, "the arrival of a parcel containing a dead child gave the duty clerk who opened it a bad shock. There was some little confusion until it was realized just what it was all about, and the point that was being made by that eccentric parson. In any case, it was a nine days' wonder at best, and all was soon forgotten. But then Mrs. Aiken arrived this morning at the Yard, and fortunately I spoke to her first, for I'm not certain what reactions would have been set in motion if someone else had heard her story."

"And you wisely sent word to me," Holmes said, now casting his gaze toward the young woman. "What is your connection to these goings-on?"

She cleared her throat, and then began to speak in a rather thick Lincolnshire accent. "I . . . I am the mother of the poor wee babe." She paused, as if awaiting comment, but when none was forthcoming, she continued. "I had married early that year to a young man from the village who was going off to soldier. He was here in London, at Victoria Station, when the Fenian bomb went off. He helped to rescue those who were injured, and seemed to be fine, but a day later, he died from breathing the smoke. I wasn't told until several days after that he'd passed. The Army said that it wasn't related to his service, and it was simply passed off as an accidental death, despite his bravery.

"A few weeks later, I found that I was with child. The burden seemed almost too great to bear, and as the months passed, I was convinced that something wasn't right with my baby, although my fears were put down as simply the nerves of a new mother. But in late October, the child was born dead.

"I was in a bad way, and didn't even understand when the Reverend asked if he could take the body for what he called 'the greater good.' Only much later did I hear that, rather than giving it a proper burial, he'd mailed my poor baby to London *in a box!*" Here she paused for a moment to breathe deeply before continuing. What she told us had occurred nearly five years earlier, but it was clearly still a raw wound.

Holmes, while not insensitive to her feelings, was also becoming a bit impatient. "Jumping ahead," he said, "what has occurred now that would cause you to visit Scotland Yard?"

"This," replied Lestrade, rising and pulling a note from his coat pocket.

Holmes was suddenly more alert, and he took the sheet with a gleam in his eye. He turned it this way and that in the morning sun shining at his back. Then, having given it an initial examination, he repeated the process using the lens that he kept on the small octagonal table beside his chair. Finally, having apparently wrung all that he could from it, he handed it to me.

I made no pretense at a similar effort. I saw that it was of good quality paper, about five inches square and folded once. It was written in a strong hand by a nib in good condition, and with black ink that seemed of expensive quality:

> Your child still lives. You have been cruelly used.
> Sir Cecil Aberforth knows the truth.
> You must force him to reveal it.

The last line was written with emphasis, the lines being somewhat thicker, as if they had been gone over twice with the pen. I handed the sheet back to Holmes without comment. He took and laid it underneath the lens on his table. "How did you receive this, Mrs. Aiken?"

"It was slipped underneath my bedroom door last night."

"And your place of residence?"

"I'm a maid at Bedford College, just along Baker Street. I came up to London soon after the baby died and found a job there. I have a room on the top floor, above the dormitories."

"Do you share the room?" She shook her head. "Is the facility so casual then that anyone may enter during the night and slide a note under your door?"

Mrs. Aiken seemed to ponder this question for the first time. "It's possible," she said. "After all, it happened."

"Do you have any ideas that it could have been placed by someone who has a room nearby?"

She frowned. "I can't imagine who might do such a thing."

"Anyone can be bought," added Lestrade.

"True," countered Holmes, "but the buyer must know whom to buy." He pulled at his earlobe for a moment, pondering. Then, "After you received this note, what were your first thoughts?"

Mrs. Aiken frowned. "First? Well, it fair rocked me back. I'll never be over the loss of my child, but the pain is less than it was. This morning, it came rushing back. And yet, it makes no sense. Why would this Sir Cecil know anything about whether my child actually lived, in spite of me being told that it had died?"

"And a dead child *was* sent," added Lestrade. "If it wasn't Mrs. Aiken's, then whose was it, and where did it come from?"

"Is any effort being made to question Reverend Mirehouse?"

"Not yet," replied the inspector. "If you recall anything about him, he's quite contentious, and was very secretive at the time as to the identity of the parents, or any other relevant information. When Mrs. Aiken presented herself at the Yard this morning, it was just good luck that I heard her story first. This is dynamite,

gentlemen—you both know about Sir Cecil, and his involvement
with certain government affairs, even if Mrs. Aiken hasn't heard
of him, and I wanted to get your opinion on it."

"So you have told no one else?"

"Well, I did discuss it with the Chief Inspector, and whether I
should approach Sir Cecil, but instead he agreed that you should
be consulted, Mr. Holmes. That's as far as he wants to take it
right now."

Holmes nodded and started absently to reach for the index book
propped against his chair. Then, instead, he rose, indicating that
the interview was over. Mrs. Aiken seemed a bit surprised, but
Lestrade and I were used to his ways. He asked me to accompany
the lady downstairs while he had a word with the inspector. I did
so, and by the time she had put on her coat, simple and a few years
out of date but still quite serviceable, Lestrade had joined us. He
nodded to me without a word and then they both passed outside.

Back upstairs, Holmes, who was by his shelf of index books,
asked, "Are you free for a few hours, Watson? I would value your
company as we run this down."

I nodded in agreement while he replaced one book and
pulled out another. Taking it to the dining table, he flipped
through it until finding what he sought. Then he called me
over and pointed at what I should read. It was a list, in his
own hand, containing several names that I recognized, the
major espionage agents operating in London: Hugo Oberstein,
Adolph Mayer, Louis La Rothiere, and Eduardo Lucas. The last
had a thin line drawn through it, as Lucas had been violently
murdered just three years before. Beside his name another had
been penciled in, Gretel Walbeck, along with an extensive note
in Holmes's neat handwriting succinctly describing her skills
and physical appearance.

Seeing a description of something that I'd recently observed—a curious mole—I straightened up with a surprised look on my face. "Surely not," I said.

Holmes nodded. "I'm almost certain. When Lucas died, there was a vacuum to be filled, and her masters were quick to do so. While Lucas was a bold personality who used his big life to distract from what he did in the shadows, Fräulein Walbeck is more of a specialist, dipping in here and there as needed, usually under a false name. She is clever, and worth ten of the other men who have performed similar functions over the last few years. I've been aware of her presence before this, but so far she hasn't directly crossed my path. Today, I knew that something was wrong as soon as she spoke—she clearly wasn't comfortable with her Lincolnshire accent, and yet her story was that she was born and raised there until moving to London. When her note involved a man of current vital importance to the Crown in a possibly seamy scandal, the connection was suddenly apparent in my mind, and then I recalled the physical description—particularly that unusual mole near her mouth. Finally, did you notice that she never actually referred to the gender of the dead baby, supposedly her own?"

"Now that you mention it, I did, but it's possible that a mother wouldn't want to know such a thing, preferring to have as little connection as possible to the deceased infant."

"I defer to your judgment, but I'm also aware that the deceased child was a girl, and if I knew it, one would think that the mother would know too—unless this story was put together rather thinly over spots like that where it was too much trouble to discover the finer details." He nodded toward the shelf where he had replaced the first scrapbook. "I refreshed my memory that my notes referred to the baby having *two* parents."

"That's right," I said. "I saw that, but assumed that it was a mistake, and didn't mention it to avoid embarrassing her."

"Just so. But in fact, she contrived her widowhood as a way to avoid addressing why she had no husband when claiming a connection to the Home Office Baby."

He moved to the door and began to don his Inverness. "I spoke with Lestrade just long enough to convey my suspicions. He isn't the brightest candle, but he understood immediately and is taking her back to the Yard, ostensibly for administrative reasons, or possibly for her own protection. In the meantime, we shall explore her room at Bedford College, before carrying on in a different direction."

The school, on the east side of the street, wasn't far away. It was located directly across from York Street, in a part of Baker Street that is still sometimes mistakenly referred to as York Terrace—the result of a misguided politician of old who had managed to use his influence to get that name, along with references to "Upper Baker Street" just to the north, incorrectly placed on a number of maps, serving to fulfill some twisted reasoning of his own. Holmes's brother Mycroft had managed to correct the mistake for the most part, but not before a great deal of confusion was sown.

The residents of Baker Street all know one another, and neither Holmes nor I were strangers to Cyrus Brownlow, the administrator of Bedford College, founded decades before as the first school of its kind in England, providing higher education for women. We knew him to be an honorable man, and more important, a trustworthy one as well. Without providing him with too many details, we explained the situation, although Holmes's identification of Mrs. Aiken as Gretel Walbeck was not mentioned.

"She has only been here a couple of weeks," explained Brownlow. "She had excellent references from the north, and asked for part-time hours, as she is interested in pursuing studies. It's an unusual arrangement, but she had some funds of her own, and I was willing to give it a try."

Holmes asked to see her file, but apparently he found nothing out of order, or of interest, and he didn't appear to expect to. "Did you verify the references?"

Brownlow hemmed and hawed, explaining that he hadn't yet had the time to do so, but that the girl seemed acceptable. It was easy, by way of his embarrassment, to convince him to let us search her room.

Knowing that my own skills lay in different directions, I remained in the doorway while Holmes made his examination. It didn't take him long to find several familiar sheets, pushed deeply into the back of one of the desk drawers. He motioned me closer and handed them to me. They were all the same type of paper as the note referring to Sir Cecil Aberforth that we had been shown in Holmes's sitting room, and written with the same pen and ink. However, these, while of a similar nature, contained commands to contact other noted members of government to ask about the truth regarding the Home Office Baby. Some of them held additional varying allegations of a most frank and vulgar description. "If these were to be made public," I murmured, "there would be quite a cat set loose among the pigeons, even when eventually disproved. It's fortunate that she approached Lestrade first."

"I agree. I doubt whether her plans included being rerouted to Baker Street and involving me."

As I finished reading, Holmes pulled out a fine pen and bottle of ink from another drawer, along with a number of matching blank sheets of paper. "Tut tut, Watson. She is too confident that the Yard would believe her story." He took back the written sheets and looked again at the various names. "Hmm, I wonder just what is going on right now in the political realm that needs to be disrupted with this rather amateur distraction. I believe that a quick visit to brother Mycroft is next on our agenda."

At that time of day, we found Mycroft Holmes in his obscurely located office in Whitehall. His days ran on fixed rails, and it was still several hours before he would walk around to the Diogenes Club for the evening. His attention was obviously pulled elsewhere, as he barely acknowledged our entrance. When we approached his desk, he simply handed a file to his brother, and rather than offer greetings, said "The Chief Superintendent couldn't keep his mouth shut. He spoke to Sir Cecil, who—most upset, as you can imagine—came to me. Here is the information that we have on Gretel Walbeck. Read it, and then tell me what you need." Then his eyes returned to a document centered before him which seemed to be mostly red ink overlaying black. He picked up a pen, dipped it into a red inkpot, and proceeded to add considerably to the editorial hieroglyphics and strike-throughs already covering the sheet.

Holmes glanced my way, his expression indicating that Mycroft's omniscience was exactly what he'd expected. He scanned through the various clipped pages in the file and then, without offering it to me, placed it back on Mycroft's desk, waiting until his brother finished his edits and laid aside his pen.

"Perhaps," said Holmes, "you should know what we found when searching Fräulein Walbeck's room at Bedford College." And he then outlined the details of additional and unsent letters, concluding by asking, "What does she hope to accomplish?"

Mycroft sighed. "We are in the early days of drafting an ultimatum to Portugal regarding a withdrawal of their military forces from the lands between Mozambique and Angola. Sir Cecil and the other names that you mentioned are very involved, and vital to this effort—their time and attention cannot be diverted, and their character and reputations cannot be besmirched at such a critical juncture. The Germans must have caught wind of what we're doing and came up with this plan. It's a pity really, from their perspective. It was obviously thrown together at the last minute, held together with spit and string, and it's a waste of one of their better agents. She must have advised against it, but I doubt if she was given the option to decline."

He waved a hand. "We maintain a number of contingency plans, ready to be modified for use at a moment's notice. I suspect that this is their equivalent of such." He took another deep breath and asked, "What do you suggest that we do?"

Holmes was prompt with his response. "Lestrade should still have her. Perhaps she can be taken into 'protective custody'—for her own safety." He went on to outline more specific details.

Mycroft considered it for no more than three seconds, but one could imagine that he perceived how this or that action would lead to another, and that each choice would open up a new direction of possibilities, spreading from one point to another like a tangled rootlike mass in every direction. And yet, three seconds were enough for him to nod his agreement and summon a secretary to prepare a satchel of documents. Then he retrieved his pen and returned to his editing, effectively dismissing us.

We retreated to the hallway, and within moments, the secretary presented us with the small leather case, which Holmes accepted without comment. Scotland Yard was only a quick walk away, and we were soon within the bowels of the convoluted building, conversing with Lestrade in the hallway while the girl remained in his office. When he was told who she was, he was rather concerned that she was left alone and able to get at his papers, but Holmes quickly explained his plan, and it wasn't very long at all before we had retrieved her, only to escort her from the building and outside to a four-wheeler.

"Where are we going?" she asked breathlessly.

"To a place of safety," Holmes told her grimly. "I've learned that the man named in the note, Sir Cecil, has threatened to kill you. There's nothing left to be done but get you out of the capital as soon as possible and into hiding. We'll be on the train shortly, and the police will pack up your belongings and send them later."

"But . . . but . . ." Even an experienced agent such as this was clearly speechless. The situation had escalated far beyond any mayhem that she and her masters had hoped to cause. She was still trying to formulate a response when Holmes spoke again.

"Hold this, Watson," he said, handing me the satchel of documents. "Don't take your eye off it for a second. Mycroft is counting on me to deliver these documents as soon as possible, or our naval forces might make a terrible blunder." Then he seemed to fall into a brown study.

Lestrade spoke not at all, but rather looked all around as if expecting the cab to fall under sudden attack. There was nothing but silence among us until our arrival at Victoria Station, where Holmes announced that we were just in time to catch the train to Horsham, where our female charge would be hidden until further notice. She looked surprised, but followed us meekly into the crowded station. We paused beside a pillar and Holmes informed us that he would go and buy the tickets. I set down the satchel, turning slightly away from it, while Lestrade took a few steps, still looking around for anything resembling a threat. I heard a sound behind me, and in a moment I glanced around to see that, as expected, Miss Walbeck had taken the satchel of supposedly vital documents—in fact a rag-bag of worthless decoys quickly assembled by Mycroft's department—and vanished into the masses.

"There is a boat train leaving in two minutes," said Holmes, returning to us. "No doubt she will be on it, her plan scotched, and hopefully that bag of useless drivel effective in confusing her masters for quite a while."

In fact, it did. Mycroft Holmes's sources learned that not only were Fräulein Walbeck's superiors more than taken in by the false documents, but later—when it was realized what she had brought them—her credibility was destroyed, to her great sorrow.

However, that afternoon, it sufficed that she had taken the bait while abandoning the pesterment of a plan that would have discredited Sir Cecil and the others at a moment when they could ill afford the distraction. Holmes, Lestrade, and I returned to Scotland Yard in the cab, and I was gratified to finally hear the surprising details of the Brune Street killing, which ended up being quite a bit more complex than I would have thought—which was really no surprise at all.

I've been writing since I was a boy, borrowing my dad's typewriter to crank out my own Hardy Boys adventures. In my twenties, I was a US Federal Investigator, and while on very long trips away from home, I bought a cheap typewriter at Walmart, and then spent the nights in the hotels writing what became a six-hundred-plus-page (unpublished) Ludlum-esque novel about my thinly disguised alter ego's adventures. That's where I learned two important author lessons: It only gets written if you sit your butt in the chair and write it, and always trust the muse that's whispering in your ear. For that massive first novel, I made an outline, but it quickly became useless once the characters started talking, and I simply raced to stay caught up, transcribing what they were saying, page after page. Years later, after having gone back to school to be a civil engineer, I found myself laid off from an engineering job, and I decided to use some of that time to write about my main hero, Sherlock Holmes. Those two author lessons still applied, leading to a lot of new Sherlock Holmes adventures. There are apparently two kinds of writers—those who outline, and those who write by the seats of their pants. I am the latter. I open a new Word document with no plan or outline and then let Watson tell me a story. That's how "The Adventure of the Home Office Baby" arrived: I'd had several of my Holmes stories published in The Strand *magazine, and it was time to submit a new one—which meant that I had to sit down and write it. As always, I just started recording what Watson was telling me (based upon what's in my head from decades of collecting, reading, and chronologizing literally thousands of Holmes pastiches) and somewhere soon after the story began, my brain recalled reading something about an 1884 incident called "The Home Office Baby" and so it went from there—and now to this book. As writers know, it isn't an easy process, but it's incredibly rewarding. I go into "The Zone" and come back several hours later with half a story that didn't exist before, and all of my coffee is gone. I'm very fortunate indeed.*

Tom Mead *is a UK-based author and translator. He is a prolific writer of short fiction whose work has appeared in* Ellery Queen Mystery Magazine, Alfred Hitchcock Mystery Magazine, Lighthouse, Flash: The International Short-Short Story Magazine, Mystery Weekly, *and various others. He recently completed his first full-length novel,* Occam's Razor, *featuring series detective Joseph Spector.*

HEATWAVE

Tom Mead

The summer of 1954, we were pushing 110 degrees in Los Angeles. Windows and doors gaped wide; you could have mistaken Downtown LA for the most welcoming place on Earth. The papers screamed about the increasing death rate: the old and the weak sizzling away in their armchairs and hospital beds. But heat like that brings with it the threat of violence. The air in those empty streets gets so thick that it eats at your mind. Some people get desperate.

The papers were promising the heat would break within a day or two; they'd been making similar promises for about two weeks. Skipping through pages of this kind of stuff, I dived straight into the police beat on page fourteen. There I found, among others, the story of a dead girl on La Cienega. A cashier at Thrifty's All-Night Drug Store. She'd been shot to death in a messy, heat-crazed robbery. The perpetrators made off with six thousand dollars from the safe and a drizzling of the young girl's blood on their clothes.

Elsewhere a family man had bludgeoned his eight-year-old daughter into a coma with a teakettle, a delirious teenager had set himself afire in Inglewood, and an elderly couple were missing (presumed dead) after their neatly piled clothes and an elegantly calligraphed suicide note were found under a rock on Venice Beach. I was reading that story when the phone rang.

I pulled up at the roadside on Washington Boulevard, letting the Pontiac amble to a halt in the shade of a camphor tree. I'd picked out the house straightaway: it was the only one on the street with all its doors bolted shut. I waited for a moment, watching for movement in either of the twin front windows. I saw none.

Loosening my tie, undoing a second button on my shirt, and tilting the brim of my lead-gray trilby to dab the sweat against my forehead, I looked bad and knew it. My face was an unshaven brick and my suit didn't fit anymore. I couldn't tell if the sweats were from the heatwave or the DTs.

I approached at a slow, lumbering pace, taking in the faded pink stucco and terra-cotta roof tiles lined up like row upon row of crooked, off-white teeth. When I reached the door, my knock was loud and businesslike. I wanted her to think that God himself might be on the other end of that knock.

She opened the door slowly and a wave of fetid warmth seeped out. "Yes?"

I didn't smile. "Mrs. Lukather?"

"Yes?"

"My name is Max Ehrlich. You called me this morning."

"Have you any identification Mr. Ehrlich?" Her tone was not unfriendly. I showed her the photostat of my license I carried everywhere, though the thin-faced thirty-something in the photo no longer looked like me.

Mrs. Lukather threw open the door to let me in and it was as if the whole house sighed, as if it had been holding its breath in anticipation. She led me through to the living room, babbling the whole time. "To be frank, Mr. Ehrlich, I'm afraid I may be bothering you unnecessarily. My phone call this morning was made while I was under extreme mental anguish—I have a tendency toward irrational emotional responses—and now that I'm in my right mind I can see that all this bother might very well be over nothing . . ." She wore a natty, cinnamon-colored gabardine suit, her hands fluttering like a couple of calloused butterflies as she spoke. When my eyes were on her, she grinned, but as my gaze wandered around the room, her face sagged.

"You mentioned your son. You said he was missing."

"Uh yes, uh, well, that's right, I haven't heard from my son Arnold in a little while, but perhaps I'm worrying too much, he always tells me I worry too much, that I should lay off once in a while and . . ."

"Mrs. Lukather, why did you call me and not the police?"

Suddenly, her face crumpled and she let out a long sob. I waited for her to catch her breath. "I'm sorry. I'm so sorry, it's just . . ."

She reached behind the couch and produced an object wrapped in a yellow dishrag. She proffered it like a holy relic and I took it from her—its dead weight was fearfully familiar. I unwrapped a snub-nosed .38.

"I found that under his mattress. He didn't come home last night, Mr. Ehrlich, and now I'm completely terrified."

I leaned back and felt the easy chair groan under my weight.

"My rates are thirty dollars per diem."

"That's not a problem, Mr. Ehrlich. I have a little rainy day fund put aside. And, though the sun may be shining out there, this looks like quite a rainy day to me. In fact, let's say I'll give you an additional seventy-five dollars if you can get Arnie back here today."

I nodded. "How old is your son?"

"Seventeen. It was his birthday two weeks ago. We had a little get-together at home, just me and him."

"When's the last time you heard from him?"

"Yesterday. Around eight. A friend of his came by to pick him up. They were going somewhere, movies I think."

"Who's the friend?"

"Just a kid, I don't know, I don't keep track of Arnie's friends, he hates it when I do that."

"Male, female?"

"Arnie's not the type to run around with girls. It was one of his high school buddies—Roy, I think the name is." She rubbed her forehead then struggled to her feet. "Hold on a second."

I waited while she shuffled out of the room, then came back bearing a small square photograph, a polaroid. It showed two adolescent males in baseball uniforms, both grinning widely and stupidly. The uniforms were nondescript: plain white, with bold vertical stripes. Each had numbers stitched to their breast pockets, like a pair of jailbirds.

"That's my Arnie," she said, pointing to the kid on the left, number nine. He was wiry, smooth-chinned, with dark eyes and wild black hair. He looked like he would make a good baseball player. "And that—" she indicated the kid next to him, number fifteen, "is Roy. Roy Moretz, I remember the name now." Roy was wider, with a belly like a beer cask. Skin and hair shimmeringly pale.

"Can I borrow this photo?"

"All yours, Mr. Ehrlich. I took it last summer."

"Uh-huh. So this Roy kid picked up Arnie last night. Do you know where Roy lives?"

"I'm afraid not."

"Did they leave in a car?"

"Oh yes. Roy owns a dreadful old Ford De Luxe, such a noisy machine, churning out black smoke. I don't know how he keeps it running. Anyway, he came for Arnie in that."

"Color?"

"Rust."

"I see."

As soon as she mentioned it, I knew the car would be the key. Who would forget a car like that?

"Does Arnie have a father, Mrs. Lukather?"

She didn't answer. She aimed her gray eyes at the window and pretended not to hear.

"Could I take a look at Arnie's room, Mrs. Lukather?"

"Well of course, right this way."

The only conclusion I drew from that little bedroom was that it did not belong to a would-be gangster. Various trophies for sporting achievement served as bookends, sealing in row upon row of trashy adventure novels: *Tarzan*, *Sinbad*, *Conan the Barbarian*, *King Solomon's Mines*. The walls were lined with posters of famous athletes. The bed was narrow, more fit for a child than an adolescent on the cusp of manhood. There was nothing of use here.

"Do you have a phone I could use?"

"In the hall."

She let me find my own way, but I could hear her bustling conspicuously in the kitchen as I gave the operator a number. I pictured her leaning toward the wall, aching to hear what I had to say about her boy. My first call was to a friend in police dispatch, who was able to give me the lowdown on Roy Moretz.

Roy, it seemed, was a problem child. Mother dead, father jailed for embezzling funds from the venetian-blind manufacturer where he worked. Roy was legally emancipated at age seventeen, only to be subsequently arrested for marijuana possession, drunkenness, and disorderly conduct, all within a six-month period. His last known address was a bungalow a couple of blocks away from the Lukather residence.

As for Arnie, he had no record of any kind. His mother must have been proud.

My second call was to ambulance dispatch. The girl I spoke to was bright and keen, her voice like sunshine over the telephone wires. I had never met her, but she knew me by reputation. I gave her a description of Roy's infamous automobile and she swiftly responded that a car matching that description had been involved in a collision at around three A.M. that very morning, somewhere up in the Hollywood Hills. Just a drunken accident which resulted in said vehicle getting wrapped around a palm tree. I waited on the line while she tried to identify the ambulance men who took the callout.

She gave me the name Jasper Monroe, and provided a direct line to the ambulance drivers' break room in the Santa Monica depot. While I waited for Monroe to come on the line, I developed a pretty firm idea of what had happened: two drunken kids had gone on a wild bender, culminating in an ugly smash. Roy and Arnie were probably being patched up in hospital rooms at that very moment.

"Hello?" said a voice on the other end of the line.

"Yes, am I speaking to Jasper Monroe?"

"That's me."

"My name is Max Ehrlich, Jasper. I understand you drove the ambulance from the scene of a crash in the Hollywood Hills this morning."

"Uh-huh." He was impatient. That was fine, my questions were easy enough.

"I just have a couple of things I need to ask, Jasper. The guys in the car, were they a pair of teenagers, one skinny and dark, the other fair and fat?"

There was a pause. "Well, you got it half right. There was only one kid in the car, though. He was skinny, like you say."

"Huh." So Arnie had ditched Roy somewhere along the way and ridden off in his car. Naughty boy. "Dark-haired boy?"

"Yeah, dark curly hair. He was unconscious when we pulled him out of the wreck."

"ID?"

"He had a driver's license on him, but I forget the name."

"Could it have been Arnold Lukather?"

A pause. "Yeah. Hey, yeah, I think that's it."

"Where did you take him, Jasper?"

"We had to drive around for a while, all the emergency rooms were so busy. In the end we wound up at Linda Vista Community."

"What time was that?"

"That would have been around four A.M."

"Wonderful. Thanks Jasper, I owe you a beer."

As I hung up the phone, Mrs. Lukather came out from the kitchen to check on me. "Success?" she inquired.

"Just putting a few feelers out there. Thanks for the use of your phone. Now if you'll excuse me, I'd better get to work."

The drive to the emergency room was strangely relaxed, in spite of the humidity. I had just made an easy thirty dollars and was well on track for an easy seventy-five. Of course, I did not know what had gone on between the two boys, Arnold and Roy, or how Arnold had come to wrap Roy's car around a tree in the early hours of the morning, but those unanswered questions were not a part of this particular job description.

I found the parking lot packed to the gills, eventually giving up and abandoning the Pontiac with two wheels bumped up on the sidewalk. No one was around to stop me. I straightened my tie and marched toward the double doors of the vast, white building.

"I'm looking for a patient named Arnold Lukather. You got a man by that name?"

The desk nurse looked up at me, unimpressed. She didn't reply, and went back to her paperwork.

"Vehicular smash. He was brought in this morning."

Still, no answer. Rolling my eyes, I removed a loose cigarette from my pocket and slipped it between my lips.

"Don't you dare," the nurse said.

"Maybe you didn't hear me . . ."

"I heard you, mister, I'm not deaf. But look here, this is a heatwave. We've been getting tens of thousands of new patients every day for the past two weeks. Every hour, it feels like. I'm just one woman here!"

"Remind me to write a letter to *Queen for a Day*. I'm sure your work is sterling, but how is that going to help me find my friend?"

The nurse exhaled slowly, and it was the most desolate sound I had heard. "Try Ward 6. Most of the new arrivals this morning ended up there."

"God bless you," I said with an antiseptic smile. I turned on my heel and marched off, dropping the cigarette to the floor unlit.

After a few minutes' bemused wandering, I found Ward 6 halfway down a long, bone-colored corridor on the first floor. I took a deep breath at the door. I removed the photo from my pocket. Then I plunged in.

Molten sunlight streaked in on row upon row of deathly pallid men. The whole ward screamed and broiled to the beat of nurses' skittering footsteps. Gurneys shrieked past. I strode up and down a few times like a commander inspecting troops. I took about ten minutes making sure none of these men was Arnold Lukather. When I'd been there so long that my presence could no longer be reasonably ignored, a stout matron (is there any other kind?) approached.

"Can I do something for you?" she said.

"I hope so. My name is Max Lukather, I'm looking for a relative of mine named Arnold."

The name meant something to her; her eyes flashed. "Oh, Mr. Lukather. Please come with me." She led me to a row of sleeping old men, which was obviously the closest this place had to a sanctuary. There, she lowered her voice. "I'm afraid I have some terrible news, Mr. Lukather. Arnold Lukather passed away an hour ago."

I breathed in the thin, disinfected air. "I see. That is most upsetting."

"My condolences. It was quite peaceful, I assure you," said the matron. The suffering in this place was so pointedly vocal that I found her second statement difficult to credit. "And anyway, he's with God now. Were you close?"

"Cousins. Yes, very close."

"Would you like to see him? Perhaps say a final goodbye?"

"That would be nice."

I found my way down to the morgue in spite of the matron's directions. Morgues are never hard to find. They are always below, isolated and sealed off by steel doors. Death is a dirty secret. When I got there, just saying "Arnold Lukather" in somber tones was all the soft-spoken mortician required. A steel body-drawer was swiftly pulled out, a toe-tag checked.

"You might want to . . ." the mortician demonstrated covering his mouth and nose. I didn't argue; I removed my handkerchief and put it to use. When the shroud was folded back, I surveyed the corpse's face dispassionately. I had seen all shapes and sizes in my time, but none quite so . . . tumescent. This one looked like an effigy in melting candlewax. I was seized by the irrational urge to reach out and poke it, to see if my fingers would sink right into the soft, yellow flesh.

In death, a body loses its shape. The muscles holding the facial features in place go slack, so the skin flaps like a pancake. Even so, and with the eyes riveted shut and the mouth gaping open, there was no mistaking: this body was not Arnie Lukather.

"This is him?" I said. "You sure?"

"I know he looks a little different. That's perfectly natural, honestly. There's no mistake. I'm very sorry."

The body was at least seventy years old—bald, liver-spotted, and toothless. Another martyr to the crippling heat, no doubt.

"Do you mind if I take a look at his records?"

The mortician was briefly flummoxed. "Sure. If you want." He covered up the body and ushered me into a tiny, crypt-like office. There, he handed me a brown manila folder. I flicked through, and realized two things. The first was that this mortician, for all his professional merits, was not an avid reader of records. The second was that by now Arnie Lukather could be, quite literally, anywhere.

The kid had switched records with this dead old man. Perhaps he had been in the same ward and watched the geezer check out.

Now he, Arnie, was officially dead, with all the freedom that brought.

"Thanks for your time," I said.

———

After a couple of minutes' contemplation at the wheel of my car, I decided to head for Roy Moretz's bungalow. Of course it was a long shot, but by now it had dawned on me that I was lucky to have any shot at all. The place was identical to the Lukather house in design, but the stucco that was so carefully tended there had all but entirely peeled away here. Most of the terra-cotta roof tiles were chipped away to nothing. The patch of garden out front was a knot of weeds. Among this mess of yellowish-green vines and leaves, I glimpsed a pair of rusted lawn chairs, most likely irretrievable.

I rang the bell a few times, to be met only by angry silence within the house. I tried the door handle and, to my dismay, the front door was unlocked and fell obligingly open. I stepped through into the hallway. It was dingy and under-decorated, with patches of mold spreading outward from the corners of the room like wandering shadows. The distant sound of flies buzzing drew me toward the closed kitchen door, and I became conscious of an insidious odor seeping out from under it.

"I wouldn't do that," said a man's voice from behind me.

I spun round, heart thundering, and found myself confronted by two men.

The man who had spoken was unimpressive. His suit, like his slicked-back hair, was gray before its time. The sole distinguishing feature of his smooth, insufferably oval face was a pair of small, circular, and very dark sunglasses shielding his eyes. He grinned fleetingly, flashing a set of angry little teeth.

At his side was another officious-looking nobody, this one dressed like an undertaker. He watched me through passive, half-lidded eyes.

"I don't think you'd like what you found in there," the first man went on. "Now let me see. Would you happen to be Mr. Max Ehrlich by any chance? We've been waiting for you. It took you longer to get here than we expected. Mind you, my friend tells me I'm looking at the most out-of-shape piece of shit he's ever laid eyes on. He says he's seen gentlemen who've been in the river for fourteen days and bobbed up in better shape than you."

"He's got a lot to say for a man who never opens his mouth."

The sidekick took a step closer, but the man with sunglasses placed a gentle hand on his forearm. "Careful," Sunglasses said, "he's got ears, you know. Perhaps I should make it plain to you, Mr. Ehrlich, just how much trouble you are in. Do you know who I am?"

"Tell me."

"My name is Frank Mellish."

I halted midbreath. "Bullshit."

"I'd tell you to check my driver's license, but they don't let me out on the roads these days."

"So is it really true that you're . . . ?"

Mellish removed the sunglasses with a practiced flourish. The eyelids beneath gaped wide and unblinking, encircled with tender, pinkish red. The eyeballs themselves were off-white globes, like twin cue balls, unmarred by pupils or irises. Everybody knew Mellish's name. When it came to contract killers, he had been top of the heap for a long, long time; a real wizard with a knife. He had style and the psychosis to back it up. But he'd dropped out of the game a couple of years ago when a punk threw corrosive acid in his face.

"Oh, it's true all right. But you should see the other guy."

I resisted the urge to swallow the lump of fear which had bubbled up in my throat.

Mellish went on, nodding in the undertaker's direction: "Meet my new eyes. His name is Ormerod, but don't bother speaking to him. He's been a mute ever since he was a little kid. Isn't that funny, the two of us ending up together? Suits me fine of course, I have plenty to say. But some people might find it funny, a blind man and a mute."

"Look Mr. Mellish, I don't know how you found me, but there's really nothing I can do for you. Honestly."

"Let's see about that, shall we. I'm told you were hired by a woman named Lukather to retrieve her errant son, Arnold."

"That's right. He's just a kid on a bender, probably drunk in an alley somewhere, no use to you at all."

Mellish smiled faintly. "Well, you seem to know an awful lot about a lot of things. You hear about a robbery last night? Old-fashioned stickup?"

I made a show of thinking about it, then shook my head.

"Out on La Cienega. Things turned messy. A checkout girl took a bullet in the throat and the two perpetrators made off with six thousand and change. Is that ringing any bells?"

I didn't reply, so Mellish continued: "Your guy, Arnie, was one of the perps." He waited a moment for that to sink in. "It was Arnie and his good buddy Roy, who you'll find in the kitchen. They were just stupid kids trying to pull off a big score, make themselves look like big men. Ordinarily this kind of operation wouldn't fall within the remit of Mr. Ormerod and myself, but that particular drug store just happened to be, shall we say, *protected*. The girl who died was the store owner's daughter, who just happens to be a personal friend of my employer. Do you see now?"

Bewildered, I nodded.

"We already caught up with Roy but, credit where it's due, he never opened his mouth. Except to scream, that is, when we turned his insides into outsides. They were kind of warm and juicy to the touch, like hamburger meat. But the smell isn't quite so appetizing, of course. Although," he added parenthetically, "I wouldn't put anything past Ormerod. Between you and me, he's crazy."

On cue, Ormerod offered the first flicker of a smile. It was not an expression so much as an absence. Just a muscle spasm.

"So now we have something of a problem," Mellish went on, mock casual. "No Arnie. And no cash."

"That is a problem."

"Yes indeed. And now it's your problem. We know you're looking for Arnie, and we know you're being paid to do it. That's fine. A man's got to make a living. But I want you to know that we'll be keeping an eye on you, so to speak. You find Arnie and collect your payoff, and then get the hell out, because Ormerod and I want to have a few words with young Arnold Lukather. Any objections?"

I cleared my throat. "None at all. May I leave now?"

"It's a free country," Mellish said.

My hands shook as I turned the key in the ignition. I drove away from the late Roy Moretz's home with my heart still racing and my chest heaving with frantic breaths. It was true that, since his injury, Frank Mellish's name was no longer synonymous with underworld supremacy. However, with Ormerod at his side he still presented a degree of danger which I'd not foreseen. No doubt Arnie and Roy had not foreseen it either.

Although, thinking it through as I drove, Arnie's behavior started to make more sense. After the robbery, he had ditched Roy, taking both the car and the money. Roy, for whatever foolish reason, had returned home to find Mellish and Ormerod waiting for him. While this was going on, Arnie had taken an ill-fated trip to the Hollywood Hills and promptly wrecked Roy's automobile.

Odd, I thought, that Arnie had chosen for his getaway those narrow, circuitous country roads. Surely LAX, the bus terminal, or even the freeway would have seemed like more agreeable options to a seventeen-year-old on the run with a sack full of cash. But the Hills? There was nothing for him there.

With this fleeting notion snagging on my brain like a thin strand of gossamer, I pulled over at the corner, next to a payphone. I got out and dialed. Eventually I got through to the ambulance driver once again.

"Jasper? It's Max Ehrlich."

"You again? I'm trying to work here! Don't you know there's a heatwave going on out there?"

"Yeah, somebody mentioned that. I'll buy you suntan lotion for your trouble. I only need to ask you one quick question and then I'll be out of your hair for good."

Jasper sighed breathily like the drama queen he was. "Go ahead."

"Where exactly did you pick Arnold Lukather up from? Where *exactly* did he have his smash?"

"Southbound on Canyon Lake Drive."

"Southbound? You mean he was headed back into Los Angeles?"

"That's what I mean."

"Did he say anything to you?"

"He was unconscious, Max. Use your noodle."

"Did you find anything in the car, Jasper? Anything unusual?"

"Such as?"

Such as a bag of blood money. "Such as anything unusual. I don't know."

"Nothing. The car was empty."

I thanked him and hung up. Supposing this ambulance man was telling the truth, the cash had already been stashed somewhere when they pulled Arnie out of his wrecked car. Roy hadn't had it, and Arnie hadn't had it. There was only a small window of time in which Arnie could have disposed of it. That would also explain his mysterious trip into the Hollywood Hills. I thought back to those old adventure stories which had lined the boy's shelves, and the whole thing made sense. Arnie had driven up there to bury his treasure.

<hr />

I found the crash site with minimal effort. There is a devilish hairpin bend a mile along Canyon Lake Drive, and it was there that the asphalt was scattered with broken glass and errant slivers of rusty metal. I pictured Arnie, delirious with adrenaline in the early hours of the morning, losing control and spinning himself off into a tree.

From there, tracing Arnie's steps back into the Hollywood Hills was surprisingly easy. The old Ford De Luxe had had uncharacteristically narrow tire treads, probably the cheapest Roy could find. The speed Arnie traveled had left frequent, serpentine black markings on the road itself. I followed these uphill for almost a quarter mile, until they unceremoniously stopped. So this was as far as Arnie had come. I pulled up at the roadside. It was reasonable to assume, therefore, that the money was stashed within walking distance of this very spot.

It was an isolated area, and easy to understand why Arnie had chosen it. If he had covered his tracks a little better, it would have been damn near untraceable. Just an anonymous stretch of road, shielded from the sun by dense clusters of trees. Above me was the Hollywood sign, beaming down on all like the smile of a benevolent God. Below me lay the city.

I climbed out of the car and wandered slowly up the road for another hundred yards. Then I wandered back down the road a similar distance. It was only on my third or fourth circuit, with my eyes fixed firmly on the ground, that I spotted familiar narrow tire treads in the dust, veering off the road to the right-hand side. I followed them through a patch of greenery into a small clearing, where they halted once more. Perfect.

The heat had dried out the terrain, giving it the texture and hue of scorched concrete. I dared not imagine how difficult it had been for Arnie digging a moneybag-sized hole in that unforgiving earth.

At the foot of a nearby palm, I found shovel marks in the smooth, dusty ground. When it's as dry as this, it's virtually impossible to smooth over. The ground does not decimate into powder; it splinters into messy chunks. There is no way to hide the fact that you have been digging. Arnie, after concealing the cash, had done what he could to rearrange the chunks over the hollow. But, inevitably, they had not quite fit. Just his luck. So, he had left the job half-finished; the money stowed in the ground with the sun-dried earth messily rearranged on top of it. Now, I did not even need a shovel. I merely kicked the dirt aside with my shoe, revealing a small black traveling case in a little cavity about eight inches deep.

I seized the bag and unzippered it a little to check that the cash was still there. It was. So Arnie had not yet returned to retrieve it. This was perfect. It meant the clearing was the one spot in the whole of Los Angeles where Arnie was guaranteed to show up. And I would be there waiting for him.

By nightfall, however, I had almost given up hope. I'd parked my Pontiac on the far side of the clearing and now sat behind the wheel, watching for the vaguest hint of movement in the seeping darkness. It was only the tangible presence of the moneybag at my side, like a loyal pet curled up in a shadow, that kept me from drifting off into a well-earned sleep. As I was breaking the seal on my third pack of Camels, I heard the chug of a car engine struggling uphill. I hastily lit the cigarette as a pair of headlamps swung into view.

It was a dirt-crusted Dodge pickup, and God knows where Arnie got it from. It rattled to a halt in the center of the clearing, the lights aimed straight at the burial site. A spindly figure that could only be Arnie clambered out, leaving the engine running. I watched as Arnie retrieved a shovel from the truck bed, then started to dig.

After about five minutes had passed and he had still not unearthed the case, Arnie gave in. In silhouette, I saw him drop the shovel and cover his eyes with his hands. Was he crying?

I gripped the handle of the Webley revolver I kept at my shoulder and slithered out of the Pontiac's driving seat. "Don't move!" I called, my voice wet with smoke and rattling in the darkness. Arnie, who had dropped to his knees in despair, sprang upright.

I cocked the hammer. "Don't you goddamn move Arnie. I'm not kidding."

Arnie was obviously itching to make a run for it, and probably could have pulled it off; it was, after all, dark and the shadows were untrustworthy. But his greed won out. He wanted his money more. "Who are you?" the kid called out, his voice cracking. Both of his eyes were blackened and he had a long, messy wound over his right brow, held together by a tangle of stitches.

I approached, the Webley still trained firmly on Arnie's bony carcass. "Don't talk. We need to get out of here." I saw that Arnie's limbs were quivering, like a half-drowned river rat.

"I ain't going anywhere with you."

I swung the butt of the pistol, catching Arnie a vicious blow across the jaw. Arnie dropped, spitting teeth. He struggled to his knees and hawked a chunk of bloody phlegm.

I knelt down beside him and seized a handful of his fulsome, oil-black hair. With my other hand I patted the kid down, removing a .45, which was stuffed down the back of Arnie's Levis. "Quite a collector, aren't you?" I said as I pulled him to his feet.

Bundling the sack full of dollars into the rear of the Pontiac, I installed Arnie in the passenger seat and calmly fired up the engine. We left the pickup with its headlights trained on the shallow ditch, and slowly snaked our way down from the Hollywood Hills. Along the way, Arnie began to snivel. "What . . . what happened to Roy?" he wanted to know. "I tried to get in touch, to say I was sorry, but he didn't pick up the phone. Did you hurt him?"

"Me? No. This whole mess is nothing to do with me. But I wouldn't make any plans on seeing Roy again anytime soon."

Arnie fell silent.

"So," I said, as if making conversation, "which one of you was it that shot the checkout girl?"

"Roy," said Arnie without hesitation, "it was Roy I swear."

I laughed. "Whatever you say."

"It was all Roy's big idea. He wanted the money so he could leave home."

"And what about you? What about your mother?"

Arnie's gaze snapped toward me. "What *about* my mother?"

"Easy now. I'm only asking."

Arnie's shoulders slumped; he deflated like a corpse. "Yeah, I guess I wanted to get away too. Things were getting a little . . . *close*, at home."

"Well, it sounds like you boys came up with the perfect crime," I said, smirking at myself in the rearview mirror.

We picked up the tail on Homebrook Street. It was a burgundy Oldsmobile, with two shadowed passengers. I made no effort to lose them. "See that car?" I said to Arnie.

Arnie looked and nodded.

"In there are the two men who killed Roy."

Arnie gasped. "You mean Roy's really dead?"

"As dead as that cashier girl. And now they're coming for you."

"No!" Arnie shrieked, making a desperate grab for the steering wheel. I put a stop to that with a swift punch to the nose. I felt the bone crunch beneath my fist and saw the gout of blood shimmer beneath the streetlamps. Arnie was quiet after that, his hands clamped to his face as fresh blood spilled out between his fingers.

We reached Mrs. Lukather's house at around eleven P.M. She came out onto the veranda to meet us, sobbing with joy and relief. When she saw the mess Arnie was in, she stopped. "Hey, what have you done to my boy, you animal?"

"Let's go inside, Mrs. Lukather. I believe you owe me seventy-five dollars."

Grudgingly, she ushered me in. Before I stepped across the threshold, I glanced along the street, where the Oldsmobile sat idling by the curb.

Mrs. Lukather positioned Arnie at the kitchen table and handed him a wet washcloth for his bloody face. "Thanks Mom," he said softly and nasally. Then she turned on me.

"Well, you found my son. I don't know how you did it, and I don't want to know, but I guess you did your job. I have your money in the other room." Not waiting for me to reply, she marched out to fetch it. I seated myself at the table opposite Arnie, who did not look up.

It was then, in the heavy silence of the kitchen, that I heard the front door quietly unlatch from outside. Arnie heard it too, and his whole body snapped upright. The boy flung the washcloth aside and sprang to his feet.

I, however, remained seated. I did not even turn around when Mellish and Ormerod entered the room. Arnie whimpered as the two men approached him. Nobody spoke.

The two assassins quickly cornered Arnie. The blind man produced a flick-knife and sliced the air with a venomous swing. Ormerod reached out and gripped Arnie around the waist. Arnie shrieked, and it was only then that I got up to leave.

From nowhere, Mrs. Lukather exploded into the room. Under ordinary circumstances, the two hitmen would have made short work of her as well, but she had caught them off-guard. They were stealthy operators and had not expected a frontal assault. She was waving a baseball bat over her head—I recognized it as the same one Arnie had clutched in the photograph. In the split second Ormerod's attention faltered, Arnie flung his leg back and kicked him square in the groin. Ormerod crumpled, his face frozen in open-mouthed, silent agony. Arnie broke free of the two killers and darted over to his mother.

Before Ormerod could struggle to his feet, Mrs. Lukather swung the bat in his direction. The wet crunch as it connected with the side of his head made me cringe. Ormerod keeled over sideways, blood spilling from the side of his head onto the bare floorboards.

Mellish, meanwhile, still had the knife. Fortunately for mother and son, without his guide dog he was powerless to use it. He swung it out in wild, desperate arcs, grunting like an animal.

Arnie, finally finding his courage, leapt on the blind man, gripping his wrist and battering it against the kitchen counter until Mellish let go of the blade. Then Arnie punched him in the stomach and watched him double up, panting helplessly. His dark glasses dropped to the ground and cracked.

Silence. Arnie and Mrs. Lukather looked at each other questioningly, then they turned to me. "What now?" Mrs. Lukather spat.

"Well, I guess that depends," I said. "You love your son, ma'am?"

"Don't play games."

I laughed. "Of course not," I nodded toward the bat. "Besides, you don't follow the rules. Now let me ask you again: do you love your son?"

She nodded.

I sauntered over to the counter, where the .38 Arnie had stuffed under his mattress now lay. I picked it up—it was cool and sturdy in my palm. Then I turned and placed it in the center of the kitchen table, with the barrel facing pointedly toward Mellish. The blind man still lay jackknifed on the floor, too winded to speak.

"Maybe you need to decide just how much you love him, Mrs. Lukather."

<hr/>

I counted out seventy-five dollars in cash from the woman's purse, and stepped out of the house before I saw anything I shouldn't. I waited on the porch for a moment, in case there came from within the startling whip-crack of a gunshot. In that moment I thought about the nameless checkout girl from Thrifty's Drug

Store. I also thought about Roy Moretz. I listened, but there was no sound at all.

Then I walked shakily back toward my car. I spotted the suitcase on the back seat and, without thinking, pulled it out and left it on the sidewalk. Gripping the steering wheel, I paused and counted to ten slowly until my heart rate steadied. A fresh summer rain speckled the Pontiac's windshield as I gunned the engine and pulled away from the curb.

---

* "Heatwave" is not the kind of story I usually write. Usually, my interest is in golden age detection and locked-room mysteries; this is neither. Here the criminals are stupid and small-time, while the atmosphere is suffocating—hence the title—and punctuated by sudden flashes of violence. But reading the story again, it strikes me that even though it's set in the '50s, and is my unabashed attempt to capture the spirit of classic noir, it's also very much a product of 2020. I find it harder and harder to tell where the story ends and real life seeps back in. In "Heatwave," you'll see a corrupt system weighted against the underdog, you'll see casual everyday violence, Beckettian cynicism, and an atmosphere of pervasive darkness. Sounds rather familiar, don't you think?

David Morrell is the award-winning author of First Blood, *the 1972 novel in which Rambo was introduced. He has an MA and PhD from Pennsylvania State University and was a professor in the English department at the University of Iowa. His* New York Times *bestsellers include the classic espionage novel,* The Brotherhood of the Rose, *the basis for the only television miniseries to be broadcast after a Super Bowl. An Anthony, Edgar, Ellis, Left Coast Crime, and Thriller finalist, Morrell has Comic-Con, Macavity, Nero, and Stoker awards as well as the International Thriller Writers' Thriller Master award and a Bouchercon Lifetime Achievement award.*

REQUIEM FOR A HOMECOMING

David Morrell

"Did they ever find who killed that female student?" Ben asked.

Despite the heat in the crowded pub, he still shivered from sitting in the open convertible during the homecoming parade. After twenty years living in Malibu, he'd forgotten how cold autumn nights could be in the Midwest. He took for granted the people he'd waved to hadn't the faintest idea why he was in the parade. They'd cheered for the actor on the movie poster propped behind him, not the screenwriter whose credit was in fine print at the bottom.

"Female student?" Howard asked.

Ben and Howard had been graduate students in the English department back then. Now Howard taught here, and Ben had accepted the guest-of-honor invitation (despite a screenplay deadline) so he could spend the weekend with his long-ago friend.

"The one that got stabbed in the library," Ben answered. "On homecoming Saturday. Our final year."

"Now I remember," Howard said, lowering his beer glass. "Of course. Her."

"Are you guys okay?" a female voice asked.

Ben looked at the waitress, who had purple hair and a ring through her left nostril. She gestured toward their nearly empty beer pitcher on the table.

"We're good," he answered. "Thanks."

As she pushed her way toward the next booth, the din of the celebrating students gave Ben a headache.

"So far as I know, they never proved who stabbed her," Howard said.

"There was a rumor," Ben said. "About Wayne McDonald."

He referred to an assistant professor, who'd joined the faculty that autumn. A week after the murder, the assistant professor had died when his car veered off a highway and flipped several times before plunging into a ravine. The deaths so close together may have been a coincidence, but after the police discovered that the murdered student had come from the same college where McDonald had recently earned his PhD, there was talk that they'd been connected in other ways, that McDonald had killed her and committed suicide.

"Nothing was proven," Howard said. "All of that happened twenty years ago. What made you think of it? Coming back to campus?"

"Do you remember her name?"

"After so much time?"

"Rebecca Markle," Ben said.

"How . . . ? You must have looked it up on the Internet."

"Didn't need to. I never forgot how terrified everybody on campus felt after her body was found in the library. When I moved to Los Angeles"—Ben had received a scholarship to the grad-school film program at USC—"I kept thinking she was in a place she could take for granted was safe. How surprised and helpless and afraid she must have been when the attack occurred. The first screenplay I sold began with a version of what happened to her."

"I noticed," Howard said.

"Do you remember what she looked like?"

"From photos in newspapers twenty years ago?" Howard shook his head.

Ben pulled his wallet from his jacket and removed a photo-graph. The edges were bent, the color faded. It showed a young, attractive woman, thin, with long blond hair, expressive eyes, and an unhappy smile.

"You keep her picture in your wallet?" Howard asked.

"From the yearbook back then. After the college invited me to be guest of honor this year, I cut it out."

"What on earth for?"

"There was a memorial section for the five students who died that year. One drowned at the reservoir. One committed sui-cide. One had cancer. One got drunk and fell off a balcony at a frat party." Ben paused. "And Rebecca got stabbed to death in a secluded section of the library. You still don't recognize her?"

"No."

"She was in the modern-novel course we took that term."

Howard sat straighter. "What?"

The din of the celebrating students seemed louder.

"Wayne McDonald taught that course," Ben said.

"I remember he taught it, but not who was in it. There must have been a hundred students. Why didn't the police make a big deal about her being in the course? It would have been another connection between her and Wayne."

"Are you sure you guys are good?" the female voice asked.

Ben turned toward their now-weary-eyed server. "I bet you could use this booth for people who drink more than we do."

"I hope you don't mind. Tips can be generous at homecoming. The more people I serve . . ."

"Here's something to make up for us hogging the booth." Ben gave her more than what she'd probably receive all week. "I used to work part-time in the kitchen here. I know how hard it is to pay tuition. Howard, if you're not tired, I'd like to walk around the campus."

After the heat of the pub, the night's chill stung Ben's cheeks. He zipped up a jacket Howard had lent him and shoved his hands in its warm pockets. The noise of the crowd remained in his ears as they crossed the street toward the college.

Arching tree branches obscured a quarter moon. A gentle breeze scraped leaves across a path.

"The trees are bigger," Ben said. "But the ivy on the buildings looks the same. How's your family?"

"Our daughter graduated from here two years ago." Howard referred to his stepchild. "She works for an advertising firm in New York."

"Great. And your wife?"

"No better."

"Sorry."

"Depression isn't anybody's friend."

Their footsteps crunched through the leaves.

"The reason the police didn't make a big deal about Rebecca Markle being in that class is they didn't know," Ben said. "Her name wasn't on the list of students taking the course. She wasn't registered."

"How do you know?"

"I dated her."

Howard turned to him in surprise.

"She and I sat next to each other at the back of the lecture hall," Ben said. "We got to talking. I asked if she'd like to go to a movie. We had a few beers afterward."

"You never mentioned it."

"It didn't seem important. All she talked about was Wayne McDonald, how brilliant he was, how she could listen to him forever. I never asked her to go on another date. I forgot about her until I saw her photo in the newspaper and realized who'd been killed."

"What about the police? Did you tell *them*?"

"Working part-time in that pub earned barely enough for my dorm fees. You know how I paid my tuition—selling uppers to guys in our dorm who waited too long to study for exams or write term papers. I helped them pull all-nighters."

"I always wondered where you got the pills."

"The police would have wondered, too. How long would it have taken them to make a drug dealer a suspect? They could've decided I was furious because Rebecca refused to go out with me again after she discovered how I earned money, or they might have decided I shut her up after she threatened to tell the police I sold drugs. Neither would have been the truth, but by the time the police realized it, my reputation would have been dirt. I'd just received a scholarship to USC. I couldn't risk losing it."

The night breeze turned colder. Ben pushed his hands deeper into the jacket's pockets.

"And you've been thinking about her ever since?" Howard asked.

"I remember her sitting across from me in the pub we just came from. The same booth, in fact. Tonight, *you* sat exactly where *she* did twenty years ago."

"You're creeping me out."

"I'm going to write about her again, but this time, it won't be only a first scene. It'll be about a man who feels guilty because his ambition might have let a murderer escape twenty years earlier. He comes back for his college homecoming to find who did it."

"You're here doing research?" Howard asked.

"And to see *you* again. It's been a long time."

"Yeah, somehow we could never get our schedules to match," Howard said. "Sounds like an interesting movie."

"Well, it has a lot of twists. For example, the main character's best friend dated the murdered woman also."

In the darkness, Howard peered down at the murky leaves. On the street far behind them, car horns blared. Engines roared. Students whooped. The night became quiet again.

"I didn't date her," Howard said.

"She pointed at you in class. She told me you went out with her."

"It wasn't a date."

"She told me she hoped I wasn't going to try what *you* did."

"It wasn't what it sounds like."

"What *was* it then?" Ben asked.

"I often visited Wayne during his office hours. You knew that."

"You were his favorite student."

"He hadn't adjusted to being a faculty member," Howard said. "He missed being in graduate school. He liked hanging out with me. A couple of times, he invited me to his apartment to have dinner with his wife and three-year-old daughter. I said 'office hours.'"

Actually he met students in the cafeteria at our dorm. It was obvious he was avoiding his office. It was also obvious he had something he wanted to say to me. Finally, he told me there was a female student who wasn't registered for his classes but was showing up for all of them. He told me she'd followed him from his previous college, that he'd given up a job offer there because of her."

Another horn blared in the distance. More students whooped.

"Why did she follow him?" Ben asked.

"Wayne swore he hadn't been involved with her. He'd been hired as an instructor in his last year at the previous college. Rebecca Markle had been one of his students. He said he'd treated her like any other student, but she thought he meant more than what he was actually saying in his lectures, that he was sending her coded messages, telling her she was special to him. Remember how he made eye contact with every student as he lectured. He scanned back and forth, making it seem he spoke directly to each of us."

"A gifted teacher," Ben agreed. "What did he want you to do?"

"To talk to her, one student to another, and persuade her to leave him alone. Not only *him*. He said his wife had seen Rebecca outside the apartment building where they lived and outside the nursery school where his wife dropped off and picked up their daughter. They were scared."

The night's chill made Ben shiver. "After Rebecca was murdered, did you tell the police about what he'd asked you to do?"

"No."

"Why not?"

"That would have made him a suspect, and I didn't believe he killed her. Where are you going with this, Ben? Is what *I* did any different from what *you* did, keeping quiet because you were afraid the police would suspect *you*?"

"Sorry for being intense. You remember how I used to get when we were students and I was working on a story. Where am I going with this? Back to the hotel to get some sleep. Tomorrow will be busy."

First came an alumni breakfast, where he told good-natured Hollywood gossip about what happened behind the scenes of the films he'd written. Then he gave advice to actors in the theater department. Then he spoke at a lunch for major donors, emphasizing how he wouldn't have had a career if not for the excellent education he'd received here.

At the football stadium, he met numerous dignitaries in the college president's skybox. When he'd been a student, he hadn't been able to afford to go to a football game. This was the first game he'd ever seen that wasn't on television. Even from the top of the stadium, he heard the crack of helmet against helmet.

When the second half started, he pretended to walk toward the nearby men's room, passed it, descended stairs, and reached the car-crammed parking lot. In autumn sunlight that made him squint, he walked past brilliantly colored maple trees toward the library. Having written a film about electronic surveillance, he noticed cameras on various buildings, cameras that hadn't been there twenty years earlier and that might have recorded Rebecca Markle's movements.

Ben passed the English/philosophy building and climbed the stately steps to the column-flanked doors that led to the vast library building. Inside the echoing vestibule, he needed a moment to orient himself after not having been here for twenty years. Then he shifted to the right, passed through an archway, and entered an area where numerous computers occupied rows of tables. On homecoming Saturday while a football game was in progress, only a few students studied the screens. There were cameras here as well. If they'd been installed twenty years earlier, they'd have recorded Rebecca Markle passing through this room and perhaps have revealed someone following her.

He went to the back of the room, passed through an arch, and climbed stone stairs. More cameras. He could have used an elevator, but he'd once written a scene in which a character got a nasty surprise when stepping from an elevator, and the intensity of writing that scene had stayed with him ever since.

On the third landing, he passed beneath another camera, walked along a narrow corridor lined with books, turned a corner, proceeded along a further corridor of books, and entered a small, square, windowless area that had a desk and a wooden chair. He'd visited here several times during his final year. In his imagination, he had returned here many times since.

It was here that Rebecca Markle had been murdered.

He peered down at the floor. She'd lain in her blood after the killer had attacked from behind, reaching around her, plunging a knife into her chest.

Plunging repeatedly.

Footsteps made him turn toward the only entrance to this area.

Howard appeared.

"You followed me?" Ben asked.

"Didn't need to."

"Oh?"

"If you're researching Rebecca's murder, the logical place for you to be is here, at 3:30 when the medical examiner estimated she was killed," Howard said. "I watched the library entrance from the far side of the English/philosophy building."

"You could have been a detective instead of an English professor."

"Or someone in a movie you wrote. Do you seriously think I killed her?"

"I never suggested that."

"Like hell. You set me up last night. 'Did they ever find who killed that female student?' you asked. You must have enjoyed listening to me pretend I didn't remember who Rebecca Markle was. Then you forced me to admit I'd gone out with her. It wasn't a date. I was trying to help Wayne."

"Okay," Ben said. "It wasn't a date."

"I can play your game in reverse. Last night, you gave all sorts of reasons for me to believe *you* killed her. Maybe she threatened to tell the police how you earned your money. Maybe you couldn't bear the thought of USC finding out and canceling your scholarship."

"That would have been a powerful motivation," Ben agreed.

"It would have made more sense than any motive you tried to invent for *me*."

"I don't believe you killed her."

Howard looked surprised.

"But role playing helps me write stories," Ben said. "If this were a detective movie, you'd be a suspect until somebody else seemed likely."

"So you're convinced Wayne did in fact kill her?"

"He had a sort-of alibi because a few people remembered seeing him at the football game. But according to the rumor, he slipped out the same way *I* did. I bet when I go back to the game, no one will realize I've been gone."

"He'd need to have brought a knife," Howard said. "I can't imagine him cold-bloodedly planning to murder someone."

"If only there'd been cameras in the library twenty years ago," Ben said. "They might have shown someone following Rebecca, just as today they showed *you* following *me*. But I don't believe she was followed."

"You think the attack was random?" Howard asked. "A predator saw her alone in here? An attempted rape turned into murder?"

"Or perhaps someone was already waiting."

"I don't understand."

"Perhaps Rebecca came here to meet someone."

"Now you're back to Wayne. No one else had a motive," Howard said. He took a step forward. The tiny space felt even smaller.

"I shouldn't have come back," Ben said.

"Maybe not," Howard told him.

"Would you like to know how my script would end?"

"Never make your audience impatient."

"The audience would suddenly realize that seemingly casual remarks made earlier were actually clues. There'd be a quick cut to a previous scene. 'How's your family?' the detective asked. 'Our daughter graduated from here two years ago,' the apparent suspect answered. He meant his stepchild. 'And your wife?' the detective asked. 'Depression isn't anybody's friend,' the apparent suspect answered. A quick cut to another scene would show the apparent suspect talking about spending time with the assistant professor, his wife, and their three-year-old daughter."

Howard stepped even closer.

"Yes, I spent a lot of time with Wayne and his family," he said.

"And with his wife and his daughter after Wayne died," Ben said.

"Dammit, *somebody* had to. People assumed Wayne was the killer. They avoided his wife. Their little girl wasn't welcome at the nursery school any longer. I was the only person who showed them kindness. She wanted to leave town, to take her daughter and live with her parents in Minneapolis while she tried to recover from Wayne's death and figure out what to do next. I told her if she ran, people would believe they were right to suspect Wayne. She had to stay, to show them they were wrong."

"You were in love with her?" Ben asked.

"From the first time I saw her."

Ben peered down at the floor where Rebecca Markle had lain. "Yes, I shouldn't have come back."

"So how is your screenplay going to end?" Howard asked.

"Wayne's wife . . ."

"Yes? What about her?"

". . . could have asked Rebecca to meet her in the library. Rebecca wouldn't have expected any trouble there. Afraid for her family, Wayne's wife begged Rebecca to leave her husband and child alone. When Rebecca refused, when she turned and walked away, Wayne's wife . . ."

"Pulled the knife from her purse?" Howard asked. "She planned it?"

"As a last resort. After she saw Rebecca at the day-care center, she was desperate."

"In the story," Howard said.

"Yes. In the story. Then maybe Wayne suspected what she'd done. Maybe he saw blood on the sleeve of a blouse or a sweater his wife had been wearing. Maybe he became so distressed he couldn't concentrate until a week later he lost control of his car and . . ."

"In the story," Howard repeated.

"Yes. In the story."

"What's that movie where everybody sees the same thing but every version is different? It's Japanese."

"*Rashomon*."

"I remember we watched it together. Your story could be like that. Different versions of what happened. None truer than the other. Me killing her, you killing her, Wayne killing her, a predator killing her."

"But not Wayne's wife?" Ben asked.

"She *couldn't* have done it. She had an alibi. She was at home, taking care of their little girl."

"Yes, to meet Rebecca, she'd have needed a babysitter," Ben said. "Someone she trusted. Someone who maybe saw blood on a sleeve when she returned home. Someone who never mentioned it to the police or contradicted her when she told the police she'd been taking care of her little girl at the time of the murder."

"Hard to find someone she could depend on that much," Howard said.

"Yes, hard to find." Ben peered down at the floor again. "I think I talked the story to death."

"When we were students, that used to happen to you."

"I'd better get back to the game. The college president has a lot more donors he wants me to convince to be generous."

"Good luck with them."

"I'll do my best since this is my last homecoming."

For much of my life, I balanced fiction writing with being in academia, first as an American-literature graduate student at Penn State, then as a professor in the English Department at the University of Iowa. When Lawrence Block asked me to write a story for his university-themed anthology, The Darkling Halls of Ivy, *I didn't think twice, so eagerly did I wish to return (in my imagination, at least) to that fulfilling classroom environment. Of course, outside the classroom, academia isn't always an ideal place—office politics can be especially annoying. I briefly considered a story about that topic or about plagiarism or about student political demonstrations. There are many dramatic aspects to the university world. But my memory kept taking me back to a murder that traumatized a university and threatened its innocent belief that it could indeed enjoy the protection of an ivory tower. "Requiem for a Homecoming" shares a few parallels with an actual event but is otherwise a work of my creation and is in no way intended to suggest a solution to the original, long-ago mystery.*

Joyce Carol Oates is the recipient of the 2021 Pepe Carvalho Prize for Noir Fiction (Spain) and the 2020 Cino del Duca World Prize (France) as well as the National Book Award and the President's Humanities Medal. Among her recent novels are Pursuit *and* Night. Sleep. Death. The Stars *and the story collections* Beautiful Days *and* Night, Neon. *Stories of hers have appeared previously in* The Best American Mystery Stories *and* The Best American Noir of the Century *edited by James Ellroy and Otto Penzler. She is currently teaching at Princeton and at Rutgers University.*

PAROLE HEARING, CALIFORNIA INSTITUTION FOR WOMEN, CHINO, CA

Joyce Carol Oates

W hy am I requesting parole another time?—because I am penitent.

Because I am remorseful for the wrongs I have inflicted upon the innocent.

Because I am a changed person.

Because I have punished myself every day, every hour, and every minute of my incarceration.

Because the warden will testify on my behalf: I have been a model prisoner.

Because the chaplain will testify on my behalf: I have welcomed Jesus Christ into my heart.

Because I have served fifty-one years in prison. Because I have been rejected for parole fifteen times.

Because I am seventy years old, I am no longer nineteen years old.

Because I cannot remember who I was when I was nineteen years old.

Because I regret all that I was commanded to do in August 1969.

Because the person I hurt most at that terrible time was—myself.

<hr />

Why am I requesting parole?—because (I believe) I have paid what is called my debt to society.

Because I have completed college while in prison. I have a community college degree, Chino Valley Community College.

Because I have taught generations of inmates to read and write.

Because I have assisted the arts and crafts instructors and they have praised me.

(I love the thrill of power, making lesser beings my slaves.)

Because I have goodness in my heart that yearns to be released into the world.

Because I would make amends.

Because I am an example to the younger women.

Because I am the oldest woman prisoner in California, and there is shame in this.

Because the other prisoners are all younger than I am, and they pity me.

Because I am not a threat to society.

Because I was a battered woman and did not realize.

Because all that happened in 1969 happened because of that.

Because it was not fair, and is not fair.

Because the person I hurt most was—myself.

—⊶—

Why am I requesting parole?—Because Jesus has come into my heart, and He has forgiven me.

Because Jesus understood it was the Devil who guided my hand to smite the innocent with evil intent.

Because the Devil whispered to us—Do something witchy!

Because I had no choice, I had to obey.

Because he would have punished me if I did not.

Because he would have ceased to love me if I did not.

Because he has passed away now and left me with this (swastika) scar on my forehead.

Because, seeing this scar I have borne for fifty-one years, you will judge me harshly.

Because the person he hurt most was—me.

—⊶—

Because I was abused by others.

Because I was trusting in my heart, and so I was abused by others.

Because I was abused by him.

Because I was weak-willed. Because I was a victim of what the therapist has called low self-esteem.

Because I was starving, and he gave me nourishment.

Because he asked of me—Don't you know who I am?

Because I dissolved into tears before him at such words. Because all my life I had been awaiting such words.

Because the Family welcomed me, at his bidding.

Because soon they called me Big Patty. Because they called me Pimply Face. Because they made me crouch down and eat from the dog's dish.

Because they laughed at me.

Because he did not protect me from them.

Because I gave my soul to him.

Because I am begging understanding and forgiveness from you, on my knees.

Because I am a good person, in my heart.

Because you can see—can't you?—I am a good person, in my heart.

Because it was easy to hypnotize me.

Because it was easy to drug me.

Because I could not say no.

Because very feebly I did say no, no—but he laughed at me and made me serve him on my knees.

Because I was ravenous for love—for touch.

Because stabbing the victims, I was stabbing myself.

Because sinking my hands into the wounds of the victims, to mock and defile them, I was mocking and defiling myself.

Because tasting the blood that was "warm and sticky," I was tasting my own blood that spurted out onto walls, ceilings, carpets.

Because, at my trial, prejudiced jurors found me guilty of "seven counts of homicide," not knowing how I was but his instrument.

Because you who sit in judgment of me have no idea of the being I am in my innermost heart.

Because you gaze upon me with pity and contempt, thinking—Oh she is a monster! She is nothing like me.

But I am like you. In my heart that is without pity, I am you.

Because it is true, certain terrible things were done by my hand, which was but his hand.

Because it is true, these were terrible acts and yet joyous, as he had ordained.

Because it is true, I showed no mercy to those who begged for their lives on their knees.

On my knees for all of my life, I did not receive mercy, and so I had no mercy to give.

Well, yes—it is true, I stabbed her sixteen times. The beautiful "movie star."

And it is true, each stab was a shriek of pure joy.

And it is true, in a frenzy I stabbed the baby in her belly, eight months, five weeks old. For a mere second it crossed my mind, I could "deliver" this baby by Caesarean, for I had a razor-sharp butcher knife, and if I did this and brought the baby to Charlie . . . But I could not think beyond the moment, I did not know if Charlie would bless me or curse me, and I could not risk it.

For the baby, too, that had no name, I showed no mercy. For no mercy had been shown me.

Because for these acts that are so terrible in your eyes, I have repented.

For these acts and others, I have repented.

⚬⟊⚬

Because in this prison I am a white woman.

A pearl in a sea of mud. A pearl cast before swine.

Amid the brown- and black-skinned, my skin shines, it is so pure.

He entrusted us with the first battle of Helter Skelter.

He sent us on our mission, to pitch the first battle of the Race War.

He kissed my forehead. He told me—You are beautiful.

Because I had not known this!—in my soul I believed that I was ugly.

Because at school, in all the schools I had gone to—there were jeering eyes, cruel laughter.

Because, when I was not yet twelve years old, already dark hairs grew thick and coarse on my head and beneath my arms and at the pit of my belly. In that place between my legs that was sin to touch. On my legs that were muscled like a boy's, and on my forearms. Wiry hairs on my naked breasts, ticklish at the nipples.

Yet of my body Charlie declared—You are beautiful.

Except: blood, like sludge, oozed between my thighs. A nasty smell lifted from me.

Go away, you disgust me, Charlie said.

Because you are saying—The poor girl!—she was abused, hypnotized.

Because you are saying—She wasn't herself.

Because none of that was true. Because love is a kind of hypnosis, but it was one I chose.

Because Charlie favored the pretty ones, even so.

Because I hated them. Because I had always hated them—beautiful women and girls.

Because it is not fair that some that are sluts, are beautiful like Sharon Tate, and some are ugly like me.

Because when we were done with her, she was not so beautiful.

Because I would not do it again!—I promise.

Because I stuck a fork in a man's belly and laughed at how it dangled from the flab of his belly, but I can scarcely remember.

Because I have been washed clean of these sins through the grace of Jesus.

Because I am a Christian woman, my Savior dwells in my heart.

Because I was not evil, but weak.

Because I was a "criminal" in the eyes of the law but a "victim" in the eyes of God.

Because the swastika scar between my eyes calls your eye to it, in judgment. Because you think—She is disfigured! She bears the sign of Satan, she must not ever be paroled.

Because the scar is faded now. Because if you did not know what it was, you would not recognize it.

Because I was a battered woman—a therapist has told me.

Because my case should be reopened. Because my incarceration should be ended. Because I have served my time.

Because sin has faded in my memory.

Because where there was the Devil, there is now Love.

❦

Because in the blood of the dying I wrote on the walls of the fancy house—DEATH TO PIGS HEALTER SKELTER

Because it was not to be that I would have a baby—so it was fitting, she could not have her baby.

Such a big belly! Big white drum-belly! Screaming, like they say a stuck pig screams, and squeals, and tries to crawl away—so you must straddle it, knees gripping her slippery, naked back to wreak the greatest vengeance.

Because she was so beautiful, the sun shone out of her face.

Because she was so beautiful, she did not deserve to live.

All of them, strangers to us—they did not deserve to live.

Do it gruesome—Charlie commanded.

Because that was the address he'd given us on a winding canyon road in the night—Leave no one alive there.

Because we did not question. (Why would we question?)

Because rage is justice, if you are the meek.

Because it is said—Blessed are the meek, they shall inherit the earth.

Because when flames burst inside you, you know that you are redeemed.

Because it is time for my parole, Jesus is commanding you—Turn my minion loose!

Because you are fools who think you see a putty-skinned plain old woman in prison clothes humbling herself before you, a harmless old bag with a collapsed face and collapsed breasts to her waist—you have not the eyes to see who I am, as with his laser eyes Charlie saw at once—You are beautiful.

Because Charlie perceived in me within a minute of seeing me, I might be a sword of God.

Because I might be a scourge of the enemy.

Because I had wanted to be a nun, but the nuns rejected me.

Because you will all pay, that the nuns rejected me.

Because if you release me, I have more justice to seek.

Because you hold the keys to the prison, but one day you will suffer as we suffer, in the flaming pits of Hell.

Because you are trying to find a way to comprehend me. So you can pity me. So you can be superior to me. She was brainwashed. She was not responsible. She was fed hallucinogens—LSD. She was weak-minded, under the spell of the madman.

Because you are mistaken. Because you have no idea what is in my heart.

Because beside Charlie, who was our beautiful Christ, you are vermin.

He would grind you beneath his feet.

Because we made her famous—"Sharon Tate."

Because the slut would be forgotten by now if we had not made her famous.

Because I dipped my hands in her hot, pulsing blood. Shoved my hands into her big belly. Eviscerate—Charlie commanded.

Because you see?—I am meeting your eyes, I am not looking away.

Because I am not servile to the Board of Parole like others who appear meekly before you.

Because I am a woman of dignity. Because prison has not broken my spirit, which is suffused with Charlie's love.

Because I can see, you are filled with loathing for me. As I am filled with loathing for you.

Because even in death her eyes were the color of burnt sugar, her skin flawless and so smooth . . . I thought that I would tell Charlie—I will go back and skin her! Should I go back and skin her!

Because I was sure that Charlie would laugh and say—Yes! Go back and skin the slut and return to me wearing her skin, then I will love you above all the others because you are more beautiful than all of them.

Because this did not happen, and yet it is more real to me than many things that have happened.

As Charlie is more real to me than any of you.

Because we would tear out your throats with our teeth if we could.

Because it is ended now—my (last) parole hearing.

Because I leave you with my curse—DEATH TO PIGS.

"Parole Hearing, California Institution for Women, Chino, CA" was inspired by the fiftieth anniversary, in August 2019, of the infamous Manson murders that so riveted the country at the time, along with the subsequent trial of Manson and several of his young female disciples. The speaker is an imagined disciple of Manson, partly fictitious and

partly based upon Leslie Van Houten who, denied her twenty-second request for parole recently by the intervention of the governor of California, was revealed to be the oldest female inmate in the California prison system.

How must it feel, I wondered, to have thrown away one's life for the (fantasized) love of a psychopathic con man? To have committed grisly murders at the bidding of another? All of Manson's "girls" denied at the time of their trial that Charlie Manson had directed the murders, so powerful was his spell over them; later, they would alter their stories and express some degree of "remorse," no doubt urged by their attorneys.

Fifty years is a long time to brood over guilt, conscience, some hope of redemption; yet, very likely, the embittered person who gleefully hacked living persons to death, stabbing one of the victims as many as forty times, probably remains unchanged in her heart, and regrets only having been punished for her crimes and having lost the love of her stunted life, "Charlie."

And yes, anyone who could revert to such savagery once might well do it again, at any age, and write upon a wall DEATH TO PIGS. And next time, the helpless victim could be a member of the parole board to whom she is speaking here, or, indeed, one of us.

LOVE & OTHER CRIMES

Sara Paretsky

1

"They're trying to frame Gregory," she announced baldly.

"Who are 'they,' who is Gregory, and what are 'they' saying he did?" I asked.

"Fucking Warshawski snob," she said. "I might have known. Like your mother, too good to walk around the planet with the ordinary mortals."

"Anyone who compares me to my mother is paying me the highest possible compliment. But I still don't—oh, Gregory? Baby Gregory? Are you Sonia Litvak?" She'd given her name as Sonia Geary when she made the appointment.

"I got married. Did you think that was impossible?" she jeered.

She saw my inadvertent glance at her bare left hand. "It didn't last. Neither did yours, what I heard, but you had to keep your own name, didn't you? No one else could be as good as a Warshawski."

"Do you want to tell me who framed Gregory for what?" I asked. "Or just needle me about my family?"

"I want you to understand I don't need any Warshawski pity or handouts. I came here for help and I plan to pay your bill."

"That assumes I agree to help you," I snapped.

"But—you have to!" She was astonished. "You're from South Houston, same as me. And I need a private cop to go up against the city, although come to think of it, your father was a Chicago cop and—"

"If you insult my father on top of my mother, you'll have to leave."

"Oh, don't get your undies in a bundle," she grumbled. "I never went to finishing school."

It was as close as she would come to an apology. I turned away to type Gregory Litvak's name into a legal database, and he popped right up: charged with second-degree homicide along with criminal destruction of property. Ten days ago, someone—allegedly Gregory Litvak—had gone through the Roccamena warehouse and smashed about twenty-five million dollars' worth of wine and booze.

Sonia was reading over my shoulder. "See, I told you—they framed him for this."

"Sonia—this doesn't prove anything about anyone."

I scrolled down the screen. Roccamena had fired Gregory a week or so before the destruction. The state—and the liquor distributor—claimed he sought revenge by rampaging through the warehouse.

He might still have made bail, but the crime held a second, more serious offense: when the cleanup crew started hauling out the debris, they'd found the body of Eugene Horvath mixed in with the broken bottles in aisle ninety-seven. Horvath was Roccamena's accountant; the state's theory was that Gregory blamed him for losing his job.

"They fired Gregory for no reason," Sonia burst out. "And then, because they feel guilty, they have to frame him for destroying the warehouse and killing Horvath. The Roccamenas probably did it themselves to collect insurance."

"What made the police pick up Gregory?" I asked.

"His prints were on the forklift. Well, of course his prints were on the forklift. He drove it for them, loading and unloading crap for them all day. Eighteen years he worked there, and then, bingo, he's getting close to being a hundred percent vested, out the door with him. I need you to prove he didn't do it."

She glared fiercely. When she'd been young, carting baby Gregory around, her hair grew in lopsided clumps around her head, as though she got her brother Donny to cut it for her. Today the thick curls, dyed bright orange, were symmetrically shaped. Her face was covered with the armor of heavy makeup, but beneath that, she was still the ungainly, needy girl of fifteen.

Sonia didn't want Warshawski pity, and I didn't want to give her any, so it annoyed me to find myself stirred by it.

"He has a lawyer, right? Or is he in the system?"

"The public defender. We're trying to put the money together for a real lawyer, but we can't even make bail right now. They set it for two million. Who can come up with that kind of money? Reggie could help, but he won't. Taking his brats to Disney World instead of taking care of his own flesh and blood."

I didn't think suggesting that his children were also Reggie's flesh and blood would help. Instead, I laboriously pried details from her. Reggie had moved to Elgin, with his own little company. Sonia was vague about what they did, but it had something to do with computers. She seemed to think Reggie had become another Gates or Jobs, and that he wouldn't help Gregory out of spite.

Donny worked for Klondike insurance. This was an agency that had the inside track on a lot of city and county business, which somehow, inevitably, also seemed to mean some of their clients were Mob fronts. It sounded as though he was the agency's handyman, repairing broken machines, changing lightbulbs, ordering supplies. I could picture him siphoning off supplies and selling them on craigslist, but not engineering the big deals that make a successful mobster.

"So it's not like Donny's got a lot of money," Sonia was continuing to whine, "and then his ex is sucking the marrow out of his bones. He doesn't even get to see the kid except weekends and then the kid doesn't want to hang around Donny because Donny doesn't have a PlayStation or any of that crap."

"Stanley can't help?" I asked.

"He dropped all the way out." Sonia snorted. "First he was in business with Reggie, but he said late-stage capitalism was draining his lifeblood, whatever the fuck that means. He lives in a cabin in the hills somewhere in Arizona and thinks great thoughts. Or maybe it's no thoughts."

That left baby Gregory.

"Gregory is super smart," Sonia said. "Like, he had really high ACT scores, so Daddy wanted him to go to college. He even got a scholarship to go to the University of Illinois, but then he never went. So Daddy threw him out of the house, which was when I was

married, and he lived with me, then Ken threw him out, which
led to me beating Ken up and him getting an order of protection
and then a divorce. Anyway, that's when Donny found Gregory
a job at Roccamena's, and he's been there ever since. Until they
fired him for no reason at all."

"They must have told him something."

She tossed her head, but the orange curls didn't move. She must
have sprayed some kind of epoxy on them.

"Ask him yourself. Maybe you can turn on some Warshawski
charm and he'll tell you stuff he won't talk to me about."

The chin beneath the thick makeup wobbled; she fished in
her handbag and blew her nose, a good loud honk. "You going to
help me or not?"

Not, I chanted silently. Not, not, not.

So why did I find myself printing out a copy of my standard
contract for Sonia? I thought when she saw my fees and the nonrefundable deposit she'd walk out, but she signed it with every
appearance of nonchalance, counted out five hundred dollars in
twenties, and swept from the office. Sort of. She was wearing a
sweatshirt that proclaimed her attachment to Liggett Bar and
Grill's Slow Pitch team; the sleeve snagged on the lock tongue on
her way out and she had to stop to pull it free.

2

Even the cockiest gang members look wilted after a week at
County, and Gregory Litvak hadn't been cocky to begin with. Like
all the Litvaks, he was short, with wide shoulders and a mass of
wiry curls. Unlike his siblings, he sat hunched on his side of the
table, looking at the floor.

I hadn't seen him since he was a baby, seemingly glued to his sister's hip, but when the guard brought him into the room for lawyers and clients, I recognized him at once.

"I used to live up the street from your family," I said, to break a growing silence. "I sold my house when my dad died. Are you still in South Chicago?"

"I, uh, moved," he mumbled, without looking up. "After Karen and Arthur died. Over to Fernwood. Sonia and Donny, they found me a place."

It took a minute for me to realize Karen and Arthur were his parents. "Did Sonia tell you she's hired me to find evidence to exonerate you?"

His thick neck bobbed fractionally. He'd been shifting boxes of liquor at the Roccamena warehouse for the best part of twenty years; his broad shoulders were also heavily muscled. I could see him easily bashing—but I was on his team. Put those thoughts firmly away. Anyway, he wasn't a fighter: the bruises all over his face and arms showed that he was easy prey in the halls and exercise yard.

"Sonia says you didn't do it."

"I didn't." His voice, even in protest, remained a monotone. "It sounds awful, what happened, but I didn't see it. I didn't do it."

"You didn't see it?" I was puzzled.

He looked up for a second. "They showed me pictures. But I didn't see it happen. I don't know who did it."

"Do you have an alibi for the night?"

"I live alone. I guess you could ask Gattara." He gave a bark of unhappy laughter. "That's my cat. It's the name of a wine we—they sell. It has a cat on the label."

"Donny says you do have an alibi."

"He told me," Gregory said, listless. "I don't know what he's talking about. I guess he thinks he can rescue me. Him and Sonia, like they've always done." His voice trailed away.

3

My dad used to say that Donny Litvak would end up in prison, but only after taking over the Chicago Mob. "Kid's constantly skating close to the edge, except on the wrong side," he grunted, "but he's got brains and the Outfit could use a few."

Gabriella would respond, "The one who should be in prison is the mother. She pays no attention to her children, so they run around like—like *teppisti*. The girl, she is even worse than the brothers. I thought maybe I could help, but—!"

There were five Litvak children—Sonia, who was a couple of years older than me, and four younger brothers. Donny was in my year, but I never saw him in school, only on the streets. He ran with the sports kids, so my cousin Boom-Boom was part of his life, but he also hung out with the guys who boosted booze from delivery trucks to help out the local bars. In exchange they got a few bucks and free cigarettes.

The cops picked Donny up a couple of times, until he got more skilled at avoiding capture. On at least one occasion, Sonia stomped to the station and stared down the desk sergeant.

"Donny was with me. Baby Gregory has croup, it takes two of us to look after him when he's feverish and coughing like that."

Except when Sonia was at school herself, baby Gregory was part of her wardrobe. When he grew too heavy for her to carry, he held on to the belt loops on her jeans. He was an unhappy baby who cried easily; the howls in the police station brought out the watch commander, who let Donny go, even though he knew as well as Sonia that her brother was guilty as charged.

Reggie and Stanley, identical twins two years younger than Donny, flew below the radar. Boom-Boom used to say they were running a gambling game that moved around in the dark, but no one ever proved anything. However, when they graduated from high school, they had saved enough pocket money to pay for college.

Mrs. Litvak was a massively fat woman who spent her days in front of the television with a cup that she refilled frequently from an unplugged coffeepot in the corner of the kitchen. It infuriated my mother that she never seemed to stir whenever any of the boys got into trouble.

Mr. Litvak was an engineer at the Ford Assembly Plant on 130th. He had a ferocious temper, and in a neighborhood of small houses divided by narrow passageways, we all knew all the fights.

Mr. Litvak claimed his wife slept around: *You're lucky I let those damned kids live in my house when not one of them is mine. That's why Donny keeps getting Cs. Your children have the IQs of monkeys. No, wait, monkeys are smart. Your children have the IQs of hamsters.*

Mrs. Litvak wasn't intimidated, or at least she fought back: her husband was a mama's boy who couldn't wipe his own ass if his mother wasn't there to do it. And so on.

The children dressed in odd, mismatched clothes. A rich aunt in New York sent Sonia her daughter's castoffs, but they were two or three sizes too small, and so the girl went to school in her mother's clothes, clumsily cut down to fit her. Once a year, for the Jewish New Year, Mr. Litvak marched the children to services, the older boys looking like clowns in their father's sports jackets, Sonia looking like a middle-aged woman in her mother's ill-fitting dress.

Kids like the Litvaks would normally be the butt of taunts and assaults, but Donny and Sonia seemed to have some kind of force field around them—it repelled attack, but it also repelled any overture of friendship. Sonia's basilisk stare dried up words in the biggest bully's mouth.

My mother either didn't sense the force field, or figured she could penetrate it. She knew what it was like to be an outsider and an outcast; she thought all Sonia needed was an adult to show her some kindness.

Each fall, when school started, Gabriella commissioned a new dress for me from Signora Rapellini, who made the few elegant outfits Gabriella herself owned. My mother had a good eye for color and fit; one September, she asked Signora Rapellini to make something for the Litvak girl at the same time.

When we picked up the clothes, I didn't want to go with Gabriella to the Litvak house. I had a nasty feeling in the pit of my stomach about what could go wrong. Sonia answered the door, Gregory on her hip. We could hear the TV in the background and Mrs. Litvak's hoarse demand to know who was at the door. The twins were fighting over something. All the noise drowned out Gabriella's little speech, offering Sonia something to bring luck in the new school year.

Sonia looked at Gabriella in astonishment, but when she saw the dress inside the parcel and fingered the fine material, her face softened and she muttered a startled thanks. However, while we were at dinner, Mr. Litvak barged into the house. He flung the dress—which he'd cut into strips—at my mother.

"How dare you come into my house and act as if I can't look after my own children? We don't need your pity, your charity, your saintly good deeds. Come near my family again and I'll have the law on you."

My father, the most peaceable man on earth, was on his feet, moving Litvak back to the door. "If you ever threaten my wife again, I will arrest you myself. You don't deserve a family. You're the only man in the neighborhood who isn't at your son's baseball games, isn't listening to your daughter's piano recitals. Not that she has any, because she's looking after your children and your home. Go away and don't come back until you've taken on adult responsibility for your family."

It was as if someone had stuck a pin into Mr. Litvak. All the air oozed out of him. He left without another word.

That was the last time I actually saw a member of the family up close: after that, Sonia and her brothers would cross the street when they saw me, making ostentatious retching noises. And then the day came when Sonia showed up in my office.

4

Before visiting Gregory at County, I had gone to see Sergeant Pizzello. She'd been transferred to the Eighth District, which included the section of South Pulaski where the Roccamena warehouse stood. She'd handled Gregory's interrogation when they picked him up.

"Was he on the run? How did you find him?"

"Solid police work, Warshawski. We knocked on the door of the crappy little hellhole he lives in. He was drinking bourbon and eating chicken wings. In his underwear. At five in the morning."

"I missed the latest set of new felonies out of the legislature. Is it the hour, the underwear, or wings with bourbon that made him a suspect?"

"You trying for Second City? Your act needs polish. When a guy with a grudge is awake at five A.M., and his place of employment was turned into a shambles an hour earlier, it raises questions. The shortest way to point B is from—"

"The right starting place," I interrupted. "Did he have glass on him? From what I read about the damage, there must have been glass dust in his hair and face—you couldn't keep it off you."

"The humble police sergeant thanks the superior intellect of the private investigator. Litvak was naked except for his Y-fronts. Any clothes that would have carried glass into the apartment he'd ditched before he came home."

"You find them?"

She shook her head regretfully. "Still, doesn't mean anything. It's a big city, and there are a lot of places you can get rid of incriminating evidence."

"Any witnesses report a heavyset white man wandering around naked at five A.M.?"

She pressed her lips together and looked away.

"Eugene Horvath," I said. "It sounds like a hideous death, buried under a mound of broken bottles."

"It was." She clicked on her keyboard and turned the screen around to show me the crime scene photos.

I sucked in a breath when I saw the destruction at the warehouse: twenty-foot-high shelves had been toppled on top of each other. Thousands of bottles had crashed as the shelves went down. Broken glass lay hip deep in some places.

Pizzello also showed me copies of half a dozen stills from the internal security cameras. They showed the forklift at the head of an aisle. The teeth were under a set of shelves in one frame. In the next the shelves had jackknifed at a crazy angle, as if a tank had crashed into them. The other stills showed piles of broken glass and pools of alcohol. The forklift had clearly been driven by an experienced handler.

"Why we picked up Litvak. Someone knew that warehouse inside and out. They were skilled with a forklift. Litvak's prints were all over the forklift."

"Anyone else's?" I asked.

She bit her lower lip, a kind of "tell" with her that she was on thin ice. "Some of the other operators."

I made a show of entering her answer into my tablet. "How long did this mayhem go on? Don't they have an alarm system?"

"Disabled. Which also points to Litvak. He *says* he never knew the codes on the door or on the internal alarms, but after eighteen years—you'd have to be a total zombie not to pick up that stuff."

If it had been Donny, yes, but Gregory seemed too listless and depressed to spy on someone typing in an alarm code.

"Who called the cops?" I asked.

"Litvak lost his head—left through the loading bays. They have bar locks that you can slide open from the inside, but if you do, that triggers the alarm system. We had a patrol there in fifteen minutes, but he'd taken off."

I made another note.

"What about the dead man? How did he end up in the warehouse during the rampage?"

"That's a mystery." Pizzello bared her teeth in a hideous parody of a grin. "Something for the suave sleuth. We don't know. His wife says he had a dinner meeting, but she doesn't know who with. His phone has disappeared and his desktop calendar was wiped clean. We don't know if he was lured to the warehouse, or if he went in to check on something—the wife says he worked odd hours sometimes, especially at tax season—or if he drove past and saw lights blazing and went in to investigate."

"The suave sleuth thinks time of death could narrow that down."

Pizzello brought up photos of Horvath's body. He looked as though he'd been through a cattle stampede, the skin flailed from most of his body, left ear dangling from the skull.

"I get it," I said, my voice thick with nausea. "Hard to pin down. I assume that applies to the cause of death too."

"What do you mean?" She stared. "You imagining some kind of superhero able to withstand a ton of glass coming down on your head?"

"I'm wondering if the murder was the sideshow or the main attraction. Maybe he was killed by the ton of glass, but maybe it was an altercation that got out of hand and was covered by a ton of glass. Or a bullet, covered ditto, or if he was even alive when he came into the warehouse."

She digested those possibilities in silence, but said, "Whether it was a sideshow or main attraction, Litvak is still in the frame."

"Then it will be my job to paint a new canvas." I left on that grandiose line and went to County, where I met with Gregory.

By the time I'd finished interviewing him, I was sure of two things: he wouldn't survive a month in the jail, and he hadn't killed Horvath or even destroyed the Roccamena warehouse.

5

Nick Vishnikov, Cook County's deputy chief medical examiner, was a fracquaintance: somewhere between friend and business contact. He'd personally conducted Eugene Horvath's autopsy.

They'd x-rayed the body: it didn't hold any extraneous metal; he had a plate in his left elbow and quite a few dental crowns, but no bullets.

"He ate his last meal about two hours before he died. Find out what time he ate and you'll know what time he was killed. Beyond that—was he dead before being mangled by glass and a warehouse tractor? No way of knowing. Not even Abby Sciuto or Ducky could tell you."

I had already exchanged emails with Gregory's harried public defender, getting his permission to be signed on as part of Gregory's legal team. That had allowed me access to him in prison, as well as to the state's case. Now I told the PD I thought we could raise significant doubts about the murder, along with the warehouse destruction; I thought it worthwhile to apply for a new bail hearing.

The PD, an anxious young man named Colin Vilot, was reluctant, mostly because he was juggling one hundred twenty-three cases, but he finally agreed to set up a hearing if I promised to put everything he should say into writing, complete with bullet points.

The new hearing was set for a week away. In the meantime, it could be worthwhile to look at Roccamena's finances. Sonia had said maybe the Roccamenas had destroyed the warehouse themselves to collect the insurance—a not uncommon strategy for a business with cash flow problems, but one that usually involves arson.

Colin Vilot refused to subpoena the Roccamena financial records. He had about three minutes for me to explain why that would help: if we could show dubious finances, we could raise additional doubts about Gregory's involvement.

"You want to take over his defense? Be my guest. I can't handle the cases I've got, anyway," he finally exploded.

I hastily demurred, mended my fences. I hadn't been a litigator for two decades—even a harassed PD could outmaneuver me. Anyway, Roccamena would fight a subpoena, we'd be in court a dozen times or more, and the clock would keep ticking on Gregory.

Instead, I went to Roccamena's offices. They were a big outfit—besides the central warehouse where Gregory had worked, they had satellites around the city perimeter, and had recently expanded to Milwaukee and Peoria. Their offices were inside their main depot, in the maze of half streets and warehouses south of Midway Airport. I often get lost there. This time I drove in circles around a multiplex and a few big-box outlets before realizing that Roccamena occupied all of a spur of Eighty-Seventh Place.

A foreman blocked my passage at the main entrance. When I explained I was a lawyer working for Gregory Litvak, he unbent slightly: Gregory had been an odd duck, a loner, but he wouldn't hurt a fly. If he had killed Horvath, it was an accident, no way should he be arrested for murder. The foreman called inside, and in a few minutes a man in coveralls and a hard hat came out to escort me to the office.

My escort took me around the side of the building to an exterior iron staircase that led to the offices. The door at the top opened from the inside only. My escort kept a finger on a buzzer until someone let us in. Once inside, I saw there was a camera and a monitor that overlooked the stairwell.

The offices occupied space built above the truck bays. They'd been pretty well soundproofed, but they still shook as the semis pulled in and dropped their loads.

As Harry Truman sort of said, if a detective wants a friend, she should get a dog. Fortunately I had two at home, because my welcome was somewhere between glacial and frigid. The HR director wouldn't tell me why Gregory had been fired.

"State secret?" I suggested. "Altering wine labels to send coded messages to Putin? Or was he spending too much time playing games on his phone?"

The HR director said that she couldn't talk to Gregory's lawyer, since his dismissal was a legal matter.

"Is he suing for wrongful dismissal?" I was startled—neither Gregory nor Sonia had told me this.

"No, no." She was impatient. "You must know—he's being tried for murder."

"No, we don't know that, Ms."—I squinted at the name plate buried behind some computer manuals—"Forde. He's a long way from being tried. There are a lot of holes in the state's case, and I am finding out more every half hour I'm on the job. So let's go back to why he was fired. Was he fiddling with the company's finances?"

Unless Gregory was the best actor since Humphrey Bogart, I couldn't picture him doing something that active. I only said it to try to force Ms. Forde into blurting out an indiscretion, so I was surprised when she looked frightened. Eyes wide, looking nervously to her office door, she said, "Of course not. What a ridiculous idea, a loser who moved boxes around knowing how to break into our computers."

The words were scornful, but the tone was quavery.

"Had Eugene Horvath discovered something wrong with the company's books?" I asked.

"I'm just the HR secretary. You need to talk to Mr. Roccamena." She tapped a couple of digits on her phone. "Ellie? It's Carmen in HR. One of Gregory Litvak's lawyers is here, and she's asking about the pension fund. Can Harvey talk to her?"

A few minutes later, a tall man with thick gray hair and a deeply lined face joined us. "Harvey Roccamena. You the lawyer?

We aren't discussing why we terminated Litvak. Just be assured it was for cause."

"The pension fund?" I said. "How did he have access to that?"

The crags between the creases in his cheeks turned burgundy. He waited a fraction of a second too long before saying, "Who knows what a punk can figure out."

"So there is something wrong with the pension fund?"

The burgundy deepened to cabernet. "We run a liquor business, not a fishing company. Off you go, counselor."

Off I went. On my way back to my car, I passed the loading dock where trucks hauling California wines, Europeans, South Americans, liquors, liqueurs, mixers, beers were lined up to water the Roccamena empire.

Every bay at the loading dock had a semi backed up to it. I hoisted myself up onto the lip of the dock. Forklifts were beetling from the semis into the warehouse, stacked with high loads of crates. So much booze made me feel unwell. Made me wonder what it meant for the son of a determined alcoholic like Karen Litvak to work in the liquor business. Pizzello had said they'd found Gregory in his Y-fronts drinking bourbon. Maybe he'd been fired for siphoning off the inventory.

At each bay, a couple stood with a clipboard, ticking off the load. One from the truck, one from the warehouse. When they'd agreed on the delivery, the Roccamena employee signed the bill of lading and the trucker took off. The insurers must have come through quickly for the restocking to be happening at this pace.

I went back to my car for the hard hat I keep in the trunk and wandered into the interior of the building. In the press of activity, no one had time to notice me.

New floor-to-ceiling shelves had been bolted into place, new signage hung above the ends of the aisles. Men were on catwalks high above the aisles, shifting crates from the lifts to the shelves. It was like watching a futuristic horror movie, maybe *Metropolis*, where people are enslaved to machines and the machines know the human addictions.

I slipped among the tractors, wondering which one had done last week's damage, looking for someone taking a break. I came to a side door, propped open, and found what I needed—a trio of smokers. When I joined them, they moved closer together, solidarity against an outsider.

"That's a zoo." I jerked my head toward the open door.

One of them stubbed out his cigarette against his boot heel. The other two took that as a signal that the break was over. Before they disappeared into the building, I said, "I'm Gregory Litvak's lawyer. One of the team, anyway."

"Don't know a Litvak," the stubber said.

I spoke to the parking lot on his left. "If Gregory didn't do all that damage and didn't kill Horvath, who did? He seems depressed and lethargic to me. Maybe that's just from being at County, but it's hard to picture him doing all the planning it took to destroy the inventory here."

The stubber paused.

"He needed to figure out the door code, needed to make sure his face didn't show up on the security cameras. Needed to get Horvath into the warehouse in the middle of the night."

"You saying he's not guilty?"

"I'm saying the proof isn't there. It's sketchy, it's circumstantial. I'd love to know why they fired Gregory. Was he stealing? Drinking on the job? I'd also love to know how Eugene Horvath happened to be in the warehouse that night. And I'd like to know if there's a problem with the pension fund. Harvey Roccamena didn't want to talk about it."

The three men exchanged glances, nodded to one another.

"Litvak. You're right about him. He did a hard day's work most of his damned life here. Not a sociable guy. Never went out for a beer or whatever at the end of his shift. You think when you first meet him he's a snob, then you realize he's scared twenty-four seven, afraid we'll pick on him, whatever. Two years ago they brought in a new floor manager, couldn't leave the guy alone. Twenty years, your pension is fully vested. They went after vulnerable targets, forced 'em to quit, and most of them did, but Litvak, what was he going to do? He didn't have a life, far as I could tell. But it got to him. He started missing shifts. Not a lot, but every month, there'd be a day, sometimes two. So they sort of had cause.

"Horvath, who knows why he ever did anything he did. He was tight with Walker. Clarence Walker, the new floor manager. Speaking of which, I need a full paycheck this week. We were off for four days while they cleaned out the mess and put up new shelves."

I handed them my business card and trailed after them into the warehouse. At the far end of the floor, an interior staircase also led to the offices I'd just visited. A few plate glass windows were cut into the wall so that management could look down on the operation, but security cameras were also plentiful: they were mounted at every aisle as well as in the corners. Roccamena had an inventory that people wanted. A determined filcher could lift a few bottles along the way, but it would be hard to lift a whole case.

I stood in the Nebbiolo aisle. After studying the cartons for a few minutes, I pulled one toward me and started to undo the staples holding it shut. It took about ninety seconds for a forty-something man in a hard hat and shirtsleeves to appear, shouting at me.

"Get the fuck away from that shelf. Who the fuck are you and what are you doing in a restricted zone?"

"You Clarence Walker?" I said. "I'm checking your security system. Do you know how easy it was for me to get into this warehouse? Is anyone monitoring your cameras, or are they only for decoration? Your insurance carrier is going to have a bucket of questions about whether you were negligent, and whether they should force you to return your claim check. You say the perpetrator of the damage hid from the cameras, but someone should have seen a feed of what he was doing."

Walker opened and shut his mouth a few times, like a beached carp. Finally he said, "Litvak knew the security code to get into the building. If he'd broken in, the alarm would have gone off on my phone, but people come in in the night sometimes. Horvath did, to catch up on his paperwork. Mr. Roccamena likes to call his Italian suppliers at three A.M. when no one's around. If someone's here on legitimate business, the alarms don't go off."

"You were tight with Horvath, right? Did he come here that night to catch up on his paperwork? Were your security cameras even functioning so that we can see whether he arrived or not?"

"Are you with the police?" Walker demanded, recovering his balance. "Let me see some ID."

"I'm not with the police. I'm an investigator who works with insurance companies. When people wreak havoc at their businesses to collect insurance, the companies I represent become very cranky. They unleash their massive array of lawyers and do ugly things to companies. If you can't let me see the full security footage for that night, then that will affect the report I write."

"Klondike was satisfied. Which makes me think you're a scam artist yourself. Let me see some ID."

"Klondike." I rolled the name on my tongue like a bad vintage. "They're your insurance agency, they're not the company that underwrote the policy."

I walked away, out past the loading bays, where the forklifts were still racing back and forth. The cigarette stubber gave me a half wave.

6

"Don't try spinning me a line, Donny. I've been watching you cheat at marbles since we were six."

I had called Sonia, demanding to talk to Donny. She'd arrived forty minutes later, her brother in tow. Donny claimed to know nothing about Klondike's client list, especially Roccamena Liquor Wholesalers, Inc. And no way had he gotten Gregory his job there.

"Besides, that was eighteen years ago. Even if someone did put a little pressure on Roccamena, they'd have fired Gregory if he wasn't up to the job. Just like they fired him two weeks ago."

"The damage to the warehouse was what—ten days ago? Two weeks? Roccamena is back up and running. Did Klondike get the carrier to cut a check, or did they advance money to Roccamena? No way would suppliers provide as much inventory as I saw unloaded today because they love Harvey Roccamena."

That's when Donny said he was just the Klondike handyman; he didn't know anything about their client base or who paid claims to whom. When I said I couldn't keep working for Sonia if he didn't tell me a few truths, he said that Klondike had gotten Ajax Insurance, who underwrote the Roccamena policies, to give them a bridge loan until the claim was settled.

This is common in the industry: an important account could get a favorable interest rate on a short-term loan to tide them over a bad patch. In this case, since the claim was almost certain to be paid, Ajax had demanded the most nominal possible interest.

"Gregory says you've promised him an alibi," I said to Donny. "We're trying to get his bail reduced, so letting the judge know he's got a believable alibi will make a big difference."

Donny cracked his knuckles. "You come up with evidence showing someone else had a bigger interest in offing Horvath. If you can't, I'll see about the alibi."

"You'll 'see' about it? Crap, Donny. Does that mean you don't have one but you'll manufacture it?"

"It means the alibi would embarrass some people, so I'd rather not have to use it."

"You'd let Gregory rot?" Sonia exclaimed.

"Sonny, Sonny." Donny patted her broad shoulders. "You know I wouldn't. Remember the time the cops arrested me but Stan told the cops it was him and Reggie said it couldn't be because Stan was with you; it was really him? We all look after each other, even Stanley, down there in Sedona communing with interplanetary forces. Even Reggie, snotty little capitalist that he is. We won't let Gregory down."

Sonia gave a reluctant smile. "Then Reggie will come up with the bail money?"

"Probably not," Donny said, "but I'm working on him."

"Tell me about Eugene Horvath," I said. "Why was he so despicable?"

Donny spread his hands. "I didn't know the guy. He's the one who—oh. You think if Gregory didn't murder him, I did? I did not kill him. He was a jerk and I'm not crying over him, but he has ten thousand clones on the South Side. I know Roccamena will find just as big an asshole, if not bigger, to take his place. Gregory didn't kill him, either. Nor did Sonia or Reggie or even Saint Stanley."

"I want to see the security tapes for that night. Not just the stills that the cops have, the whole footage for the whole evening."

"Can't help you," Donny said.

"Give me the code to the warehouse and I'll find them myself."

"How would I know the code?"

I shook my head. "Maybe Klondike has it in their client database. Or you have a friend at the alarm company. They've probably changed it since the bust-up, but I have enormous faith in your ability to weasel it out of any file or hiding place where the numbers are buried."

Donny's shoulders went back, preening. He corrected the move at once: no one was supposed to notice that he could be flattered.

7

Melanie Horvath bore her grief quietly, in the middle of a very quiet subdivision on the outer reaches of Chicago's exurbia. We don't dress for mourning anymore; she greeted me in skinny jeans covered by a man's white shirt.

She took me to a sunroom at the back of the house, which overlooked a flower garden. Beyond it a field stretched away into the hills.

"I didn't want to see his body, not when the police described it to me, but then it showed up on social media. A kind neighbor thought I should look at it. Will I ever get that image out of my head?"

It was a rhetorical question, but I assured her it would fade in time. "If the picture comes to you, try to think at that moment of a time when he was laughing or intent on a project. Some people find that helpful."

I apologized again for disturbing her but explained that there were ongoing questions about the murder—in particular, what time her husband went to the warehouse.

"The crew on the floor say he was often there in the middle of the night, that he liked to work on accounts undisturbed. It seems as though he could be pretty peaceful here."

She smiled, a small bleak smile. "I worried at first that he was using that as an excuse for an affair. I worried so much that I followed him several times, but, in fact, he'd go into the warehouse and leave after a few hours. I never saw anyone else there, except sometimes Harvey Roccamena."

A trio of horses appeared at the fence behind her garden. Horvath saw me looking at them.

"My hobby. My lifesaver now: you cannot leave animals unattended. They force me to get dressed and go outside."

I made a sympathetic noise, but I wondered about the income that supported three horses, a house that might include five thousand square feet, and the BMW I'd parked next to in the driveway.

We continued a desultory chat. She had last seen her husband when he left for work the morning he died. "He told me he had a dinner date and that he would probably be late. I finally went to bed at midnight. The police woke me at six with the news."

Her voice was steady with an effort; the tendons in her neck stood out and she twisted the ruby on her right hand until the prongs caught on a knuckle and made her bleed.

I asked if she could look up her husband's credit card on the chance he had paid for dinner. She did so, but he hadn't charged anything to his personal cards that day. She didn't have access to his corporate cards.

"I hope your coworkers or your neighbors are looking after you," I said as I left.

"My coworkers. Yes, it would be good if I had a job, something besides the horses to get me out of bed in the mornings. I'll think about that."

When I got back to my office I found a message under the door: *parking lot across from warehouse midnight*. It was in the rough handwriting of someone who seldom wrote; I took for granted it was from Donny Litvak.

8

At midnight, most of the massive warehouses and plants were down to skeleton crews. The parking lots were nearly empty. I left the Mustang near a twenty-four-hour diner so it wouldn't stand out and provide a target for the knots of teens who swarmed and evaporated through the area.

The Roccamena warehouse was about half a mile away, across a vast stretch of asphalt. The empty lot unnerved me. I walked along the perimeter, keeping away from the circles of light the streetlamps created, but close enough to the road I could sprint from danger if I had to.

When I got to the lot entrance, facing Roccamena, I squatted on the pavement. I was wearing a black cap, loose black clothes, running shoes with the white trim painted black.

A few semis were still huffing in the loading bays, a few cars still parked nearby. It was one before the last truck drove off, the last worker jumped down from the dock lip and into his car. One SUV remained, a late-model Lincoln. After another twenty minutes, Harvey Roccamena himself came through a side door, typed the code into the pad next to it, and took off in the Navigator.

After its taillights vanished, two figures walked down the road toward me. They were both bulky, broad shouldered, but I waited for them to get near before I got to my feet. When they reached the entrance to the lot, I could hear one say, "She'd damned well better be here, after you dragged me into Gregory's mess."

"Present and accounted for," I said softly, from my shadow.

"Fuck, Warshawski!" Donny swore. "You fucking gave me a heart attack."

"Wanted to make sure this wasn't a setup," I said. "Is this Reggie?"

The second man grunted. "Yeah. Donny can't handle technology. Has to come to little brother. Slobbering and groveling."

"You could have come up with the bail money," Donny said.

"I could not come up with two hundred thousand in cash. Stop playing on that string, Donny, or I'll head back to Elgin. In fact, I'd like to be there right now instead of running the risk of arrest with you. And what kind of lawyer did you grow up to be, Warshawski, breaking into warehouses in the dead of night? You could be disbarred if you're caught."

"Then we'd better not get caught," I said. "And the easiest way to avoid that is to stop arguing on a public street where no one else is loitering. I saw both Chicago and Bedford cruisers roaming through the lot while I was waiting."

I took gloves from my pocket. I offered some to the brothers, but they'd brought their own. I put on mine and followed the pair across the road to the warehouse. Despite their bulk, the Litvaks moved quickly. At the side door where Roccamena had exited, we flattened ourselves against the wall while Donny stuck up an arm to put a piece of chewing gum over the camera eye. Reggie held his camera lens over the keypad. Whatever app he'd installed communed with the keypad's brain; in another minute a light flashed green, and we were inside.

The warehouse had security lights in the ceiling tiles. Their glow was just bright enough that we could see the crates and ladders cluttering the aisles.

Donny knew what arcs the security cameras traced. Reggie and I followed his lead, getting down on the floor and sliding, snakelike, between the edges of the camera ranges. We were all out of breath, holding back adolescent giggles, when we reached the door that led to the warehouse offices.

Reggie once again held his phone to the keypad. On the other side of the door, we tiptoed up a metal stairwell to a small room that overlooked the warehouse floor. Here were the computer monitors, showing the cameras at work. I watched as they tracked the shelves, checking for pilfering, but not sweeping low enough to have seen us on the floor. A big monitor with a keyboard in front was connected to the company's main computer.

This room didn't have any windows to show a light to the outside; we turned on the desk lamps.

"Okay, nerd, work your magic," Donny said to Reggie.

"Right, punk. Go beat someone up and don't bother me."

Reggie settled himself at the monitor, removing his gloves to make it easier to type. Donny entertained himself by going through the drawers in the small desk. I stood behind Reggie, watching the screen.

It took him about twenty minutes to get into the system and to find his way around the files. I watched, impressed, as he found the reports from the night Horvath was killed.

Action began at 2:32 A.M. It showed a forklift emerging from the back of the warehouse, from the area around the loading bay.

It was impossible to see the driver but easy to follow the action: Godzilla going through New York City, picking up high shelving and toppling it.

At one point, the driver stuck his torso out at right angles to the machine and waved at the cameras. He was masked, wearing work gloves. You couldn't see who it was, but if the state was basing Gregory's arrest on his prints on the machine, this frame showed he didn't leave them that night.

A few minutes after that, the machine started down aisle ninety-seven. We saw the driver pick up a shelf, try to resettle it, and back away as it crashed in front of him. He maneuvered through the wreckage and disappeared into the service bays.

"Poor bastard—must have seen Horvath's body," Donny said.

I swerved to look at him. "How do you know that, Donny?"

He met my gaze with a limpid smile. "Police report; dude was found in aisle ninety-seven. Must have been a hell of a shock to see a body on the floor."

"Right." My voice was as dry as glass dust. "As you pointed out, Gregory's alibi could embarrass someone."

I waited another minute, but he wasn't going to say anything else; I turned back to the monitor.

The program only played camera activity if something triggered their motion detectors. A clock at the top of the screen reported how many minutes they idled between reports. Twelve minutes had passed before the warehouse was filled with cops.

Roccamena appeared, talking to whoever was leading the patrol unit.

"Back that up," I told Reggie. "Where did he come from?"

He backed up the video, but Roccamena seemed to appear from nowhere.

"You can't get inside the offices from the outside staircase, so he had to still be in the building," I said. "If he'd come in through the side entrance or the bays, he'd be on camera four or seventeen. Go back to the start of the night. When did the last person leave the building?"

Reggie found someone bolting the last of the loading bays at 11:00 P.M. He left through the side door, shutting off the lights on his way out. After that, nothing triggered the sensors until 11:30, when a man came in through the side door. The cameras went black.

Reggie went through all his file-revival tricks, but the cameras hadn't found anything until 2:32, when the forklift appeared from the loading bays.

"Was that Horvath? Can we look at him again?"

Reggie went back to 11:30 and froze the frame. None of us knew Horvath by sight, but his picture had been all over the news immediately after the murder.

"Send all these files to me, will you?" I said to Reggie. "We need these pictures if we end up going to court. Of course, the real driver of the forklift may step forward."

"I wouldn't count on it," Donny said. "He'd be afraid of being framed for the murder."

"Maybe he'll grow a conscience," Reggie growled.

"Maybe his overgrown conscience led him to the warehouse that night," Donny growled back.

"We'll turn the alibi holder over to Sonia in the morning," I said. "Right now, I want to make sure we have our own copy of the camera footage. And then get out before someone finds us in here."

"Sonia," Donny said in a strangled voice.

"Your sister is my client. She needs to know about Gregory's alibi." I grinned in a friendly way.

Reggie muttered curses at Roccamena's IT administrator—he couldn't find file compression software. "They've got 7-Zip now and they'd better thank me for it."

He closed the files he'd opened, used an alcohol pad to wipe off the keyboard, and followed Donny out the door. I was behind them when I realized Donny had left one of the drawers he'd been fiddling with open.

When I couldn't get it to shut all the way, I squatted and saw a sheaf of crumpled paper had slid between the back of the drawer and the desk wall behind it. I eased the pages out. It was a printout of financial data, as far as I could tell—most of the paper was so crusted in dried blood I couldn't read it.

9

I was between the stairs to the office and the side door when I saw the flashlight dancing across the floor.

"I know you're in there. I have a gun and I'm prepared to use it," a deep voice cried.

"And I have the blood-covered report on your pension fund. Which I am prepared to use," I called back.

I'd stood in the office too long, trying to read through the dried blood. I'd finally seen that this was a printout of the Roccamena pension fund activity for the past six years. Names that I couldn't decipher were highlighted.

I'd heard the side door shut behind Donny and Reggie; Donny texted me to hurry it up, they wouldn't wait forever. I stuck the report into an envelope and left the office—about five minutes too late.

Harvey Roccamena charged around the corner of aisle 114, gun out. I hit the floor, rolled up against the shelf. He lifted his hand to fire and I swept all the bottles from the bottom shelf into his path. He sidestepped and his shot went wide, shattering the whiskey behind me.

I scrambled to my feet and flung a bottle at him. It went high, flying over his head to shatter against the shelf behind him. I threw again as he fired. My fourth bottle hit his shoulder and he dropped the gun. He scrabbled for it as I tried to kick it. My toe slammed into his hand, but he held on to the gun and pointed it at my head.

I twisted around, swung my left foot into his gut. Dropped to the floor as he fired, grabbed his leg, upended him into the broken glass.

The gunshots were so deafening that I didn't hear the forklift engine until it was almost on us. Donny was screaming at me. I jumped onto the forks and clung to the mast as the lift made a tight circle and trundled to the loading bays.

One of the doors was open, waiting. We jumped from the machine and ran. Roccamena stood in the doorway shooting at us.

10

"They should never have fired Gregory," Donny said.

"So you decided to destroy Roccamena's inventory in revenge?" I said.

"Of course not." That was Sonia. "Donny was with me that night. I needed help filling out my tax return."

"And Donny, tax whiz that he is, was just the man for the job," I agreed politely. "Reggie would have been a better choice, but he was with Donny at the warehouse, using his snazzy app to undo the keypads at Roccamena's."

"I most certainly was not," Reggie huffed. "I was right here at home with Cassie, wasn't I, darling? Our home security photos prove it."

He showed me the date-and-time-stamped pictures on his monitor, Cassie working on a quilt in the family room, him at his desk, doing something on his computer. Their two sons were playing a video game.

"You do remember that I grew up with you, I hope. I remember when you and Stanley worked a racket with the numbers runners outside US Steel. That guy, what was his name? Lime Pit or something—he ratted you to the cops, and each of you claimed it was the other until Sonia stepped in and said you'd both been with her."

"So?" Reggie said. He sounded blasé, but his shoulders were tense.

"So I learned the only way to tell you apart was Stanley's birthmark on his left temple." It was tiny, barely the size of a sunflower seed, but visible in the security photo.

"Stanley drove straight through from Sedona, stayed here with Cassie, and drove home."

"You can't prove that," Sonia cried.

"I can't prove the driving part," I agreed, "but the birthmark is there. Anyway, the SA had to release Gregory. The documents I pulled from Roccamena's desk were Harvey's printout showing how Horvath had been defrauding the pension fund.

"Horvath created phantom employees. He was sending their benefits to a bank in Saint Kitts. Roccamena finally figured that out—he had a forensic accountant audit the books. He confronted Horvath, killed him, and left him on the warehouse floor. When Donny came in an hour later and started knocking over the inventory, it was gravy. No way to prove how Horvath died or who killed him, but Roccamena and Harvey must have fought—blood from both was on the report. It was good enough for the cops. They figured Roccamena did the damage to the warehouse himself to cover the crime."

"So Sonia and Donny saved me again." That was Gregory. He looked better in jeans and a T-shirt than he had in the jail, but he was still slouched in his chair, looking at the floor. "I'm such a fuckup."

Sonia went over to him and put an arm around his neck. "You're not a fuckup, Gregory. You just need a little extra support. That's what we're here for."

"What I'd really like to know, Sonia, is why the hell you put me through that song and dance of hiring me, when you Litvaks already had the whole story covered."

No one spoke for a long moment until Donny said, "She didn't know. It was all I could do to talk the clean virtuous twins into helping out. Reggie made me promise not to tell Sonia—he didn't want word getting back to his investors."

"I have a life," Reggie snapped. "You can't grow up, Donny. I gave up all that crap when I left South Chicago. It was only when you told me you were going ahead regardless that I got Stanley involved, and he hated it as much as I did. But we needed him here for the time stamp, and so he came, but he sure as hell won't do it again, and neither will I."

"Oh, Reggie," Sonia said reproachfully. "Your own brother? If he was in danger again I can't believe you'd let him suffer."

"Then keep him out of danger." Reggie scowled.

After another pause, Donny said, "I hear the whole company has shut down. I thought Roccamena's kids could keep it going."

"They could if they had the capital," I said. "Ajax canceled the bridge loan they'd provided while they waited for their adjusters to figure out the bottom line on the claim. Roccamena's is gone, which is sad. They had a wonderful whisky supply."

Donny grinned. "Someone told me you were a whisky drinker. I just happened to have a case of Oban delivered to me. I kept a bottle for you. Along with whatever Sonia's paying you, of course."

11

I set the bottle of Oban on my dining-room table, in between two of the red wineglasses my mother had brought with her from Italy all those years ago. Next to them I set my framed photo of my parents, not the formal one—Tony in his dress blues, Gabriella in her burnt velvet concert gown—but a snapshot I'd taken with the Brownie camera they'd given me for my tenth birthday. They were sitting in plastic garden chairs in our minute garden on South Houston, fingers loosely linked. Tony was watching her, his beloved wife, while Gabriella smiled at some private thought.

I wondered what my dad would have done with Donny, if he'd have let him off the hook or made the arrest. Would he have seen him as someone protecting his vulnerable brother, or just the punk who never even committed grand enough crimes to qualify for a federal prosecutor?

"It was the dress, Mama," I explained to Gabriella. "Why couldn't Mr. Litvak let Sonia have that one beautiful thing? Maybe her life would have moved onto a different track if she'd seen herself as someone special, someone who got to wear that dress."

Although I grew up in rural Kansas and V. I. Warshawski comes from the South Side of Chicago, I always feel freest in writing about her when I can mine her memories of the people in her old neighbor-hood. "Love & Other Crimes" grew out of my own revenge fantasy: a person I'm close to was fired from a job where new management was getting rid of long-standing employees to cut payroll costs. I thought if I was half as good a friend as I wanted to be, I would have wreaked havoc on the offending business. Instead, it all came out on the page, and in the Litvak family, who turn dysfunction into an art form.

Joseph S. Walker is a college instructor living in Bloomington, Indiana. He has a PhD in American literature from Purdue University. He is a member of the Mystery Writers of America, the Short Mystery Fiction Society, Sisters in Crime, and the Private Eye Writers of America. His stories have appeared in Alfred Hitchcock Mystery Magazine, Ellery Queen Mystery Magazine, Mystery Weekly, Hoosier Noir, Tough, and a number of other magazines and anthologies. In 2019 he won the Al Blanchard Award and the Bill Crider Prize for Short Fiction. Recent and upcoming anthologies from small presses (which are helping to keep short crime fiction alive out of love and dedication, and are richly deserving of support) containing his stories include Mickey Finn: 21st Century Noir *(Down & Out Books)*, Peace, Love, and Crime: Crime Fiction Inspired by the Songs of the Sixties *(Untreed Reads)*, Cozy Villages of Death *(Camden Park Press), and* Heartbreaks and Half-Truths: 22 Stories of Mystery and Suspense *(Superior Shores Press)*.

ETTA AT THE END OF THE WORLD

Joseph S. Walker

After she left the truck stop south of Jacksonville, Etta kept passing signs with names she'd heard all her life from TV and people with the time and money for vacations. Orlando. Tampa. Daytona Beach. It all felt imaginary, but then Florida felt imaginary, like a giant billboard for itself. She passed a lot of palm trees before she accepted that they were real. She couldn't always see the ocean off to her left, but she knew it was there, knew it by the wind and a smell that would never touch Iowa. The sky was big and blue and untouched until the late afternoon, when mountainous clouds started to rise up out of the east. It was like driving into a 3D antidepressant commercial, but she felt an itch at the back of her neck all day. She was cutting herself off. There was only one direction to go now, and if they found her, no place else to run.

Of course, running wasn't really the idea.

She pulled off in Boca Raton. It was still light out, but she had no chance of making Key West before sunset, and her back wouldn't take another night in the car. She found a run-down motel, not one of the big chains, a few blocks away from the beach. The Sandcastle Lodge. It was a long L, two stories high, sheltered from the main drag by a mini-mall and backed by a big, abandoned lot full of scrub pine trees. She'd put up with the roaches for the sake of a desk clerk who wouldn't find cash strange.

Her room was on the first floor, near the swimming pool tucked into the elbow of the building. A man in the pool was drinking a can of beer and roughhousing with a couple of kids, while a plump woman perched on one of the deck chairs made dismayed noises every time one of them went under the water. The only other person near the pool was a teenage girl, sleeping on her stomach on a lounger, wearing sunglasses and a red swimsuit that said she thought her body was a little slimmer than it actually was. Etta only glanced at her as she walked by, but the clearly defined bruises on the girl's upper arm jumped at her like they were lit up in neon. She'd seen their match often enough in her own mirror. Four angry purple blemishes perfectly staking out the shape of a man's hand. The girl's arm was the most real thing she'd seen all day.

The room was as bad as she'd expected, but the sheets were clean and the water in the shower hot enough to satisfy. She let it pound onto her aching shoulders for more than half an hour. There'd been a time when she could have driven for four straight days and then partied all night, but fifty was creeping up on her a lot faster than she'd like. She dried herself with the surprisingly adequate towel and fell across the bed, intending to get up in a few minutes and go in search of some kind of dinner.

The next thing Etta was aware of was a heavy thud that shook the whole bed. She jerked upright, with no idea for a moment of where she was or what was happening. She was nude, sprawled across the bedspread, shivering with cold. She could see the outline of the window behind the drapes, but the room was pitch dark. Heart pounding, she tried to figure out what had woken her.

There was a yell from behind the headboard, a deep man's voice. She couldn't make out the words, but the anger was clear. It was cut into by another voice, a female voice, this one pleading and tearful. The second voice got out only a few words before the initial thud happened again: Something heavy being thrown up against the wall. She remembered now—the imprint of those fingers on that arm.

She sat still for the next ten minutes, listening to what could have been the soundtrack of most of her life. At some point she noticed the faintly glowing dial of the clock beside the bed. If it was remotely accurate, it was just past three in the morning.

When the noises ended she still did not move, unable to decide if she could still hear crying from the room next door or if her mind was filling that in. Eventually she stood, moving as quietly as possible to the chair where her backpack rested. A T-shirt and shorts were the closest thing she had to sleeping wear and she pulled them on. Then she stuck her hand back in the bag and felt the grip of the gun. She held it for a long minute, biting her lip, then went back to the bed and crawled under the blankets. She brought the backpack and put it next to her pillow and stared into the darkness, willing the room next door to stay silent.

Shooting Tyler had been like a power outage. That instant when everything falls dark and all the hums of a house, the ones you don't hear until they're not there to hear, end. She'd put the barrel against the base of his skull and pulled the trigger and he'd simply dropped, first face forward onto the table and then rolling to the floor. He didn't flop or gasp for breath or spit out bitter final words. He didn't even bleed that much. He just . . . stopped. Twenty minutes later Etta was on the interstate outside Davenport, deciding where she would stop to steal a different car. Tyler had taught her how to steal cars. He'd taught her about guns too. He was a good teacher. That didn't come close to making up for all the things he was bad at.

The knock at the door the next morning was so light that Etta wasn't sure she'd heard it. Just dressed after another shower, she was looking out the bathroom window at the wild tangle of trees and vines that ended about ten feet from the motel, picking out all the plants she'd never seen before.

Surely the cops wouldn't knock?

She looked through the peephole and wasn't really surprised to see the girl. For a moment she just stood with her hand on the knob, trying again to project silence, but the girl must have heard something because she knocked again.

Etta opened the door a few inches. "Can I help you?"

"Um, yeah," the girl said. She was wearing the sunglasses again, but with jeans and a T-shirt with sleeves long enough to obscure the bruises Etta had seen. "I lost my ID? And I was wondering if I could give you some money to go to the liquor store for me." She pointed at the mini-mall. "There's one right at the road there."

"Lost your ID," Etta said. "Clerk didn't believe that either, right?"

The girl just stared blankly at the door.

"It's a little early in the day for a beer buzz," Etta said. She was about to add "dear" but bit it off, horrified to be talking like an old woman.

"I don't need beer," the girl blurted. She shifted from foot to foot. "Ma'am, it's not for me. Honest. Tone . . . the man I'm with . . . he wants me to get him a bottle of Jack. I tried yesterday and . . . look, he's gonna be real mad if I don't get it again today."

"The man you're with," Etta said. "Not your husband."

"I ain't married," the girl said forcefully.

Etta sighed. She wanted to close the door. She wanted to crawl back on the bed and just wait until somebody found her. Instead she said, "Is there a place to eat around here?"

The girl cocked her head. "There's a restaurant next to the liquor store."

Etta nodded. "I'll make you a deal. Come have breakfast with me and I'll buy the liquor."

<hr />

The restaurant was a diner where everything was coated with a thin layer of grease. All the employees were slender young dark-skinned men who shouted Spanish at each other and seemed perpetually annoyed by the customers wanting attention. The girl left her sunglasses on and kept touching the bottle of booze in its plain brown bag as if to assure herself it was real. She'd insisted on going to buy it before eating, though she had waited outside.

Etta ordered eggs and toast and watched the girl work on a stack of pancakes. "So, Tone," Etta said carefully. "Is he underage too?"

"No, ma'am," the girl said. "He's old. In his thirties."

This definition of *old* made Etta decide she'd been ma'amed enough. "Call me Etta," she said. "So why doesn't he buy his own whiskey?"

The girl shrugged. "He's real busy."

"Too busy to go into a liquor store right outside his door?"

"He's supposed to be meeting a guy." The girl pushed her food around a little. "He's gone all day waiting for him."

Etta nodded as though that made sense. "But what does he expect you to do if they're carding?"

The girl didn't say anything. She stared down at her plate.

"Let's try this again," Etta said. "My name is Etta, and you are—"

"Grace," the girl said quietly.

"It's nice to meet you, Grace." Etta took a sip from her coffee and waited.

Grace finished the pancakes. She put the fork down and took off the sunglasses and looked Etta in the face for the first time. Etta carefully didn't react to the black eye she had known she would see.

"He gets off on making me do stuff. He told me to shoplift," Grace said. "Only I tried that yesterday and they caught me. That's why I waited outside. So then he told me." She looked out the window. "He told me to offer to blow the clerk."

A waiter came up and slapped the check down on the table, where part of it immediately turned translucent with grease.

Grace put her sunglasses back on. Etta dropped a twenty on top of the check. "Do you have to stay at the hotel all day?" she asked.

Grace shook her head. "Tone won't be back until late."

"I thought I'd walk down to the beach," Etta said. She stood up. "Join me?"

They went back to the hotel first, so Grace could drop off the bottle and Etta could pay for another night. She got directions to the beach from the clerk, who warned her not to go into the lot behind the hotel. "Snakes back in there," the man said in an accent Etta didn't even try to identify. "Gators."

"I think he was putting me on," she told Grace as they walked.

The girl shrugged. "He told us the same when we checked in," she said. "Then a couple of days ago a gator ate some lady's dog a few blocks from here."

Unreal Florida again. Etta tried to imagine scaly monsters strolling around in Davenport and people just accepting it.

The beach seemed unreal too. They sat a few yards above the waterline, Grace propped up against her backpack, watching the waves come in and dead-eyed gulls scurrying down onto the wet sand as the water receded. It was still early in the day on Monday and there were only a few other people around, mostly just watching the water themselves.

Etta thought she could watch it all day. "I've never seen the ocean before," she told Grace. "I've spent my whole life in Iowa."

Etta dug her hand into the sand, looking for shells. *Souvenirs*, she thought, then wondered when she expected to ever enjoy such a thing. She'd always thought of sand as light, but this was heavy, shifting, hard to walk through. The breeze from offshore kept the sun from being too hot and she was mesmerized by the perpetual motion of the water.

"Just think," she said. "It's been doing that since before we were born and it'll keep doing it until the end of the world."

There was no answer. Grace was sleeping. Etta kicked her shoes off and buried her feet in the warm sand. There was nobody in the world who knew where she was or what she was doing. Nobody in the world to tell her to do something different.

She dozed some herself and was startled when Grace suddenly spoke. "You just here on vacation?"

"Sort of," Etta said. "I'm on my way to Key West. Thought I'd make it today, but there's nothing wrong with tomorrow."

"What's in Key West?"

"The end of the world," Etta said. She dug up a scalloped white shell, no bigger than her thumbnail but exquisite and perfect. She turned it over in her fingers. "It's the last island in this group of islands that hangs off the end of Florida. It's where the road ends. Where all the roads end. My parents honeymooned there, sixty years ago. My mother said until the day she died that if you hadn't seen the sun set in Key West you hadn't lived a complete life."

"That's nice," the girl said. "Now you're finally gonna see it."

"That's the plan," Etta said. She dug into her backpack and found a rolled pair of socks and carefully put the shell inside them. She tucked the socks back into the bottom of the bag, near the other pair of socks concealing what had been Tyler's emergency stash of hundreds and twenties. "What about you?" she asked. "You said Tone is here for business?"

Grace was quiet for so long that Etta was sure she'd fallen asleep again. "Sort of business," she finally said. Etta waited.

"His name is Tony," Grace said. "He makes people call him Tone because he thinks it makes him sound tough. Gangster."

"And is he a gangster?"

"He wants to be." Grace rolled over on her stomach. "He works for my daddy. Now my daddy, *he's* a gangster. Runs meth labs around the whole state."

Etta wanted to ask if Grace should be talking about this, but she bit her tongue.

"Daddy wants to branch out," Grace said. "So Tony is down here to buy coke. He set up a deal where a guy is supposed to meet him at a spot a couple of miles out on the water, but the guy says he has to wait for a day when he's sure it's clear. So Tony's been going out and waiting for the last four days. He's in a pretty bad mood when he gets back to the room."

"And he takes it out on you," Etta said. Grace didn't answer, but it wasn't really a question. "Grace, why are you with this guy? What do you see in him?"

Grace barked out a laugh. "See in him? Jesus. I hate him." She pushed her fingers roughly into the sand. "Daddy *gave* me to him. Said I'm a useless shit like my mother but maybe I can make a grandson to carry on the business."

Etta sat silently for several minutes. She thought about patting the girl's shoulder, making comforting noises, but that would have taken something she didn't quite think she had. She thought about all the ways the girl might be playing her, about the fact that she could go back to the hotel right this second and leave. Eventually she surprised herself by speaking.

"You've got better taste than me," she said. "My husband Tyler was like Tone. A crook, somebody who wanted everyone to know how tough he was. My parents tried to warn me about him, but I fell for it. God, I thought he was everything." She stared out at the water. "I thought I must deserve the things he did." She didn't look, but she knew Grace was listening.

The waves came in, the waves went out. They'd been doing it long before Etta was born. They'd be doing it long after she was gone.

Etta stood up. "I passed a library yesterday," she said. Grace looked up at her and Etta held out a hand to help her up. "Come on. I want to show you something."

⁂

The library, a couple of blocks off the beach, was a low-slung stucco building with pastel awnings and red terra-cotta tiles on the roof. Etta couldn't help but wish it were just a plain old concrete black. *Jesus, Florida*, she thought. *We get it already.*

The few people inside were dressed as casually as those they'd seen on the beach. Etta found the computer stations and chose one in a private corner. Grace stood next to her, hip cocked against the desk, looking around from behind her pitch-dark shades. Etta had the feeling she didn't spend much time in libraries.

It took her only a few minutes to find the article she was looking for in the online version of the *Quad-City Times*. "Here," she said. She stood up and steered Grace into the chair. "Read this."

Grace took off the sunglasses and began scanning the article. After a few seconds her eyes opened wide. Etta didn't need to look; she'd read it at another library, in Georgia, two days ago. Local man Tyler Hession found dead in his home of a single gunshot wound. Troubled history. Grand theft, domestic abuse. Wife, Etta, missing and being actively sought by police as a person of interest. If you have any information . . .

"Holy shit," Grace hissed. She looked up at Etta. "Did you do that?"

"Yeah," Etta said. She pulled over another chair and perched on the edge, leaning forward. "Tell me something. Does Tone shower when he comes back at night?"

⊶

That night Etta sat in the chair in her room. She'd cleaned and reloaded the gun, every step reminding her of Tyler's impatient lectures, his warnings about a gun that jams at the moment when you need it. As though he'd ever done anything with a gun other than wave it around. She put the gun on the nightstand and forced herself to leave it alone. She turned on the TV with the volume all the way down so she'd have something to look at. She nibbled on cookies and drank soda to stay alert. A hospital show. Lots of very earnest, very serious young men and women in scrubs, frowning at helpless-looking people in beds.

After a while they were replaced by the local news. From what she could tell without any sound, it was exactly the same as the local news in Iowa. She'd come here because Florida felt like the end of the world, but there were people who lived here every day. They'd probably find a few miles of unbroken cornfields as bizarre as Etta had found the beach.

The talk-show host who came on after the news was on his second guest when Etta heard a door open and the mumble of voices through the wall behind her. She turned off the TV and listened. She still couldn't make out words but it didn't sound like he was hitting her this time, though he still sounded angry. Probably pleased to have his Jack. She listened to the two voices rising and falling, the indistinct movements around the room. It was hard to be sure what was happening. Was that Tone throwing himself onto the bed? Grace moving around to get him a drink? What was she going to do if Tone decided not to shower tonight? Grace had said he always did, that he couldn't stand sleeping coated in the sweat and sunscreen of a long day out on the water, but now, sitting alone in her room, Etta didn't think that sounded like much to base a plan on. Maybe they should have gone with their first idea, having Etta hide under the bed, but she hadn't been able to stand the idea of being under there in God knows what filth for God knew how long.

The bedsprings in the next room creaked again. Tony said something that had a nasty edge to it and laughed loudly. Then footsteps, then a moment of silence, and then a pipe somewhere creaked to life and three soft but distinct knocks came against the wall.

So this was it. Etta seemed to watch herself from a distance as she picked up the gun with her right hand and covered it with a folded towel held in her left. Moving quickly, she went out the door and turned and came to the door of the next room, which was cracked open. She pushed through. Grace was on the other side, her eyes wide. She closed the door behind Etta and put the chain on, just as they'd rehearsed, and Etta dropped the towel and walked to the bathroom, seeing nothing but what was immediately in front of her.

The shower curtain was not quite closed. She could see Tone, facing away from the door, scrubbing at his crotch. He was a small man, shorter than Etta, but his frame was wiry and muscular. He had more body hair than any man she'd ever seen.

He must have heard something or caught a glimpse of something because he started to turn and raise his hand and the shot Etta had intended for the back of his head, the same place she'd shot Tyler, instead hit the corner of his jaw. His head jerked back and his eyes widened and she shot him two more times, both in the head, and now he dropped and she saw the tile behind him spattered with blood.

Tyler always had said she was a good shot.

She kept the gun raised and watched him not moving. There was quite a lot of blood but the running shower was swirling most of it away down the drain. She replayed the three shots in her head and thought about the people in adjoining rooms, imagined them jerking awake or suddenly looking up from the TV, wondering about the bangs. They'd sit still, like she had after the thud last night, waiting to see what else would happen, convincing themselves that it was a car or something equally meaningless. Nothing they needed to be involved with.

After she had counted off five minutes in her head and heard no sirens she lowered the gun to her side. There was no new blood coming from Tone and the one eye he had left was milky and unfocused.

She stepped out the bathroom door. Grace was sitting cross-legged on the bed, clutching a pillow to her chest and shaking. "It's over," Etta said. "Go get the stuff." Grace nodded and jumped from the bed and ran outside. In a minute she was back with the plastic bags holding the supplies they'd bought this afternoon. Cleaning solution, paper towels, plastic bags, duct tape, flashlight, and, just because Etta had damn well wanted some, Oreos.

"You don't have to look," Etta said.

Grace shook her head. "I didn't have the balls to do it," she said. "Least I can do is look at it." Etta stepped aside and Grace dropped the bags on the bed and walked into the bathroom. Etta let her take her moment, let her make it whatever it needed to be for her, as she ran through a list of everything that needed to be done. Clean up the bathroom. Use the duct tape and plastic bags to cover any part of Tone that might leave a blood trail. In a few hours, when it was the deadest part of the night, shove his body through the bathroom window, then go around the building and move him as far as they dared into the wooded lot. If there were gators, they were in for a nice breakfast. Then, hopefully just before dawn, take off. They would leave Etta's stolen car in a parking lot with the keys in it. Tone's Mustang would be a safe ride for a while. It wasn't like Grace's father was going to file a missing person report on his drug mule.

Grace came out of the bathroom. For the first time since Etta had met her she looked completely composed. "Thank you," she said. "Let's get started."

The sunset in Key West was everything Etta's mother had promised, fantastic bands of pink and orange remaking the sky continuously, the colors edging into the impossibly vibrant. Seemingly just to keep living up to the postcards, Florida was even kind enough to provide a couple of magnificent sailboats perfectly silhouetted against the spectacular sky. Etta couldn't even bring herself to resent it.

She and Grace watched from a restaurant on a boardwalk thronged with tourists and street performers. They seemed to be the only people actually watching the sky, as opposed to filming it on their phones. Etta had left hers in Iowa, and Tone had never allowed Grace to have one. It was hard to feel they were missing anything. Between Tyler's stash and Tone's unspent coke money, they could always get a burner phone if they needed to. Or a dozen.

When the sky was finally dark she lifted her margarita glass and clinked it against Grace's diet soda. "I have to say that was worth the trip," she said.

"It was fantastic," Grace said. She was still looking out over the water but now she turned to look at Etta. "So what were you going to do after the sunset?"

"I hadn't decided," Etta said. She leaned back in her chair. "I was either going to blow my brains out on the beach or walk into the water and wait to drown."

Grace looked shocked. "You wanted to die?"

Etta shrugged. "I thought that's what you came to the end of the world to do."

"And now?"

"Why rush?" Etta said. "It'll happen sooner or later. Might as well go for later. Why, do you have any plans?"

Grace looked down at the table. "I thought maybe we could go see my daddy."

Etta smiled and drained the last of her drink and set the glass down.

"Why the hell not?" she said.

---

*Every tourist has had the experience of going to some long-anticipated destination and being disappointed, but some things do live up to their advance billing. One is the sunset at Key West, which I got to see when my wife Mary and I vacationed in the Keys in 2017. It was every bit as spectacular as I'd heard, painting the sky in bands of colors many times richer and more vibrant than any film could capture. A happy, raucous, mostly drunken crowd watched from the beaches and bars, as silhouetted sailboats drifted by. It was all so transcendent, and to my Midwestern eyes so unreal, that I wouldn't have been surprised to see Travis McGee pulling up to the dock in the Busted Flush.

Something that struck me forcefully about the experience was the sense of being at the end of every road, and I started thinking about the kind of person who might risk a great deal to get there to see it, perhaps with the expectation that it would be the last thing they'd ever see at all. By the time we flew back to Indiana a few days later, Etta was already beginning to talk to me. I'm grateful to Linda Landrigan (who, back in 2011, gave me my first professional fiction sale) for letting me tell Etta's story in the pages of Alfred Hitchcock, and to Otto Penzler and Lee

Child for giving her another home in this volume. I'd be remiss if I didn't also thank my wife, my parents, and the many friends (hi, Leslie, Angel, Penny, and Eric!) who have been endlessly encouraging of my writing.

Of course, by the time "Etta" was published it read like historical fiction, with its mobs of innocently unmasked people traveling about at will, and the very notion of the end of the world had become considerably less figurative than it was when I was writing. Living through this strange, dark, closed-down time has made me very grateful for the friendship and society I've found among the community of mystery writers and readers. In particular, the members of the Short Mystery Fiction Society (and especially the heroic Kevin R. Tipple) are unfailingly generous in their advice and support, and many of my stories would never have found their way into existence without them.

Here's hoping that, like Etta, we can all find a way to keep going beyond what at times seems like the end of the world.

Andrew Welsh-Huggins is a reporter for the Associated Press in Columbus, and the author of seven novels featuring Andy Hayes, a former Ohio State and Cleveland Browns quarterback turned private eye, including the Nero Award–nominated Fatal Judgment. Welsh-Huggins is also the editor of Columbus Noir *from Akashic Books, and his short fiction has appeared in publications including* Ellery Queen Mystery Magazine, Mystery Weekly, *and* Mystery Tribune. *Andrew's nonfiction book,* No Winners Here Tonight, *is the definitive history of the death penalty in Ohio.*

THE PATH I TOOK

Andrew Welsh-Huggins

Any hopes I'd had of a peaceful morning of work that day evaporated the instant I opened my email and saw the single word in the subject line.

Ireland.

My heart raced. Was this the moment I'd dreaded for so long—the unmasking of the truth? The beginning of the end of the journey I'd begun so long ago?

I calmed down after a moment, scrolling through the body of the message. The writer was a student reporter for *The Beacon Star*, the paper at the small, liberal arts college in Ohio where I teach. An Irish politician was coming to speak on campus, she explained. A former member of the Irish Republican Army turned peace activist. A controversial figure at home whose tour of the United States featured protests outside several of his appearances.

I believe you studied in Ireland in the 1980s, when the IRA was active, the student wrote. *I was wondering if I could ask you a few questions for my article.*

A new thrill of panic. How had she known? It was hardly something I advertised. I do my best to maintain a low profile without gaining a reputation as a recluse—easier said than done as a teacher of Greek and Latin. After a moment I relaxed again. I realized my long-ago sojourn abroad was on my CV—how could it not be?—and likely inserted on a faculty bio someplace. The Internet takes unkindly to the preservation of secrets like that. This tech-savvy student no doubt located it in the time it takes me to make my morning cup of tea.

Yes, I wrote back carefully. *I was in Ireland then. What would you like to know?*

Anything you'd like to tell me, she replied.

Like the day I found the body? I said to myself, leaning back in my chair and collecting my thoughts.

It all began in the fall of 1983, when I found myself living in a village on the far west coast of Ireland where Irish—Gaelic—was still the predominant language. A *Gaeltacht*, as such enclaves are known. *Next Parish Boston* went the saying in that part of the world, which boasted of being at the tip of the westernmost point of Europe. I settled there thanks to a fellowship I'd secured for postcollege research. I'd been to Ireland briefly in high school, and was captivated by the fact that people still spoke Irish in certain isolated communities. I put off graduate studies in Greek at the University of Illinois for a year and instead pursued the romantic notion of immersing myself in the literature and legends of old Ireland by gaining fluency in the island's first language.

My parents were skeptical, to say the least. If anything, they thought I should have gone to France to improve my already near-fluent language skills in that idiom. Still, they couldn't argue with the generosity of my stipend, some multiple thousands of dollars, or the fact that, unlike many of their peers' children, I would be immediately self-sufficient after graduation. With their half-hearted blessing, I flew into Shannon Airport in early July. After a few false starts, I rented a vacationer's cottage a few kilometers west of Dingle in County Kerry and settled down to pursue my unlikely project on the outskirts of a tiny town called *Baile na Farraige*, literally place of the sea, known more generally by its prosaic English pronunciation, Ballynafarragy.

At first, the fishermen, farmers, and retired pensioners who constituted the majority of the town's population weren't sure what to do with me. They had plenty of experience with Americans, of course, with half the region's population having emigrated at one point or another, and with hordes of Yankee tourists descending on the peninsula each summer to consume breathtaking views of the old country along with gallons of Guinness in authentic Irish pubs. But how to react to a shy, slight boy who knocked on their doors, introduced himself in faltering Irish, and explained he wanted nothing more than to chat a bit and take some notes? Much is made of Irish hospitality, but it turns out it's only skin deep when you start intruding on personal matters like a language people simultaneously held dear to their hearts and considered a bit of an embarrassment in the modern age. Still, to their credit, the villagers accepted me in the end, and warmly at that, since Ireland is hardly immune to the presence of peculiar people, homegrown or otherwise. It didn't hurt that I was the only American spending money in Ballynafarragy after August.

Gradually, I fashioned a routine. Each morning I would rise and walk the mile into town along a narrow road. My journey took me past fragrant fuchsia hedges, green fields, a few scattered houses, and, at the base of a series of rock outcroppings leading up a hill, a large, stone-carved Celtic cross of unknown age but deemed of enough antiquity to merit its own historical marker, in Irish and in English. The sea, of course, was everywhere around me, a vast, looming presence that became my constant companion as I tramped along the road.

Once in the village, I seated myself at a wooden table in the tiny shop that doubled—or tripled—as Ballynafarragy's café, post office, and general store, drank a cup of tea, and ate a scone or two.

"*Dia Duit,*" I said each morning to Mrs. Donnelly, the proprietor. Literally, *God save you,* a phrase equivalent to *Good day.*

"Good morning," she replied curtly, in English, each day for the first week of my stay. I persisted, and finally, whether through a softening of her heart or a decision that it was easier just to play along—my daily purchases probably didn't hurt—she responded one day with "*Dia is Muire duit,*" or *God and Mary be with you.* Progress.

Thus ensconced, I read the *Irish Times* for the next hour, dutifully starting with the pages printed in Irish, consulting an Irish-English dictionary I carried with me everywhere, and then moving on to the English-language news.

One thing that struck me immediately was how little we knew back home of the violence in Northern Ireland. The execution of a suspected collaborator, the ambush of a British soldier, the death of a child from crossfire. Like the daily shootings in America today, The Troubles blurred together in a profusion of daily, deadly headlines. I blushed to think of the carefully curated tour I'd taken of Ireland after my junior year in high school, the way it avoided mention of the bloodletting in favor of Irish language tutorials and tales of mythological heroes like Cúchulainn. Once I lived in Ireland, even so far away from the North, the true extent of the conflict hit home.

Finished at the café, and depending on the day, I would pay a visit to the local priest, a kindly, middle-aged man with perpetually red cheeks and a monk-like tonsure of thinning brown hair who always seemed to have time to chat with me, usually half in Irish and then in English, over a cup of tea.

"*Buachaill cróga is ea tú*," he said with a smile the first time we met, translating it roughly as, "You're a brave lad."

"Why do you say that?"

"You, coming here alone like this, not knowing a soul? Trying to gain the trust of the likes of us. It's inspiring, is what it is."

"*Buíochas*"—thanks—I said, not sure how else to reply.

Afterward, near lunchtime, I walked home and spent a few hours at the kitchen table in my cottage studying grammar, learning vocabulary, reviewing notes, reading, writing letters, and doing my best to stave off loneliness. Like Ballynafarragy's priest, Father Seamus, you can marvel at the determination it took to transport a shy young man from the middle of Ohio to the heart of Gaelic-speaking Ireland. I marvel at it sometimes too. But despite how introverted I was, I was passionate about at least one thing: the desire to throw myself head-on into the task at hand. To become good at something, anything, even if it was learning a moribund language with far fewer than twenty thousand living speakers.

Most early afternoons I napped, wrapping myself in my bed's woolen blankets to stave off the chill of the sea air, even in summer. And then, rested up, I set out on the path that very nearly cost me my life.

Ballynafarragy nestled above a small bay that was home to an equally small fishing fleet. From there the lone road out of town wound its way along a rocky peninsula jutting into the Atlantic. Halfway along, it crossed a bridge that carried the road over a splinter of an inlet carved by the sea millennia ago, a sight to behold with its jagged rocks at the bottom and cliff walls rising sheer on either side.

From there, the road continued to the even smaller village on the other side, called simply *Cuas*, or "The Cove," my destination most afternoons and evenings. Everyone there down to the handful of bright-eyed children spoke Irish from dawn till dusk. Some of the elders, people whispered to me, might even have trouble speaking English. A generation earlier, many of them lived on the island half a mile beyond, its craggy outline jutting from the ocean like the tip of a sunken mountain. Eventually, as the island's population waned and the price of cod plummeted, the remaining villagers moved across the bay with the government's help and resettled in Cuas. On any but the most gray and rainy days it was still possible to make out the stone walls and tic-tac-toe design of abandoned farm fields across the water, along with the cluster of thatch-roofed houses that constituted the old village. *Oileán na Rón*—Seal Island—loomed as a daily reminder of lost heritage, a stunningly beautiful landmark of what once was and never could be again.

On my first forays to the village I trekked along the road on foot, skirting the edge of the peninsula, always pausing at the bridge to stare into the dark interior of the inlet. It was a walk of nearly an hour. Later, I bought a bike and cut the trip's duration considerably, though the coast's frequent and heavy rains meant biking wasn't always an option. I didn't mind the trip because of the view, which also kept the road thick with rental vehicles from

May to September. Drivers could look out their window and see ocean waves crashing in an arcing cascade of green and white along the sharp rocks at the base of the peninsula. Beyond that rose Seal Island, shrouded in mist one moment, drenched in sunlight the next, waves exploding in an emerald dance along the base while above the water gulls and puffins and terns wheeled and rose and fell all day long.

It was Moira who first told me about the shortcut. I met her one day as I emerged around the hedge lining an old farmer's property whose house I had just visited. Startled, she took a step back and placed her hands on her hips.

"So you're the American," she said.

"Ah, yes."

"And you're here to learn Irish?"

"That's right," I stammered.

"Why?"

I didn't answer right away. I couldn't. I was transfixed by her, not in small part because she was the first woman anywhere close to my age who I'd spoken to that summer. And she was—well, what? Not conventionally beautiful, since even then, in what must have been her late twenties, the toll of a rural life lived frequently outdoors was taking its toll on her creamy, freckle dappled skin, with hints of crow's feet already around her eyes and a weariness to her furrowed brow. But her green eyes shone, and her riot of curly black hair was a wonder, and she had a smile that was genuine and welcoming in a way I'd missed, trying to explain myself and my mission to her more guarded elders over the past few weeks. She asked me where I was going and I explained I was about to make the return trip home walking along the road.

"There's a faster way," she said. "If you're feeling brave."

I wasn't, particularly, despite Father Seamus's teasing. But at the moment I would have followed her anywhere.

For all intents and purposes, the shortcut—the path, or *cosán*—was invisible to outsiders. To reach it, we tramped behind a stone chapel that Moira explained was opened now only on special occasions. From there, we followed a cow lane along a wall of carefully layered stones. The ground steadily rose and I struggled to stay with her. She walked without hesitation, taking confident steps in her brown corduroy pants and heavy green Wellies. At the end of the wall she turned right, around a massive boulder, and then scampered up a small set of steplike rocks. Suddenly, I was staring at a well-trodden path that cut up and across the hill like the thrust of a broad sword.

"What is this?"

"It's your way home," she said with a laugh.

We climbed higher and higher, pausing only once to raise the hoods on our oilskin raincoats as a late-afternoon shower passed over. At the top, a shoulder-high spur of black, lichen-covered granite bisected the trail. For the first time Moira slowed, then stopped. I paused, sneaking a glance at her face, which was set off in heart-stopping fashion by the ringlets of her hair, before directing my attention to Seal Island in the distance.

"Stand back a bit," she said, taking my right elbow and pulling me toward her.

"Why?" I said, my heart pounding from her touch.

"There," she said, pointing.

At first I didn't see it. Following her instructions, I took a couple of steps forward. I swallowed hard. Just a few feet off the path loomed a precipice, below which the earth dropped away hundreds of feet. Through a quirk in the topography the drop-off wasn't visible from the path and only appeared as you crested a low swell in the ground, at which point it would be too late to avoid the plunge if you weren't looking. I inched closer. Far below, white spray from a wave crashed into rocks. I realized I was staring at the inlet carved into the peninsula, the same one I saw from the opposite vantage point on the bridge below. It was a long way down. A very long way.

"It's beautiful, but it's deadly," Moira said. "Any cow that gets loose is more or less doomed if they make it up this far." She trained her green eyes on me. "It's fine enough in the day, but don't ever try it at night. Even I won't do that. One slip . . ." she said, and pushed her hand out into the air with a frown.

I nodded, not sure how to respond. We lingered a few minutes longer, staring at the island in the distance. She asked me about my project, and then posed a question in Irish. *"An dtaithníonn na Rincí Gaelacha leat?"*

"Taithníonn! Taithníonn na Rincí Gaelacha liom," I said, gratified by the surprise on her face. *Yes, I do like Irish dancing.*

"I'm glad to hear that," she said with a smile. "I was afraid from what I was hearing you were a hermit as well as a dreamer."

Over time she told me her story. Moira's grandparents grew up on Seal Island. Once relocated, they settled in Cuas with no thoughts of moving elsewhere. Moira's own mother, however, would have nothing to do with such a life and left as soon as she could. Moira was raised in the small city of Tralee, farther into the interior. In college she met her husband, Connor, a Dublin boy who'd never set foot in an Irish-speaking village but spoke passable Irish thanks to his grandfather. Fired by a combination of young love and national pride, Moira and Connor moved to Cuas, determined to participate in the country's attempts to reclaim a heritage lost to English domination and global homogenization.

They even harbored dreams of repopulating Seal Island with a new generation of Irish speakers. They bought a small farm and Connor hired onto a fishing crew. Moira gave birth to boy and girl twins whose first word, she recounted with pride, was *daidí*: "daddy."

And then Connor set off to sea one day and a storm blew up and by nightfall Moira was a widow.

I'd like to report that meeting Moira was the beginning of a great romance. The pretty Irish lass and the quiet but adventurous American boy at play in a landscape of achingly harsh beauty. Our love deepening as I helped her heal from loss and she unleashed my inner confidence. But it wasn't anything like that. I was a shy boy, as I've already explained. I'd kissed exactly one girl in college, and though nice enough, it turned out she was a lesbian trying to figure things out, and that was that. Moira had a spirited side but she was also practical. Even with her background, an Irish widow with two young children knew better than to take up with an American whose preoccupation in life was with dead or dying languages.

What followed instead was a friendship that occasionally danced on the edge of something else. I continued my routine of visits and studies, slowly winning the trust of nearly every villager both in Ballynafarragy and Cuas. I still experienced stretches of loneliness and depression as I questioned my mission. But I also rapidly gained fluency in Irish, to the point that later that fall, a visiting scholar from Cork insisted I attend a symposium on Gaelic that coming spring as a featured speaker. Never one for the pubs, I overcame my insular nature enough to spend a night or two a week drinking Guinness and speaking Irish in Ballynafarragy's lone bar. I achieved what I thought of as equilibrium after months of unrest.

And then I found Sean Murphy's corpse.

For several weeks I followed Moira's admonition about the path and walked it only during daylight hours. I came to appreciate both its utility—it cut the travel time from Cuas to Ballynafarragy by thirty minutes or more—as well as the vistas it provided of Seal Island to the west and the lonely, stony fields stretching behind it to the east. But as the days shortened and I spent more and more time in Cuas, either visiting Moira and her twins or huddled in the kitchens of elderly Irish speakers, the thought of the hour-long trek home along the road appealed less and less.

One day after breakfast—it was now mid-November—I purchased a flashlight from Mrs. Donnelly. That night, I returned along the path in the dark for the first time. I halted when I reached the lichen-covered outcropping at the peak, where just a few short feet away the steep canyon walls of the inlet opened up like a jagged wound. Creeping past, I made it safely down and home and felt a thrill of pride in my accomplishment that nearly rivaled the self-esteem I'd gained from my language acquisition. From that point on, I traveled the path exclusively, including at night.

The day before my gruesome discovery, I spent the bulk of the afternoon and early evening helping an elderly woman named Nell care for her chickens and tidy her gardens, now put to bed for the winter behind her stone cottage. Grateful for the company and the help, she served me boiled ham and potatoes and carrots and tea and we sat by her fireplace chatting in Irish as she poked bricks of peat with a poker until past nine o'clock.

"*Caithfidh mé bóthar a bhualadh,*" I said at last. *I need to get going.* I thanked her for the meal, promised to return soon, and set off for the path and home. As was often the case, I glanced over at Moira's cottage and to my surprise saw that a light was on; she was usually asleep early, often just minutes after putting the twins down. Perhaps emboldened by my success that day—Nell had taught me a long Irish ballad—I diverted my course and decided to stop by.

"*An bhfuil sé ródhéanach?*" I said, reading the surprise in her eyes when she answered the door. *Is it too late?* To my wonder, she said that it wasn't and I was more than welcome. Inside, I saw that she'd been looking at photographs, and as she made me a cup of tea she explained it was the anniversary of Connor's death. We sat and talked for nearly an hour. Then, before I knew exactly what was happening, I leaned over and kissed her, and she didn't resist and kissed me back, her lips wonderfully soft and warm. We kept it up for several minutes on her small couch, holding each other. And that was all. No fumbling in the dark as we stripped off our clothes, no groans of rapture as the sea crashed against the rocks outside. After a while we stopped and she said I should probably go. I stood up and put on my oil slicker and opened the door and stared out at pouring rain interrupted only by gusts of howling wind.

"Sure and you can't go out in that," Moira said softly, coming up beside me.

She offered to let me drive her car home for the evening. I resisted, reluctant to strand her on such a night with her children, in case something happened. Instead, as a compromise, I slept on the couch, fully dressed, falling asleep with the thought of her just a few feet away, tucked into her own bed in the small room across the hall from the bedroom her twins shared.

I startled awake hours later. Fumbling about, I saw by the dim glow of the kitchen clock that it was just past five in the morning. I sat up, rubbed my face, and glanced briefly in the direction of Moira's room. I retrieved my notebook from my satchel, scribbled a note of thanks and explanation and left it on the kitchen table. I carefully opened her door, looking around for early risers who might object to the sight of me leaving the widow's house that time of day, shut the door, and started up and along the path.

Feeling tired and dejected, I was safely over the top and past the precipice and halfway down the opposite side when I heard a car engine. I stopped, listening, thinking it odd for a vehicle to be on the road so early. A minute later I heard men's voices and a door opening and closing and then the sound of a car driving off. After a few moments I continued on.

On the opposite side of the peninsula the path emptied out by the Celtic stone cross and its historical marker. I had passed it dozens of times at this point, often in the dark. This morning I saw right away it didn't look right. Something was propped against the front of the cross. Not something, I saw, as I approached and raised the beam of my flashlight. My heart raced. Someone. A man was slumped against the cross. He was naked, and as I shone the light I gasped at the sight of the gaping hole between his eyes. I looked closer and saw something had been carved into his chest, a jagged mess of lines and curls, blood drying at the edges of deep wounds. It took me a moment, but I realized I was staring at a word.

Grass.

Panicked, I stumbled down the road toward the center of Ballynafarragy. Not sure what to do, I ran to the café and pounded on the door. Mrs. Donnelly lived upstairs, and I was hoping she might be awake, readying for the day. As it turned out she wasn't, and was in little mood to be awakened that early in the morning. The expression on her face changed as I explained what I'd seen. In my panic, I abandoned Irish and blurted everything out in English. She beckoned me inside and I stood, shivering, while she used the phone to call the nearest police station, in Dingle, a good ten miles away. While we waited she made more calls, and then after running back upstairs to dress she left the shop and marched to the church to summon Father Seamus. The result was that by the time the first *Garda* car arrived with its blue and red flashers a crowd of onlookers had gathered around the body, alternately gawking and trying to shield anyone from drawing too close.

"Grass?" I asked Mrs. Donnelly.

"Informer," she whispered, not meeting my eyes.

Later that morning I was interviewed at length by an officer from the Dingle *Garda* office named Flaherty suspicious of my explanations for being out that early. Making things worse, he couldn't understand why in the world an American would stoop to learning, in his words, "a useless language like Irish." But his interrogation was nothing compared to the conversation I had the next day with two men with stern expressions and unfamiliar accents who I eventually determined to be police security officials from Belfast.

It turned out the body was that of a local boy named Sean Murphy. He'd grown up in Ballynafarragy, and then—like the majority of young people his age—left seeking work at eighteen, first to Limerick, then to Dublin. At some point he'd joined the IRA—it was never clear to me in exactly what capacity, whether as gunrunner or low-level thief funding their operations or some kind of muscleman—and ended up in the North. And then, apparently, he'd crossed someone or done something or said something that raised suspicions, and he'd been tortured and killed and his body deposited back home as a lesson to anyone in the Republic seeking to help the cause without the purest of motives.

"You've stuck your foot in it now, lad," Father Seamus told me in the rectory at the end of the second day, after I'd finally been told I was free to go.

"I've never seen anything like that."

"Nor have we," he said, getting up and pouring me a second glass of whiskey. "And I hope that's the last we ever do."

I tried visiting Moira the next day, but she didn't have time to talk. Her daughter, Siobhan, was down with a fever, and her son,

Connor Jr., was in a bad way at school and needed help with his maths. There was no mention of our evening together three nights earlier. I wished her well and said I hoped to see her soon, once things were better. She smiled noncommittally.

I saw her sooner than I expected, however. Much sooner.

I tried to resume some semblance of my routine the following day, but to little avail. Doors that had opened to me for months now stayed shut, the voices behind them apologizing about busyness and suggesting another time, perhaps. Locals who cocked their head with a familiar nod as they passed me in trucks while I tramped along the peninsula road now stared straight ahead, ignoring me.

"They're just nervous," Father Seamus said to me late that afternoon as I sat again in his living room. "It took a lot for them to accept you here, a stranger like you were. Now they're rethinking it all."

"But all I did was find him—find the body, I mean," I protested.

"They know that. But, I'm sorry, you Americans don't grasp what it's like over here, with what's happening up north. The brutality. It's not the movies for us. It's real. And when the Troubles show up here, people look for explanations. For someone to blame, or at least suspect. You're a big target, as a Yank."

"I didn't do anything."

"Of course you didn't. It's not you—it's where you're from. If Paddy the potato farmer had found the body, someone we all knew, it would be different. Don't worry. It'll pass. You'll be parsing your verb tenses again in no time. *Gan dabht.*"

Without a doubt. I wasn't so sure, I thought as I walked back to my cottage. Under different circumstances, I should have been preparing for a visit to Cuas, or perhaps the pub. Instead, I stepped into the kitchen and set the kettle on for tea. I fixed a cup, settled down at the table, and read and took notes for an hour or more, absorbing hardly anything.

Night had fallen when I was startled by a pounding at the door. Cautiously, I walked across the living room and opened it. Moira stood before me, dripping wet from a chill rain, a look of what can only be described as sheer terror on her face. Behind her, down the lane leading to my cottage, sat her small car, running with its lights on.

"There's men," she said, trying to catch her breath. "In the village. Looking for you. You've got to go."

"Men?"

"Two of them. They're not from here. They've something to do with Sean. They're asking after the American."

"Are they police?"

"No!" she said, shaking her head violently. "You don't understand. They're trying to find whoever found Sean."

"Why?"

"Are you thick?" she said, exasperation coating her voice. "They think you saw them dump his body."

"I didn't see anyone."

"They don't know that. And they're not going to listen to you. They're going to—"

"To what?" I said, fear gripping my insides.

"*Leave, you fool*. While you still can."

"Leave? To where?"

"Anywhere. Just go."

In confusion, I said, "Father Seamus. Perhaps he could—"

"No," Moira hissed.

"Why not?"

"It's him who's helping them, you idiot."

"You can't be serious—"

"Hurry," she said, and turned and ran down the lane to her car.

I closed the door and stumbled into the kitchen. I sat down, stunned. My heart pounded with terror. I had no context for what she'd just told me. Men—after me? Just because I'd found Sean Murphy? Father Seamus—helping them?

A phone. If I could just get to Mrs. Donnelly's café, call over to Dingle, explain to someone official what was going on. Perhaps the impatient *Garda* officer, Flaherty, who'd interviewed me. Because this couldn't be real. This sort of thing didn't happen. I was a language student, nothing more or less. I was from Ohio! I stood up and ran into the bedroom. I tugged on my walking boots. I threw a fisherman's sweater over my shirt and stepped back into the living room and slipped on my oilskin coat. I made for the door, stopped, bent over and retrieved the flashlight I kept beside a small drying rack for socks. A phone, I thought. A phone and I would be all right.

I opened the door. Two men stared at me below, standing on the road in the rain. Men I didn't recognize. Men with faces of stone. They said nothing, but started to walk quickly toward my cottage. I slammed the door shut and threw the dead bolt, knowing instinctively it would slow them but a little. I dashed into the kitchen and went out the back way, into a little garden I'd tried half-heartedly to tend. Behind me I heard the sound of something crashing and the deep baritone of a man shouting. I wiped the rain from my eyes, lowered my head, and started to run. The path, I thought.

I was halfway to the summit when I heard a grunt, followed by a curse. They were right behind me—no surprise, since I'd foolishly kept the flashlight on to guide my way. One of them had fallen, but a quick glance around showed he was up again and they were both coming on fast, ominous moving shadows in the dark and rain. Near tears, I switched the light off and picked up my pace. One thing I had gained in recent months was a physicality I'd lacked in nearly all my youth. Even taking the path as a shortcut, I'd become accustomed to walking three to five miles each day, often more, and my stamina had increased considerably in turn. Now I ran hard in the dark, trusting my knowledge of the path's twists and turns gained after so many crossings. The sounds behind me faded.

When I reached the top and the lichen-covered granite spur I stopped to catch my breath. I realized I had no idea what I was doing. Continuing on would take me to Cuas, where shelter might or might not be forthcoming in the homes of the now suspicious villagers. I could try tramping east, across the moor, but that was uncertain territory for me. I could confront the men, but with what? The flashlight? My fluent Irish?

The sound of another grunt interrupted my thoughts and sent me into a new panic. I took a few steps forward, but it was too late. The men had been coming faster than I thought. They were nearly at the peak and would see me in another few moments. As my blood froze I stepped around the tall stone outcropping and crouched low, praying they'd pass by.

They didn't. From my hiding spot I could just make out their silhouettes as they stopped, breathing hard, but also glancing around and listening, their heads turned to the side. Predators sniffing the air for prey. I saw in their hands the dark, cruel outlines of guns.

"Show yourself," the man on the left said.

"We just need a few words," the other man said.

For a moment nothing happened. The only sounds were the falling rain and the crashing of waves far below at the base of the inlet. The inlet. The precipice leading to it nearly invisible in the day, let alone at night. Slowly, quietly, heart crashing, I placed my right hand on the ground and felt through the cold, stiff grass. After a moment I found what I was looking for. A stone. I had no idea whether this would work. I assumed I would die anyway. But it was something.

Carefully, judging the distance in my mind, praying the dimensions I was envisioning were exactly as I'd seen them so many times on my daytime jaunts, I lobbed the stone underhanded through the air. A moment later it landed with a click as it struck a rock on the edge of the drop-off. The man on the left turned and rushed toward the sound, his right arm raising the gun in one smooth, practiced motion. And then he disappeared, plummeting over the side, his scream swiftly swallowed up by the dark and the rain and the wind.

"Tommy!" the other man yelled, turning in that direction. His back was to me. As if in a dream I left my hiding spot, moved around the granite spur, and ran toward him. I shoved him hard, in the direction Tommy had fallen. But he didn't follow his mate. He was prepared, even in his unconsciousness. You didn't live in his world and die quite that fast.

With a speed that stunned me he turned and grasped my right arm with his free hand even as he stumbled, pulling me toward him. Toward the precipice. He stared at me with a glance of controlled fury, features etched in anger, but a cold anger, like a face chiseled from ice. He was raising his gun when I jerked my arm back, through instinct or reflex or sheer terror, and he realized with a slight widening of his eyes that he had no purchase—the rain on my oil slicker caused his hand to slip away like butter falling from a hot knife. He tottered, shot a glance of outrage at me, and he, too, was gone, tumbling down to the sea and the rocks below.

Once I was sure there weren't others, I returned quickly to my cottage. I gathered my notes, my wallet and my passport, and my flashlight, stuffed everything into my satchel, pulled the hood of my slicker over my head, and set off in the pouring rain. I wasn't staying there another moment. I moved unseen through the village, its lone street abandoned thanks to the driving rain, though I saw lights on in the pub and heard voices and music. I glanced at the church rectory, numb with the thought of the priest's betrayal. Its windows were dark.

It took me four long hours to reach Dingle because of the caution I took, ducking behind fuchsia hedges and stone walls each time I saw the lights of a car from either direction. Once in the small city I huddled under the eaves of a mausoleum in the graveyard of a church until dawn. When I saw the sky lighten I made my way to the harbor, waited until I saw a truck driver who seemed trustworthy, and asked for a ride east.

I didn't go home, though. As irrational as it seems now, I worried that my presence there would bring trouble to my Ohio town, which when all was said and done was only a ten- or twelve-hour car ride from Boston and neighborhoods where someone might know the name Sean Murphy. Instead, I rode buses and trains until I reached Rosslare Harbour on the country's southeastern coast, a grim determination to my passage that was new and different from the will that had taken me to a *Gaeltacht* to learn Irish. This was something more raw, and yet harder-edged. More than one tough on the street or in a railcar decided against approaching me during that journey after I shot a dead eye in his direction.

Three days later I landed at Le Havre on the southwestern coast of France. Emboldened that no authorities seemed to be seeking me, I made my way to Paris and the small suburb where I'd spent a sheltered semester abroad two years earlier, reading Balzac and memorizing verb conjugations while my fellow study abroad classmates partied in bars and dance clubs and soccer stadiums. I inquired after and found a position teaching English that came with a small apartment and few questions asked. I hunkered down and waited. For what, I wasn't sure.

During that time I met a girl, another American, a public health student examining French medical care for a master's thesis. Things between us went a lot faster than between me and Moira, and a lot farther. But after each time we were together, it was always Moira, with her shining green eyes and cream-textured face framed by black ringlets of hair, who I dreamed of holding.

"I'll tell you what I can," I wrote back to the reporter from the *Beacon Star*. And it's the truth. I will give her a sanitized version of my time in Ireland. If I'm feeling generous I'll provide her with a copy of a monograph I produced in graduate school at Illinois comparing Homeric and old Irish epic poems, featuring my own translation of each language.

I will not tell her of Paris, and the eventual knock that came on my apartment door. Of the meeting I took in the basement of a drab concrete office building with polite, nameless American men with flat Midwestern accents, buzzed haircuts, and black off-the-rack suits. Of the offer of funding for my graduate studies I received in exchange for assistance in certain matters of strategic interest in western Europe that a man with a talent for languages, and for extricating himself from difficult situations, might be able to provide. The names Sean Murphy and "Tommy" and, for that matter, Father Seamus, were never uttered. But an arrangement was reached.

No, I won't tell the student any of that. I will explain to her, in vague terms, how I learned to admire the resilience of the Irish nation at the time of the Troubles, the little I saw of them. I will commend the coming speaker's apparently legitimate conversion to peace. And I will relate, with a smile, that as odd as studying a language like Irish seemed at the time, the undertaking changed my life forever.

When the student is gone I will open my email and check the flight arrangements for a trip I'm taking in just a few weeks, over our ridiculously long Christmas break. To Helsinki first, and then points farther east. Ostensibly to study similarities between the Finnish and Basque languages that have always fascinated me. But it's possible I'll follow other paths as well.

"The Path I Took" is based on my experience more than thirty-five years ago—absent the discovery of a body—learning Gaelic in a tiny village in Ireland's County Kerry. I'd traveled there on a post-college scholarship that disallowed university study in favor of pursuing a creative project of your choice. Aside from language learning, one of the many eye-opening aspects of that experience was reading the daily accounts of violence in Northern Ireland, which didn't receive nearly the same coverage in the States. After achieving passing fluency in Irish-Gaelic, I traveled to other regions where so-called "minority languages" were dominant, including Wales, Spain's Catalonian region, and the Faroe Islands. Fast forward to 2017 and my overdue return to Europe to celebrate our older daughter's wedding to her Catalonian husband (talk about foreshadowing). That trip revived memories of my months in Ireland, including the impact of "The Troubles" in Northern Ireland, and I plotted most of the story in my head on the flight home. Assisting me were the retrieval of typewritten reports I'd compiled from my original trip and an Irish language instructor at University College Cork who, via email, helped me dust off my rusty Gaelic so I could include phrases of the language in the narrative. After a couple rejections and lots of rewriting, my story found a home at Mystery Tribune, for which I'm forever grateful.

BONUS STORY

Ambrose Gwinnett Bierce (1842–1914?) *was born in Meigs County, Ohio, but grew up in Indiana with his mother and eccentric father as the tenth of thirteen of children, all of whose names began with the letter* A. *When the Civil War broke out, he volunteered and was soon commissioned a first lieutenant in the Union Army, seeing action in the Battle of Shiloh.*

Often described as America's greatest writer of horror fiction in the years between the publications of Edgar Allan Poe and H. P. Lovecraft, Bierce also became one of the most important and influential journalists in America, writing columns for William Randolph Hearst's San Francisco Examiner. *His darkest book may be the devastating* Devil's Dictionary, *in which he defined a saint as "a dead sinner revised and edited," befriend as "to make an ingrate," and birth as "the first and direst of all disasters." His most famous story is probably "An Occurrence at Owl's Creek Bridge" in which a condemned prisoner believes he has been reprieved—just before the rope snaps his neck. It was filmed three times and was twice made for television, by Rod Serling for* The Twilight Zone *and by Alfred Hitchcock for* Alfred Hitchcock Presents.

In 1913, he accompanied Pancho Villa's army as an observer. He wrote a letter to a friend dated December 26, 1913. He then vanished—one of the most famous disappearances in history, once as famous as those of Judge Crater and Amelia Earhart.

"My Favorite Murder" was first published in the September 16, 1888, edition of The San Francisco Examiner; *it was first published in book form in* Can Such Things Be? *(New York, Cassell, 1893).*

MY FAVORITE MURDER

Ambrose Gwinnett Bierce

Having murdered my mother under circumstances of singular atrocity, I was arrested and put upon my trial, which lasted seven years. In charging the jury, the judge of the Court of Acquittal remarked that it was one of the most ghastly crimes that he had ever been called upon to explain away.

At this, my attorney rose and said:

"May it please your Honor, crimes are ghastly or agreeable only by comparison. If you were familiar with the details of my client's previous murder of his uncle you would discern in his later offense (if offense it may be called) something in the nature of tender forbearance and filial consideration for the feelings of the victim. The appalling ferocity of the former assassination was indeed inconsistent with any hypothesis but that of guilt; and had it not been for the fact that the honorable judge before whom he was tried was the president of a life insurance company that took risks on hanging, and in which my client held a policy, it is hard to see how he could decently have been acquitted. If your Honor would like to hear about it for instruction and guidance of your Honor's mind, this unfortunate man, my client, will consent to give himself the pain of relating it under oath."

The district attorney said: "Your Honor, I object. Such a statement would be in the nature of evidence, and the testimony in this case is closed. The prisoner's statement should have been introduced three years ago, in the spring of 1881."

"In a statutory sense," said the judge, "you are right, and in the Court of Objections and Technicalities you would get a ruling in your favor. But not in a Court of Acquittal. The objection is overruled."

"I except," said the district attorney.

"You cannot do that," the judge said. "I must remind you that in order to take an exception you must first get this case transferred for a time to the Court of Exceptions on a formal motion duly supported by affidavits. A motion to that effect by your predecessor in office was denied by me during the first year of this trial. Mr. Clerk, swear the prisoner."

The customary oath having been administered, I made the following statement, which impressed the judge with so strong a sense of the comparative triviality of the offense for which I was on trial that he made no further search for mitigating circumstances, but simply instructed the jury to acquit, and I left the court, without a stain upon my reputation:

"I was born in 1856 in Kalamakee, Mich., of honest and reputable parents, one of whom Heaven has mercifully spared to comfort me in my later years. In 1867 the family came to California and settled near Nigger Head, where my father opened a road agency and prospered beyond the dreams of avarice. He was a reticent, saturnine man then, though his increasing years have now somewhat relaxed the austerity of his disposition, and I believe that nothing but his memory of the sad event for which I am now on trial prevents him from manifesting a genuine hilarity.

"Four years after we had set up the road agency an itinerant preacher came along, and having no other way to pay for the night's lodging that we gave him, favored us with an exhortation of such power that, praise God, we were all converted to religion.

My father at once sent for his brother the Hon. William Ridley of Stockton, and on his arrival turned over the agency to him, charging him nothing for the franchise nor plant—the latter consisting of a Winchester rifle, a sawed-off shotgun, and an assortment of masks made out of flour sacks. The family then moved to Ghost Rock and opened a dance house. It was called 'The Saints' Rest Hurdy-Gurdy,' and the proceedings each night began with prayer. It was there that my now sainted mother, by her grace in the dance, acquired the sobriquet of 'The Bucking Walrus.'

"In the fall of '75 I had occasion to visit Coyote, on the road to Mahala, and took the stage at Ghost Rock. There were four other passengers. About three miles beyond Nigger Head, persons whom I identified as my Uncle William and his two sons held up the stage. Finding nothing in the express box, they went through the passengers. I acted a most honorable part in the affair, placing myself in line with the others, holding up my hands and permitting myself to be deprived of forty dollars and a gold watch. From my behavior no one could have suspected that I knew the gentlemen who gave the entertainment. A few days later, when I went to Nigger Head and asked for the return of my money and watch my uncle and cousins swore they knew nothing of the matter, and they affected a belief that my father and I had done the job ourselves in dishonest violation of commercial good faith. Uncle William even threatened to retaliate by starting an opposition dance house at Ghost Rock. As 'The Saints' Rest' had become rather unpopular, I saw that this would assuredly ruin it and prove a paying enterprise, so I told my uncle that I was willing to overlook the past if he would take me into the scheme and keep the partnership a secret from my father. This fair offer he rejected, and I then perceived that it would be better and more satisfactory if he were dead.

"My plans to that end were soon perfected, and communicating them to my dear parents I had the gratification of receiving their approval. My father said he was proud of me, and my mother promised that although her religion forbade her to assist in taking human life I should have the advantage of her prayers for my success. As a preliminary measure looking to my security in case of detection I made an application for membership in that powerful order, the Knights of Murder, and in due course was received as a member of the Ghost Rock commandery. On the day that my probation ended I was for the first time permitted to inspect the records of the order and learn who belonged to it—all the rites of initiation having been conducted in masks. Fancy my delight when, in looking over the roll of membership, I found the third name to be that of my uncle, who indeed was junior vice-chancellor of the order! Here was an opportunity exceeding my wildest dreams—to murder I could add insubordination and treachery. It was what my good mother would have called 'a special Providence.'

"At about this time something occurred which caused my cup of joy, already full, to overflow on all sides, a circular cataract of bliss. Three men, strangers in that locality, were arrested for the stage robbery in which I had lost my money and watch. They were brought to trial and, despite my efforts to clear them and fasten the guilt upon three of the most respectable and worthy citizens of Ghost Rock, convicted on the clearest proof. The murder would now be as wanton and reasonless as I could wish.

"One morning I shouldered my Winchester rifle, and going over to my uncle's house, near Nigger Head, asked my Aunt Mary, his wife, if he were at home, adding that I had come to kill him. My aunt replied with her peculiar smile that so many gentlemen called on that errand and were afterward carried away without having performed it that I must excuse her for doubting my good faith in the matter. She said I did not look as if I would kill anybody, so, as a proof of good faith I leveled my rifle and wounded a Chinaman who happened to be passing the house. She said she knew whole families that could do a thing of that kind, but Bill Ridley was a horse of another color. She said, however, that I would find him over on the other side of the creek in the sheep lot; and she added that she hoped the best man would win.

"My Aunt Mary was one of the most fair-minded women that I have ever met.

"I found my uncle down on his knees engaged in skinning a sheep. Seeing that he had neither gun nor pistol handy I had not the heart to shoot him, so I approached him, greeted him pleasantly, and struck him a powerful blow on the head with the butt of my rifle. I have a very good delivery and Uncle William lay down on his side, then rolled over on his back, spread out his fingers and shivered. Before he could recover the use of his limbs I seized the knife that he had been using and cut his hamstrings. You know, doubtless, that when you sever the tendon achillis the patient has no further use of his leg; it is just the same as if he had no leg. Well, I parted them both, and when he revived he was at my service. As soon as he comprehended the situation, he said:

" 'Samuel, you have got the drop on me and can afford to be generous. I have only one thing to ask of you, and that is that you carry me to the house and finish me in the bosom of my family.'

"I told him I thought that a pretty reasonable request and I would do so if he would let me put him into a wheat sack; he would be easier to carry that way and if we were seen by the neighbors en route it would cause less remark. He agreed to that, and going to the barn I got a sack. This, however, did not fit him; it was too short and much wider than he; so I bent his legs, forced his knees up against his breast and got him into it that way, tying the sack above his head. He was a heavy man and I had all that I could do to get him on my back, but I staggered along for some distance until I came to a swing that some of the children had suspended to the branch of an oak. Here I laid him down and sat upon him to rest, and the sight of the rope gave me a happy inspiration. In twenty minutes my uncle, still in the sack, swung free to the sport of the wind.

"I had taken down the rope, tied one end tightly about the mouth of the bag, thrown the other across the limb and hauled him up about five feet from the ground. Fastening the other end of the rope also about the mouth of the sack, I had the satisfaction to see my uncle converted into a large, fine pendulum. I must add that he was not himself entirely aware of the nature of the change that he had undergone in his relation to the exterior world, though in justice to a good man's memory I ought to say that I do not think he would in any case have wasted much of my time in vain remonstrance.

"Uncle William had a ram that was famous in all that region as a fighter. It was in a state of chronic constitutional indignation. Some deep disappointment in early life had soured its disposition and it had declared war upon the whole world. To say that it would butt anything accessible is but faintly to express the nature and scope of its military activity: the universe was its antagonist; its methods that of a projectile. It fought like the angels and devils, in mid-air, cleaving the atmosphere like a bird, describing a parabolic curve and descending upon its victim at just the exact angle of incidence to make the most of its velocity and weight. Its momentum, calculated in foot-tons, was something incredible. It had been seen to destroy a four-year-old bull by a single impact upon that animal's gnarly forehead. No stone wall had ever been known to resist its downward swoop; there were no trees tough enough to stay it; it would splinter them into matchwood and defile their leafy honors in the dust. This irascible and implacable brute—this incarnate thunderbolt—this monster of the upper deep, I had seen reposing in the shade of an adjacent tree, dreaming dreams of conquest and glory. It was with a view to summoning it forth to the field of honor that I suspended its master in the manner described.

"Having completed my preparations, I imparted to the avuncular pendulum a gentle oscillation, and retiring to cover behind a contiguous rock, lifted up my voice in a long rasping cry whose diminishing final note was drowned in a noise like that of a swearing cat, which emanated from the sack. Instantly that formidable sheep was upon its feet and had taken in the military situation at a glance. In a few moments it had approached, stamping, to within fifty yards of the swinging foeman, who, now retreating and anon advancing, seemed to invite the fray. Suddenly I saw the beast's head drop earthward as if depressed by the weight of its enormous horns; then a dim, white, wavy streak of sheep prolonged itself from that spot in a generally horizontal direction to within about four yards of a point immediately beneath the enemy. There it struck sharply upward, and before it had faded from my gaze at the place whence it had set out I heard a horrid thump and a piercing scream, and my poor uncle shot forward, with a slack rope higher than the limb to which he was attached. Here the rope tautened with a jerk, arresting his flight, and back he swung in a breathless curve to the other end of his arc. The ram had fallen, a heap of indistinguishable legs, wool and horns, but pulling itself together and dodging as its antagonist swept downward it retired at random, alternately shaking its head and stamping its fore-feet. When it had backed about the same distance as that from which it had delivered the assault it paused again, bowed its head as if in prayer for victory, and again shot forward, dimly visible as before—a prolonging white streak with monstrous undulations, ending with a sharp ascension. Its course this time was at a right

angle to its former one, and its impatience so great that it struck
the enemy before he had nearly reached the lowest point of his arc.
In consequence he went flying round and round in a horizontal
circle whose radius was about equal to half the length of the rope,
which I forgot to say was nearly twenty feet long. His shrieks,
crescendo in approach and diminuendo in recession, made the
rapidity of his revolution more obvious to the ear than to the eye.
He had evidently not yet been struck in a vital spot. His posture
in the sack and the distance from the ground at which he hung
compelled the ram to operate upon his lower extremities and the
end of his back. Like a plant that has struck its root into some
poisonous mineral, my poor uncle was dying slowly upward.

"After delivering its second blow the ram had not again retired.
The fever of battle burned hot in its heart; its brain was intoxicated
with the wine of strife. Like a pugilist who in his rage forgets his
skill and fights ineffectively at half-arm's length, the angry beast
endeavored to reach its fleeting foe by awkward vertical leaps as
he passed overhead, sometimes, indeed, succeeding in striking
him feebly, but more frequently overthrown by its own misguided
eagerness. But as the impetus was exhausted and the man's circles
narrowed in scope and diminished in speed, bringing him nearer
to the ground, these tactics produced better results, eliciting a
superior quality of screams, which I greatly enjoyed.

"Suddenly, as if the bugles had sung truce, the ram suspended
hostilities and walked away, thoughtfully wrinkling and smoothing
its great aquiline nose, and occasionally cropping a bunch of grass
and slowly munching it. It seemed to have tired of war's alarms and
resolved to beat the sword into a plowshare and cultivate the arts of
peace. Steadily it held its course away from the field of fame until it
had gained a distance of nearly a quarter of a mile. There it stopped
and stood with its rear to the foe, chewing its cud and apparently

half asleep. I observed, however, an occasional slight turn of its head, as if its apathy were more affected than real.

"Meantime Uncle William's shrieks had abated with his motion, and nothing was heard from him but long, low moans, and at long intervals my name, uttered in pleading tones exceedingly grateful to my ear. Evidently the man had not the faintest notion of what was being done to him, and was inexpressibly terrified. When Death comes cloaked in mystery he is terrible indeed. Little by little my uncle's oscillations diminished, and finally he hung motionless. I went to him and was about to give him the coup de grace, when I heard and felt a succession of smart shocks which shook the ground like a series of light earthquakes, and turning in the direction of the ram, saw a long cloud of dust approaching me with inconceivable rapidity and alarming effect! At a distance of some thirty yards away it stopped short, and from the near end of it rose into the air what I at first thought a great white bird. Its ascent was so smooth and easy and regular that I could not realize its extraordinary celerity, and was lost in admiration of its grace. To this day the impression remains that it was a slow, deliberate movement, the ram—for it was that animal—being upborne by some power other than its own impetus, and supported through the successive stages of its flight with infinite tenderness and care. My eyes followed its progress through the air with unspeakable pleasure, all the greater by contrast with my former terror of its approach by land. Onward and upward the noble animal sailed, its head bent down almost between its knees, its fore-feet thrown back, its hinder legs trailing to rear like the legs of a soaring heron.

"At a height of forty or fifty feet, as fond recollection presents it to view, it attained its zenith and appeared to remain an instant stationary; then, tilting suddenly forward without altering the relative position of its parts, it shot downward on a steeper and steeper course with augmenting velocity, passed immediately above me with a noise like the rush of a cannon shot and struck my poor uncle almost squarely on the top of the head! So frightful was the impact that not only the man's neck was broken, but the rope too; and the body of the deceased, forced against the earth, was crushed to pulp beneath the awful front of that meteoric sheep! The concussion stopped all the clocks between Lone Hand and Dutch Dan's, and Professor Davidson, a distinguished authority in matters seismic, who happened to be in the vicinity, promptly explained that the vibrations were from north to southwest.

"Altogether, I cannot help thinking that in point of artistic atrocity my murder of Uncle William has seldom been excelled."

Like virtually every word he wrote, "My Favorite Murder" is dark and cynical, Bierce's preferred style and tone. His relentlessly sharp wit and cruel pen earned him the sobriquet "Bitter Bierce." This story is a splendid example of how hilarious he could be, even as he was describing nothing less than a murder.

THE BEST CRIME STORIES 2021 HONOUR ROLL

Additional outstanding stories published in 2020

Garrett, Cheryl
"Breath," *Crossing Borders*, ed. Lisa Brackman and Matt Coyle
(Down & Out)

Hockensmith, Steve
"The Death and Carnage Boy," *Ellery Queen Mystery Magazine*
(July/August)

Martin, Lee
"Pull," *Story*, Issue #7

Oleksiw, Susan
"Kenny Orslow Shows Up on Time," *Mystery Weekly Magazine*

Perona, Elizabeth
"The Ear Witness," *Murder 20/20*, ed. M. B. Dabney, Lillie
Evans, and Sherri Held (Speed City Press)

Sibi-Okumu, J. E.
"Belonging," *Nairobi Noir*, ed. Peter Kimani (Akashic Books)

Simpson, Chad
"Notes Towards a Story Called Streetlight Superman," *Story*,
        Issue #8

Terrell, Stephen
"In the Deepest Darkness," *Murder 20/20*, ed. M. B. Dabney,
        Lillie Evans, and Sherri Held (Speed City Press)

Todd, Marilyn
"Burning Desire," *Ellery Queen Mystery Magazine* (September/
        October)

Wilson, Matthew
"The Wretched Strangers," *Ellery Queen Mystery Magazine*
        (January/February)

ABOUT THE EDITORS

LEE CHILD is the author of the #1 *New York Times* bestselling Jack Reacher thrillers. All his novels have been optioned for major motion pictures, and foreign rights in the Reacher series have sold in one hundred territories. He lives in New York City.

OTTO PENZLER is the founder of the Mysterious Press (1975), Mysterious Press.com (2011) and New York City's Mysterious Bookshop (1979). He has won a Raven, the Ellery Queen Award, two Edgars and lifetime achievement awards from NoirCon and *The Strand Magazine*. He has edited more than 70 anthologies and written extensively about crime fiction.